EVAN HUNTER

hit the literary headlines with *The Blackboard Jungle*. He followed this with *Second Ending* and *A Matter of Conviction*, by which time he was firmly established as one of the most exciting talents of the day.

Strangers When We Meet has the same brilliance of narrative and sensational power—a novel of deep and searching characterisation which explores the adulterous affair between Larry Coles and Maggie Gault, two mature people who loved their families, yet who found themselves drawn together as though by a magnet.

Strangers When We Meet was made into a successful film starring Kirk Douglas and Kim Novak. The novel tells the story with an intimacy the screen could never portray.

Photographs by courtesy of Columbia Pictures

Evan Hunter

Strangers When We Meet

CORGI BOOKS
TRANSWORLD PUBLISHERS LTD
A National General Company

STRANGERS WHEN WE MEET

A CORGI BOOK 552 01489 3

Originally published in Great Britain by
Constable & Company Ltd.

PRINTING HISTORY
Constable Edition published 1958
Corgi Edition published 1960
Corgi Edition re-issued 1961
Corgi Edition reprinted 1961
Corgi Edition reprinted 1961
Corgi Edition reprinted 1962
Corgi Edition reprinted 1963
Corgi Edition re-issued 1964
Corgi Edition reprinted 1964
Corgi Edition reprinted 1965
Corgi Edition reprinted 1965
Corgi Edition reprinted 1967
Corgi Edition reprinted 1967
Corgi Edition reprinted 1968
Corgi Edition reprinted 1971

Corgi Books are published by Transworld Publishers Ltd.,
Cavendish House, 57-59 Uxbridge Road,
Ealing, London, W.5.
Made and printed in Great Britain by
Hunt Barnard Printing Ltd., Aylesbury, Bucks.

This book is dedicated to my wife
ANITA

I WOULD LIKE *to express my sincere gratitude to Scott and Sidney Meredith, my agents, who from the very beginning provided honest enthusiasm and encouragement for what I was attempting; to Peter Schwed and Herbert Alexander, who, through creative and fastidious editing, opened for me previously non-existent avenues of writing; to Gerry Ash, who, reading the manuscript pages as they left the type-writer, became a responsive and illuminating touchstone; to Ingram Ash, my friend and neighbor, who graciously carried the manuscript or portions of it to and from the city more times than I can remember; to Bill Breger, who patiently corrected and explained and shared the joy of completion as only an artist could; and most of all to Anita, who suffered on the bleak days and rejoiced on the good ones, who mirrored the many defeats and small victories, who criticized and comforted, assuaged and assured—and who was always there.*

E. H.

Now is the world of grandeur dwindled, shrunk
To what the stupidest can understand;
The shabby treasures of an exile's trunk
Include no passport to that wonderland,
Though you are told you are its citizen.
The scenery is changed, the climate dull,
The fateful masks are faces, gods are men,
Most nights are long, and none are magical.
But there are strangers even here. . . .

—From "Then and Now" by BABETTE DEUTSCH
Published by Henry Holt and Company,
© *by Babette Deutsch*

Strangers
When We Meet

1

MONDAY morning.

Gray October, and an early-morning chill in the house and a sullen sky pressing against the windowpanes. The sound of the children in the kitchen, Chris haggling with David, hounding the younger boy over the fact that he'd wet his bed again the night before.

Another day.

There is a routine in this house, as prescribed as the steady cadence of minutes ticking off time on the face of the bedroom clock. There is a routine here, he thought, and it governs the people living here, and the routine is broken only on Saturdays and Sundays, and even then it is replaced only by another routine, as disciplined and relentless as the first.

"Better get up, Eve," he said, and beside him, her head under the pillow, one arm tangled in the blanket, Eve mumbled something incoherently.

He looked across at the clock on the dresser, the drill-master, the sergeant who handled the Early Awakening Detail. 7:00 A.M. What a ridiculous hour to be facing the world! By 7:10, the sergeant would relinquish his duties, pass them on to the white-faced disciplinarian who scowled down from the kitchen wall. You could see him from the bathroom. You could poke your head around the door jamb while you were shaving and there he was, tocking off minutes in his rigid voice.

Time.

He rose and stretched. He was a tall, sinewy man with brown hair and dark-brown eyes, eyes which were almost black. He had high cheekbones, and a straight nose, and a full mouth which looked amused even when it was not. He raised muscular arms to the ceiling and opened his jaws wide in a great lion yawn, and then he unbuttoned his pajama top, took it off and threw it onto the chair alongside the bed.

"Eve," he said, "let's . . ."

"Is it time?" sh . . .

"It's time," he . . .

Time.

In the kitchen, C . . . . . . houldn't wet the bed at nig . . .

"I di'n wet the . . .

With perfect adu . . .

11

"A fairy made it in my pants," David said.

Abandoning the logic, Chris laughed hysterically. David joined him. Together they bellowed until they'd forgotten what was so funny, until the house reverberated with their delighted cackling.

"Quiet down in there," Larry called. He reached behind him, touched Eve's warm shoulder. "Hey," he said. "Come on."

"Are you up, Daddy?" Chris asked from the kitchen. "Will you make pancakes?"

"Pancakes are for Sunday. That was yesterday."

"What's today?"

"Monday."

"Do I go to school today?"

"Yes."

"Does David go to school?"

"No." He paused. "Are you dressed yet? How about it?" He pulled on his trousers and then shook Eve vigorously. "Hey, honey," he said, "get up and supervise Chris, will you?"

Eve sat bolt upright. "What time is it?" she asked.

He looked at the clock. "Seven-ten."

Eve rubbed her eyes. Her eyes were blue, and they always looked faded in the morning, as if the color somehow drained out of them during the night. She had long black hair, and he knew her next gesture even before she made it. Yawningly, she put both hands to the back of her neck and then ran them up toward the top of her head, lifting the black hair, stretching the sleep from her body.

"Oh, God," she said, "I had a horrible dream. I dreamt you left me."

"I will if you don't get out of that bed," Larry said, tying his shoes.

"Seriously. You were a beast."

"Are you getting up?"

"I was pregnant when you left."

"Bite your tongue."

"It was terrible," Eve said. She shuddered slightly, and then swung her legs over the side of the bed. The shudder seemed to dispel all memory of the dream. She smiled sleepily and said, "Good morning, beast." He kissed her gently, and she said, "Pwhhh, I haven't brushed my teeth yet."

"You're not supposed to brush them until after your first meal."

"That's what dentists say. What do they know?"

His hand had settled on her knee. Effortlessly now, it glided onto the smooth flesh of her thigh, and his fingers settled in the pocket of warmth where the short nightgown ended.

Eve wriggled away from him, smiling. "Stop it," she said. "I have to go to the bathroom."

"You always have to go to the bathroom."

"Doesn't everybody?" she asked lightly. She winked at him

12

and then started down the corridor to the bathroom at the end of the hall.

"Ma," Chris said, intercepting her.

"Don't call me 'Ma.'"

"Mother . . ."

"That's better."

"Does David go to school?"

"No."

Chris turned. He was five years old, with his mother's black hair and blue eyes. "See, David?" he said. "You can't go to school because you wet the bed."

"Did you wet again, David?" Eve asked.

"Yes," David answered in a small voice.

"I don't know what I'm going to do with you."

"A fairy made it in my pants, Eve," David said, hoping his earlier joke would convulse his mother, knowing too that she thought it devilishly cute of him to call her by her first name.

"I'll talk to you later," Eve said, and she closed the bathroom door behind her.

"Are you dressed yet?" Larry asked, coming from the bedroom.

"No," Chris answered. "What shall I wear?"

"Ask your mother."

Chris banged on the bathroom door. "Ma, what shall I wear?"

"I'll be out in a minute," Eve answered. As an after-thought she said, "Larry, will you put up the coffee water?"

"Sure." He walked into the kitchen. David followed him like a penitent shadow. David had brown hair and brown eyes, and he was three years old. His wet pajamas hung limply on his spare frame.

"Hi, Dad," he said.

Larry filled the tea kettle and then tousled David's hair. "Hi, son. Have a good sleep?"

"I wet the bed," David said matter-of-factly.

"You've got to be careful," Larry answered, taking the kettle to the stove.

"I know," David solemnly agreed, "but it just happens without my knowing, Dad."

"Well," Larry said, "you've got to be careful."

"Oh, sure," David said.

The bathroom door opened. Eve disappeared down the corridor.

"Hurry it up, hon," Larry said.

"What time is it?"

"Almost seven-twenty."

He went into the bathroom and closed the door. He could hear the sounds of the house around him while he shaved, the oil burner thrumming in the basement below, the vents expanding as heat attacked the aluminium. Another day. Another day to gird on the armor and step into the arena. Lawrence Cole, knight in shining. Available for dragon slaying, honor salvation, and holy-grail searches.

"Hurry, Larry!"

Eve's voice. Part of the routine. Somewhere during the early-morning rush on his city days, the clocks and Eve would join forces, combining in their efforts to shove slothful, lethargic, lackadaisical Lawrence Cole out of the warmth of Abode into the coldness of Arena. He rinsed his face and dried himself. He went quickly to the bedroom then, opened the second drawer of the dresser—top drawer belongs to Eve, invasion of privacy—and hurriedly unwrapped a white shirt, noticing at the same time that there was only one other shirt in the drawer.

When he came into the kitchen it was 7:35. His juice, cereal and coffee were waiting on the table. Miraculously, Chris was fully dressed and eating a soft-boiled egg. David sat morosely in his damp pajamas.

"How do I look, Daddy?" Chris asked.

"Fine, Chris." He picked up his juice glass. "When's the laundry man coming?"

"Today. Why?"

"I'm almost out of shirts."

"Again? Why don't you buy a few more? A man could get neurotic worrying over whether his shirts will last the week."

"Maybe I'll get some today, after I'm through with this character."

"You say you will, but you won't. Why do you hate to buy clothes?"

"I love to buy clothes," Larry said. He grinned. "I just hate to spend money." He drank his orange juice. "Good stuff."

"They had a sale at Food Fair."

"Good. Better than the stuff you had last week."

"You look handsome, Dad," David said.

"Thank you, eat your egg, son."

"You'll have to take Chris to the bus stop this morning," Eve said. "I'm not dressed."

"Are you going to the Governor's Ball, or are you dropping your son off at the school bus?"

"I'm doing neither. *You're* dropping him off."

"A mother's job . . ."

"Larry. I can't go in my underwear! Now don't—"

"Why not? That would set lovely Pinecrest Manor on its ear."

"You'd like that."

"So would all the other men in the development."

"That's all you ever think of," Eve said.

"*What's* all he ever thinks of?" Chris asked. He shoved his cup aside. "I finished my egg."

14

"Go wash your face," Eve said.

"Sure." Chris pushed his chair back. "But *what's* all he thinks of?"

"S-e-x," Eve spelled.

"What's that?"

"That's corrupting the morals of a minor," Larry said. "Go wash your face.

"Is s-e-x Santa Claus?" Chris asked.

"In a way," Larry answered, smiling.

"I could tell," Chris said triumphantly. "Because everytime you spell, it's Santa Claus."

"Is it almost Christmas?" David asked.

"Come on, come on," Larry said, suddenly galvanized, reaching for his coffee cup. "Wash your face, Chris. Hurry."

Chris vanished.

"You're not having cereal?" Eve asked.

"I don't want to stuff myself. I'm meeting this guy for breakfast."

"You'll never gain any weight the way you eat."

"Who wants to? A hundred and ninety-two pounds is fine."

"You're six-one," she said, studying him as if for the first time. "You can use a few pounds."

Larry shoved back his chair. "Chris! Let's go!"

Chris burst out of the bathroom. "Am I all right, Ma?" he asked.

"You're fine. Put on a sweater."

Chris ran to his room. Larry took Eve in his arms.

"Be good. Don't make eyes at the laundry man."

"He's very handsome. He looks like Gregory Peck."

"Did you brush your teeth?"

"Yes."

"Do I get a kiss now?"

"Sure."

They were kissing when Chris came back into the kitchen. The moment he saw them in embrace, he began singing, "Love and marriage, love and—"

"Shut up, runt," Larry said. He broke away from Eve. "I'll call you later."

They went out of the house together. David and Eve stood in the doorway, watching. "When I get big next week, can I go with them?" David asked.

"First you've got to stop wetting the bed," Eve said absently.

From the car Chris yelled, "Bye, Ma!"

Larry waved and backed the car out of the driveway, glancing at the line of his small development house and hating for the hundredth time the aesthetic of it. Pinecrest Manor, he thought. Lovely Pinecrest Manor. His wrist watch read 7:50. He waved again when they turned the corner. The bus stop was five blocks

15

away on the main road which hemmed in the development. He pulled up at the intersection and opened the door for Chris. "Have fun," he said.

"Yeah, yeah," Chris said, and he went to join the knot of children and mothers who stood near the curb. Larry watched him, proud of his son, forgetting for the moment that he had to catch a train.

And then he saw the woman, her head in profile against the gray sky, pale-blonde hair and brown eyes, her head erect against the backdrop of gray. She held the hand of a blond boy, and Larry looked at the boy and then at the woman again. One of the other women in the group, one of Eve's friends, caught his eye and waved at him. He waved back, hesitating before he set the car in motion. He looked at his watch. 7:55. He would have one hell of a race to the station. He turned the corner onto the main road, looking back once more at the pale blonde.

She did not return his glance.

The man's name was Roger Altar.

"I'm a writer," he said to Larry.

Larry sat opposite him at the restaurant table. There was something honest about meeting a man for late breakfast. Neither of the two had yet buckled on the armor of society. The visors had not yet been clanged shut, concealing the eyes. They sat across from each other, and there was the smell of coffee and fried bacon at the table, and Larry made up his mind that all business deals should be concluded at breakfast when men could be honest with each other.

"Go ahead, say it," Altar said.

"Say what?"

"That you've always wanted to be a writer."

"Why should I say that?"

"It's what everyone says." Altar shrugged massive shoulders. A waitress passed, and his eyes followed her progression across the room.

Larry poked his fork into the egg yolk, watching the bright yellow spread. "I'm sorry to disappoint you," he said, "but I never entertained the thought. As a matter of fact, I always wanted to be exactly what I am."

"And what's that?"

"The best architect in the world."

Altar chuckled as if he begrudged humor in another man. But at the same time, the chuckle was a delighted release from somewhere deep within his barrel chest. "I enjoy modesty," he said. "I think I like you." He picked up his coffee cup with two hands, the way Larry imagined medieval kings might have. "Do you like me?"

"I don't know you yet."

16

"How long does it take? I'm not asking you to marry me."

"I'd have to refuse," Larry said.

Altar exploded into real laughter this time. He was a big man wearing a bulky tweed jacket which emphasized his hugeness. He had shaggy black brows and hair, and his nose honestly advertized the fact that it had once been broken. His chin was cleft, a dishonest chin in that it was molded along perfect classical lines in an otherwise craggy, disorganized face. But there was nothing dishonest about Altar's eyes. They were a sharp, penetrating brown, and they seemed to examine every object in the room while miraculously remaining fixed on the abundant buttocks of the waitress.

"It's a pleasure to talk to a creator," Altar said. "Are you really a good architect, or is the ego a big bluff?"

"Are you really a good writer, or is the ego a big bluff?" Larry asked.

"I try," Altar said simply. "Somebody told me you were honest. He also said you were a good architect. That's why I contacted you. I want someone who'll design a house for me the way he wants to design it, without any of my half-assed opinions. If I could design it myself, I would. I can't."

"Suppose my ideas don't jibe with yours?"

"Our ideas don't have to jibe. Only our frame of reference. That's why I wanted to meet you."

"And you think a breakfast conversation is going to tell you what I'm like?"

"Probably not. Do you mind if I ask a few questions?" He snapped his fingers impatiently for the waitress. "I want more coffee."

"Go ahead. Ask your questions."

"You'd never heard of me before I called, had you?"

"Should I have?"

"Well," Altar said wearily, "I've achieved a small degree of fame."

The waitress came to the table. "Will there be anything else, sir?" she asked.

"Two more coffees," Altar said.

"What have you written?" Larry asked.

"You must be abysmally ignorant," Altar said, watching the waitress as she moved away from the table.

Larry shrugged. "If you're shy, don't tell me."

"I wrote two books," Altar said. "The first was called *Star Reach*. It was serialized in *Good Housekeeping* and was a Book-of-the-Month Club selection. We sold a hundred and fifty thousand copies in the hard cover and over a million in the paperback. Ray Milland starred in the movie. Perhaps you saw it last year?"

"No, I'm sorry. What was the second book?"

"*The Debacle*," Altar said. "It was published last June."

"That's a dangerous title," Larry said. "I can see a review starting with 'This book is aptly titled.' "

"One started exactly that way," Altar said, unsmiling.

"Was this one serialized?"

"*Ladies' Home Journal*," Altar said. "And Literary Guild, and Metro bought it from the galleys. They're making the movie now."

"I see. I guess you're successful."

"I'm King Midas."

"Well, in any case, I haven't read either of your books. I'm sorry."

"Don't be. We can't expect to enlighten everyone with two brilliant thrusts."

"Jesus, you're almost insufferable," Larry said, laughing. "Will you get me a copy of *The Debacle*? I'm assuming that's the better of the two."

"If it weren't, I'd quit writing tomorrow."

"Will you get it for me?"

"Go buy one," Altar said. "I run a grocery store, and I don't give away canned goods. It sells for three-ninety-five. If you're cheap, wait until next June. It'll be reprinted by then, and it'll only cost you thirty-five cents."

"I'll buy one now. It may break me, but I'll buy it. How much do you want to spend on this house of yours?"

"About seventy-five thousand."

"I guess you *are* King Midas."

"Making money isn't the hard thing to do," Altar said, suddenly serious.

"What kind of house do you want?"

"Something to live in."

"I don't design gingerbread or colonials or ranchonials or any other bastard forms. I'll design a contemporary house, and that's all."

"What else would a contemporary architect design?"

"You'd be surprised."

"Just show me pictures of what you've done," Altar said. "After that, it's up to you. I don't tell a plumber how to fix pipes, and I don't like people telling me how to write books. I won't tell you what to design."

"You may not like the houses I show you. They were designed for other people."

"So what? Each book an author writes is a separate entity, but they all bear the same man's stamp. I like you, but your stamp may stink. I want to see it."

"How old are you, Altar?"

"Thirty-two. You?"

"Thirty-one."

"Good. I like young people."

"Suppose we agree my houses are good, Altar?"

18

"We've got a deal. Don't call me by my last name. That's for the critics."

"What's the matter? Weren't they kind to your books?"

"As a matter of fact, they weren't." Altar stopped and shook his head. "The hell with the critics. Will you design my house?"

"Maybe."

"When will you know?"

"After I've read your book."

"Why?"

Larry grinned. "I want to see *your* stamp," he said.

There was, Larry discovered that night, a polish about the prose of Roger Altar which seemed in antipathy to the bluff, earthy exterior of the man, a contradiction which made the reading experience puzzling. Try as he might, he could not associate the book with Altar. The book simply did not seem to be the man.

He could not understand the disagreement. He knew with certainty that every house he designed revealed at least a part of himself. He had hoped similarly to find a clue to Altar's identity within the pages of his book, but he was sorely disappointed. The book seemed to be nothing more than quick entertainment.

Altar wrote in a clear, crisp magazine style. A succession of slick polished words helped Altar to create a world within which flesh-and-blood characters lived. The trouble with the characters, Larry supposed, was that they approached all their problems in terms of half truths. The novel seemed to be a collection of tired household verities, and by the time Larry reached page fifty of *The Debacle*, he seriously wondered if he wanted to design a house for a man who was utterly lacking in integrity.

As he went deeper into the book, his feelings changed.

Altar *was* trying to speak, but something constantly intruded to prevent the naked statement. It was a fear, perhaps, a holding back, a refusal to commit completely to the printed page. The struggle was immense, entirely overshadowing the characters Altar had created. Page by page, the intricate plot development became meaningless when juxtaposed to Altar's tortured personal combat. He could not have said why Altar struck a sympathetic chord within him. He knew only that he was rooting for the man, that he was mentally screaming, "Get it out! For God's sake, please get it out!" The effort left him exhausted. More so because it ended in defeat; the half truths triumphed.

When Larry closed *The Debacle* it was four o'clock in the morning. He had started reading after dinner, and he hadn't been aware of Eve in the house all night long. He realized now that she'd gone to bed long ago and that she'd probably given him a good-night peck, but he couldn't remember when. He sat in the easy chair with the circle of light around him, the novel closed in his lap. He sat that way for ten minutes, and then he went into the bedroom and dialed a number.

"Hello?"

"Altar?"

"Yes?"

"This is Larry Cole."

"Man, it's the middle of the night. What—?"

"I just finished your book."

"Oh."

There was a long silence.

"I want to design your house."

Altar laughed a curiously relieved laugh.

"Thanks," he said.

2

SHE did not like autumn, would never like it.

Autumn was a time of dying, the death of her grandfather in November the biggest dying of all, but other dyings too, little dyings, death falling from the trees, rattling underfoot. The splendid deceptive coloration of death, a spreading fungus which lapped the bright green of summer with decaying reds and oranges and yellows. The sun, too, died in autumn. Bright and golden, it turned pale and sickly yellow, pasted against a lusterless sky, intimidated by the sharp bite of a new wind. October was a paradox, a frigid month which dressed itself in the hot-blooded colors of a streetwalker—but only to attend a funeral.

I'm too morbid, she thought. I must stop being morbid. It's because winter is coming. Still, I must stop.

It was all a matter of routine, she supposed. The new routine of getting Patrick off to school every day, and then moving around in a house gone suddenly still. The Cape Cod seemed larger with him gone. In its silent immensity, there no longer seemed a need for the third bedroom they'd put upstairs. But Don had insisted on a guest room for his mother's visits, and so of course the shift had taken place: master bedroom into the finished attic, Patrick into the old master bedroom, and the smallest bedroom saved for Mrs. Gault, always clean and waiting for her descent.

I might as well get started, she thought, and doggedly she went upstairs to the bedroom in the finished attic of the Pinecrest Manor house.

Don's tee shirt and shorts lay on the floor in the center of the room, rumpled and white against the multicolored scatter rug. The canopied bed stood against the far wall of the room, the blankets trailing onto the floor. Distastefully, she picked up the underwear and took them to the hamper. There was something that annoyed her about his clothes. Not just his dirty clothes, but all of his clothes, even the clean white shirts lined up with precision in the cherrywood dresser, fresh from the laundry, the curlicued DG monogram over each breast pocket. Or his newly pressed suits and jackets in the closet, wide shoulders stretched taut over the hangers, trousers neatly folded over the wooden supporting bars. Unworn clothes were false and pathetic, but the fact was that she disliked Don's clothes even when he was inside them.

With intuitive female logic, she understood there was something wrong with her attitude. She had seen other women wearing their husbands' shirts or jackets with a curious sense of proprietorship. She had known from their expressions that they gained more from the experience than the simple female advantage of looking fragile and protected in the overlarge male garments.

But she could remember the boat ride, the dark inland waters of the Hudson, the timid assault of new stars on a deepening dusky sky, the chill wind blowing off the water, a cutting wind that penetrated to her bones. Sitting with the women, listening to talk of babies and toilet training, she had felt the wind. Don, the man among men, the only husband who had not drunk too much that afternoon at Bear Mountain, had left the male company of dirty-joke tellers and come to her, offering his sweater.

With the sweater around her, with the coarse wool against her flesh, she had begun trembling. Even the wind had not caused her to tremble so. There was the smell of her husband on the sweater, his hair tonic, his after-shave, his body. In the tight circle of bellowing male voices and simpering female echoes, she had felt suddenly nauseated. Quickly she had taken off the sweater and handed it back to him. And then she'd made her way aft, turning her face to the cold breeze that swept off the swirling waters of the Hudson.

She had hurt him badly that night. They had made the long drive home from the pier in silence, but his eyes told her all there was to say. Blue, flecked with white, they seemed to echo the stiff regularity about Don which first impressed you. It was not until later that you felt any warmth from him; it was not until later that you realized the blue eyes were gentle and easily penetrated by daggers of pain.

In the darkness of their attic bedroom, in the rectangular canopied vastness of their bed, with the modern air conditioner anachronistically humming beneath the ruffled curtain in the Cape Cod house, with the summer sounds of hushed automobile tires far away bruising the insect drone of the night, his hand had touched her shoulder tentatively. She had not turned. His hand had rested on her flesh lightly, unmoving. There were words in his hand, so many words, but lying stiffly naked beside him, she chose not to understand the gentle pressure, so that he was forced finally to speak.

"Should we make love?"

"No," she said.

"Oh."

A single word, and she was glad she could not see the blue eyes in that moment. He drew back his hand, and again the room was silent, and at last he sighed and said, "Good night, Margaret."

He never mentioned the sweater to her. Nor did he ever wear it again.

She turned from the hamper now and walked to the bed. Downstairs the doorbell chimed. Unhurriedly she started down the steps. The dormer windows behind her threw a shuttered cold light onto the steps, limning her pale-blonde hair. She wore black tapered slacks and a white sweater, and she navigated the steps with unconscious, uncalculated femininity. Again, the doorbell chimed.

"I'm coming," she called.

The attic steps terminated just inside the entrance doorway. She opened the door, backing instinctively away from the wind, telling herself that Don would have to be reminded again about putting in the storm-door glass.

Betty Anders stood on the front stoop, cocking a disciplinary eyebrow. Betty was a petite brunette with high cheekbones and wide blue eyes. She was twenty-five years old and usually attractive except when her hair was in curlers as it was this morning. The scarf around her head hid some of the intricate beautifying machinery, but not all. Betty didn't seem to care very much. Betty always did pretty much as she pleased. She was the daughter of a Presbyterian minister and her tendency toward independent expression had caused a serious explosion when she married Felix, a devout Catholic. Her defiance eventually won out. Now, in direct defiance to the October briskness—and also because she had good legs—Betty wore shorts. She held her pose of petulant anger for a moment and then burst into the house like a hand-grenade explosion.

"Were you asleep?" she asked, her voice loud and booming.

"I was upstairs cleaning."

"Give me a cup of coffee," Betty said. "How do you manage to look so goddamn beautiful at ten o'clock in the morning?"

She was moving toward the kitchen with the easy familiarity of a person who is at home in any house. She had tossed her question over her shoulder, not expecting or wanting an answer, in a light tone which completely belied the fact that any display of beauty at ten in the morning disturbed her immensely. She further felt that no woman had the right to be so blatantly beautiful as this woman. And so, as a defense against the beauty,

22

and as a salving to her own hair-in-curlers womanhood, she decided to let the world—and especially this woman—know that she too, in her own way, was also desirable.

"I'm a wreck," she said. "All that man wants to do is make love."

She underlined the last words as if she expected Margaret to wince. Margaret did not.

"If I don't get some sleep soon, I'll die," Betty persisted.

"I'll heat the coffee," Margaret said.

She moved to the stove, and Betty watched her. She would have been lying to herself if she'd pretended that the sight of Margaret Gault did not delight her. When she looked at Margaret, she saw an ash-blonde whose brown eyes were fringed with thick lashes. She saw a well-shaped nose, and a full mouth with a wide lower lip. She saw an enviable bosom, a narrow waist, wide hips, good legs, an over-all picture of total femininity.

There was, she supposed, a certain flamboyancy to Margaret's good looks. They bordered on the narrow edge of cheapness but only because of their plenitude; and generous endowment was not, to Betty, a saving grace. Had the hair been less blonde, the eyes less brown, the bust less emphatically pronounced, the legs turned not quite so splendidly, the woman could have been forgiven. Had the smile been less radiantly perfect . . . there, the smile. Even the smile. Margaret Gault carried a scar below her right cheek, the result of a childhood accident. The scar was in the shape of a small cross, almost invisible when her face was in repose. But when she smiled, the scar became a deep dimple in her cheek, enhancing the smile. The one-sided dimpling of her face, the sudden revealed whiteness of her teeth behind the red lips made her smile a startlingly radiant thing.

It was unfair. Her beauty remained consistent, and its consistency rankled. But, curiously, Margaret's beauty was the only thing about her which Betty could find to dislike. And even that, paradoxically, delighted her traitor eye.

"I think he's oversexed," she said.

"Do you really?" Margaret asked.

"I think they *all* are, if you want to know the truth."

Margaret shrugged.

Betty watched her shrewdly. Nothing would have pleased her more than the thought that something was amiss in the Gault relationship. Unfortunately, though, the signs as Betty read them did not point in that direction. Being an avid sign reader, but only of those which pertained to where she was going, she dropped the thought as quickly as she had picked it up.

"I wanted to watch Steve Allen," she said. "I certainly don't think that's too much to ask after a day of running around after *his* monsters."

"Do you take cream?" Margaret asked.

23

"And sugar. Six months she knows me, and she still asks." She stirred her coffee and then sipped at it. "Steve Allen had Louis Jordan as his guest. I like him."

"I do, too," Margaret said, sitting down at the table opposite Betty.

"He sang this thing, 'Beware, Brother, Beware.' It's a hot sketch. I was getting a kick out of it. That's when Felix came in with his ideas. I can smell his ideas six miles away, even before he gets off the train. If it was up to Felix—"

"What else did he sing?"

"I don't know. Felix turned off the set." She leaned forward confidentially. "He carried me upstairs like a hero. Except that he had his hand under my skirt all the way. You don't see that in the movies, Miss." Betty chuckled in reminiscence. "I'll tell you the truth, it wasn't so enjoyable. I've got to be in the mood, and right then I was in the mood for Steve Allen." Betty paused. "Do you ever feel that way?"

"What way?"

"As if you just don't feel like it?"

"Yes."

"Felix always feels like it. But always! There must be a difference between men and women. Don't you find Don that way?"

"What way?" Margaret asked again.

"Always ready."

"Oh. Yes. Yes."

"Sometimes I don't even feel like looking at him, let alone going to bed with him. Sometimes he bores me stiff." Again Betty paused. "Does Don bore you?"

"No," Margaret said quickly.

"Never?"

"No, he's always very interesting."

"Well, a girl like you . . ." Betty started, and then let the sentence trail.

Margaret stared through the kitchen window, past the chintz curtains, and she wondered why the women she knew eventually confided to her the intimate details of their married lives. She was not unaware of her good looks and she suspected that most women, as well as men, unconsciously equated beauty with sexuality. Their automatic assumptions annoyed her. In female company she invariably started the game at a disadvantage, putting women on the defensive the moment she stepped into a room. And even if she'd sat in a corner all night mentally reciting the Lord's Prayer, no woman present could look at her without imagining that the most sensual thoughts lay concealed behind her pretty face.

Having reached the primitive conclusion that where there's smoke there's fire, they then progressed to the next level of their dubious reasoning. Margaret Gault automatically received attention from men, and the women assumed she provoked it by cold premeditation. They all wanted to know what Margaret had that they didn't have—even though the answer smacked them squarely between the eyes. And so they engaged her in conversation, and the talk was a curiously preordained thing. Having decided that a face so beautiful, a body so provocative, were made for nothing but sin, they then proceeded to impute to Margaret a sexual wisdom which, in the beginning, she truly did not possess. At the same time, they treated her like the classic and decorative dumb blonde who was good for one thing alone, so that it was almost impossible for her to venture into any other fields of conversation without being laughed off as an ambitious nitwit.

". . . when it was all over. So what can you say to a man like that?" Betty stopped abruptly. "Are you listening to me?"

"What? Oh, yes, of course."

"Where were you?" Betty wanted to know.

"I was just thinking . . . It'll be winter soon."

"You're too cheerful for me, Miss," Betty said. "I'm going home."

"Have another cup of coffee."

"No. Thanks."

She was already out of the kitchen and walking through the living room. In the entrance hallway she paused. She seemed about to say something, then abruptly changed her mind, opened the door, and left. Margaret stood at the door, watching her cross the street. The leaves whipped about her small figure like a horde of multicolored birds in frenzied flight.

The telephone rang.

For a terrified moment Margaret stood frozen at the door. The piercing clamor of the phone shrieked through the silent house.

"I'll let it ring," she said aloud, and then she began counting the rings—*three, four, five* . . .

"I'll let it ring," she said again, hearing her own words in the stillness of the hallway, hearing the phone shrilling in the kitchen —*eight, nine, ten* . . .

She closed the door and walked through the living room, and then to the phone, where it rested on the counter top near the sink. She stared at it, biting her lip, not wanting to pick it up. And then her hand reached out, and she took the receiver from the cradle and held the phone to her ear, not speaking for a moment, waiting, not knowing for what she was waiting.

When she spoke, her voice was very low.

"Hello?" she said.

"Margaret?" the voice asked.

"You," she said.

3

"PEOPLE sing songs about Indian summer," Altar said, "but they very rarely recognize it when it's all around them."

"Like the Lucky Pierre joke," the blonde said. "Everybody knows the punch line, but nobody remembers the story."

"That's not exactly what I meant, doll," Altar said. He glanced at Larry and added, "She's stupid, but she's a doll."

Coming from Altar, the Broadway cliché sounded like an accurate description. The blonde *was* a doll, a round doll's face and round blue doll's eyes and a doll's Cupid's-bow mouth. There was nothing doll-like about her body, though, or about the way she managed to cross her legs with expert abandon on the front seat of the convertible. She was, Larry realized, one of the few single women with whom he'd come into contact socially for a good many years, and he found her realistic approach to the basic necessities of life bewildering but refreshing.

The first thing Altar had said to him when he stepped into the car was "This is Agnes. You want to lay her?"

Agnes had not batted an eyelash. Agnes had smiled doll-like and said, "Not now, Mr. Cole. I just had breakfast."

The presence of the blonde, the light banter between her and Altar, the way she consciously appreciated Larry as a male, gave the Saturday excursion an unbusinesslike aspect which left Larry feeling somewhat guilty. This was, after all, a business trip to the site of Altar's proposed house. Eve had strenuously objected to business on Saturday, "the one day you can devote fully to the kids." Larry had pointed out that Sunday could be as equally devoted, and he had further elaborated on the "business is business" concept which he'd trained Eve to accept as one of the cruel facts of life. Now, though, with the day unfolding in such splendor, with the crossed legs of the blonde beside him in the open car, he guiltily felt the day might have been well spent with his family.

"I'm an autumn guy," Altar said. "There are different kinds of people, you know." He drove the way he ate, his eyes traveling everywhere, to Larry's face, to the blonde's legs, to the road, the trees, the sky. "I think it has something to do with when you were born. When were you born, Larry?"

"July," Larry said.

"What's your favorite month?"

"October."

"You only said that to blast my theory."

"No, seriously. It's October."

"When were you born, Agnes?" Altar asked, undefeated.

26

Agnes considered the question for a moment. "December," she said. "I came for Christmas."

"What's your favorite month?"

"I like them all."

"You've got to have a favorite," Altar said. "What pleases you most? A nice nip in the air, or a hot sunny day?"

"I like them both."

Altar seemed to be losing his patience. "You've got to like one more than the other."

"Why? How could I appreciate hot days if there were never any cold ones?"

Larry smiled and said, "She's got a point."

"On the top of her head," Altar said. "Why do I always go for dumb girls?"

"He can't stand to lose an argument," Agnes said, giggling. "It makes him furious."

"She's known me for two weeks, and she's already psychoanalyzing me," Altar said. "I've got some advice for you, Larry. Never live with a woman for more than five days."

"Your advice comes late," Larry said. "I've been living with a woman for eight years."

"Your wife, you mean? Who's talking about wives? Wives are a different thing again."

"He knows all about wives," Agnes said, winking. "He chases more wives than any man. . . ."

"You'll note that once the fifth day has been passed," Altar said dryly, "a certain attitude of possessiveness sets in. You'd think women would realize that possessiveness, even though they invented it, is their downfall." And then, without pausing for breath, he added, "We're almost there."

"Do you know what your trouble is, Altar?" Larry asked.

"Yes," Altar said.

"What?"

"I speak the truth."

"No. You speak banalities as if they were profundities."

He had not intended to injure Altar. He had delivered his words in the same light tones which had prevailed since they'd started the drive. But he realized in an instant that he had touched too close to the quick. He saw the momentary pain flicker on Altar's face, and he was immediately sorry.

And then Altar grinned. "I'll let you in on a secret," he said lightly. "The truth always sounds banal. Clichés are nothing to be ashamed of. They're the folk legend of truth."

"I don't understand him at all," Agnes said.

"Oh, go to hell," Altar said playfully. "It's down this road."

"Hell?"

"No, the property, doll."

He made a sharp left turn and began climbing a steep hill. The hill leveled into a gently rolling landscape patched with the faded green of autumn lawns.

"I don't see any contemporary houses," Larry said.

"No? What do you call these?"

"Eyesores."

"You'd call the Taj Mahal an eyesore."

"I would if it were set here," Larry said.

" 'Time is always time,' " Altar said, " 'and place is always and only place.' "

"What's that?"

"Eliot. 'And what is actual is actual only for one time and only for one place.' "

"He an architect?" Larry asked.

"You're joking!" Altar said, appalled.

"I'm joking."

"You're not! By God, I can tell you're not!"

" 'Because I do not hope to turn again, because I do not hope,' " Larry quoted. " 'Because I do not hope to turn, desiring, this man's gift and that man's scope . . .' "

"If you know the goddamn poem, why'd you ask what it was?"

"I only remember the first few lines," Larry said. "It makes me sound intelligent."

"Who's Eliot?" Agnes asked. "I don't know him."

"T. S.," Altar said.

"You don't have to get nasty," she answered, and Altar snorted in delight and turned the car onto a sharply sloping dirt road.

"It's right at the bottom of this road," he said. "What do you think of it?"

"I haven't seen it yet, Altar."

"Why don't you stop calling me Altar?"

"Because Roger sounds as if I'm acknowledging flight instructions."

"Well, I'm sorry all to hell, believe me. I didn't know you were a temperamental ex-pilot."

"I'm neither. I was in the Infantry."

"Officer?"

"Yes."

"I was a Seaman First Class," Altar said somewhat proudly. They were at the foot of the hill now. He pulled up the hand brake and said, "How do you like the view?"

"Beautiful," Larry said. "Is there one for the enlisted men?"

Altar broke up, remembering the Mauldin cartoon. "You're a son of a bitch," he said. "I can't understand why I like you. Come on, let's look at the land."

Larry got out of the car and extended his hand to Agnes. She took his hand and stepped out, showing complete unconcern for her skirts, her long legs flashing at him. For a moment, the pressure of her hand increased. Altar slammed the door on his side. Agnes smiled briefly and dropped Larry's hand.

"Well, what do you think of it?" Altar asked.

"It slopes," Larry said.

"Is that bad?"

"No, I'm just thinking out loud. The house design'll have to take that into consideration. How many acres are there?"

"Six." Altar looked out over the land. "How are the trees?"

"They look fine. Come on, let's walk through it."

"In there?" Agnes asked, her eyes taking in the fallen branches and the brambles and the thick overgrown weeds. "I'm wearing heels."

"If you like, you can stay in the car," Altar said.

"No. I want to see how an architect works," she said, and she looked at Larry archly. For a moment Larry thought he'd imagined the look. He had not been looked at in quite that way for eight years. There was open invitation in the blue eyes, baldly stated, and all he had to do was pick up the dropped cue. He chose to let it lie where it was.

Together, they started into the woods. Autumn lost some of its splendor when viewed leaf by leaf. Like the pointillism of a Seurat painting, the tiny areas of pigment lost their force unless viewed at a distance as an overwhelming whole. Piece by piece, autumn built her jigsaw puzzle around them. The woods were curiously still. There were no bird sounds, no animal sounds. There was only the rattling crush of leaves underfoot, and a sense of time unchanging, unmoving so that Larry felt almost suspended, disoriented as he walked with a man he didn't yet know and a blonde who wanted to know him better.

He could not put her invitation out of his mind. Nor could he dismiss her physical presence. She was there by his side, her hand touching his arm whenever she navigated a difficult stretch of ground. He felt, oddly, as if he were being unfair to Altar, and he did not like the feeling. But he could not rid himself of the appealing idea that this girl had found him attractive, and he cursed his own ego for responding as it had.

In an attempt to get his mind back to the task of studying the land, he asked, "Have you got a survey, Altar?"

"Yes, in the car. Want me to get it?"

"It would help."

"Okay," Altar said, and he turned abruptly and started up toward the convertible.

Agnes sat on a large boulder, crossed her legs and examined her nylons for runs. Larry watched her. The stillness of the woods seemed intense.

She looked up suddenly and said, "Why don't you call me?"

"What for?"

"Don't you want to?"

29

"I don't know," he said honestly.

"Rhinelander 4-4598," she said. "Think it over."

"I already have."

"Good," she said, as if convinced he would call.

"I'm married, you know."

"I know."

"Well . . ."

"I'm not," Agnes said flatly. "Rhinelander 4-4598."

Altar came thrashing through the woods.

"Here are the surveys," he said, handing the photostated copies to Larry. "Are you going to lay her?"

And Larry burst out laughing.

The day with Altar and Agnes had been something of a narcotic.

There was about Altar the glamour of the unattached, irresponsible stud living in Bohemian abandon. This week's blonde was Agnes, and when she was gone there would be another blonde, or a redhead, or a brunette. Altar owed allegiance to no woman; the idea was sinfully stimulating. And on the heels of such a heady concept had come the girl's invitation, awakening in Larry a male ego which he thought had died in his teens.

That he responded, that he felt flattered at first, and then puzzled, and then terribly masculine, had disturbed him. He did not mention the incident to Eve, and his conscious concealment of something on his mind produced a feeling of guilt out of all proportion to what had actually happened.

By 5:30 the next afternoon, the feeling of guilt—inert to begin with—was totally immobilized by the dissipating power of two martinis.

"You are pretty," he said to Eve. He recognized a certain fuzziness about his speech, and he wondered why a drink so subtly beautiful should possess such hidden muscularity.

He reached for the shaker, and Eve sitting opposite him in a straight black skirt and a pale-blue sweater, said, "Don't get drunk."

"Why not?"

"Because you get idiotic."

"I get amorous."

"You get incapable."

"Well, you look pretty." He nodded in agreement with himself.

"Those are the martinis talking, and I'm not flattered."

"You should be flattered," he said.

"Why?"

"Because," he started, and he almost added, "a girl gave me her phone number," but he clipped the word off so that it sounded like a simple childish declaration.

"I'm going to get dinner," Eve said, rising.

"Let's finish the drinks first."

"No. You're going to get romantic, and I'm hungry." She paused. "Besides, the kids are still up."

"We'll invite them in."

"Oh, Larry, for God's sake."

"What's the matter?"

"There's a time and a place," Eve said. "I hate to see you silly."

"What's so silly about drinking a few martinis?"

"Nothing."

"Are you sore or something?"

"No."

"Then what?"

"Nothing. We need bread. Will you go up to the store?"

"The stores are closed. This is Sunday."

"The delicatessen is open. You can get bread there."

"Man does not live by bread alone," he said, grinning.

"Listen, don't . . ." Eve paused. "Larry, there's always later. Will you go for the bread?"

"Sure. Will you be waiting for me when I come back?"

"I'm not going anywhere."

"That's not what I meant."

"I know what you meant."

"Well?"

Eve smiled. The smile to Larry was a thing of a mystery and promise. "I told you," she said. "I'm not going anywhere."

"That means no."

"Does it?" she said, and still she smiled.

"Do you want me to go to the delicatessen?"

"Yes."

"Okay." He rose and started unsteadily for the front door.

"Be careful driving."

"I'm always careful driving. I'm too talented to die in an automobile accident."

"A loaf of white bread."

"Yes, ma'am."

"You're drunk already, aren't you?"

"No, ma'am."

"If you had any idea how absurd you look with that silly grin on your mouth . . ."

"Yes, ma'am."

"Don't get killed." She studied him concernedly. "Maybe I ought to go for the bread."

"I'll go for the bread," he said emphatically, and walked out of the house.

There was a cruel bite on the air, but he was just drunk enough to appreciate it. He liked this idea of sunny days and cool evenings—that was good weather provided by a most provident providence—what did we poor humans do to deserve it? He walked

31

to the car, a '52 Dodge, part of the prize money, he thought, did I once win a prize, did I really win a prize, where's that money now, where's the promise of the shining young star, why am I designing harems for the crazy-bastard writers, what's the matter with you, Cole, what the hell is the matter with you?

He twisted the key in the ignition and started the car, looking at his house, the brick and shingle, the ridiculously outsized gable, the goddam shabby architectural pretense of lovely Pinecrest Manor, the affront, the insult, the padded cell of an eagle. I live there, he thought. Dammit, I *live* there!

"Gracious Living," she had called it. Not the house, never such a sin for an architect's wife, certainly not Eve, whose eye was true, who recognized the falseness of Pinecrest Manor, who could dissect the development with the cold logic of an Aesthetics professor. But the drinks. Eve's idea, and Eve's title. The first time he'd come out of the small third bedroom which served as his office to find hot hors d'oeuvres and a private cocktail hour. Had they ever been that naïve? Had "Gracious Living" been capitalized in quotes even then, or had they really *discovered* the before-dinner drink and then later given the title sarcastic overtones in defense of their earlier naïvete?

He backed out of the driveway and executed a screeching left turn.

He could remember the night they'd fed the children and then settled down to a most ungracious hour of getting completely plastered, forgetting their own dinner. God, how long ago was that? Are people ever really that young? Gracious Living. Boy, do we live graciously!

He gripped the wheel tightly and said aloud "Pinecrest Manor, I hate your guts!"

The center's parking lot was almost empty, the way it always was on a Sunday. The delicatessen and the drugstore were the only open shops. He pulled up alongside a pale-blue Chevy, slammed on the brakes and snapped open the door almost in one continuous motion. There was a man with a crew cut sitting at the wheel of the Chevy.

Go ahead, say something, Larry thought.

The man said nothing.

Larry sauntered toward the delicatessen, feeling somewhat proud of himself. He pushed open the glass door, spotted the bread shelf immediately and was walking toward it when he saw the woman. The pale-blonde. The woman from the bus stop. He walked past the loaves of bread. He stopped a foot away from her and said, "Hi."

Margaret Gault turned.

An uncertain smile formed on her mouth, and he watched the spreading cushion of her lips and the revealed brilliance of her

32

smile, the deep dimple in her right cheek and he thought, She's beautiful.

"The bus stop," he said. "I'm Chris's father."

"Oh." The smile widened. "Yes."

They stood opposite each other, silent for a moment. She seemed reluctant to leave, and yet he sensed an eagerness to leave, and he suddenly had the idea that she was afraid of him, and he thought, Am I that drunk?

And then for no reason that he could understand—it was not what he was thinking; it was the furthest thing from what he was thinking—he said, "You're not so pretty."

The smile faded from her mouth. There was, he noticed, a minuscule scar on her cheek. She seemed flustered for a moment, and then she picked up her package from the counter and said, "I must go. My husband's waiting," and she left the store.

When he got outside, the blue Chevy was gone. He drove home, pulled into the driveway, went into the house, and threw the bread onto the kitchen table.

"I just talked to a gorgeous blonde," he said.

"Really?" Eve asked.

"Yeah."

"What's her name?"

"I don't know."

"You couldn't have talked very long," Eve said. "She from the neighbourhood?"

"I think so. I saw her at the bus stop once."

"Oh." Eve nodded knowingly. "Margaret Gault," she said. "Go wash your hands. Dinner's ready. Chris! David! Dinner!"

4

DON GAULT walked into the house with his hands in his pockets.

It was Monday evening, and he had put in a long, hard day at the plant. He had pulled down his tie and unbuttoned his collar the moment he'd stepped out of the automobile. Then, hooking his jacket over his arm, he had put both hands into his pockets, removing one briefly to open the front door, returning it to his pocket as he entered the house.

He wore a slender gold chain around his neck. A small locket containing a picture of his mother was cradled in the hollow of his throat, exaggerating the muscularity of his neck. He looked for Patrick in the living room, then crossed to the windows, walking past the cobbler's-bench coffee table, and glanced out at the back yard. His son was nowhere in sight.

"Margaret!" he called.

"Don?" Her voice came from the upstairs bedroom.

"Hiya."

"I'll be down in a minute, honey."

"Where's the mail?"

"Kitchen table."

"Okay."

He threw his jacket over one of the chairs and went into the kitchen. The mail had already been opened, and Margaret had neatly stacked the slit envelopes in a little pile near the sugar bowl. He sat at the large round pine-top table and picked up the stack, thumbing through it quickly. Bills. Naturally, there'd be bills. There were always bills. He sat in the deepening darkness of the kitchen, the envelopes in his square, compact hands, his face vaguely troubled.

The face of Don Gault was curious in that it was absolutely clean. He wore his blond hair in a skull-tight crew cut which completed the immaculate square of his face. There was a geometric regularity to his features, an unblinking monotony about the straight blond eyebrows, the clean sweep of the nose, the hard unbroken line of the mouth. Only the eyes softened the face. Bright and blue, scattered with random flecks of white, they seemed at first as cold and clean as the rest of the face. But there was warmth there, and gentleness.

He was five feet nine inches tall, some four inches taller than Margaret in her stockinged feet, but inches did not matter with Don Gault. He was one of those perfectly proportioned men whose bodies have the flat, obdurate gleam of polished stone surfaces. The eyes were the only contradiction in the unbending geometry of Don Gault. And perhaps the eyes were the man.

It did not disturb him that Margaret had opened *all* the letters, including some addressed to him. He believed that marriage was an absolute partnership and the thought simply would never have entered his mind that there was anything in his mail which Margaret should not see.

Troubled, he thought only of the bills and of how difficult it was to earn money and hang onto it. For perhaps the fiftieth time he told himself he should have gone to college on the G.I. Bill after the war. He shouldn't have let that opportunity go by. He always felt slightly inadequate in the presence of college men. He couldn't exactly pin-point what it was about them that made him feel awkward. A certain slick façade, perhaps, or the arrogant knowledge that they were better equipped to lick, to defeat, life than he was.

In his heart he knew he would have been an absolute flop at school. He'd never had any patience with books or reading or sitting still and listening to another man talk. He was good with his hands, had always been. He could still remember the jewelry box he had made for his mother in a junior-high-school wood-working class.

"Did you make this, Donald?" she asked. "For me?" And he had nodded wordlessly, basking in her open admiration. "With your own hands? With your own hands?"

With his own hands, with these hands.

He held them out in front of him. They were good hands. They had been good to him.

I killed a man with these hands, he thought.

He immediately shoved the thought out of his mind. But like a nail driven too far into a narrow plank, the sharp tip of the thought protruded, catching at the fabric of his mind.

"Margaret!" he shouted, suddenly angry.

He put his hands into his pockets and walked into the living-room and then to the foot of the steps leading upstairs.

"Margaret!"

"Yes," she said. "I'm coming."

He waited, annoyed, and not knowing why, blaming it on the fact that he was hungry and there were no cooking smells in the house. She appeared at the top of the steps. She wore a tight black sweater and a flaring white skirt and exceptionally high heels.

"What are you supposed to be?" he said.

"What's the matter?" She was smiling. She stood with one hand on the wooden railing, the other on her hip.

"Why do you always have to look like—" He bit off the sentence.

"Like what?" The smile was brilliant. Her hair, always wild, looked now as if she had purposely disarranged it before coming out of the bedroom.

"Like I don't know," he said harshly. "What are you always getting dressed up around the house for?"

"Don't you want me to look pretty?"

"I don't want you to look like a—"

"Like a what?" she asked quickly.

Her smile was beginning to infuriate him. "Never mind," he said.

"I haven't got anything on underneath," she said.

"Margaret! For the love of. . . .!"

She came down the steps slowly, her hand gliding along the railing, burlesquing a movie siren, slithering down the steps, undulating her body, moistening her lips, the smile never leaving her mouth. In a sultry, sexy voice, she said, "Come on, big boy."

"Where's Patrick?" he asked.

"I sent him over to Betty's."

"Got this all planned out, huh?"

"Um-huh."

She was a step above him now, so that her eyes were almost

35

level with his. Her eyes were impishly bright, and the smile was fixed on her mouth, and he wanted to kiss her, pull her to him and cover her mouth with kisses. Her hand touched his shoulder, rested there a moment, and then slid over his chest, down, trailing fire behind it. She touched him, and he ached with the touch, and he felt himself come instantly awake, and her smile widened, widened until there was nothing in the room but her smile and her hand on him, and he thought, This is evil, this is evil.

"Come upstairs," she said.

"What . . . what's today?"

"It's all right."

"Are you sure?"

"Yes," she said.

"I don't want any accidents. I don't want—"

"I'm sure."

"When will Patrick be back?"

"I told her I'd call."

"Does she know what—?"

"Come upstairs."

"Margaret . . ."

"Come upstairs."

"It's still light."

"It'll be dark soon."

"Margaret . . ."

"Come with me, Don. Come upstairs with me."

"What about dinner? Have you—?"

"Don't you *want* me, Don?"

"I . . ."

"Don't you want to be inside me?"

"Don't talk like that!"

"How do you want me to talk?"

"You're a mother, for God's—"

"Don, Don . . ."

Her fingers tightened, and there was no smile any more, only her hand, and his entire life clutched in the warm full palm of her hand, and then she released him suddenly and turned and started up the steps. She walked swiftly, the skirt swirling around her legs, the sharp heels leaving tiny rounded squares in the pile of the rug. Dusk had invaded the living room, spreading into the corners, spreading darkness into the silent house. In the basement, the oil burner started with a sudden click.

He brushed his hand across his eyes, and then he started up after her. She was naked when he entered the bedroom. He could see the line of her body against the deep blue of the blanket, softened by dusk. She stirred when he came into the room, twisting the familiar golden head on the white pillow.

He went into the bathroom. He did not turn on the light. He stood looking into the sink for a long time, the darkness growing around him. He took off his clothes then and folded them neatly over the edge of the tub. Then he washed his hands and went out to her.

The room was very dark. He found his way to the bed, and he sat, and her hand went to him instantly, and he climbed onto the bed feeling immense and clumsy, and then he lay beside her on his back, and whispered, "Make love to me."

"Do you think I'm pretty?"

"Yes."

"Do you love me?"

"Yes."

"Do you think of me when you're working?"

"Yes."

"What do you think?"

"I don't know."

"Do you think of going to bed with me?"

"Don't talk like that."

"What do you think?"

"I don't know."

"Don . . ."

"Make love to me."

"What do you want to do to me? What do you think of doing to me?"

"Nothing. I don't think anything like that. You know I don't."

"What *do* you think then?"

"I think of you."

"What?"

"You."

"What about me?"

"I just think of you."

"How?"

"I don't know."

"In bed?"

"No."

"Naked?"

"No."

"How?"

"I don't know. Are you ready?"

"I've been ready all day."

"Help me."

"Why?"

"I want you to."

"Don't you know where it is?"

"Don't make fun of me."

"I'm not."

"Then help me, Margaret."

"Why?"

"Because."

37

"If you really wanted me . . ."

"I do, I do."

"Say it."

"Help me, Margaret."

"No."

"Margaret . . ."

"Tell me you want me."

"Margaret . . ."

"Tell me what you want to do to me."

"Oh, Margaret, Margaret . . ."

"Why won't you touch me?"

"Honey, can't we . . . ?"

"Kiss me."

He kissed her, and her hand tightened, and he pulled his mouth from hers.

"Touch my breasts. Don't you like my breasts?"

"I love them."

"They're good. They're big and soft, and the nipples—"

"Don't talk like that!"

"Why don't you ever touch them?"

"I do. You know I do. There. There."

"Do you like the way they feel?"

"Yes."

"Tell me."

"I like them."

"Tell me why."

"Because I do."

"Tell me. Talk to me, Don. *Tell me!*"

"Honey, honey, help me!"

"No! Do it yourself."

"Honey, I can't. I don't want to."

"Why not?"

"I don't . . ."

He stopped. The room was very silent. When her voice came, it came as a slow, sepulchral command.

"*Touch me!*"

"No."

"Touch me."

"No."

"Don, why? Why? Why?"

"I don't . . . I don't want to get you dirty," he said.

He heard her heavy sigh, and he held his breath for a moment, and then he felt the weight of her body on him, her hands guiding him, and he closed his eyes tightly and said again, "Make love to me."

38

5

IN THE second act of *The Pajama Game*, Eddie Foy, Jr., had trouble with his trousers, and Larry almost fell out of his seat laughing. His laughter was both surprising and encouraging to Eve. She had known Larry for ten years, been married to him for eight, and still could not understand what made him laugh.

She knew he had a good sense of humor. The things he said were truly funny, and he was the first to laugh at a good joke. But he would sit at a play or a movie when a comic line came along, and the house would collapse into waves of uncontrolled hilarity while Larry remained steadfastly deadpan. And then one of the actors would say or do something which no one else considered comical, and Larry would erupt into secret laughter which continued long after the line was broken or the gesture made.

Having resigned herself to this peculiarity after years of puzzlement, she was pleased on Friday night to see Larry laughing along with the rest of the house on the trousers routine. His response added to the surprise-party atmosphere surrounding the entire evening.

He had come home Wednesday evening after a day in the city and announced "We're being wined and dined this Friday."

"By whom?" she asked.

"Baxter and Baxter."

"And who are Baxter and Baxter?"

"Just about the biggest architectural and planning firm in New York," Larry said smugly.

"My! What's the occasion?"

"They have a proposal to make."

"I thought you liked working at home. You don't want to join any firm do you?"

"No, but this isn't that kind of proposal. They want my advice on something."

"Really? Larry, that's wonderful. Aren't you flattered?"

"Yeah, I guess so," he said, as if first coming to the realization.

"I'll have to get a sitter," Eve said, and she started for the phone. Larry followed her into the bedroom.

"Make it early, Eve. We're meeting them for dinner, and they're taking us to a show."

"I'm thrilled," Eve said, her eyes glowing as she dialled. "Will Baxter *and* Baxter be there?"

"No, just Harry Baxter and his wife."

"What's she like?"

"Never met her."

"Do you think . . . ?" She paused. "Hello?" she said into the phone, and then began the intricate womanly business of exchanging cordialities with a seventeen-year-old sitter.

Eloise Baxter had turned out to be a mild-mannered woman in her middle forties. She was a native New Yorker, but there was about her the aura of an out-of-towner who is bewildered by the clutter and noise of a big city. At dinner, Eve confessed to her that this was the first time she'd been in Sardi's. With simple honesty, Eloise answered, "The food is good and they get you to the show on time. Besides, the waiters know Harry. When they call him 'Mr. Baxter,' he feels like a celebrity."

Harry Baxter was a short man of fifty-four with a craggy face, an unkempt mustache, and a deep rumbling voice. He seemed stuffy and insensitive until you noticed his eyes and his hands. And then, all at once, you got the feeling that this unattractive little man could design wonderful buildings. He and Larry hit it off instantly, and by the time dessert was being served they were talking familiarly of Gropius, Le Corbusier, and Mies.

"Well," Baxter said at the end of the discussion, "our Puerto Rican project will undoubtedly be prefab. That's why I brought up Gropius to begin with."

"I understand," Larry said.

"How does it strike you?"

"It sounds good, so far."

"That's encouraging," Baxter said. "Think about it." He glanced at his watch. "Say, if we're going to see that show, I'd better call for a check."

Eve had heard the reference to Puerto Rico, and it aroused her curiosity without satisfying it. Nor did the topic come up again until they were sitting in Lindy's after the show, and then Eve, who was reading her menu, almost missed Baxter's second mention of the project.

". . . and, of course, it would necessitate going to Puerto Rico."

"Naturally," Larry said.

"I imagine a week's time would be sufficient," Baxter said. "That is, of course, if the proposal appeals to you."

"Well, I'm really pleased you thought of me," Larry said, and Eve turned her complete attention to the conversation at the table.

"But you're not interested, is that it?"

"I'm interested, but I'm working on another job right now."

"Oh, what kind?"

"A house."

"How far along are you?"

"Well, to be truthful we've barely started."

"Then postpone it awhile."

"No, I couldn't do that. The client is anxious to begin, and I'd like to present some ideas to him."

"I understand. When will you show your rough sketches?"

"I'm meeting with him on the twenty-ninth."

"And after that?"

"I'd want him to study the drawings for a while."

"Then you could conceivably leave by the first of the month?"

"Yes. If I took the job."

"What job?" Eve asked. "Leave for where?"

"Puerto Rico," Larry said.

"My firm is designing a factory for the island," Baxter explained. "A lot of new industry is being seduced to the island by the lenient taxes. Actually. it's a wonderful thing for the economy, and it doesn't hurt the manufacturers one bit. Our factory is to have its own housing development for the employees." He paused. waiting for Eve to grasp his meaning.

"Oh, I see," she said, nodding.

"Naturally, since your husband won a prize back in 1952 for—"

"Oh, did he?" Eloise Baxter interrupted. "I didn't know that."

"Yes, El," Baxter said. "In an international competition. Larry designed a housing development for a typewriter factory in Milan. Six hundred families. His scheme won second prize. Seventy-five hundred dollars, wasn't it, Larry?"

"Yes." He paused. "Actually a little less after the lire exchange."

"tI'm not attempting flattery when I say you should have got first prize. I studied both schemes when they were published, and yours was superior by far."

"Well, thank you."

"I always thought so, too," Eve said.

"You're prejudiced," Larry answered.

"I'm not," Baxter said, "but the devil with prize-awarding committees. The important thing is that I saw your scheme and liked the thinking in it. I can use that level of thinking on this project. Please don't misunderstand me. I have a staff inferior to none, and I think our factory design is excellent. Nor do I doubt we'll turn in a competent job on the development, too. But if I can bring flair to it, if I can bring the sort of sweeping imagination you showed in your Milan scheme, I'll be achieving something more than the merely adequate. Do you follow me?"

"Yes," Larry said.

Baxter turned to Eve. "That's why I've asked your husband to work with us in an advisory capacity. I want him to go to Puerto Rico to get the feel of the site. It's as easy to plan well as to plan badly, and I'd like to begin the right way."

Eve nodded. She could feel pride for her husband swelling into her throat.

"I can pay you fifteen hundred dollars, Larry. Plus all expenses, of course. I'd want an imaginative site layout, recommendations

41

for the kind of buildings you'd want on the site, and a schematic of one of the buildings."

"That's worth a lot more than fifteen hundred dollars," Larry said, and Eve felt a slight pang at his audacity.

"How much more?"

"I'd want three thousand. Plus expenses. If you want to save the expenses, I can work from photographs of the site."

"No, I think the feel is important. Would you settle for twenty-five hundred?"

Eve looked to Larry nervously. "That sounds fair," Larry said.

"What's the trouble, Mrs. Cole?" Baxter asked.

"Why, none. It's entirely up to my husband."

Baxter smiled. "Have you ever been separated before?"

"No."

"I see."

"Oh, don't be silly," Eve said. "Really, it isn't that at all. I'd like Larry to go. It's entirely up to him."

"Larry," Baxter said, "would you be more inclined to say yes if your wife could go along?"

"Well, I . . ."

"Take her with you."

"Well, that's very kind of you. But . . ."

"It's not kind at all. Architecture is an art, but it's also a business. And I've never yet met a successful businessman who doesn't speculate. If this design is superior, other projects will come to my firm. The housing development is an integral part of the factory. I want your ideas. I'll pay for them now because I'll profit from them later."

Baxter paused. The table was suddenly silent.

"Can you and Eve leave by November first?"

Larry looked at Eve. Eve nodded.

"All right," Larry said.

"Good," Baxter answered. "Then we've got a deal." He extended his hand and Larry took it. Then he grinned broadly and said, "Ah, here comes the coffee."

They were both silent until they approached the bridge.

The radio was on in the car, and Larry was listening to it in seeming contentment. Eve had learned not to push conversation upon him, especially after a new idea was presented. She knew that the idea needed time to jell and that once the excitement of it—or the disappointment, in some cases—had caught up with him, there was no stopping his torrent of words.

So she would not have brought up Puerto Rico, even though she was bubbling with the excitement of it, had the disk jockey not begun playing a mambo. And then, because she normally associated mambos with Spanish-speaking peoples, and because she was thinking of lush tropical growth and sunny skies to begin with, she automatically said, "I'll have to get some new bathing suits."

He realized she was only thinking aloud, and there was certainly nothing in her words to precipitate an argument. Yet he felt an awakening of anger, even though he answered her mildly.

"He seems like a pretty decent fellow," he said. "Baxter, I mean."

"Yes, he does."

"I hope we're not taking advantage of him."

"What do you mean?"

"Well, you know."

"No," Eve said innocently.

"Taking you along," Larry said. There still was no anger in his voice. But he felt himself frowning, and he wondered why.

Eve thought for a moment and then said, "Well it was his suggestion."

"More or less," Larry answered.

"More or less?"

"You did sort of cue him."

"Cue him?"

"Yes." Gently, although he was aware of his own increasing irritation, he added, "Honey, you don't have to repeat every word I say."

"But I didn't cue him. I didn't do anything."

"Well, you smiled sort of wistfully. You know what I mean."

"Wistfully?" Eve repeated.

"Sort of like a newlywed, you know, who couldn't bear to be separated from her husband."

"Oh, Larry, please, I didn't," Eve said, laughing somewhat embarrassedly.

Her laugh annoyed him. "It seemed that way to me," he said. "I hope he doesn't think you're . . . well, pushy."

"Pushy? Me?" Now Eve frowned.

"Yes, yes."

"Pushy? Are you talking about *me*?"

"Eve, you're raising your—"

"Well, I simply don't like to be called pushy."

"Nobody *called* you pushy," he said, his own voice rising. "I just hope Baxter didn't get the wrong idea and *think* you were pushy."

"I don't see how he could have got *that* impression," Eve said loftily.

"Well, you did—you did sort of . . . well, dammit, you looked pretty upset when you thought I was going down there alone!"

He felt anger full upon him now, and he thought, We're going to have a fight, but he was helpless to stop the anger or the argument which he was certain would erupt around them. He didn't even know why he was angry, and his inability to pinpoint the cause of his irritation made him angrier still.

"In fact," he said, "it was pretty embarrassing."

"What was embarrassing?" Eve asked.

"Business is business," he said flatly. "I thought you knew that."

"How did I do anything to—?"

"You could have kicked this right out of the window," he said, gathering steam, "right out of the window! We were lucky, that's all. Baxter's reaction could have been the complete opposite."

"Baxter's reaction to *what*, damnit!" Eve said.

"To your wanting to come along, damnit?" Larry said.

"But it was his suggestion!"

"Come on!" Larry snapped.

"It—"

"You could have killed this opportunity. The first *real* chance since that rotten prize. Do you think I enjoy designing—designing unimportant things? Don't you think I want something bigger for myself? You could have—"

"Me?" Eve asked.

"Yes, you! You! Who the hell do you think?"

"What did I *do*, would you mind telling me?"

"Why'd you have to insist on making the trip with me?"

"Insist?"

"Yes, insist, insist! And stop repeating every damn word I say!"

"I didn't insist on anything. Baxter made the suggestion."

"Sure, he made the suggestion. And you sat there like a wilted flower with an apologetic smile. Oh, no, really," he mimicked, "really, Mr. Baxter, it's entirely up to Larry, really it is."

"Well, it was. And I didn't sit there like a wilted flower or *anything*. The decision was yours."

"Sure, provided you could go along. I'm going there to work, you know, not to—"

"Who's stopping you from working? I was perfectly content to have you go alone. Baxter said—"

"Baxter said, Baxter said—"

"Well, he did! Now cut it out, Larry! You're getting me angry!"

"Oh, am I? Well, isn't that too damn bad!"

"You can go to Puerto Rico alone if you like. You can go to China, for all I care. You can go and *stay*, for that matter."

"Sure, sure. Now I'm the one who's anxious to get away from you. I'm the one who's dying to flop into some Spanish brothel and—"

"Maybe that's *exactly* what you want!" Eve snapped.

The car went dead silent.

He sat with his hands on the wheel and his foot on the accelerator and he looked out at the road ahead, his anger dissipating, to be replaced by a deep puzzlement.

"I'm sorry," he said softly. "I didn't want to argue."

"This could have been fun, you know," Eve said, thoroughly infuriated now. "You didn't have to spoil it."

"I'm sorry," Larry said again.

They drove home in utter silence. The baby sitter greeted them at the door with the assurance that neither of the children had awoken. Larry paid her and drove her home. When he got back to the house, Eve was asleep. He undressed quietly and then climbed into bed beside her. It grew cold sometime in the middle of the night, and Eve curled up against him, and his arms unconsciously circled her, and his hands found her breasts, and in her sleep she murmured, "You stinker," but she did not move away from the warmth of his body.

6

MONDAY morning.

He felt logy and puffed with sleep, and he vowed to turn down the thermostat at night so that the house would be cool and right for sleeping, but how could you do that with children in the house, David still wetting the bed; the boy would catch pneumonia.

He was sullen and uncommunicative at the breakfast table. He planned an extended session at the drawing board that morning, and he hadn't bothered shaving. He sensed Eve's disapproval, and he told himself he would shave right after lunch. They had patched up the argument over the weekend, had in fact discussed the coming Puerto Rico trip with great enthusiasm, and he did not want to risk a fresh breach over something as ridiculous as a beard.

"I'll walk you to the bus stop," he told Chris. "I need some fresh air this morning."

"Can I come, Dad?" David asked.

"I don't think there's time to get you all bundled up, David."

"Is there, Eve?" David asked.

"I don't think so, son."

"I never go anyplace," David said unfairly. "Only Chris goes."

"That's because I'm five," Chris said.

"I'm five, too."

"You're not."

"I'm five," David said firmly.

"Is he, Daddy?"

45

"No. But you'll be five soon, David. You stay here and help your mommy."

They put on their coats and left the house. The air was sharp and crisp. It attacked his cheeks and his teeth like a cold needle-point spray.

"I saw a squirrel yesterday," Chris said.

"Yeah?"

"He was burying nuts."

"That's good," Larry said.

"That's so he'll have something to eat this winter."

"I know."

"Sure. I know, too."

He was coming awake. He could feel his mind returning to his body, as if it had been away for a long time and was now tentatively trying out the furniture. It was a cold day, but there was beauty in the cloudless blue of the sky, the barren streets rushing off to a vanishing point on the horizon.

"I'll have to put in antifreeze," he said aloud.

"What?"

"Nothing."

"He holds the nuts in his hands," Chris said. "Just like a person."

"His paws."

"Sure, his paws."

He saw Margaret Gault when he was a block away from the bus stop. Unconsciously he quickened his step so that Chris had to trot to keep up with him. She was standing alone with her son, and the boy had his arms wrapped around her, his head buried in the protective folds of her skirt.

"There's Patrick," Chris said, and he ran off to join the other boy. Larry slowed his pace, assuming an air of nonchalant ease. When he was close enough to her, he smiled and said, "Good morning."

"Good morning," she answered, returning the smile, her right cheek magically dimpling.

"Got cold all of a sudden, didn't it?"

"Yes," she said, and she shuddered a little at the thought, and then pulled her son closer.

"Think the frost'll hurt the rhubarb?" Larry asked.

"What?" she said.

"The fr——" He smiled. "Forget it. It's a bad joke."

"I just didn't hear you," she explained.

"It's still a bad joke."

They were silent for a moment. He watched her. She seemed embarrassed in his presence. For a fleeting instant he wondered how the scene appeared to their neighbors, the two standing alone on a windswept street.

"You're all dressed up today," he said.

46

"I'm just going shopping."

"New York?"

"No. Just the center."

"You look nice."

She smiled. The smile was uncertain, as if she didn't know whether or not to accept his compliment. "Are you on vacation?" she asked.

"Me? Vaca—— Oh. Oh, no. I work at home most of the time."

"I was wondering."

"Yes, I work at home."

She paused, and he could see her thinking, and then she smiled and said "A cousin of mine is a bookie, too."

He burst out laughing, surprised by her humor, surprised that she had taken the trouble to want to make him laugh. He had the feeling that she was stupid, and the further feeling that he was stepping into a timeworn cliché, falling for the stereotyped idea that all beautiful women are stupid. In a vague way, too, it annoyed him that he had so readily accepted the fact of her beauty or so warmly responded to her little joke.

Her son snuggled closer to her, his head tight against her thighs.

"He's the lucky one," Larry said.

Again she seemed embarrassed. She glanced down quickly, seemed undecided whether to push the boy away from her body or pull him closer. Her lashes fluttered and Larry couldn't tell whether she had consciously maneuvered them or whether she was truly as bewildered as she appeared.

He suddenly wondered if she had suspected any *double entendre* in his words, and he quickly explained, "He's nice and warm," and then just as suddenly realized he had fully intended a double meaning.

Mothers were appearing in the streets now. Storm doors clicked shut behind them, and they stepped into the well-ordered streets of the development, wearily leading their charges off to another day of school. They descended on the bus stop, and Margaret began talking with them, and he noticed an instant change in her attitude, a lighter tone in her voice, a smile that was forced and not so genuine as her earlier smile had been. And then the big yellow school bus rumbled around the corner and ground to a stop, and the doors snapped open, and the little boys fought for first place in the line, and one of the little girls squeaked, "Ladies first, ladies first!" and Chris ran to him and planted a cold, moist kiss on his cheek and then scrambled aboard the bus, and he was aware all at once of the fact that he had not shaved. The women began to disperse almost before the bus got under way. He waved at Chris and then turned.

"Well," he said to Margaret, "so long."

She nodded briefly, smiling, and he turned and walked back to the house.

In two days' time, the walls of his office were covered with sketches.

The room was a small one, the smallest in the house, a perfect eleven-by-eleven square. The wall opposite the door carried a bank of windows which rose from shoulder level to the ceiling. A good northern light came through the windows even though the blank side of a split-level was visible not fifteen feet away.

The room was devoid of all furniture save his drawing board, a stool, a filing cabinet for blueprints, and a filing cabinet for correspondence. A fluorescent lamp on a swinging arm hung over the drawing board for use on days when the natural light was insufficient.

The drawing board was large, a three-by-four-foot rectangle set up against the window wall. Thick tan detail paper had been stapled to its wooden surface. He liked to work in an orderly fashion, and so the board was uncluttered except for the tools he considered essential to his trade. These were a box of mechanical pencils, a second box containing leads of different hardness (H and 2H were the ones he used most frequently), a T square hanging on a cup hook at the right of the board, a scale, a ruby eraser and the item he considered indispensable: an erasing shield. Rolls of tracing paper in various widths—twelve inch, twenty-four inch, and thirty inch—lay on top of the flat green surface of the blueprint cabinet together with his typewriter, a portable machine which had seen better days.

He had used the typewriter when he'd first begun the Altar job, listing an outline of requirements for each room. He had not concerned himself with general requirements. These he retained in his memory and there was no need for a typewritten reminder. At the same time, the notes—while being detailed—did not consider such specifics as furniture sizes, which he knew by heart and which automatically came to mind when he was considering the size of any room.

The notes then, detailed but not specific, looked like this:

STUDY—MOST IMPORTANT ROOM IN HOUSE! Desires open view and feeling of spaciousness. Does not like to work near walls. Desk unsurrounded. Space for many books. Would like balcony overlooking short view as opposed to longer open view from desk. Exposure irrelevant, but not looking into sun. Works from ten in morning to four in afternoon generally. Does not want look or feel of an office, needs area here for small refrigerator and hot plate as well as space for hidden filing cabinets. These for correspondence and carbon copies of manuscripts. Desk will be large. Other furniture: slop table, sofa, bar.

BEDROOM—Sleep two people. View unnecessary. Likes to wake to morning sun. Fifteen square feet closet space. Accessibility to study. Balcony if possible. (Tie-in to study balcony?) No need for . . .

The notes went on in similar fashion for each room in the house. There was a time when Larry, fresh out of Pratt Institute and beginning practice, would have made a flow diagram of the proposed house. The diagram would have been a simple series of circles, each representing an area, and its purpose would have been to define the relationship between the areas. He still used a mental flow diagram, but he no longer found it necessary to commit such elementary planning to paper. Unless, of course, he were working on something with as many elements as a hospital. A house rarely contained more than ten or twelve elements, and these he safely juggled in his mind.

With most houses, Larry found it best to begin his thinking with an over-all theme which came from the client. These, capitalized in his mind, were necessities or concepts like Ideal Orientation, Maximum Economy, Soar Heavenward, Cloistered Silence and the like. Roger Altar wanted to spend seventy-five thousand dollars on his house, and he had given Larry a virtual *carte blanche*. Unstrapped economically, unlimited architecturally, he had only to concern himself with expression, and so his early thoughts about the house did not consider the economical placing of toilets back to back but only the type of statement he wanted in the house: Powerful? Dramatic? Natural? In short, he asked himself what kind of an experience the house would be and, thinking in this manner, he began by drawing perspectives first rather than floor plans.

Would Altar accept all spaces in one space?

Or would he prefer a different experience for the living spaces as opposed to the bedroom spaces?

Or should the house be a tower rather than a low horizontal?

Would Altar prefer something more serene, a scheme of sunken courts?

Using the yellow tracing paper, he allowed his mind to roam, creating the doodles of free expression. Would Altar consider a cube on stilts? The land sloped sharply. Should he take advantage of the slope the way Wright would do; or should he fight it, present the house as a statement against the terrain, like Corbusier?

He did not discard any of his sketches. By Wednesday morning, they were all Scotch-taped to the walls of his office and, like a connoisseur at a gallery exhibit, he stood in the center of the small room and studied them carefully. He would not show Altar all of the sketches. He would eliminate those he disliked and then work over the remainder into $\frac{1}{8}''$ scale drawings. These exploratory sketches would be presented to Altar for thought and comment. Once they had decided on an approach, he would then attack his preliminary drawings, using white paper rather than the rough tracing paper.

The weeding-out was not a simple job. He worked all through the morning and then went into the kitchen for lunch. He felt the need for a short break after lunch and so he drove up to the shopping center to buy the afternoon newspaper. He did not expect to see Margaret Gault, nor was he looking for her.

Mrs. Garandi, the widowed old lady who lived with her son and daughter-in-law in the house across the street, was coming out of the super market with a shopping bag. Larry tucked his newspaper under his arm and then walked quickly to her.

"Can I help you with that, Signora?" he asked.

Mrs. Garandi looked up, surprised. She was a hardy woman with white hair and the compact body of a tree stump. She had been born in Basilico, and despite the fact that she spoke English without a trace of accent, everyone in the neighborhood called her Signora. There was no attempt at sarcasm in their affectionate title. She was a lady through and through.

Larry's fancy, in fact, maintained that the Signora had been high-born in Italy and had learned English from a governess at the same time she'd learned to ride and serve tea. Nothing could have been further from the truth. Mrs. Garandi had been born in poverty, married in poverty, and had come to America with her husband to seek a new life. She knew she couldn't start with a language handicap and so she'd instantly enrolled at night school, where she'd learned her flawless English.

"Oh, Larry," she said, "don't bother. It's not heavy."

"It's no bother. Where's the car?"

"I walked."

"Well, come on, I'll drive you home."

"Thank you," she said. "I am a little tired."

He took the shopping bag from her and together they walked to the car. He closed the door behind her and then went around to the driver's side. When he was seated he said, "Whoo! Cold!"

"Terrible, terrible. Do you really think it'll snow?"

"Is it supposed to?"

"The radio said so."

"Today?"

"Supposed to come this afternoon."

"I don't believe it," he said. "The sky is clear."

He started the car and backed out of his space. He was slowing down at the exit when he saw Margaret.

She walked with her head bent against the wind, one hand in her coat pocket. Her right hand held her lifted coat collar, and her cheek was turned into the collar. He tooted the horn, and she looked up instantly, recognized him, and waved. He waved back. Margaret walked closer to the car. She was saying something but he couldn't hear her because the window was closed.

He rolled it down and said, "What?"

"I said, 'Do you go around picking up all the women in the neighborhood?'"

Larry laughed. "No," he answered. "Just the pretty ones."

"Oh," she said, and she laughed with him, waved, and then continued walking toward the shops. Larry rolled up the window.

"*É bella*," Mrs. Garandi said, using Italian for the first time since he'd known her. "*É bellissima*."

The girl who admitted him to Roger Altar's apartment on the twenty-ninth was not Agnes.

He didn't know whether or not he expected Agnes, but he was nonetheless disappointed to find a stranger. The girl was a tall, relaxed brunette with a bored expression on her face. She wore no make-up, and a pair of brass hoop earrings decorated her ears. She was dressed entirely in black—a black sweater, black slacks, black belt, black Capezio slippers. Larry wondered if she had just come from someone's funeral.

"Who are you?" she asked.

"Larry Cole."

"Oh, sure. Come in. The Genius is working."

He stepped into the apartment. The place was a masterpiece of disorderly living. A pair of trousers was hung over the blue couch in the center of the room facing the bar unit. The bar itself was covered with empty bottles and unwashed glasses. A table rested near a long window wall and was covered with dirty breakfast dishes even though it was three in the afternoon. The sink was piled with last night's dinner dishes.

For no apparent reason, a half-empty bottle of milk was under the easy chair to the left of the bar unit. Phonograph records were piled in a haphazard heap in the center of the room. A man's shoe was on the table, and its mate was in the far corner of the room. A pair of red socks had been hung on the open door of the hi-fi setup.

"You're the architect, huh?" the girl said.

"Yes."

"Another genius. I've had geniuses up to here." She studied Larry. "You're not even a good-looking genius."

"I'm not even a genius," he answered.

"The modest ones are the worst kind," the girl said. "My name's Marcia."

"How do you do?"

"Fine. Want a drink?"

"No, thank you."

"Too early for you?"

"No."

"What then?"

"I just don't feel like one."

51

"Mind if I have one?"

"Go right ahead."

"Thanks." The girl walked to the bar and poured a water glass half full of bourbon. "Choke," she said, and she drained the glass. From somewhere in the apartment, Larry heard the sound of a typewriter. Marcia looked up, pulled a face, and said, "The Genius."

"Want to tell him I'm here?"

"Me? If I stick my head in that room, he'll bite it off. Not me, thanks."

"What's he doing?"

"That's a stupid question, all right. Don't you hear the typewriter?"

"I don't know you well enough to insult you," Larry said, "but I wish you'd cut it out."

"Cut what out?"

"The aggression."

"I didn't realize you were so sensitive."

"I'm not. Go put on some lipstick. It'll make you feel better."

"I feel fine the way I am, thanks."

"How long has he been working?"

"He got out of bed at two in the morning. He's been going ever since."

Larry looked at the dishes on the table. "He stopped for breakfast, didn't he?"

The girl followed Larry's glance. "Those are yesterday's." She paused. "Are you his friend?"

"I don't know," Larry said.

"I think he's nuts."

"Maybe he is."

"You think he's a good writer?"

"I don't know."

"I thought *Star Reach* stank. As a matter of fact, I didn't like *The Debacle*, either. I should have listened to the reviewers."

"Maybe you should have."

"Damn right I should have. When I spend money for a book, the author makes a contract to entertain me."

"And he didn't?"

"He let me down. I think he's a lousy writer. The critics think so, too. I read all the reviews, every single one. In the New York area, anyway. They think he stinks. I agree with them." She paused. "I also think he's nuts. Or did I already say that?"

"You did."

"That makes it doubly true."

A door opened at the back of the apartment, and Roger Altar stepped out. "Hey, Larry," he said, "I thought I heard you." He came toward him, his hand extended. "When did you get here?"

"About five minutes ago," Marcia said.

Altar blinked at the girl. "Are you still here?" he asked. "I thought you'd left."

"I want to see how long your spurt lasts."

"Bad way to write," Altar said to Larry. "By inspiration, I mean. A pro sits down and bangs it out whether he's inspired or not. Only way to make this crazy racket pay off." He wiped a hand across his mouth. "This is the first time this has ever happened to me. I'm winding up the first draft of the new book. All of a sudden I had to get up in the middle of the night and get to the typewriter. How do you like that? Has that ever happened to you?"

"No."

"It's the goddamnedst feeling. I must have batted out sixty pages since last night, and I'm still going strong. It's going to be a great book, great! Have you had breakfast yet?"

"*And* lunch," Larry said.

"Yeah? What time is it, anyway?"

"It's past three."

"No kidding? How do you like that?" Altar rubbed his hand across his chin lazily. He looked very contented and very weary and almost out of touch. "I need a shave," he said. "I'm also hungry." He seemed to discover that he was wearing a pajama top with his trousers, and he began unbuttoning it. "Turn your back, honey," he said to Marcia and then began chuckling. "A great book, Larry, best I've ever done. I can feel it right down in my bones, where it counts. Oh, Jesus, it's going to be magnificent!"

"You look excited," Larry said.

"I *am* excited. The words are running off me like sweat in August. I can't believe I'm writing them, they're so terrific. I'm not that good."

"See?" Marcia said. "He admits it."

Altar looked at her steadily, wearily, his eyes taking in the black costume. "Who's she playing?" he asked Larry. "The Flowers-for-the-Dead Vendor in *Streetcar*?"

"He thinks he's literate," Marcia said. "He's the most ignorant genius I ever met."

"Oh, baby, go fly a kite," Altar said gently, as if he didn't have the energy to argue.

"He was lucky with two books, so he thinks he's an important American writer."

"I am an important American writer," Altar said, as if the question didn't even need discussion.

"The critics blasted both your books," Marcia said. "I know. I read the reviews."

"Critics," Altar said, shrugging.

"They said you wrote commercial tripe."

Altar shrugged and said nothing.

"They said you wrote for the Hollywood machine."

Again Altar shrugged, but he no longer seemed to be shrugging from weariness. He seemed instead to be withering before the onslaught of Marcia's quotations. Altar did not deny the accuracy of the quotations, and Larry instantly realized the girl was not inventing the reviews. But he had not expected Altar to shrink before them. He kept waiting for Altar to strike back at the girl, but he was seemingly quite defenseless in the face of her verbal barrage. He had taken off the pajama top, and he stood now like a shaggy giant dancing bear being whipped by an irate owner.

"One review said, 'Roger Altar has set the wheels of his fiction factory turning to produce a new vehicle for Tab Hunter.' Do you remember that one? I got a kick out of that one."

"Well, critics," Altar said, retreating still further.

Larry watched him. All of the man's enthusiasm seemed to have vanished. He had come out of his office feeling confident and sure and excited and weary with honest sweat. The girl had punctured all that, and he stood deflated and unsure now, and he seemed to have completely forgotten that Larry was in the room.

"The one I love the best," the girl said, as if she were telling a favorite joke, "is the one that started '*The Debacle* is aptly titled.' That was priceless! A classic!"

"Critics don't know," Altar said quietly. "What do they know?" He shrugged aimlessly.

"They said you wrote with facile ease, but they don't think you have anything to say. Not a thing to say."

"I have things to say," Altar said.

"They don't think so."

Altar kept staring at the girl. "I have things to say," he said more firmly.

"Then why don't you say them?" Marcia goaded. "Why do you write commercial tripe?"

"I don't write commercial tripe," Altar said, and he seemed at last to be getting angry. "The critics don't know. If you believe them, you go nuts. I don't listen to the critics."

Fight her back, Larry thought. Come on. Altar, fight her.

"The critics know what they're talking about," Marcia said, grinning. "They're trained to—"

"They don't know anything!" Altar said angrily.

"You're dying because the critics pan your books," Marcia said. "It kills you. It's destroying you!"

Altar pulled back his shoulders and thrust out his unshaven jaw. Give it to her, Larry thought. Tell her!

"I cried all the way to the bank!" Altar shouted.

Larry blinked at him, disappointed. And then he realized that Altar had picked up the only weapon available to him. Success was lying at his feet, and he had picked up Success and wielded it like a club. And having used it, he seemed embarrassed by the

54

ineffectiveness of his ultimate weapon. He would not meet Larry's eyes. He turned his back to Marcia and, with a great show of bravado, stamped barefooted to the refrigerator. He pulled out a package of sliced American cheese, tore off the cellophane wrapping, folded six slices of cheese in half, and stuffed them into his mouth.

"Critics," he said. "I eat them like the pieces of cheese they are!"

The room was silent. Altar chewed his food. The girl went to the bar and poured herself another bourbon.

"I brought you some rough sketches," Larry said.

"Oh, yeah."

"We had an appointment for three, remember?"

"I'm sorry. I forgot." Altar opened a bottle of milk, tilted it to his mouth, and began drinking. He wiped away the milk mustache with the back of his hand and then said, "I can't talk sketches today. I'm too busy."

"Okay," Larry said. "Look them over and we'll discuss them when I get back."

"Back from where?" Altar asked, interested.

"My wife and I are going to Puerto Rico."

"What the hell for? That's the asshole of the Antilles."

"Business," Larry said. "I'm on my way now to pick up the plane tickets."

"Okay, don't say I didn't warn you." Altar turned to the girl. "Listen, Critic," he said, "instead of guzzling my booze, why don't you clean up the place a little? It looks like a pigsty." He turned back to Larry. "She's trying to make me live like her goddamn stereotype of a writer. She knows too many Greenwich Village phonies."

"I'll get around to cleaning it," she said.

"Oh, forget it," Altar said. "Pack a bag and go live with a reviewer, why don't you?"

"I like it here."

"You're the most unimaginative, insulting bitch I've ever met in my life," Altar said.

"I inspired your creative spurt," Marcia said.

"Sure. There isn't a woman alive who doesn't believe her body is a deep soulful well from which a terribly stupid man grabs a handful of divine inspiration. Well, baby, I hate to disillusion you, but—"

"Don't," Marcia said.

"I'm going," Larry interrupted. "I'll call you when I get back."

"Okay," Altar said. He led Larry to the front door, and then added, "Give my regards."

"To whom?" Larry asked.

And Altar, remembering the joke, suddenly kicked Larry in the seat of his pants and shouted, "Why, the governor!"

7

It was the day before Halloween, and there were pumpkins to buy.

Don would have to cut grinning faces into them—how Patrick loved to see the faces appear in the orange globes. And Indian corn, of course, to hang outside the house next to the mailbox. How quickly it was Halloween, how quickly summer had died.

She shuddered.

She did not like the word Halloween. The word to her meant terror, the boy chasing behind her, hitting her with the chalked stick, shouting, "Halloween! Halloween!" and then circling around in front of her, still shouting, the chalked stick pointed and sharp. She could remember it clearly, she had been twelve, two years after her grandfather's death, could remember running, and then stumbling, and suddenly the sharp penetrating end of the stick hitting her cheek, and the blood, and the boy's eyes going wide with sudden fright.

They had taken two stitches to close the curiously shaped miniature X on her right cheek. The cross I bear, she mused, but she did not smile. And even the more timid boys on other Halloweens had chased her with stockings full of flour, marking up her clothes. Halloween meant terror to her, huge bonfires in the Manhattan streets, the kids rushing to the leaping flames with their booty; old chairs, crates, bundles of newspapers, signs ripped from grocery stores; dancing around the fire like hobgoblins, their watch caps pulled over their eyes and their ears, or some of the boys wearing their leather pilot's helmets, the goggles pulled down against the billowing smoke, glowing weirdly in the light of the fire. Terror. She did not like the word Halloween.

Pumpkins, she told herself, and Indian corn. And candy for the kids who come to the front door. And she'd better get some of those little trick-or-treat bags to put the candy in. God, there wasn't a holiday now that didn't cost a fortune.

She walked with her head bent, watching the pavement.

There was a wind, and her head was ducked partially in defense against it. But even if it were summertime, she'd have walked with her eyes cast downward. She had grown used to automobiles slowing and offering her rides, had grown used to the whistles from truck drivers, and so she walked now with her own thoughts, erecting the shell of a false indifference around her. She kept one hand in her coat pocket. The other held the flap of her collar against her scarred right cheek. She wore long dangling earrings, and a kerchief of bright blue, and her heels made hurried chatter with the pavement.

When she heard the automobile horn, she did not look up. The car pulled to the curb just as she was about to cross the street. It stopped, and then she heard the horn again. Slowly she raised her eyes.

She recognized the Dodge almost instantly, and she was surprised by the smile which appeared on her mouth. She realized abruptly that she didn't even know this man's name, except as "Chris's father." He was smiling, and his eyes in the sunlit interior of the car were almost black, and she found herself looking at his face for the first time and thinking it was not a handsome face, except for the eyes. The eyes were a deep, warm brown.

"Hi, Maggie," he said, and the name stabbed deep within her because no one but her grandfather had ever called her Maggie.

"My name is Margaret," she said, aware that her voice had trembled a little, unable to hide her resentment, and remembering that he had told her she wasn't so pretty, allowing the memory to add to her resentment.

"Mine's Larry," he said. "Larry Cole. Pleased to meet you. Want to see something terrific?"

She wanted to say, "No, I don't!" firmly and emphatically. But there was an eager boyishness on his face, shining in his eyes, and she got the feeling that this was very important to him, and she could not for the life of her burst his bubble.

"What is it?" she asked.

"For Allhallows' Eve," he told her. He held up a forefinger. "One moment, please," he said, and then he ducked below the window of the car.

She waited, thinking, Allhallows' Eve, and suddenly his face appeared at the window, but it wasn't his face. He was wearing a grotesque rubber mask, an exaggerated Neanderthal man thing that caused her to reel back in shock for a moment. The mask had a massive nose, and thick livery lips, and matted black hair clinging to the forehead. He began laughing behind the mask, and she laughed too, and then he pulled the mask from his face, and his eyes sought hers for approval.

"Isn't it great?"

"Where'd you get it?"

"Up at the center. I couldn't resist it." He was out of breath now. He glanced at the mask and said, "Go on, say it."

"Say what?"

"Put on the mask again."

She laughed. "No, don't. It's better this way."

"You walking to the center?" he asked.

"Yes."

"You'll freeze. Come on, I'll give you a lift."

"No, I don't mind walking."

"Okay," he said. He turned back to the wheel, seemed about to go, and then came to the window again. "I'm going where it's warm."

"Where's that?"

"Puerto Rico."

"Really?" she asked, her eyes wide.

"Day after tomorrow." He paused. "Will you miss me?"

She didn't answer. She felt very warm all at once, and she turned her head from the car.

"Maggie, will you miss me?"

"Don't call me Maggie!" she snapped.

He smiled, and she detected nervousness in the smile, withdrawal. He sat in seeming indecision for a moment, and then he said, "I'll talk to you when I get back."

"What about?"

He grinned uneasily. "Oh, I don't know. There must be lots of things to talk about."

"Well, you think of some," she said. "I've got shopping to do."

She began walking away from the car, and behind her she heard him say, "So long, Maggie," and then she heard the sound of the gunned engine, and the tires grasping the asphalt. She did not turn to look at the car. She ducked her head against the wind again and continued walking, and, oddly, she could think only, Maggie, Allhallows' Eve.

"I don't know why you have to fly," Mrs. Cole said sweetly. "There are other ways of going places, Lawrence. It's not necessary to fly."

"It takes a little longer the other way," Larry's father said, "but what's the big rush?" He puffed on his pipe and then said, "You'd better put the pants on the hanger first, don't you think, son?"

"Yes, I guess so," Larry mumbled. He cast an eye about the living room and wondered how in God's name such a simple thing had been turned into a brawling farce. Eve had arranged to divide the children among their grandparents while they were gone, and that was fine; he had never known Eve to manage badly. Chris would stay with her folks, and David with Larry's, and that too had been sound judgment since she'd apportioned the kids according to the grandparents they favored. But she'd asked only her dad to drive out to pick up the kids. Instead, both families had driven out *en masse* in two separate cars so that the living room was filled to brimming while they packed their bags.

"Did you pack your cuff links?" Eve asked.

"Yes."

"You read about so many plane crashes," Mrs. Cole said sweetly. "Why do you have to fly, Lawrence?"

"Mom, everybody flies," Larry said patiently.

"Just catch me in a plane," Mr. Cole said. He shook the dottle out of his pipe and turned to Mr. Harder. "You ever been in a plane, Alex?"

"They don't scare me a bit," Mr. Harder said.

"They don't scare me, either," Mr. Cole said. "But have you ever been in one?"

"Nope," Mr. Harder replied, chuckling. "And never hope to, either, Phil."

Larry could never understand how his father managed to leave the business whenever anything unimportant came along. Just ask him when it was a matter of life or death and then the shoe-store couldn't possibly be left in the hands of inexperienced clerks. But take a thing like this, where he was about as necessary as a sixth finger, and there was good old Dad giving advice about airplane travel. Silently, he thanked God that his brother Pete was married and practicing law in Pennsylvania. Otherwise he was sure *he'd* have trotted along for the festivities, too.

Unfortunately, Eve's twin sisters were not married. Unfortunately, they were both seventeen, entering their senior year at high school, and very proud of the fact that they at last had breasts, the lack of which up to six months before had caused Eve's mother to seek the advice of a specialist at Murray Hill Hospital. As was characteristic with Mrs. Harder, she was now disturbed because her daughters wore sweaters which were three sizes too small.

"Eve never dressed that way," she was fond of repeating. "Eve was sensible. Sensible."

The twins, Lois and Linda, managed to show a total disregard for anyone's wishes but their own in the matter. The sweaters they chose continued to be snug and emphatic. Mr. Harder, florid and puffy at fifty-two, was somewhat embarrassed by them. But he could remember the Sloppy Joes which Eve had worn to high school, and he wondered now which was the lesser of the two evils.

"When I get big, can I go to Puerto Rico?" David asked.

"Sure," Larry said. "Mom, could you take the kids for a walk or something? We're never going to be packed in time."

"You should have packed last night," Mrs. Harder said. "I don't know why you two always leave things to the last minute."

"Some neighbors came in last night," Eve said.

"What time is your plane leaving?" Mrs. Cole asked.

"I'd love to be an airline hostess," Linda said. "Come here, Chris. Let me blow your nose."

"It isn't running," Chris said.

"What time, Lawrence?" Mrs. Cole asked again.

"Four-thirty," Larry said, and his mother shook her head and clucked her tongue as if he had just announced the exact moment of his death.

"You've got plenty of time," Mr. Cole said.

"We're supposed to check in at three-thirty."

"They always give you more time than you actually need," Mr. Harder said.

"Don't you like boats, Lawrence?"

"What, Mom?"

"Boats. Couldn't you take a boat?"

"Mom, we've only got a week. We're not going to Staten Island, you know. We're going all the way to Puerto Rico."

"Don't get sarcastic," Mrs. Cole said. "Boats go to Puerto Rico, too."

"You can't tell them anything, Louise," Mrs. Harder said. "They know it all."

"Well, really," Eve interrupted, "there *is* a time element involved."

"One week," Larry repeated. "That's all we've got."

"Ike and Mike," Mrs. Cole said. "They think alike."

"Eve, did you take the alarm?"

"Do we need it?"

"I don't trust hotel switchboard operators."

"It's in the bedroom. I'll get it."

Eve left the living room, and Lois followed her. She was unplugging the electric clock when Lois said, "Do you think this sweater is too tight, Sis?"

"Well," Eve said judiciously, "it does make you look a little busty."

"I *am* busty," Lois said.

"Darling," Eve said, "you're leggy, too, but you don't run around in your panties, do you?"

"I guess not," Lois said dubiously. She studied Eve for a moment and then asked, "What's it like? Being married, I mean?"

"It's fun," Eve said.

"Do you have to do whatever he asks you?"

"What do you mean?"

"I mean, in bed."

"Lois!"

"A boy kissed me with his mouth open last Saturday night," Lois said.

"What did you do?"

"I opened mine, too. It was better."

"I think maybe you'd better have a long talk with Mama," Eve said, sighing.

"Mama doesn't know anything," Lois said. "All she knows how to say is 'Never, never, never sit on a boy's lap.' What's so terrible about sitting on a boy's lap?"

"She used to tell me that, too," Eve said, laughing. "And I haven't yet figured it out."

60

"Did you ever?" Lois asked. "Before you got married, I mean?"

"Sit on a boy's lap?"

"No. You know."

"Lois . . ."

"I mean, with Larry."

"That's none of your business," Eve said. "Listen, when I get back we'd better have a talk." She wrapped the wire around the clock, sighed, and as she walked out of the bedroom, mumbled, "If it isn't too late by then." She handed Larry the clock.

"Take out insurance at the airport, Lawrence," Mrs. Cole said. "Do you hear me?"

"Will that stop the plane from crashing, Mom?"

"Don't get smart," Mrs. Cole said. "I used to change your diapers."

Mr. Cole laughed and said, "Leave him alone, Louise. He can take care of himself."

"Certainly," she said. "That's why he's *flying* in an airplane!"

"Airplanes aren't really too bad, Louise," Mrs. Harder said, and Linda turned to look up at her mother in surprise.

Of the two girls, even though they were identical twins, Linda was perhaps the prettier. It was difficult to realize this until you'd known the girls for some time. In the beginning, they seemed absolutely alike, and their sameness nearly drove you to distraction. Later on, you recognized the subtle differences in their faces. Lois's face belonged to the first born and was more perfectly formed, as if it were the master mold from which both faces were cast. But there was about Linda a quality of serenity which Lois would never possess, a tranquillity which quietly contradicted her sister's vivaciousness and actually made her prettier.

Combing Chris's hair now, she said, "You're very lucky, Eve. I wish I could go."

Eve turned to her only briefly, but their eyes met in that moment, and they exchanged gentle, almost tender smiles.

"He always wanted to fly," Mrs. Cole said. "When the war came, I thought he'd drive me crazy. He'd come home from school every day and stick that Air Corps application under my nose, begging me to sign it."

"Did you?"

"I should say not!"

"I know a boy who's in the Air Force," Lois said, coming from the bedroom. "He's a rear gunner."

"I won't let her date servicemen," Mrs. Harder said.

"That's very wise, Patricia," Mrs. Cole said.

"I wouldn't let Eve date them, either."

"I was only thirteen when the war started!" Eve said.

"That's old enough," Mrs. Harder said. "You were very developed for your age."

61

"She's still developed," Larry said from the suitcase. "What time is it, hon?"

"I just gave you the clock," Eve said.

Larry started to look at the disconnected electric clock and then pulled a face. "Dad?" he asked, and both Mr. Harder and Mr. Cole looked at their watches simultaneously.

"It's almost two," Mr. Harder said.

The telephone in the bedroom rang. Larry turned and said, "Who's that?" Impatiently, he strode out of the room.

"He gets very nervous," Mrs. Cole said. "He was always like that. Peter is calm, but Lawrence is the nervous one."

"Well, this is a big thing for him," Mrs. Harder said.

"Do you remember when he won the prize?" Mrs. Cole asked. "I thought he would jump through the ceiling."

"He's a good architect," Linda said to no one, and again Eve turned to her tenderly.

Larry came out of the bedroom, a disgusted look on his face.

"Who was it?" Eve asked.

"The airport," Larry said. "Our flight's been delayed. Check-in time is now four-fifteen."

"Delayed?" Mrs. Cole asked quickly. "Why?"

"Some mechanical difficulties," Larry said.

"Oh, my God! I knew it!"

"Now, Louise, Louise . . ."

"Mom," Larry said, exasperated, "we're flying and that's that!" He turned to Eve. Gently, he said, "Honey, can you make some coffee or something?"

"I'll do it," Linda said, rising from her cross-legged position on the rug.

"Where's my watch?" Larry asked.

"On the dresser. Your watch, wallet and keys are all laid out."

"The traveler's checks?"

"Those too."

"And the checkbook?"

"Yes."

"I'll take a hundred in cash in my wallet, honey," Larry said, "and I'll pack the checkbook and traveler's checks in the suitcase that locks. Okay?"

"Fine," Eve said absently. "Linda, honey, the coffee is in the cabinet over the stove. The instant."

"I see it, Eve," Linda called from the kitchen.

"Is that what you're wearing on the plane?" Lois asked, studying Eve's simply tailored skirt and blouse.

"Yes. With the jacket to it. Why?"

"Nothing," Lois said. She paused. "Haven't you got anything dressier?"

"Darling," Mrs. Harder said, "your sister doesn't need any advice on how to dress."

"I just thought for a plane ride, something dressier might—"

"Perhaps you'd like to lend her one of your shrunken sweaters."

"Mama," Lois said flatly, "have you ever seen yourself in that red cocktail dress?"

"What?"

"You're half naked in it," Lois said. "I'd be ashamed to—"

"Now that's enough of *that*, young lady," Mr. Harder said firmly.

"You're lucky you never had girls, Louise," Mrs. Harder said.

"Boys are no picnic," Mrs. Cole said.

Eve very softly said, "I'd like a little girl."

Packing his suitcase beside her, Larry whispered, "I'll see if that can be arranged," and Eve chuckled quietly.

"Does everybody want coffee?" Linda asked from the kitchen.

"I don't want you girls drinking coffee," Mrs. Harder said. "Eve, darling, don't you have any milk?"

"Of course we've got milk," Eve said, annoyed by the negative assumption.

"Some milk for you and Lois, darling," Mrs. Harder called to the kitchen.

"You'd better give the children something, too," Mrs. Cole said. "God knows what time they'll be eating tonight."

Mrs. Harder took Eve aside and whispered, "Did you pack everything?"

"Yes, Mama."

"I mean, did you pack *everything*, darling?"

"I packed everything."

"Everything? Do you know what I mean?"

"Mama," Eve said patiently, "*everything*."

"All right," Mrs. Harder said, nodding. And then, unwilling to let it go, she added, "You know what I mean, don't you?"

"Yes, Mama. I packed the damn—"

"Coffee!" Linda shouted from the kitchen.

At the airport, David burst into tears when Eve kissed him, and Chris shouted, "I want to kiss Daddy, too. I want to kiss Daddy." Larry pulled Eve through the loading gate as the uniformed attendant stretched out his arm to hold back the well-wishers waiting for the plane's departure. He bent down and kissed his son under the man's outstretched blue sleeve, and then he stood up and shouted "So long! We'll see you in a week!" and together he and Eve ran across the field, the wash from the airplane's propellers lashing at the coats they wore, up the ramp and into the plane where a smiling hostess greeted them. There was the sudden smell of human beings, the muted hum of the engines inside the ship, the long walk down the center aisle, squeezing into their seats past a little Puerto Rican man who held a guitar on his lap. There were the lighted signs at the front of the air-

63

plane, "No Smoking" and "Fasten Your Seat Belts," and then there was the sudden angry roar of the engines, and Eve leaning over him to wave out of the curtained window, and then the plane taxiing across the field, gathering speed, the buildings rushing past in a blinding whitish-gray blur, the plane trembling with the power of its engines, and the little Puerto Rican man praying quietly in Spanish.

And then they were airborne.

8

HE AWOKE. For a moment he didn't know where he was. He sat up, blinked, and then remembered he was in Puerto Rico.

This was the Caribe Hilton. The unfamiliar hum in the room was the air conditioner, and the unfamiliar light was the tropical sun filtering through the drapes on the wall-length windows which faced the ocean.

Quietly, so that he would not awaken Eve in the other bed, he rose and went to the dresser. He lighted a cigarette and then tiptoed to the windows and peeked around one end of the drapes. The room was on the sixth floor of the hotel. There was a little balcony outside the window. He and Eve had sat on that balcony last night before going to bed.

The plane had put down at International Airport at 12:30 A.M., Puerto Rican time. They'd disembarked and waited for their luggage, only to discover it was coming down on a later plane, and then caught a cab to the hotel. By the time they'd registered and asked the desk clerk if they couldn't get something to eat, it was close to 1:45. At 2:00 A.M. a bellhop knocked on their door. He explained that he had got them sandwiches and coffee from the gambling casino, the grill was closed, he hoped they would understand, he hoped it would be all right. Larry had tipped him extravagantly and then wheeled the tray onto the balcony. Ravenously, he and Eve devoured the food and drank the entire pot of coffee. Then, weary and satiated, they had sat back to smoke a last cigarette before turning in, the Puerto Rican sky peppered with stars above them.

Now, at eleven-fifteen in the morning, Larry looked through the window and felt wonderfully glad to be alive.

Far below him, the hotel's amoeba-shaped pool gleamed a bright indigo in the sun. There were girls around the pool, and sailors in their summer whites, and gaily colored canvas chairs and luxuriant palms. Beyond the pool, directly opposite the vertical façade of the hotel, the white and sprawling beach encircled a calm blue lagoon in a huge overgrown C. Off to the right, where the sea wall blocked the lagoon, the ocean leaped against the boulders in splendid white and green fury.

"Eve," he said.

"Mmmm?"

"Eve, come look at this."

"What time is it?"

"Eleven-twenty."

"Chris, up yet?"

"Wh——?" He grinned. "Yes, I've already taken him to the bus stop."

"Good. Good. Put up the coffee?"

"Yes."

"Good."

"Honey?"

"Mmmm?"

"Watch."

He drew the drapes open quickly, and sunlight splashed into the room. She turned her head away and then blinked and then sat upright, and then rubbed her eyes, smiled foolishly, and said, "Oh. Puerto Rico." Sleepily, stretching lithely, she put her hands to the back of her neck and then moved them upward, lifting the black hair, letting it fall again in a glittering ebony cascade.

"Come look," Larry said.

"I haven't got anything on. Did our suitcases arrive yet?"

"I haven't checked. Come on."

"Larry, I'm naked."

"So what? I'm in my shorts."

"Did you sleep in those?"

"My pajamas are in the suitcases someplace."

"Give me your shirt," she said.

"A lot that's going to cover."

"It'll do. Give it to me."

He handed her the shirt and then asked, "Do you want the cuff links?"

"Ha-ha," she said. She buttoned the shirt and went to the window, pulling the drape over her waist so that it hid her legs where the shirt ended. "Oh, it's beautiful," she said. "Did you order breakfast?"

"I just got up."

"All right, call down and order breakfast, and then find out if the airport sent over the bags."

He snapped a salute at her and said, "Yes, sir, right away, sir!"

"If that sun is as hot as it looks, I'll die in the skirt I wore down."

"Why don't you just go out on the balcony with my shirt?"

"I would, darling, believe me," Eve said lightly, "but then what would *you* wear, sweetheart?"

He slapped her on the rump and went to the phone. He watched her while she dressed, talking first to Room Service and then to the Bell Captain. When he hung up, she said, "Well?"

"Breakfast'll be up in a minute, Puerto Rican time."

"The bags?"

"They haven't arrived yet."

"Well, for Pete's sake!" she said, and then went into the bathroom. When the breakfast arrived, Larry asked the bellhop to wheel the tray onto the balcony. He signed the check, tipped him, and then went to join Eve, who was already sitting at the table.

"Do you want some coffee first?" she asked.

"Leave it in the pot until I'm ready for it."

"What did you order?"

"A veritable feast." He began poking around the tray, lifting napkins and covers. "Orange juice, corn flakes, ahhh, hot corn muffins, coffee."

"No eggs?"

"I didn't feel eggy."

"How's the juice?"

"Haven't tasted it yet."

They raised their glasses, and Larry clinked his against Eve's. "Here's to a wonderful stay on the Enchanted Island," he toasted.

"Is that what they call it?"

"Yes." He drank some of the juice.

"How is it?"

"Canned."

"No! Are you joking?"

"I'm serious."

"Oh, hell." Eve thought for a moment. "Call down for a grapefruit, will you?"

"Oh, come on, Eve. Drink the juice."

"Can't you call down?"

"Sure I can." He paused. "Do you really want me to?"

"Well, you know how I feel about canned juice."

"Yeah, but . . ." He drank a little more of his own juice. "It's not so terrible. It's good and cold."

"Here. You can have mine."

"You want me to call down?"

"No, never mind."

"I will if you want me to."

"No, it's all right."

"It's just that I can't see getting a bellhop to come up here just to bring a grapefruit." He paused. "I will if you want me to."

"No." She sliced a corn muffin and began buttering it.

"Aren't you having any cereal?"

"No."

"Shall I call down for the grapefruit?"

"No. We don't want to overwork the bellhops."

"If you're going to get angry—"

"No, Larry, honestly. By the time he got here, the coffee'd be cold, anyway. Forget it. I'm not angry or even annoyed." She paused. "But the longer I live with you, the more I think I don't know you at all."

Larry narrowed his eyes. In a low, sinister voice, he said, "You think I'm your husband, don't you?"

"What?" Eve asked.

He laughed evilly and continued to watch her. "I inhabited your husband's body a long time ago."

"Oh, Larry . . ."

"The Martians are afoot," he said. "And now that you know, you still can't stop us."

"I believe you," she said, shaking her head. "This coffee is strong."

"But good."

"If you like it strong."

"I like strong coffee and weak women."

"I think I resent your use of the plural," Eve said. She drank more coffee and then lighted a cigarette. "What's on the agenda for today?"

"I have to make a half-dozen phone calls, people Baxter asked me to see. I don't imagine I'll get much else done today. I suppose we can just relax."

"Oh, good. I was hoping you'd say that. Can we go into San Juan later?"

"If you like."

"I guess I won't trade you in after all," Eve said, and she leaned over the table and kissed him quickly on the cheek.

At one o'clock a bellhop brought up their bags. As soon as he was gone, Larry unlocked the one lockable valise and began a frantic search for the traveler's checks. When he found them, he sighed, held them up, and said, "I was getting a little worried."

"What for?" Eve asked. "When you're stranded in a strange land and can't speak the language, who needs money?"

Larry laughed. "Want to take a swim?"

"Are all your calls made?"

"All but one, and I can make that later. I've got two appointments for tomorrow, and I also got us a dinner invite for tonight. Guy named Hebbery."

"Good. Then let's swim."

They changed into their swim suits and took the service elevator down. Following the signs, they walked through the cool basement corridor and emerged in the hot Puerto Rican sunlight. They found chairs for themselves, dropped their towels, and went to the deep end of the pool. Larry dove in first. Eve followed with a clean dive, surfacing again and then breaking into a strong, fast crawl. She touched the tile lip at the shallow end, reversed her body and—as if she were in a high-school swimming match—s.arted back toward the deep water. Larry watched her, pleased with the way she swam. He came up the steps, waited for her, and handed her a towel when she came dripping from the pool.

"Cigarette?" he said.

"Yes. That was good. I feel all tingly."

She pulled off the cap, and her black hair tumbled to her shoulders. Larry put two cigarettes into his mouth, lighted them, and handed one to Eve.

"Mmm," she said, inhaling. "Now let's go back to the chairs and just toast for a while."

They soaked up sun for a half hour. At the end of that time they both conceded it was a treacherous sun and moved into the shade of a palm. Eve's lip was beaded with perspiration. She lay in the chair limply and said, "I feel as if I'd been flogged."

"It's hot," he said. He was propped up on his elbows, looking toward the breakwater. "I wonder what that is."

"What?"

"Over there. All the commotion."

Eve rolled over. She squinted into the sun. "Looks as if they're taking pictures."

"Let's walk over," he said.

Leisurely, they strolled to the breakwater. A tripod was set up facing the ocean. Two young girls, a redhead and a blonde, smiled prettily at the man behind the camera.

"She's a *Vogue* model," Eve whispered. "I recognized her."

"Which one?"

"The redhead."

"She's pretty."

"She photographs beautifully," Eve said, "but I'm a little disappointed. She's very thin."

"I don't think so."

A woman wearing a wide-brimmed straw hat went over to the girls and adjusted their dresses. She said something to the photographer then, and both girls smiled more broadly, holding their poses.

"The dresses are pinned in the back with clothes pins," Eve said. "So that no wrinkles will show in the front."

They watched in silence for a while. The photographer, the models, the woman in the straw hat, went blithely about their business.

"That sun is beginning to get me again," Eve said. "Can we go back to the shade?"

"I want to watch a little," Larry said. "It's interesting."

"The photography or the redhead?" Eve asked.

"Oh, come on."

She looked at him curiously and said, "Well, I'll be under the palm when you've had enough."

"All right."

She looked at him again, the same curious expression on her face, and then she turned and walked back to the beach chair.

Larry's two Saturday appointments were with men who were willing to accommodate him even though they did not normally work on Saturdays. The first was at the Autoridad Sobre Hogares de Puerto Rico in Rio Piedras.

With a man named Fiente, Larry discussed the basic minimum housing needs as experienced in the island's public housing program. He approached the problem of factory housing the way he would approach any architectural problem. He wanted to use space in a way that would be satisfactory both functionally and aesthetically to the people who would occupy that space. And whereas Baxter was footing the bill, Larry nonetheless considered the Puerto Rican factory worker his client.

Fiente was an intelligent, farsighted man struggling with perhaps the biggest problem on the island: slum clearance. He spoke enthusiastically of his own program and of the strides they'd made in eliminating the *fanguitos*. At the same time he showed grateful appreciation for incoming industries which considered housing a basic component of their factory operation.

Larry talked with him for almost three hours. He did not speak a word of Spanish, and he discovered that talking to a man who spoke only hesitant English was a trying task. The long pauses while the mind searched for a translation, the mispronunciations, the monosyllabic exchange of ideas, the limiting of oneself to a basic vocabulary in deference to the man struggling with one's language made communication a grueling experience. He was fatigued when he left Fiente for his appointment at the Planning Board in San Juan. But he thanked him warmly for his time and stepped out of the office into a sudden Puerto Rican shower.

At the Planning Board, he spoke to a man named Miguel Dominguez. Again, in their discussion of materials which would be most satisfactory and most economical for the proposed development, the language complication stood between them like a solid stone wall. They talked of lumber and cement and doors and windows and crushed stone and pipe and floor tiles and interior and exterior paint and galvanized iron sheets and sand. And if simple conversation with Fiente had been difficult, the problem of translating "galvanized iron sheets" from the Spanish was almost insurmountable. Larry was anxious to get back to the Caribe and the simple, sweet, clean American English Eve spoke.

As he was leaving, Dominguez said, "I enjoy your visit, Señor Cole."

"Thank you," Larry said. "I enjoyed talking to you."

"When you arrive, I think perhaps is Tyrone Power. My secretary come in an' say, 'There is han'some American wants to see you.' " Dominguez grinned. Left-handedly, he added, "They don' see many mainlan' visitors here."

Larry was tired enough to have taken the remark as an insult. But Dominguez was smiling, and he sensed that no offense had been intended. The man, in his own confused English way, was offering a compliment. He took his hand, thanked him again for his time, and left.

When he got back to the hotel room, Eve had already showered and was lying on one of the beds resting. "How'd it go?" she asked, not opening her eyes.

"Pretty rough. Why didn't I take Spanish in high school?"

"Did you get to see the site?"

"Not yet. We'll discuss that with Hebbery tonight. Maybe he'll take us out there tomorrow."

"Out where?"

"Vega Alta. That's the factory town."

"Is it far from San Juan?"

"I don't know. Hebbery'll tell us all about it."

Eve nodded. "I'm going to catch a nap," she said. "Wake me when you're almost ready, will you?"

"And then spend the next half hour waiting for you."

"Oh, the hell with you," Eve said, and she rolled over.

Grinning, he went into the bathroom to shower.

The room phone rang at 7:20 while Eve was still making up at the dressing table in her bra and half-slip. Larry, fully dressed, answered it.

"Cole?"

"Yes?"

"Frank Hebbery. We're a little early."

"Where are you?"

"Downstairs in the lobby. You dressed?"

"I am, but Eve isn't."

"Want to join the wife and I for a drink?"

"Just a minute." He covered the mouthpiece. "Hebbery. Wants me to come down for a drink while you dress. Okay?"

"Sure."

"Fine," Larry said into the phone.

"We'll be in the outdoor bar. Do you know it?"

"I'll find it," Larry said. "Give me a few minutes."

Hebbery was a small, thin man with piercing brown eyes and lank brown hair. He wore a tan linen suit which was meticulously pressed, and he sported a neatly clipped mustache under his nose. He stood up the moment Larry entered the bar, and he walked toward him quickly.

"Cole?" he said.

"Hebbery?"

70

"Yes. Glad to know you. Come on over to the bar. How do you like Puerto Rico?"

"Fine, so far."

"*Bueno*," Hebbery said. "Come on, I'll introduce you to the wife."

They walked to the bar, an oval island in the center of the open patio. Easy chairs were pulled up to the bar, and the bar was of a height to permit comfortable drinking while seated in the low chairs. A plump brunette in a white dress sat at the bar toying with a Tom Collins. Hebbery walked directly to her and said, "Honey, this is Larry Cole. Mr. Cole, my wife Anne."

"How do you do?" Anne said.

"Mrs. Hebbery," Larry said.

"Oh, make it Anne."

"Anne it is."

"*Bueno*," Hebbery said. "What are you drinking, Cole?"

"Make it Larry."

"*Bueno*. And the drink?"

"Do martinis mix with the climate?"

"I wouldn't."

"Gin and tonic then."

Larry pulled out one of the chairs and sat. Hebbery snapped his fingers at the bartender and said, "*Mira, mira!*"

"You must tell me all about New York," Anne said. "I haven't been there in ages."

"How do you like Puerto Rico?" Hebbery asked. To the bartender he said, "Gin and tonic, *por favor*."

"I like it fine," Larry said. "I had a long talk today with—"

"You'll love it," Hebbery interrupted. "Once you're here a while, you'll love it. There's no place on earth like it, believe me."

"Well, we'll only be staying a week."

"That's a shame. You hit a bad time, too. We've been having a little rain."

"We're always having a little rain," Anne said.

Hebbery patted her knee. "Anne and I have been here for six years now. No place on earth like it."

"Thank God," Anne said.

"It seems very nice," Larry said.

The bartender came over with a gin and tonic. He started to put it down before Hebbery, and Hebbery said, "*No, no, alli,*" and he pointed to Larry. The bartender put the drink down. "*Muchas gracias,*" Hebbery said, "a wonderful people here, Larry, wonderful, you can't beat them. Poor, yes. But happy? Ah, you can't beat them for happiness. Not anyplace on earth. How's the drink?"

Larry tasted it. "Good," he said.

"*Bueno*. You ready for another, Anne?"

"I'll wait for Mrs. Cole. Larry, is New York—?"

"*Bueno*. Have you done any shopping, Larry?"

"Well, we went into San Juan yesterday."

"Wonderful city, isn't it? Old San Juan, I mean. Rio Piedras is another thing again. Beautiful, of course, but with none of San Juan's charm. How did you like the old cobble-stoned streets?"

"They—"

"Built by the Spaniards, you know. Centuries ago. No automobiles then. Built for horses. Give the city an old-world flavor. Wouldn't change it for all the tea in China. Can't you just picture the *conquistadores* riding down those streets in full armor?"

"Well, I—"

"Have you been out to Morro?"

"No, we didn't get—"

"You mustn't miss El Morro," Hebbery said. "A wonderful treat."

"We'll try not to—"

"Has Christmas shopping started in New York yet?" Anne asked.

"No, it's a little early yet—"

"She talks as if we're out in the middle of the Pacific someplace," Hebbery said.

"No," Anne replied, "we're out in the middle of the Atlantic."

"The Caribbean, honey," Hebbery said. "The romantic Caribbean."

"Yeah," Anne said flatly.

"Here's Eve now," Larry said, rising and signaling to her.

She had come into the bar and paused, looking about her somewhat aloofly. He knew the manner was affected, but she nonetheless presented the portrait of a poised, self-sufficient, faintly bored young lady. She was wearing an ice-blue satin sheath, pearls at the throat.

"Excuse me," he said, and he went to meet her. He took her hand and whispered, "Hi, beautiful."

"Hi. Do I look all right?"

"You look very sweet."

"That's not what I want to hear."

"No?"

"No. Tell me I look sexy."

"Oh?"

"Mmm," she said, and she smiled knowingly.

"Well! Well, well."

"Forewarned is forearmed," Eve said. "How's Hebbery?"

"*Bueno*," he said.

"Huh?"

"Come on, we'll join them."

"It got nice and cool, didn't it?" Eve said.

"Did it?" He grinned. "I thought it got warmer all at once."

He squeezed her hand and, both grinning, they walked to the bar.

9

WINTER arrived on Sunday.

Like an old man coming home to die too early, it appeared grayly and suddenly on the horizon.

And while Eve and Larry Cole listened to an endless succession of "*Buenos*" from Frank Hebbery as he showed them through the Rain Forest in the Bosque Nacional del Caribe, with the burning Puerto Rican sun shielded by the arch of trees; as they stood beside a cascading waterfall, the water leaping and rushing over a smooth sheer wall of rock; as they stood in the secret, shrouded silence of growth as old as time, confronted with the immensity of nature's construction; as they stood in El Yunque on a tropical island, Margaret Gault sat in the kitchen of her Cape Cod development house 1,425 miles to the north and listened to her mother, and winter stared bleakly through the window-panes.

"I want to know what happened to you this summer," Mrs. Wagner said.

They sat across from each other at the round pine-top kitchen table which Margaret had bought at an antique shop in New Jersey, the twenty-seven-year-old blonde, and the fifty-two-year-old blonde who was her mother.

The fifty-two-year-old blonde was a handsome woman with brown eyes that did not miss very much. She was somewhat plump, with the bosom of a matron, and there were age wrinkles at the corners of her eyes, and her chin was getting weak, and her neck was loosening in the dissolute pattern of age. But you could tell that Elizabeth Wagner had once been a beauty. You could know with certainty that she had danced the Charleston and the Bunny Hug, bound her breasts tightly in an era when boyishness was considered girlishness, so tightly that she'd almost damaged the supporting muscles but not quite, thankfully, so that they were still firm and rounded when girls got back to being girls.

Elizabeth Wagner no longer sported the natural ash-blonde hair which had been hers when she'd sampled gin from a bathtub at distillation parties, scooping it up in a teacup so that after the fourth cup the gin tasted mellowed and aged in the wood, even though it was the same horrible gut-rotting stuff which had been drunk hours before when the aging, mellowing process began. The hair now had expert care under the hands of a beautician and it combined with the brown eyes to lend a look of hardness to the woman.

She leaned across the table, her bosom on her folded arms, and hoped there was motherly concern in her eyes. But concern had gone out of those eyes a long time ago, and her daughter knew it, and so they sat, strangers who had once an eternity ago been attached with a cord through which the same rich blood has surged.

"What happened this summer?" Mrs. Wagner said, and Margaret watched her and thought, I would no more tell you what happened this summer than I would tell the milkman.

"Lots of things," she said. "There were parties and barbecues. You know how it is in a small development."

"You know what I mean, Margaret. You know exactly what I mean. Don't start telling me about parties and barbecues. I'm not interested in them."

"What *are* you interested in, Mother?"

She had stopped calling her "Mom" or "Ma" or "Mama" on the day her grandfather died. On that day her mother stopped being a blood relation and became only another woman named Elizabeth Wagner, a woman who had done something unspeakably horrible. She would have called her Elizabeth now except that it was not in her make-up to call this other woman by her first name. And so she had chosen the coldest word she knew within the limitations of the mother-daughter relationship she denied, and that word was "Mother."

"I'm interested in *you*," Mrs. Wagner said.

"You're interested in me?" Margaret asked, and a small sardonic smile touched her mouth.

"You're like me," Mrs. Wagner said. "You're my daughter. You look the way I looked when I was your age, and I can see in your eyes what was in mine. So I don't have to hear what happened this summer. I know what happened."

"Do you?"

"Yes."

"Then don't ask me."

"But not the way it happened with me, Margaret, not that way at all. That's in your eyes, too. Whatever happened wasn't good." Mrs. Wagner paused. "Margaret, I don't care what you think of me, or what—"

"Mother—"

"Or what—"

"Mother, lower your voice."

"They're watching the football game in the parlor, the two he-men. Don't worry about them. Listen to me, Margaret. When it happened to me, it was *everything*—and that's the difference. And that's what you'll never be able to understand, that's what you don't want to understand."

"I don't—"

"Nothing else mattered, Margaret. Not your father, and not

74

you, and not . . . not your grandfather, either. There was only—"

"I don't want to hear it!"

"When will you want to hear it?"

"Never."

"Don't judge me, Margaret. I'm not to be judged by you. I'm still your mother, you know."

"Are you?"

"Yes, damnit, I am. And I know a little more about life and living than you might imagine."

"I imagine you know a great deal about life and living, Mother," Margaret said.

Mrs. Wagner sighed heavily. "You're a very cold person, Margaret," she said. "You're very cold."

"I'm sorry if I—"

"Very cold. I would like to talk to you. I would really like to be able to talk to you. I used to wonder, when it happened, how I could explain it to you, how I would tell you when you were old enough to listen. That was what bothered me most, do you know? What will my daughter think, what will my daughter think? Oh, I know how you feel about what I did later, but that was a part of it too, all a part of it, and only because of what happened, only because I was so desperately—"

"Mother—"

"Margaret, I'm not a whore."

"Mother—"

"Please understand that, Margaret. I'm not a whore. It's important to me that you under—"

"Please, please," Margaret said.

She looked across at her mother, and there were tears forming in Mrs. Wagner's eyes, and for a moment she wanted to reach across the table and take her mother's delicate hands, the wedding ring and engagement ring large on the third finger, take her mother's hand in her own and say, "It's all right. Please don't cry, please."

The moment hung suspended.

And then Margaret said, "I don't want to hear it, Mother."

"I hope your life is never threatened, Margaret. I hope your blood supply is never cut off."

"I don't want to hear it," Margaret said, more firmly this time.

"Whatever happened to you is your business, but I can tell it meant nothing." Mrs. Wagner studied her daughter, and her eyes were clear now. "Do you know what I wish?"

"What?"

"I wish you fall in love some day. I wish to God you really fall in love."

"The way *you* did, Mother?" Margaret asked, vast sarcasm in her voice.

"Yes," Mrs. Wagner said slowly, her eyes bright and hard, "the way I did."

On Tuesday morning, in the town of Vega Alta, Larry saw the funeral.

The town was hot and dry and dusty. The shops lined the main street, and Larry stood on the sidewalk waiting for Hebbery, who had stepped into one of the shops to buy some "*cigarillos*" after showing Larry the site. There was a hush to the town, the silence of bare feet on dust-covered roads. There were few shoppers, and there was a feeling of almost complete inactivity, a laziness sponsored by the sun, washing the road and the sidewalk and the colorless, faded pastels of the shop fronts in a monotonous warm bath of sun yellow. The silence seemed suddenly to mushroom in upon itself. There had been silence before, but it deepened now as if before a sudden summer cloudburst so that Larry looked unconsciously skyward, expecting rain.

At the far end of the street, he saw the procession. It took him a moment to realize what it was, and then another moment to realize it had caused the deepening of silence.

The procession started with the little girls in white. He counted an even dozen of them, walking in pairs, each holding a bunch of flowers, walking in slow cadence, the dust rising around them on the painfully silent street. Six pairs of girls in white dresses, young girls with tan faces and brown faces, each clutching a bunch of blood-red flowers at her waist. And behind the little girls, the pallbearers marched with stiff solemnity, carrying the huge black coffin on their shoulders, the weight evenly distributed so that it appeared the coffin was not heavy at all, seemed as if they walked effortlessly beneath this huge black box which hovered magically on the air over their shoulders.

Behind the pallbearers, behind the coffin, the townspeople marched in mourning. They spread across the width of the small street, marching shoulder to shoulder with the slow, uneven beat of stragglers, their faces serious with the serious business of death.

The shoppers were lining the curbs now. Men removed their hats as the coffin passed. Storekeepers came out onto the sidewalk and closed the doors of their shops behind them. Up and down the street as the coffin passed, the wood louvered doors eased quietly shut, and the hats were lifted silently from heads, and the straggling mourners raised giant clouds of dust that sifted up silently on the bright, golden, sunlit air.

He felt like an outsider. He felt like a scientist watching bugs perform under a microscope, and he didn't want to feel that way, didn't want these people to think he was scientifically and coldly watching death go by, didn't want them to think he was the proud, aloof *Americano* who watched dispassionately while they put a friend and neighbor to rest. He was suddenly involved in the funeral, very involved in it, suddenly feeling the pure white innocence of the flower girls, the burden the pallbearers carried, the sadness that showed on the faces of the mourners who walked in sloppy disorganization, the awkwardness of their hands hanging at their sides, knowing they did not know what to do with their hands.

And he felt suddenly on the thin edge of realizing something very important about life. Here in this dusty town, in this town gone awkwardly silent in the presence of death, here where he did not know why they were closing the doors of the shops, or who the man in the coffin was, here he felt something start in the pit of his stomach and burn there with ferocious intensity and then work its way into his blood stream like a narcotic, rushing for his brain. He tried to channel it, tried to organize it into something he could grasp, something that would have meaning. He knew there was profundity in what was happening, something very deep and very meaningful, something about values and goals, about the incompleteness and startling brevity of life, something about clinging, living, building, something about the finality of death, but he could not think, he could only feel, and his inability to make this feeling coherent, to lay it out like a floor plan, to put it into meaningful symbols and ciphers he could manipulate frustrated him so that he stood silent and thoughtful, wracked with agonizingly elusive thought as the coffin passed and the shop doors closed and the dust rose on the street washed with sunlight.

"They close the doors because a friend is passing," Hebbery said at his elbow. "They won't do business while a dead friend goes by. It's respect."

He nodded, but he was not listening to Hebbery, did not know how long Hebbery had been standing by his side. The procession had passed, and behind it was the cloud of dust. He could no longer see the little girls in white. There were only the backs of the mourners now, spread across the street like a solid wall of sorrow. He had the feeling that once they were gone, if he allowed them to go, he would never be able to understand what he'd almost grasped, what was still within reach of his grasp, if only he could organize it, hold it.

A bell was tolling somewhere in the distance. The procession was turning a corner at the end of the street, and Hebbery said, "They're heading for the church. It's a beautiful thing, isn't it?"

He nodded. He wanted to say, Yes, yes, it's a beautiful thing, but that isn't it, help me, Hebbery, this is the whole meaning of life here if you'll only help me put it into words.

The last of the mourners turned the corner, following the coffin. The dust settled, the shop doors opened again. The men replaced their hats. Slowly the street came back to lethargic life.

In the distance he could hear the steady, unrelenting toll of the church bell.

77

The plane left Isla Verde, the island's international airport, two days later at dusk. They sat side by side, and they could see condensed moisture rising from the island's greenery as evening set in with its cool sea winds.

Eve took his hand when the wheels left the ground, and she did not let go of it until the tension inside her relaxed an hour later, and then she fell asleep.

10

HE WALKED with Chris rapidly.

He had shaved and put on his favorite woolen sports shirt. He wore it open at the throat, a sports jacket thrown over it, even though it was much too cold for such light attire. When he saw her, he smiled and then quickly pulled the smile from his face. He saw the recognition in her eyes, and he studied her face and then the ash-blonde hair and then the dangling earrings. Her eyes avoided his. Again she seemed embarrassed in his presence, and he wondered what caused the embarrassment.

"Hi," he said.

"Hi."

They stood in silence. He was beginning to feel the cold. He should have worn a coat.

"You have a nice tan," she said.

"Thanks."

"It makes your eyes . . ." She stopped.

"Yes?"

"Brown. Browner."

He didn't know what to answer. He nodded, and they were silent again, and he began to anticipate the appearance of the other neighborhood women, and found himself consciously willing their late arrival.

"Did you have a nice time?" she asked.

"Yes, very nice."

The silence closed in again. He had the feeling that the conversation was completely undirected, that neither knew where it was leading. But at the same time he felt it would run its course without conscious direction from either of them. He could not think of a single thing to say. He realized abruptly that Margaret Gault was only a passing stranger, and he wondered why he had come to the bus stop this morning.

And then he said, "Are you going shopping again?"

"No," she said. "Why?"

"You looked dressed up."

"No."

The words sprang from his mouth. "When *are* you going again?"

He did not expect the suspicious narrowing of her eyes, or the sudden coldness in her voice. He felt instant panic and doubt when she said simply, "Why?"

"I don't know," he answered, backing down.

She would not allow him to retreat. The coldness was growing in her voice. Her eyes told him he was pinned to a slide, and she was going to dissect him dispassionately. "What's so important about my going shopping?"

But he sensed, too, that the subject could have been closed by her instantly—and it had not been. The thought came to him full blown, giving him a sudden feeling of power.

"Will you be going tomorrow?" he asked.

"Maybe." Her answer told him he had not been wrong. She did not want to close the subject. He grinned slightly, surprised by the feeling of power which was growing within him.

"What time?" he asked.

"Why?"

"Why not?" he answered quickly. "I'll buy you a cup of coffee."

She started to nibble at her lower lip and then stopped. Falteringly she said, "I don't know if I'll be going shopping tomorrow."

"In the morning?"

"I don't know if I have any shopping to do."

"The afternoon?"

"I don't know."

"When?" he asked, his eyes full on her face. Her eyes locked with his. They stood silent, staring at each other.

And then as if she were leaping a hurdle in slow motion, she very slowly and cautiously said, "Tomorrow's Saturday. If I do any shopping, Don'll be with me." She kept staring at him steadily, as if struggling to keep his complete attention, as if trying to make certain he would not miss a word she was saying. "My husband."

"Oh." He paused. Somehow the hurdle had been leaped, and he felt an almost immediate relaxation of tension. "When will you go again?" he asked easily.

"I don't know." He thought he detected an archness in her voice, a coquettish quality which had not been there before. She smiled flirtatiously. "I hear you're an architect."

"Where'd you hear that?"

"One of the women. You won a prize."

"That's right."

"You must be good."

"I am," he said. "How about Monday?"

"Monday's a school holiday. My son is home."

"Tuesday?"

"I don't know. Are any of your houses in magazines or anything?"

"Yes. Is Tuesday—"

"Which magazines?"

"A lot of them. One was in September's *House and Garden*." He looked at her curiously. "Why?"

"I want to see what kind of houses you design," she said, and he was suddenly reminded of his first meeting with Altar and the words "I want to see your stamp." He looked at her, puzzled, wondering if the hurdle had indeed been leaped. Over her shoulder, he saw the other women beginning to appear, saw a little boy break into a trot for the bus stop.

Quite calmly, he said, "I'll be at the center Tuesday afternoon at two o'clock. Will you be there?"

A frightened look came into her eyes. She hesitated a long time before replying, and then she said only, "Maybe."

"I'd like you to," he said. "I'd like—"

She interrupted, her words overlapping his. "I'll see. Maybe. I wish I knew why—"

And one of the approaching women said, "Hello, Margaret," and the mechanical smile appeared on her mouth as she turned away from him.

The hi-fi unit was going full blast when Larry knocked on Roger Altar's door. He had heard the music the moment he entered the building, listened to it get progressively louder as he climbed the steps to Altar's flat. Now, standing just outside the door the sound was almost unbearable. He knocked again, harder this time, certain he could be heard by no one in the apartment.

"Come in!" Altar shouted. "It's open."

He pushed open the door. Altar was lying on the couch, smoking. He wore slacks and slipper socks and a dress shirt open at the throat. He did not rise when Larry entered the room, and this somehow annoyed Larry. Altar had called him the night before, while he'd been working on his recommendations for Baxter and Baxter, telling him he'd looked over the sketches and would like to discuss them. Larry had made the trip into the city this Monday morning and now that he was in Altar's apartment he felt that Altar should at least extend the courtesy of greeting him when he arrived.

"That's a little loud, isn't it?" he said.

"What?" Altar answered.

"The music!" Larry shouted.

"Oh. Turn it down if you like."

Larry walked to the hi-fi cabinet. He found the gain control and turned it all the way down. Altar still lay motionless on the couch.

"Don't like music, huh?" he said.

"I like it fine," Larry answered.

"But not loud."

"I like it loud, too. But I didn't come here for a concert."

"What's biting you?" Altar wanted to know.

"Nothing."

"I hope not. I hope you're in a good mood."

Altar was smiling, but the smile was a crud-eating one, and Larry's years in the service had taught him to recognize the crud-eating grin and to know what it usually preceded. He felt himself stiffening.

"Sit down," Altar said. "Want a drink?"

"No." Belatedly, he added, "Thanks."

"Well, sit down anyway."

"Sure." Larry sat in the easy chair to the left of the bar unit, facing the blue couch upon which Altar still sprawled.

"I don't like to do this," Altar said. "I don't like it when it's done to me, and Christ knows it's done often enough. But I think there's a difference here, and if I'm wrong I'll apologize. Can I talk to you like a man, Larry? Or do I have to give you the schmaltz?"

"What do you mean?"

Altar shrugged and blew out cigarette smoke. "A bad review is a bad review. No matter how you slice it, it adds up to rejection, and nobody likes being shoved away from the breast. I don't like bad reviews, and I'll probably never like them. But I prefer the ones that give it to me straight from the shoulder without the gingerbread."

"Spit it out, Altar."

"Your sketches stink."

The room was silent except for the muted cello tones coming from the phonograph.

Altar started to say, "Maybe you're the kind who needs the schm—" and Larry interrupted with, "This is your considered opinion, is it?"

"I'm not trying to hurt you, Larry," Altar said. "I wouldn't have opened my mouth if I thought you'd get sore."

"I'm not getting sore."

"You are, and I can tell it."

"No, I'm not. Don't try to tell me how I feel. It just strikes me as amusing, that's all. You're the guy who doesn't tell plumbers how to fix pipes."

"That's right."

"But you look at a set of rough sketches and deliver the exalted opinion that— What the hell makes you think you're a competent judge?"

"What makes you think I'm not?"

"How can anyone who doesn't know architecture from a—',

"Larry—"

"You're an egomaniac, Altar! You look at a set of rough sketches and tell me they stink. What do you think you're doing, browsing through a light-love story in one of your slick-paper magazines? You're looking at plans and perspectives! Do you know how to read a plan?"

"Yes, I do."

"Where the hell did you learn to—"

"I once worked with a construction gang. Larry—"

"You're a pretty successful hero, aren't you?" Larry said, his anger rising. "What else have you done? Climbed an active volcano? Wrestled aligat—"

"You're not sore, huh?"

"I *am* sore, and the hell with you!"

"Sit down. We'll start from scratch."

"I'm going home. *You* can start from scratch. You can design your own damn house."

"Sit down," Altar said firmly. "For Christ's sake, sit down and stop behaving like—"

"Don't order *me* around, Altar!" Larry snapped. "I don't give a damn if you've sold *ten* million copies of your books."

"All right," Altar said, grinning. "*Please* sit down. All right?"

Larry sat. Altar studied him. "The schmaltz," he said, "begins this way—"

"Go to hell."

"Dear Mr. Cole. Whereas your rough sketches for the Altar residence show technical knowledge—"

"All right," Larry said.

"Do you want—"

"I said all right." He sighed heavily. "I just don't like being jumped on, Altar."

"Who does? Once you commit something to paper, you're open to attack. Want me to tell you why I don't like the sketches?"

"I'd appreciate it. That is, if your omnipotent, omniscient—"

"You're getting sore again."

"Okay, okay, tell me. I'm listening."

"We're still in business?"

"It depends on what you have to say."

"One: I don't think you gave my house any more thought than you'd give a garbage-disposal unit."

"I gave your house all my time for—"

"All your time, but none of your real thought, Larry. These sketches are routine, hack. I know what you can do. I've seen it."

"Go on," Larry said tightly.

"Two: I don't think you designed this house for *me*. I think you simply culled a lot of clichéd crap that was left over in the

82

basement of your mind from an Architecture One course."

"Goddamnit, that's not—"

"Three: I don't think you *want* to design my house. I don't know why. Maybe your mind is elsewhere. Maybe it isn't a big enough challenge. But whatever—"

"This is all nonsense!"

"Is it? Look, Larry, you know me fairly well by now. You should have some inkling of the kind of house I'd want surrounding me. These sketches have nothing whatever to do with Roger Altar. He doesn't enter into them at all."

"They're only exploratory. They're supposed to—"

"What's worse, *you're* not in these sketches. There's nothing of you here at all, and you're the goddamn architect! Where's your stamp? What are you trying to sell me?"

"I'm not trying to sell you any—"

"Are you trying to cheat me?"

"I've never cheated anyone in my life!" Larry said, beginning to rise again.

"Well, you're cheating me here. And you're cheating yourself, too!" He paused. "Don't be a jerk. Sit down."

"Why don't you get yourself another architect?"

"I won't need one unless you tell me flatly you're finished."

"You don't like my sketches, you don't like my—"

"Do you want to design my house, or don't you?"

"I don't know," Larry said harshly.

"Why do you resent me?"

"I don't resent you."

"Because I'm a success?"

"What!"

"If that's it, say so. Lots of men do. I don't hold it against them any more."

"Don't be absurd. We're not in competition."

"Then why? Because I'm a bachelor?"

"What's that got to do with it?"

"How do I know? Why *do* you resent me?"

"I told you I don't resent you. I think you're marvelous. I think you're the world's greatest living author. I don't know what literature would have done without you. I kiss your feet."

Softly Altar said, "You're just a kid, aren't you?"

"Don't start on me personally, Altar. Your ten per cent doesn't buy my soul."

"All I expect it to buy is your mind."

"A part of it."

"*All* of it where it concerns architecture."

"I could design a house you'd be afraid of."

"Try me."

"I could design a house you wouldn't understand."

"My stories are too good for the pulps," Altar said.

83

"What?"

"A local bromide. Forget it."

"What do I owe you, Altar? I could use one tenth of my brain power and still design a better house for you than any hundred architects in the country."

"When do you stop talking the good game, Larry?"

"When do you stop talking like an old friend of mine? For Christ's sake, I barely know you!"

"I'll go you one further. I don't think you *want* to know me."

"Why does every tinhorn writer in the world consider himself a psychiatrist?"

"How many other writers do you know?" Altar asked.

"None, thank God. Wise up, Altar. Do a little self-analysis. You're not attacking me. You're attacking *yourself*!"

"That's not true, Larry!"

Altar squashed his cigarette angrily into the ash tray on the coffee table. He swung upright at the same moment, as if he were buckling on his armour to do battle. His eyes narrowed, and his shaggy brows descended.

"Isn't it?" Larry asked. "You're sick of the commercial hack—"

"That's not true!" Altar snapped. "Maybe you think it's the same but it isn't. When I'm in that room, I'm working every damn minute, and I'm *trying*! I care deeply about what I'm doing. And you don't!"

"Commercial tripe, the critics said. They hit it right on—"

"The critics don't know how I bleed!" Altar shouted. "I open a vein on every page! I give everything I've got, my blood, my good red blood! What in God's name do you give? What are you afraid of? That you'll have to *give* something of yourself? Those sketches are the plotting of a guy who lives in a shell. Well, I don't live in a shell. I take, I take a lot—but I try to give something back. If you want to work for me—"

"*Work* for you! Holy—"

"What's the matter, is work a dirty word? Don't architects work? What do you prefer? Do you want me to call myself your client? Will that improve our relationship? Okay, if you want me to be your client, you've got to give. Everything. I'm treating you like a thoroughbred, and all I'm asking is that you get out there and run for me. I don't want excuses about a muddy track or a bowed tendon. All I want you to do is run. Do you know how to run, Larry? *Can you go the distance?*"

Larry was silent. Altar lighted another cigarette. He blew out a stream of smoke, and still the silence persisted. Slowly, Altar nodded and said, "Okay, forget it. It's been swell. Send me a bill for the work you've—"

"I'll design your house," Larry said.

"Don't do me any favors. If you don't want to—"

84

"I want to. I'll run. You don't deserve it, but I'll run for you."

"Why don't I deserve it? Does there have to be a prize attached before you turn on the steam?"

"That was below the belt, Altar. That damn prize didn't mean a thing, and you know it."

"Sure." Altar paused. "Maybe *none* of the prizes mean anything, Larry. Maybe there's only one prize that really counts."

"Which one?"

"You tell me."

"I'm not a big thinker," Larry said. He rose. "I'll bring you new sketches. I'll give them everything I've got, and if you still don't like them, that's that. I can't spend the rest of my life trying to please you."

"Nor can you spend it trying to please yourself, either."

"What does that mean?"

"How the hell do I know?" Altar said, grinning. "Another one of my profound banalities."

"You son of a bitch," Larry said, returning the grin. "You don't forget anything anyone ever says, do you?"

"Never. I'm a big sponge. I'm a brain picker. I'm recording secretary for the world at large. Don't ever tell me your life story. I'm liable to use it."

"Not a chance," Larry said. "It's pretty dull." He went to the door. "You can turn off the record player now," he said, smiling. "We don't need the string accompaniment any more."

He heard Altar's laugh erupt as he went in to the hall way.

11

AT FIFTEEN minutes to two on the Tuesday he was to meet Margaret Gault, Larry told the first of what was to be an endless succession of lies.

He did not particularly relish telling the lie, especially since Eve had been so understanding when he'd related the Altar incident the night before. Her earnest sympathy had carried over into the new day. While he worked out a tentative schematic for one of the housing-development buildings, she hovered over him constantly, bringing him coffee and toast, coming in every hour, trying to let him know that she, at least, thought he was a damned *good* architect.

He could not deny that Altar's attack had hurt him. He would not admit to himself that its most penetrating aspect had been its utter truthfulness. But he had allowed the attack to fire an indignation and then fill him with a fervent desire to design a house that would knock Altar's eyes out. He was grateful to Altar for having given his incentive a shove. But faced with the factory schematic, he did not appreciate the residential designing itch that tickled his unconscious. And faced with the kindnesses Eve showered upon him that morning, he did not appreciate the lie he was about to tell her.

He became conscious of the steadily advancing hands of the clock during lunch. He listened to Eve chatter, watched David pick listlessly at his food, and all the while he was thinking. This is Tuesday, she will be at the shopping center at two.

He was a little afraid of meeting her. He didn't know what he would say to her, and wondered indeed if he actually *wanted* to meet her. The thing could be dropped now. Nothing had really been said or done. Pursuit, on the other hand, might lead anywhere. Margaret Gault was still a total mystery to him, and he could no more determine exactly what might happen than he could explain to himself the tentative commitment he'd already made with her. He knew that he'd debated meeting her a hundred times, and he knew that he *would* meet her and, oddly, he felt there was nothing he could do to prevent the meeting. The concept was a peculiarly fatalistic one, especially for a person who'd flatly rejected the *Rubaiyat* at seventeen. But he knew that he had to see Margaret Gault again, if only to tell her he was crazy ever to think, ever to think *what*? He did not know.

He would see her. He would explain to her. Explain *what* to her?

Again, he did not know.

So he sat during lunch and plotted the lie he would tell Eve, and he felt an enormous sense of shame when she turned to him and asked, "Are you listening to me?"

He sprang the lie at one-forty-five.

He left the drawing board, wiping his hands on the rough tweed of his trousers. "Eve!" he called.

"I'm in the basement, honey," she answered.

He took the steps down, entering the dim concrete vault. The washing machine was making discordant music in one corner of the basement. Eve stood over her wash basket, sorting clothes. He did not want to see her face when he told the lie. From the steps he said, "I want to run into town a minute, Eve."

"All right," she said.

"I may be a while. Few things I have to get."

"All right," she said. "Will you be near the drugstore?"

"I can stop. Why?"

"Get some St. Joseph's aspirin. I think David is coming down with something."

"Okay," he said. He turned quickly and went up the steps. His heart was pounding. She had accepted the lie, had almost abetted it, but his heart was pounding nonetheless, pounding so hard that he began trembling as he put on his overcoat. From the front door, he felt compelled to say something else to her.

"I won't be too long, honey," he shouted.

He waited for an answer, but the washing machine had probably drowned him out. He sighed, left the house, and walked to the car. Sitting in the kitchen across the street, clearly visible in the large picture window, was Mrs. Garandi. He smiled pleasantly and waved at her. He unlocked the car, got in, and looked at his watch. It was ten minutes to two.

His heart was still pounding. He realized that he was very frightened, and he wondered whether he had looked peculiar to the Signora, wondered suddenly whether Eve had detected the lie in his voice, wondered what he could bring back from town to make his trip look legitimate. The simple assignation was somehow assuming gigantic proportions. He backed the car out of the driveway, and then self-consciously nodded and waved to Mrs. Garandi again, thinking he saw suspicion on her face.

He half expected Eve to appear accusingly at the front door, but she did not. Sighing in what he supposed was relief, he turned the corner and headed for the shopping center. It did not occur to him until he was almost there that Margaret Gault hadn't even said she'd definitely come. In a strange way he was beginning to hope she would not be there. But at the same time he wanted her to be there; and he knew that if she did not keep the date, he would seek her out again.

He felt suddenly trapped.

He wanted to turn the car, head back for the house, and he almost did. But his hands remained firm and steady on the wheel, and he pulled into the parking lot, stopped the car, and looked for her.

She was not there.

Nervously, he lighted a cigarette and began waiting.

Adrienne Gault was a widow.

She did not drive, and she found the train trip to her son's house tedious, but she nonetheless made the trip every week. She usually arrived on Wednesday, slept overnight, and then left Thursday morning.

This week she arrived unexpectedly on Tuesday.

At 1:35, while Margaret stood in the bathroom combing her hair, Mrs. Gault stood in the doorway and said, "If you're going shopping, I'd like to go with you."

"I'd rather you didn't," Margaret said.

"Why?" Mrs. Gault asked, knowing very well why. This girl simply didn't like her. In Donald's home, in her own home, she was always treated like some sort of a visiting dignitary. She did not mind being made comfortable, but she did object to feeling tolerated. It certainly would not have killed Margaret to generate a little ~~warmth~~. Well, that was the way it went. You raised your children and then you lost them.

"I want to get it done quickly and then come straight home," Margaret said.

"I've been shopping since I was eleven years old," Mrs. Gault said. "I'm certainly not a slow shopper."

"Besides, I'll be walking. Don took the car."

The idea of walking did not appeal to Mrs. Gault, but she did not think badly of her son for having taken the car. Her son, as she saw him, was a warm and genuine person who happened to have married a cold fish. Actually, he was warmest when Margaret wasn't around. It was then that they recaptured old times, when she told him of little things he'd done or said as a boy, told him of how terrible it had been after his father—God rest his soul—had died. They had been very close then, and talking alone they recaptured some of that closeness, a mother and son talking the way no two strangers could ever talk, flesh and blood, *her* flesh and blood. It was good to reaffirm the bond. It was good to talk to her son without Margaret around.

Margaret put down the comb and picked up her lipstick brush. Mrs. Gault watched while she traced the outline of her lips. She could feel indifference emanating from the well-built girl who stood before the mirror. What is it? she thought. Am I not a good mother? What does this girl want from me now that she has my son? And her thoughts almost always ended with the identical four words: The hell with her.

"What are you going to buy?" she asked.

"Oh, just some odds and ends."

"Well, if you're absolutely set against my going with you . . ."

"I'm not. I just don't want to make this an expedition."

". . . will you buy me a newspaper?"

"Certainly."

"The *Journal-American*. It should be out by now."

Margaret blotted her lips, then touched her little finger to the lipstick and dabbed each cheek lightly, spreading the color.

"Shouldn't it?"

"I'm sorry, Mom. Shouldn't *what*?"

"Shouldn't the paper be out by now? Where are you, anyway?"

"I just didn't hear you, that's all."

"Maybe I'd better go with you. You're in a fog. You'll probably get killed by a car."

"No," Margaret said quickly.

Her mother-in-law stared at her.

"I . . . I want to go alone."

"I wouldn't force myself on you, believe me," Mrs. Gault said, and she walked away from the open bathroom door and into the kitchen. The clock on the kitchen wall read 1:45. She sat at the pine-top table thinking how sad it was that her daughter-in-law didn't love her. When Margaret came out of the bathroom, she studied her with a dispassionate eye. She honestly couldn't see any resemblance whatever.

Adrienne Gault was a handsome woman with brown hair and blue eyes. Her bosom was large and firm, and she had the wide hips of a peasant woman, with the narrow waist of a young girl. But she certainly didn't look like Margaret, and she resented anyone's mistaking them for mother and daughter, as so often people did.

"Well, have a good time," she said blandly.

"I'm only going shopping," Margaret said. She glanced up at the clock. "I'd better go now."

"Do you always dress that way to go shopping? You'd think you were going to a dance."

"I like to be neat," Margaret said.

"What time will Donald be home?"

"The same time as always."

"He'll be so surprised to see me," Mrs. Gault said, and her eyes sparkled in anticipation.

"Yes," Margaret said unenthusiastically. "I've got to go now. I'll be back soon."

The clock on the kitchen wall read 1:57.

He saw her instantly.

She was very easy to see, he realized. You looked, and you saw her at once. He stepped out of the car and said "Maggie" softly, so softly that he was sure she would not hear him. But she lifted her head as he spoke, and then she hurried toward the car. She wore a black tailored coat and black pumps, and there were dangling rhinestone earrings on her ears. She held the coat collar against one cheek as she walked with her head down, the ash-blonde hair catching the feeble wintry sunlight.

"Get in," he said, smiling. He was very nervous. It amazed him that he could smile. What possible excuse could he offer to Eve should anyone witness this girl's getting into his car?

"Why?" she asked.

"We'll take a ride. I want to talk to you."

"I don't know what this is all about," Margaret said. "I really don't. I wish—"

"Let's not argue here," he said. "Won't you get in?"

She looked at him for just an instant. Then she shrugged, went around to the other side of the car, and got in. He pulled out of the parking lot the moment she slammed the door behind her. She sat very stiffly, her hands folded in her lap. She had looked at him only once, and now she sat staring through the windshield, apprehension in her eyes.

"Where are we going?" she asked.

"I don't know." His own fear was growing. He had expected

89

some measure of composure from her, but she sat stiffly tense and alert and her panic was spreading to him. The whole matter was taking on the aspect of a foolhardy, impulsive risk with nothing whatever to gain. He found his eyes darting all over the road, searching for faces he knew, faces he wanted to avoid. He began making excuses in advance to explain away the beautiful blonde who sat beside him on the front seat of his car. When the shopping center fell away behind them, he knew instant relief. He could feel his hands loosening their knuckle-white grip on the wheel.

"Where are we going?" she asked again. "What do you want from me?"

"I don't know."

"Whatever it is, the answer is no."

Her words shocked him. Coupled with the fear he already knew, came the horrifying presentment that he had made a grave mistake. He had approached this woman erroneously, and she would now spread the story through the whole development, and he could see himself trying to explain it all to Eve. He stepped on the accelerator.

"Well?" she said.

"Well what? For God's sake, relax, can't you?"

"I'm sorry. Where are you taking me?"

"I told you, I don't know. I'm just driving. It's broad daylight. You're absolutely safe."

"From what?" she asked. "Don't think because—" She stopped. She seemed to be very annoyed. "Don't jump to the obvious conclusion, that's all."

"I don't know what you're talking about."

"I'm talking about my anatomy!" she said.

Coupled with his first fear and his later fear, there came a new and partially suspected terror. The girl was either stupid or incredibly direct, and both failings were dangerous. All he wanted now was to get away from her as quickly as possible in the hope she would keep silent once this was over.

Nervously, he said, "I only wanted to talk to you. Because you seemed so interesting. I wanted to find out more about you." He looked at her hopefully. His words seemed to have had no effect on her. "Really," he went on, "I wasn't thinking . . . whatever . . . whatever you thought I was thinking."

"I'll bet."

"I'll turn back right now, if you say so."

"Turn back," she said.

"Sure," he answered, relieved. He swung the car to the side of the road, waited for the car behind him to pass, and then executed a U turn.

"You do this often, don't you?"

"No."

She laughed derisively. "I'll bet you don't." She seemed very angry with him, and he suddenly wondered what possible reason this complete stranger could have for being so damned annoyed. He hadn't forced her into the car, and no one had pushed her to the shopping center.

"What are you doing in my car?" he asked impulsively.

"I . . . you said you wanted to take a ride."

"And what did you think would happen on this ride?"

"I'm sure I don't know."

"Did you think I'd ask to see you again?"

"Yes. I guess so."

"Suppose I did?"

"I don't want to."

"I'm not asking. I only said suppose."

"I shouldn't be here with you. You shouldn't have asked me to meet you."

"Why *did* you meet me?"

"I wanted to know what makes you tick."

"And do you know now?"

"No. Look . . ." She was ready to say something, and then she shook her head.

"What is it?"

"Never mind."

"Go ahead. We'll never see each other again, so say it."

"It's not what you're thinking."

"I'm not thinking anything."

"It's . . . look, I was very lonely this summer. My husband was away and I . . ." She stopped. She turned away from him and stared through the windshield again. "I was very lonely."

She did not say more than that, but it was enough to tell him he had not been wrong about her. He glanced into the rear-view mirror and then at the road ahead, slowed the car, and made another U turn.

"What . . . ?"

"I don't want to go back yet, do you?"

"I . . ." She wet her lips. "You're driving."

They drove in silence for several minutes. "You asked me what I want from you," he said. "I know."

"What?"

"I want to see you some night."

"Oh, God, you're so damned practiced. How often have you done this before?"

"Never," he said flatly.

"You don't even know me. You met me in the street! How do you know me?"

"I don't. That's why I want to see you. To—"

"I don't want to know you," she said.

"All right, then leave it at that. I'll take you back."

"Please."

"Fine."

He swung the car around a third time. He was beginning to feel a little foolish. The conversation so far had been completely ridiculous. But what had he expected? What do strangers talk about, anyway? The car was silent. He drove slowly. Now that he'd had his say and been refused, he was in no real hurry to get back. He felt only relief now and, curiously, a sense of peace.

"I saw your house," she said suddenly. "The one in *House and Garden*."

"Did you like it?"

"Yes, very much. It's a . . . a strong house."

"Thank you." He paused. "Where did you find it? The September issue, I mean."

"At the library."

"You looked for it?"

"Yes."

Again they were silent. He wondered what she was thinking, but he was almost afraid of knowing. He could feel her beauty beside him, a live presence that filled the automobile. His fear had evaporated, to be replaced by an extrasensitive awareness of her closeness. But she's stupid, he thought, and then he wondered just how stupid she really was.

"What did you mean?" she asked.

"About what?"

"When you said I wasn't so pretty."

"Only that . . . sometimes you look pretty and sometimes you don't," he lied.

"How do I look now?"

"Lovely." His eyes touched her face. "Look, do you want to see me or don't you?"

"Will you be very hurt if I say no?"

"Hurt?" He felt completely confused all at once. Why should she care whether or not he was hurt? "I'll be disappointed, yes," he said. "Look, the hell with it. I'm married, you're married, this is crazy. Let's forget it."

"When did you want to see me?"

"When can you get away?"

"You name it. You do it."

"Tonight?"

"No."

"Tomorrow night?"

"No."

"Thursday night?"

"I think so."

"You'll see me?"

"Yes. But please don't think I'm a pickup. Please don't think that."

"I don't." He looked at her curiously. "Eight o'clock?"

"Don will be going out, too. I'll have to get a sitter."

"Is eight too early?"

"No, it's all right. But please don't think—"

"I'm not thinking anything."

"It's not that I don't want—" She shook her head. "What will we do? Thursday night?"

"Anything you like."

"No, no. You tell me."

"I'll surprise you. All right?"

"Yes." She nodded, but she seemed troubled. "Are you sure you want to see me?"

"Yes. Aren't you sure?"

"No," she said. "I'm not sure at all."

"Well," he said, disappointed by her unexpected honesty. There didn't seem much else to say. Everything was wrapped up, it seemed, somewhat confusedly but nonetheless securely. He did not feel at all excited. Now that it was over, he felt almost let down.

"Where shall I meet you?" she asked.

"Oh. Yeah." He thought a moment. "The post office? Do you know where that is?"

"Certainly. Eight o'clock, you said?"

"Yes."

"I'll be there. You're . . . you're sure you want to?"

"Yes, I'm sure," he said. "We're almost to the center. I'd better leave you off somewhere here."

"All right."

They were both tensely alert again. He pulled to the curb and when she reached for the door handle, he said, "Wait!" She waited obediently, not questioning his command. The car Larry had seen in the rear-view mirror flashed by.

"Okay," he said. "Thursday night, the post office, eight o'clock. Please don't leave me waiting."

"I'll be there," she said. She opened the door, and as she got out of the car, she whispered, "Larry."

"What is it?" he asked.

She smiled. "Nothing. I just wanted to try your name."

He drove into town, bought a soap eraser, a new typewriter ribbon, and a roll of tracing paper. He stopped at the drugstore to pick up the aspirin for David, and then he went home.

The huge wingless fuselages stood on the assembly line like giant hibernating insect slugs, the aluminium glistening under the glare of the overhead fluorescents. There was something eerie about the scene, Don thought, the welders with their masks pulled over their faces, the goggled eye pieces reflecting the blue flame of their torches; the staccato trip of the riveters, the resounding beat of hammered aluminium; the maze of wires

93

trailing from the plane like intestines ripped from a soldier's corpse; the people rushing over the factory floor, each with a job to do, yet each seeming like an undirected ant frantically scurrying over the orderly structure of an ant hill.

Just like the Army, he thought. Everybody running around with no place to go. Still, the Army hadn't been bad. He'd been well liked in the Army. There, in the vast faceless morass of men, he had worn his pfc rating with humorous anonymity, and he'd been content. Until. Until, of course.

Everything ends, he supposed. All happiness ends. All contentment ends. We die.

Well, the hell with that. The Army was then, and this was now, and he was certainly well liked at the plant too. Nor was it the phony deference generated by fear which some men automatically gave to muscular men. Don was excellently built, and he was also foreman of his floor, a combination which easily could have led to a false display of friendship from the men with whom he worked. But he liked to think he was a nice guy with easygoing warmth and humor who never took the little problems of aircraft production too seriously, who was always ready to look at the brighter side of a factory snarl. That was why he got along with the men. He was simply part of their team.

It was something like being on an Army patrol, where the well-being of each man depended on every other man. He could still remember the night patrols, and the tight feeling of a small group pitched against a larger unseen group, the enemy. He could remember the misty black silence of the jungle, the sense of impending danger, the sorrow that no one but the men involved in the patrol were there to see such movie heroics.

He'd have liked Margaret to have seen him on patrol, his face and hands blackened, his hands covered with soot, covered. It was a shame she hadn't seen him holding a BAR, the immense lethal length of the rifle, the hand grenades dangling from his waist, as he stalked the unseen enemy, the bodiless enemy, the enemy who was not one, not a live person who breathed and smiled and smoked cigarettes and talked, not that sonofabitching enemy.

The war is over, he thought.

He put his hands in his pockets and walked over to one of the welders. He stood watching him and the steady flame which spurted from the slender welding rod. The man cut the flame, lifted his mask, and grinned up at Don. Don stood spread-legged over him. He brought his hands behind his back and clasped them there.

"How's it going, Pete?" he asked.

"So-so." Pete grinned. He was a gnomish man with crooked black eyebrows and a bright smile. Black curling hair hung onto his forehead where the welding mask was pushed up like the visor of a helmet. Squatting beside Don, who stood muscular and fair, his blond crew-cut hair reflecting the fluorescent glow, his hands behind his back, Pete looked like a squire kneeling to fasten a knight's leg armor.

"How you like to get bombed by this bastard?" he asked, grinning.

"I wouldn't," Don said. He liked Pete. He liked the smiling face and the glowing brown eyes. Pete was a nice guy, and also a good welder.

"Me neither. We keep buildin' them bigger an' bigger. Pretty soon we won't be able to fit them in the factory. Why you think they gettin' so big, Don?"

"To carry more bombs, I guess."

"What for? An atomic bomb you could fit in a lady's pocket-book."

"We won't use no atomic bombs," Don said.

"We use them already, dint we?"

"Sure, but that was a necessity."

"So they'll be other necessities. War makes its own reasons. Some guy someday'll just say, 'It's a big necessity we got to drop an atomic bomb.' *Boom*! Up your mother's poop!" Pete laughed.

Don did not laugh with him. "I don't think we'll use atomic bombs again," he said.

"What then? Hydrogens? The same thing. *Boom*! Up your mother's . . ."

"Nobody with sense is going to use nuclear weapons," Don said quickly.

"Hey, there's a real strength word," Pete said. "Nuclear."

"What's a strength word?"

"I bought this book about strength words. Don't you want strength, Don?"

"I got all the strength I'll ever want," Don said, smiling, thinking Pete was joking and figuring he'd ride along with the gag.

"Pithy," Pete said.

"What?"

"Pithy. That's a strength word."

"What's so strong about it?"

"You know what it means?"

"Pithy?"

"No, pithy. Pithy."

"Sure. It means meaty."

"That's right," Pete said, surprised. "Did you buy that book?"

"I don't need a book to tell me what pithy means," Don said. "Give me another strength word."

"Fructify. That's a really advanced strength word. That's near the end of the book."

"Fructify, huh?" Don thought for a moment. "I don't think I know that one."

95

"It means to bear fruit. It's a dilly, ain't it?"

"It's a good word," Don agreed. "I'll have to tell it to Margaret. She likes new words. She's got a pretty good vocabulary."

"Fructify," Pete repeated, rolling the word on his tongue. "It sounds dirty, don't it?" He burst out laughing.

"Well," Don said, displeased that Pete was beginning to joke. He was enjoying the strength words. It didn't hurt a man to try improving himself.

"Tell it to Margaret," Pete said. "Margaret's so beautiful, she needs to be smart, too. It's absolutely necessary, otherwise people won't even look at her." His laughter exploded merrily.

"Well," Don said, putting his hands into his pockets.

"The kind of strength Margaret got," Pete said, "is the kind of strength I like."

"Well," Don said.

"She's the most passionate-lookin' woman I ever seen, all due respect."

"Well," Don said, embarrassed.

"You ever get tired of her, you give me a buzz. I leave my wife and run away to China with Margaret. I abscond. That's a strength word."

"Well," Don said, grinning.

"Is she as passionate as she looks?"

"Aw, come on."

"Come on, *is* she? I only seen her once but—"

"I don't know."

"What do you mean, you don't know? Is she or ain't she?"

"Well, not so much. You know. Not so much. She's just a woman. They all get their moods. You know."

"Sure," Pete said. He paused, laughed secretly, and then said, "Maybe you don't fructify her enough." He exploded hysterically. "Oh, brother, that word breaks me up!"

"Come on, come on," Don said. "Go back to your welding. We ain't building airplanes talking about women, that's for sure."

Pete's laughter trailed off. He sighed, lowered his mask, and went back to work. Don walked away from him, his hands in his pockets.

"You were always getting into accidents," Mrs. Gault said that night. "From when you were a little baby. Oh, my, were you a handful!"

They sat in the living room—Don, his mother, and Margaret. The television was on, and Margaret was trying to watch an hour-long dramatic show, but Mrs. Gault kept telling stories of Don's childhood. Margaret wondered how he managed to sit through the same stories over and over again with such a seemingly interested smile on his face. She had heard each story at least forty times since they were married, and God alone knew how many times Don had heard them before he and Margaret met.

"When you were only three," Mrs. Gault said, "I can remember it as plain as if it was yesterday. Your father—God rest his soul—and I were getting dressed for a wedding. Your Aunt Marie. Well, you were running through the rooms with a bottle in your mouth, just chewing on the nipple, and you tripped over the door jamb between the rooms. You split your chin wide open."

"I had to have three stitches, Margaret," Don said.

"Uhm," Margaret said.

"Oh, that was a time!" Mrs. Gault said. "The doctor rushing in. I never saw so much blood in my life, and us waiting to go to a wedding. Oh, my God, you were a terror!"

"Well, I lived through it," Don said.

"Certainly, *you* lived through it! But the heartache! Do you remember the time in Spotswood, New Jersey? At your Aunt Gussie's? That was another time."

"I remember that one," Don said.

"You were pumping water outside. Your aunt had one of these old-fashioned pumps. This was after your father died, poor soul. You were pushing the handle up and down, but you didn't realize you were building pressure in the pump. Then you let go of the handle and it snapped up and hit you right in the mouth! I swear to the Lord above, it's a miracle you didn't knock every tooth out of your mouth. Oh, my God, it was terrible! I remember I was wearing a white sun dress, and I held your head against me, and your lip was bleeding. Oh, I hate to even think of it! Blood all down the front of my dress! It soaked right through to my brassière, Margaret!" She shook her head, vividly remembering the incident and its terror.

"I remember that," Don said. "I was never so surprised as when that pump handle came up and hit me." He smiled. "But I suppose it was funny, in a way."

"Oh, that wasn't the funny one," Mrs. Gault said, leaning forward as if on cue. "The funny one was when we had that summer bungalow at the beach, you and I. Oh, that was the funny one." She began laughing.

In a bantering voice, Don said, "I'm sure glad you think it was so funny, Ma."

"Donald, you were so comical that day! I have to laugh just to think about it."

Don looked at Margaret, grinning, anticipating the story.

"I was down at the beach," Mrs. Gault said. "You were thirteen years old at the time, we had that nice little cottage at Rockaway, remember? And there was this bed, a cot actually. Oh, this is ridiculous!" She began laughing again, wiping the tears from her eyes.

"I'll never forget that cot," Don said.

"Anyway, I heard you yelling, and I couldn't imagine what had happened to you. I came running up from the beach in my bathing suit, and there you were. You'd sat up too suddenly and got yourself caught on the cot."

"I got caught on the cot, Margaret," Don said, smiling.

"But you can't imagine *how*, Margaret!" Mrs. Gault said. "He was just a boy, but it was so funny, the way he caught himself. Actually, I shouldn't laugh. He could have been seriously hurt. Oh, but it was so funny. I couldn't stop laughing when I saw him."

"And I kept crying," Don said.

"I think you were embarrassed," Mrs. Gault said. "I think it hurt, too, but mostly you were embarrassed. I shouldn't have laughed. But it was really comical, Donald. Even you began laughing after I'd got you loose. Oh, my, that was a day, all right. I can remember holding your head against me and both of us laughing to beat the band when it was all over. Do you remember?"

"Yes, I remember. Sure, I do. You smelled of suntan oil. You got very brown that summer."

Mrs. Gault nodded, lost in reminiscence.

In the kitchen, the telephone rang. Margaret rose.

"We had some good times, didn't we?" Mrs. Gault said. "Remember how our house was a meeting place for all your friends? That little apartment? I used to get a kick out of them. Since you got married, none of them come around any more. Not one of them. Wasn't I good to them when you were a boy?"

"Oh, sure you were, Ma. But they were *my* friends. You know how it is."

"Sammy . . . Was that his name? The short fat one?" Mrs. Gault burst out laughing. "But he was always eating, that one! Always!"

Margaret was certain, as she lifted the receiver from its cradle, that the caller would be Larry Cole and that he would break the date they had made for Thursday night. She'd been expecting him to back out ever since she'd left him, and the call now did not surprise her.

"Hello?" she said softly.

"Margaret?" the voice asked.

It was not Larry Cole. She was startled by the voice because she had not heard it for some time. And then, recognizing it, remembering it, she began trembling and was incapable of speech for a moment.

"Margaret?"

"You," she said. "Wh . . . what do you want?"

"Don't hang up. Please."

"He's home," she said.

"Please. I only want to talk to you."

Margaret glanced toward the living room. She could hear Mrs.

Gault's laughter through the closed door. "What about?" she asked.

"Margaret . . ."

She could feel his voice weakening, and his weakness brought a surge of strength. "Say what you have to say."

"Can't I see you?"

"No."

"For just a few minutes?"

"No."

"Please. Margaret, please. Say when, and I'll come. I'll meet you wherever you say."

"I say no place, never."

"Margaret . . ."

"Listen to me," she said. "I'm going to hang up."

"No! Please! Don't!"

"I have nothing to say to you. Don't call me again. If I hear your voice, I'll hang up right away. Do you hear me?"

"I hear you, but—"

"I don't want to see you, I don't want to talk to you, I don't want you to call me ever again. If you call again, I'll tell him. I swear I'll tell him everything, and he'll kill you. You know he'll kill you."

"He doesn't scare me."

"He'll kill you," she said. "Now stop annoying me."

"Margaret, I can't stop thinking about you. I can't help it. I think about you every minute. I can't help it. I can't help it." He began weeping, and she heard his sobs, and her lashes fluttered, and a bewildered look came into her eyes. Her hand was sweating on the receiver.

"Stop it," she said.

"I can't help it."

"Stop crying. I can't stand it. Are you a man, or what are you?"

"Margaret, how can you forget what happened? How can you—?"

"I want to forget! Stop calling me!"

"Margaret, I have to call you. I have to hear your voice, just—"

"Stop it, stop it!"

She thought for a moment that she'd spoken too loudly. She whirled toward the living room, but Don and his mother were still talking together.

"I'm hanging up now," she said coldly.

"No! Don't! If you do, I'll call you back. The minute you hang up, I'll call again."

"Are you crazy? What's the matter with you? I told you he's home."

"I don't care. When can I see you?"

"Never!" she said, and she hung up and then fell against the

99

counter. She put her hand to her mouth, biting her knuckles, her eyes squeezed shut tightly. Nothing ever ends, she thought. You pay and you pay. In the other room, she could hear Mrs. Gault's laughter, and the laughter infuriated her. She leaned against the counter and waited, her teeth clamped into the flesh on her hand. She expected the phone to ring, but when it did, it nonetheless startled her.

She debated answering. But if she didn't, Don would surely come into the kitchen. Nothing ever ends, she thought, and she picked up the receiver.

"Hello?"

"Margaret—"

She slammed the phone down, kept her hand on it as if that added finality to the gesture. In the living room, she could hear the muffled sound of television voices and the accompanying infuriating laughter of her husband and his mother. She watched the clock. Five minutes passed. Her breathing was even now. She looked at her hand and saw the white marks where her teeth had pinched the flesh. She sighed heavily and then went back into the living room. Her mother-in-law was still talking about a boy named Sammy. Don, sitting at her feet, looked up when Margaret entered the room.

"Who was that, hon?" he asked.

"Betty Anders," she said.

12

THE RADIO pushed a rock-and-roll ballad into the girls' bedroom, adding to the fever of preparation. For this Wednesday night alone, Mrs. Harder had broken her stringent rule forbidding anything but weekend dates. Apparently Lois's engagement was an important one, and since Linda had found a beau for that night too, the law had been temporarily revoked.

Lois was an active, nervous dresser. She could not sit still or lie still for a moment. Even brushing her hair, as she did now, she stood before the mirror and her feet tapped a constant jig in time to the radio music. Linda sat at the dressing table applying lipstick to her mouth, watching her sister's gyrations.

"Can I or can't I?" Lois asked.

"If Mama heard that, she'd flip," Linda said.

Lois put her hands on her hips and assumed an expression of extreme patience. Standing in her half-slip and bra, she looked full-breasted and narrow-waisted, quite womanly except for the childish petulance of her face.

100

"Mama would flip if she heard you say 'flip,' too." Patiently, she corrected herself. "*May* I or *may* I not wear the tan belt?"

"You may," Linda said. "Mama's always flipping about something or other. Did you notice that?"

"It's change of life," Lois said knowingly.

"Do you think so?"

"Certainly. When you get as old as Mama, your organs get all mixed up, and everything bothers you." She began stroking her hair viciously. "I'd like a cigarette," she said. "Do you have any?"

"If you're going to smoke, go to the john."

"She knows, anyway," Lois said. "Every time she goes in there, she damn near chokes on the smoke. You'd think she'd loosen up and say 'Go ahead, kids, smoke.' But not Mama." Lois shook her head. "She's silly about some things."

"Eve wasn't allowed to smoke until she was eighteen," Linda said.

"Eve's a different generation," Lois answered. "Besides, I'll bet she smoked, too."

"Not in the house."

Lois was searching through Linda's bag. When she found the cigarettes she lighted one instantly, went to the window, opened it, and stood there puffing feverishly.

"I don't know why you're dating MacLean," she said suddenly. "He's a spook."

"He doesn't seem like one."

"He is. I've dated him, and I know. He's a spook."

"Well," Linda said, and she shrugged.

"Where's he taking you?"

"To a movie."

"That's about his speed, all right. He'll buy you an ice-cream soda later. He's a big spender, MacLean. He hasn't got Scotch blood for nothing. Whatever you do, don't order anything expensive like a banana split or anything. He'll die right on the spot."

"He didn't seem tight."

"How do you know? You've never gone out with him."

"Just talking to him, I mean."

"I'll bet you ten dollars he tells you about his father's clan, and his kilt. If you want to see him blush, ask him what a Scotchman has under his kilt."

"Did *you*?"

"No, but I wanted to. He's a spook. He doesn't even know how to kiss."

"He seems nice," Linda said.

"Are you going to let him?" She paused. "Kiss you, I mean?"

"Not on the first date. That's what we decided, didn't we?"

"Sure, but it seems sort of silly. I think we ought to change it. I think we left out a lot."

101

"I think the rules are fine," Linda said.

"I think we ought to include petting. All the girls do it, Lindy. Seriously. I get awfully tired of pulling hands away."

"I don't."

"Besides, I wonder what it feels like."

"Lois, Mama wouldn't—"

"Oh, Mama, Mama! Daddy touches *her*, doesn't he?"

"They're married."

"Am I saying we should go *all* the way? Am I saying that?"

"No, but . . ."

"Well, I think we ought to change the rules. Even if you don't want to, I'm going to."

"Do what you want to do," Linda said.

"Well, what fun is it if you don't do it, too?" Lois protested. She began pacing the room. "Why are you wearing that dress to a movie?" she asked. "It's a little dressy, isn't it?"

"No, I don't think so."

"It's pretty low, too. You'll shock MacLean right out of his kilt in that dress, Lindy. You should see how it looks across your behind."

"It looks fine," Linda said. "I looked in the mirror."

"It looks a little tight to me. If you don't mind showing your backside to the world, I'm sure I—"

"It's not tight at all. Mama already let out the seams."

"I was thinking . . . Do you know my blue dress?"

"Yes?"

"I was going to wear it tonight. This is my first time out with Alan, you know."

"Yes, I know."

"He's twenty-three, Linda, twenty-three. And this is a Phi Sig party, right at his fraternity house. All his brothers'll be there."

"So?"

"So I was going to wear the blue dress. You can't just go in anything to a Phi Sig party."

"Why don't you?"

"I got gook on it. It's still at the cleaners." Lois was silent for a moment. "My beige is too severe. And the only other one I have is that green horror with the big bow that makes me look pregnant."

Linda began laughing.

"Don't laugh, Sis. Can I wear a sweater and skirt to a Phi Sig party? How can I do that?"

"Well, what else can you do?" Linda asked, still laughing.

"I *could* wear your dress. If you'd loan it to me."

"Oh, what a sneak," Linda said.

"Can I?"

"No."

"It *is* too tight, you know. I wouldn't lie about that."

"No."

"Linda, for hell's sake, this is important!"

"So's my date with Hank."

"That spook? Linda, don't be selfish."

"I'm not being selfish. I'm all dressed, Lo. He'll be here any minute."

"How long would it take you to change?"

"No."

"You can wear what I was going to wear. The black skirt and my tan cashmere."

"No."

"Linda, my *cash*mere, not just a junky orlon or something."

"Lois—"

"Lindy, please. Have I asked you for anything recently?"

"No, but—"

"I wouldn't ask now if this wasn't such a big thing. Lindy?" She paused. "Lindy?" She paused again. "Please?"

"I'm all *dressed*."

"Pretty please?"

"How can I—?"

"Pretty please with sugar on it?"

"Oh, go ahead," Linda said. "I'll . . . Oh, go ahead. Unzip me."

"I'll let you wear my pearls," Lois said happily, unzipping the dress.

"I don't want your pearls," Linda said. "I have my own pearls." She stepped out of the dress and handed it to Lois.

"You've got a run," Lois told her.

"Dammit, that's all I need."

"I've got a pair of stockings for you," Lois said generously. She went to the dresser. Over her shoulder, she said, "If Alan tries to pet, I'm going to let him."

"Do what you want to do," Linda said.

"Will you?"

"No."

"With *your* dress on," Lois said, "he'll try it. I know he will." She handed Linda the stockings. "Here."

"Thanks."

"It *was* too tight for you, you know," Lois said. "It made you look like all ass."

"Sometimes I think I *am*," Linda said.

Disgustedly, she extended one leg and began putting on the stockings.

It seemed to her that everything, sooner or later, passed into the no man's land of community property. She could count on the fingers of one hand the possessions which she could call exclusively, inviolately her own. The rest of the accouterments of everyday living were shared equally within the corporate structure of sisterhood and twinship. There were only three things she truly owned and these were jealously coveted in an old tin candy box at the back of the second dresser drawer.

The first of these was a pink shell as exquisitely turned as a water nymph's ear.

She had found it one summer at Easthampton while walking alone on the shore, just before a storm. She was nine years old, and she watched the sky turn ominously black and the waves beating the sand in windswept anger. When she found the shell, she picked it up and held it cradled in the palm of her hand; it was a delicate thing, the pink luminescent against the gathering fury of the storm. The thunder clouds broke around her. Barefoot, her hair and her skirts flying, she had run back to the cottage across the suddenly wet sand, the shell clutched in her small fist.

The second possession was an autumn leaf, thin and fragile, carefully mounted with Scotch tape on a piece of stiff paper, losing its structure nonetheless, so that only the tracery of delicate veins remained in some spots.

She had been eleven when the leaf fell.

She had been sitting alone on a bench in the park across the street from her apartment building, her black hair pulled back into a pony tail, an open book in her lap, her wide blue eyes full with the lyrics of Edna St. Vincent Millay. It had been a quiet day, wood smoke still with the splendor of fall. She had sat alone with her book of verse and read:

> Silver bark of beech, and sallow
> Bark of yellow birch and yellow
> Twig of willow.

> Stripe of green in moosewood . . .

The leaf fell.

It spiraled silently on the still air to settle on the open page of the book. Yellow and brown, it lay on the open page, rustled as if to flee, settled again when she covered it with her hand. For no reason, her eyes suddenly brimmed with tears. She had taken the leaf home and mounted it.

The third possession in the candy tin at the back of the second dresser drawer was an Adlai Stevenson campaign button.

These were her own.

Everything else she shared with Lois; even her face and her body. She did not resent the sharing as persistently as she had long ago, but just as strongly. All she wanted to be, she supposed, was Linda Harder. And the chance division of a cell had made that the most difficult aspiration in the world.

In the beginning, of course, she had not known.

There was Mama, and Daddy, and Eve, and Lois. Lois seemed

to be just another person, as different from Linda and everyone else as she could possibly be. They were sisters. Just the way she and Eve were sisters.

After a while it became apparent that she and Lois were somehow special. She had never been able to understand why Mrs. Harder dressed them alike. Why didn't she dress Lois and *Eve* alike? Eve was a sister in the family, too, wasn't she? She began to wonder about it. And she began to hear an oft-repeated expression: "Oh, how cute! Are they twins?"

One day she went to Mrs. Harder and asked, "What's twins?"

"You and Lois are twins, darling," Mrs. Harder said.

"I know, but what's twins?"

"That means you were born together. You look alike."

"Were Eve and me born together?"

"No, darling."

"Well, *we* look alike."

"But not exactly alike. You and Lois are identical twins. That means you look *exactly* alike."

Linda pondered this for a grave moment. Then she said, "I don't want to look exactly like nobody but me."

And even though Mrs. Harder had laughed and said something about *both* her girls being adorable little darlings, Linda was not pleased at all.

After that, whenever anyone mistakenly called her "Lois," she would whirl angrily and say, "I'm *Linda!*"

She did not enjoy the confusion their sameness bred. She did not smile when her nursery-school teacher reported, "One of your girls was very naughty today, Mrs. Harder. I can't remember which one. They're *so* hard to tell apart."

She did not appreciate other children referring to her and Lois as "Harder One" and "Harder Two." To one of these children, she angrily replied, "I'm not a number. I'm *Linda!*"

Nor did she enjoy the constant comparison.

"Well, Linda doesn't draw as well as Lois, but she likes to work with clay."

"No, Lois is the one who tells the stories. Linda's a little shy."

"You can tell if you really look closely. Linda's hair isn't as glossy."

"Now eat your cauliflower, Linda! See how nicely Lois is eating?"

It took her a long while to learn that there were compensations for loss of identity.

There was, to begin with, the protective coloration of the pack. Both girls, she discovered, could raise holy hell together and get away with it, simply because it was considered adorably cute in tandem. Both girls could utter completely stupid inanities which were considered terribly advanced and grown up, simply because they were spoken by twins. At any party, the Harder twins—

dressed exactly alike, their black-banged hair sleekly brushed, their blue eyes sparkling beneath long black lashes, their petticoats stiffly rustling—stole the show from the moment they entered. There was sanctuary and notoriety in twinship.

But most important of all, there was companionship.

There was no such thing as a lonely rainy day indoors, no such thing as a long solitary bout with the whooping cough or the mumps. Lois was constantly by her side, an ally and a friend. It was not so bad being a twin at all.

Except sometimes, when you remembered sitting alone on a park bench, alone, Linda Harder.

When you remembered the fall of a solitary leaf.

At eight-twenty, when Linda came out of the bedroom, Hank MacLean was sitting in the living room talking to her parents. He was a tall boy with sandy brown hair and dark brown eyes. He wore a gray tweed suit and a blue tie, and he rose instantly when Linda entered the room.

"You look pretty," he said.

"Thank you. Was Dad telling you how tough business is?"

"As a matter of fact," Hank said, "*I* was telling *him* about fencing."

"I didn't know he was on the fencing team, Linda," Mr. Harder said.

"The *second* team, Mr. Harder," Hank corrected. "That means I only get to stab people every now and then."

Mr. Harder chuckled. Mrs. Harder inspected her daughter and said, "You look very lovely, darling."

"Thank you. Shall we go, Hank?"

"Sure. If you're ready."

Linda kissed her parents and then walked to the closet. "Is it cold out?" she asked. "Do I need something for my head?"

"It's just brisk," Hank said.

She took her coat from a hanger, and he helped her on with it. She felt rather strange. She always did when she was dating one of Lois's cast-offs. She had the feeling that, having failed with his first choice, he was now dating a mildly reasonable facsimile of the original. Invariably, boys who expected a carbon copy of Lois were disappointed. She did not know Hank at all, except that he had dated Lois several times and then suddenly called Linda one day last week. But she couldn't shake the feeling that she was second choice, second best, and she remembered him helping Lois into her coat just two short weeks ago, and the memory was painful.

"I didn't know whether you and your sister would be dressing alike," he said. She turned, puzzled, buttoning her coat. "Even though you're not going out together, I think it's nice for people to know you apart, don't you?"

106

"What?" she said, thoroughly puzzled.

He lifted a box from the hall table. "This is for your button-hole," he said. "So I'll know you when we meet at the out-of-town newspaper stand."

She was too surprised to speak. She lifted the lid from the box, parted the green paper, and then picked up the corsage.

"I guess roses go with everything," he said. "I hope."

"This . . . this was very thoughtful, Hank," she said. "Would you help me pin it?"

"I'm only on the second team!" he said, backing away from the pins.

Linda laughed. "Mom?" she said, and Mrs. Harder came to pin the corsage.

"There," she said. "That's a beautiful corsage. You look lovely, Linda."

Hank nodded. He didn't say anything. He simply nodded, and Linda saw the nod and the strange sort of pride in his eyes, and she looped her hand through his arm suddenly.

"Not too late, Hank, please," Mrs. Harder said. "This is a weekday."

"Okay," he answered. "Good night, Mr. Harder."

"G'night," Mr. Harder said from the living room.

From the bedroom, Lois called, "Have fun, Lindy! Hi, Hank!"

"Hi," Hank called back.

Gently, he loosened Linda's hand from his sleeve and captured it with his own.

13

ON THURSDAY night, in the darkness of the parked automobile, Larry sat and waited.

He was grateful for the darkness. He did not want to be seen in town when he was supposed to be in New York. In the light of the dash, his watch read 8:15 and he wondered for the fifteenth time since eight o'clock whether she would come. He had never liked waiting. She should have realized it would be painful for him. She certainly could have shown the consideration of being on time.

If, of course, she were coming at all.

What am I doing here, anyway? he asked himself. Am I crazy? Why did I lie to Eve? This girl means nothing to me. She's stupid and cheap and she's probably been had by a thousand men. What do I want from her?

He admitted to himself what he wanted from her.

Not sparkling conversation, not a charming dinner companion, not a twinkle-toed dancing partner. He knew exactly what he desired. Knowing it, admitting it, the lying had seemed essential.

But it disturbed him, and not because it hurt Eve, who had accepted the falsehood with faithful innocence. It was her very trust, instead, which had turned his deception into a barbed shaft that twisted in his chest. He had been untruthful before, but never with Eve. And those lies had never been outrageously false; they had been only the polite inaccuracies of society, small falsehoods that oiled the machinery of American culture, designed to promote harmony, almost merciful in character.

The untruth he told Eve was a bald-faced, monstrous lie invented for deception alone.

"I have to see Altar in the city tonight," he'd said.

Delivered and accepted, deceit its avowed reason for existence, the lie assumed a life of its own; and it was then that *he* began working for it rather than *it* working for him.

With David in for his afternoon nap, Eve left the house to do some shopping. He watched her drive away, debating again in his mind the big question of whether or not he should keep the date with Margaret Gault. Then he thought of the lie.

And it occurred to him that, should the water tank develop a leak, or should Eve suddenly discover she was pregnant, or should any of ten or a hundred or a thousand things happen, Eve might try to contact him at Altar's. Altar's number was listed in their personal telephone directory, and he did not feel he knew Altar well enough to beg an alibi. The deception, nonetheless, had to be protected.

He went into the bedroom and found the black book next to the telephone. He looked up Altar's number. The last digit of the number was a 5. Painstakingly, as diligently as a forger working on a check, he inked over the 5, changing it to a 6. The first part of protecting the falsehood was completed. If Eve called Altar, she would get a wrong number.

But she would then, logically, go to the Manhattan directory to check the number. Larry picked up the bulky phone book and leafed through the A's, fully intending to rip out the page bearing Altar's name and number. He discovered, to his relief, that Altar was not listed in the directory. But if Eve really wanted to reach him, she would carry the phoning to its ultimate conclusion, and so Larry could not leave it at that.

He dialed Information and asked for Roger Altar's listing. The operator told him it was an unpublished number which she could not divulge. He told her it was an emergency, but she remained adamant. Satisfied that Eve could not expose him by calling Altar, he hung up. In a curious way, he was pleased that he was protecting Eve. At the same time, he could not elude the enormity of his deception or the knowledge that his mind was adjusting to it and elaborating upon it.

He felt, too, a tremendous waste of energy.

He had just spent twenty minutes of extreme concentration in an effort to protect his lie. He knew that more energy would be expended in concocting a fiction about what had transpired at Altar's apartment. Eve would certainly want to know what Altar said and did. He would have to fabricate a conversation and then relate it as if it had actually taken place. He felt suddenly delighted that he had chosen Altar. He could now invent the most fantastic architectural philosophy and pretend that Altar had spouted it. From what Eve knew about the writer, she would accept the most absurd statements as originating in his mind. But again, though he was pleased with the precautions he seemed automatically to take, he felt guilty about the facility and rapidity of his mental adjustment to deceit.

When he drove away from the house that night, the guilt was still strong within him. In a way, it served as a reagent to the fear he might have felt. Tonight he was not frightened. He pulled out of the driveway with strange determination. And though his mind toyed with the idea of meeting her and saying, "Look, Maggie, let's forget all this. There's not much sense to it, and I feel guilty as hell," the idea was rejected immediately upon invention.

Sitting in the parked automobile, he knew he had come this far and could not now retreat. There was a need deep inside him, and he told himself it was a need for the body of Margaret Gault, and for the time being that explanation satisfied him.

A car came up the street.

Its headlights illuminated the interior of the Dodge, and Larry automatically brought his left hand to his face, shielding it. As the car passed, he saw it was a pale-blue Chevy. He followed it in the rear-view mirror. The Chevy pulled up a little past the post office. The motor died. He counted the seconds. The front door opened and he saw her get out of the car and lock it. He instantly turned the key in the ignition and started the engine.

She waited until the light traffic permitted her to cross the street and then, without hesitation, walked directly to the Dodge. He had reasoned that the two most dangerous moments of tonight's meeting would be those when she entered and left his automobile. For these were the moments of assignation and departure and each would—if observed—be almost impossible to explain. Nervously, he awaited her approach, hearing the clatter of her heels against the sidewalk.

She wore a kerchief, which hid the blonde hair, and he was grateful for her precaution. She paused for a moment before opening the door, as if uncertain this was the right car. Then she reached for the handle and the interior lights snapped on when she opened the door, and she seemed startled by the sudden

109

illumination. She sat quickly, pulling the door shut behind her. The lights went out. There was darkness and silence.

"Hi," he said.

She smiled uneasily. "Hi."

He had already flicked on his headlights and pulled away from the curb. "I didn't think you were coming," he said.

"I said I would. Could we get away from town quickly, please?"

Her tone worried him. As with the last time she was in the car, there was a stiff nervousness about her, an anxiety around her mouth, an alert darting of her brown eyes. He fought to keep her panic from spreading to him. Someone had to keep a level head and obviously it wasn't going to be she. "Did you have any trouble?" he asked.

"No. Don gave me the car, but I had to drop him off. Can't you drive faster?"

"I'd hate to get a speeding ticket," he said. "It might be a little difficult to explain."

She nodded. "Where are we going?"

"I thought we'd head north."

"All right." She paused. "Suppose someone sees us?"

"Who's going to see us?"

"I don't know. One of the neighbors."

"This is Thursday night, shopping night. They're all up at the center."

"Yes," she said. "I feel terrible. I feel very guilty. Do you feel guilty?"

"Yes."

"I'm so ashamed. Maybe you ought to take me home."

"If you want me to."

"He brought me flowers. Because he was going out tonight. He belongs to the Democratic Club. They're having a meeting."

"Where do they meet?"

"At the American Legion hall."

"We won't be going near there. What time do you have to be back?"

"Eleven."

"So early?"

"Twelve? It doesn't matter. He'll get a lift home with one of the men. He thinks I'm going to a movie with a girl friend."

"Which girl friend?"

"I didn't say. He won't ask. He never asks."

"Won't he want to know what the movie was about?"

"Maybe. It doesn't matter. I'll make up something."

They were on the parkway now. Darkness surrounded them, and she seemed to relax with the darkness. She took off the kerchief and put it into her purse. Sighing, she said, "Larry, are you sure we're doing the right thing?"

"I'm sure we're doing the wrong thing," he said honestly.

110

"We can still . . . I mean, there's still time."

"Do you want me to take you back?"

"No."

"Good. I thought we might go through that whole U-turn routine again." She laughed, a low throaty chuckle that surprised him. "You've got a sexy laugh," he said.

"Don't say that. It's what everyone says."

"I'm sorry. I'll try to be more original."

"I want to laugh, Larry. Don't make me . . . don't make me think when I laugh." She paused. In search of common ground, she said, "I took your house out of the library yesterday. The magazine, I mean. I'd love to live in that house. I studied all of it—the floor plan, everything—last night before I went to bed. He thought I was crazy. He thought I wanted to move again. Do you know what I liked best about it?"

"What?"

"That big round fireplace jutting up in the center of the living room. What made you put it there?"

He shrugged. "The cave man huddling against the darkness, I guess. This way he can huddle on all sides." She laughed. Encouraged, he added, "A very primitive school of architecture. Maintains that all a man needs is a roof over his head, a fire, and a hole to look out of."

She laughed again. "It's a strong fireplace. It sweeps you right up to the sky. I'd like to see that house sometime. Would you take me to see it?"

He had not, up to that second, thought past tonight. She had, in two sentences, added continuity to their relationship, and he did not yet know if he wanted continuity.

"Sure," he said. "I'll take you to see it sometime."

"Good. Do you read a lot? I was reading all last night. First the magazine with your house in it, and then some poetry."

"Which?"

"You wouldn't know it."

On impulse, he said, *This Is My Beloved*?"

She turned on the seat in surprise. "Why . . . why, yes! How did you know?"

"A lucky guess. I used to work in the public library on Fifth Avenue when I was still a kid going to Pratt. I used to mark the books with the library's seal as they came through. I remember that when it was still a pamphlet, before a hard-cover publisher did it. There was a lot more to it then. They cut out a lot."

"I love it."

"Why?"

"I just do. Do you still feel guilty?"

"No," he lied. "Do you?"

"Yes."

Her answer surprised him. She should have lied, she should

111

have said no. Her honesty puzzled him, or was it stupidity? He still didn't know.

"Well, look, Maggie," he said, "we're here, we're together, it's done. There isn't much sense brooding about it."

"Why do you call me Maggie?"

"Doesn't everyone?"

"No, you're the only one. Even *he* calls me Margaret."

"Then I'll call you Maggie. I'll be the only one in the world who calls you Maggie."

"But why?"

"Because it's an ugly name. And you're so beautiful that you make the name beautiful simply by wearing it. It's a name like Kate or Bess. Those are ugly names, too."

"What's your favorite name?"

"Eve," he said instantly.

"Oh." He felt her stiffen beside him. He wanted to say, "I didn't mean *that*. I meant . . ." and then he wondered why he felt he should apologize for liking his own wife's name.

"I have a lot of favorite names," he said in compromise.

"Do you?" she asked coldly.

"Yes. Gertie and Sadie and Myrtle and Brunhilde . . ."

She tried to stifle the laugh but couldn't. "I have favorite boys' names, too," she said, laughing. "Percy, and Abercrombie, and Irwin . . ."

"Don't forget Maximilian."

"Yes, yes," she said, and her laughter mounted.

"Do you know Fundgie?" he asked. "It's really Fotheringay, but the British pronounce it Fundgie."

"You're joking."

"I'm serious." He paused. "Or Sinjin?"

"Like in Sinjin the Baptist?" she asked immediately.

Surprised by her quick response, he said, "You're not so stupid."

"Did you think I was?"

"No, no." He hesitated. "Well, yes, I did."

"I'm not so pretty, either. Remember?"

"You are."

"But you said I wasn't."

"Only sometimes."

"Which times? When you notice the scar?"

"Who ever sees that?" he said.

She smiled. "Am I stupid sometimes, though?"

"Yes. No. I don't *know*," he said, surprised.

"You're very smart, aren't you?" she said seriously. "You won a seventy-five-thousand-dollar prize. You must be very—"

"A *what*?"

"I know," she said, pleased with her knowledge.

112

"It was only seventy-five *hundred*! My God, who told you that?"

"One of the neighbors."

"Is *that* what they think? Wow!" He began laughing. "That would have been very nice indeed. You can buy a lot of beer with seventy-five thousand bucks."

"Do you like beer?"

"I hate it. That was just an express—"

"I loathe it."

"Good. We have something in common."

"We have a lot in common," she said, suddenly quite serious. He turned to look at her, and she smiled quickly, like a young child who had put on her mother's heels and was waiting now for her father's approval. He smiled back at her, suddenly wanting to touch her hand. He did not.

"Where are we going?" she asked. "You said you'd surprise me."

"Well, I don't know exactly. I thought we'd stop for a drink first."

"Then what?"

"Then . . ." He hesitated. "Well, let's have the drink first."

"Will you teach me to drink?"

"Well, sure, I . . ." He paused, puzzled. "What do you mean, *teach* you? You mean what to order?"

"Yes. And how to hold the glass. I don't know how to hold the glass."

He knew she was lying. You held whisky the same way you held water. Facetiously, he said, "Sure, I'll teach you to hold it."

"After the drink, what will we do?"

"We'll have another drink."

"And then what?"

He made his decision in a split second. "We'll go to a motel."

A small sharp cry escaped her lips. She sat bolt upright, and all the nervousness, all the fear, all the tension, seemed to come back into her in a rush.

"I'm sorry," he said.

"I was right."

"About what?"

"Anatomy!"

"What?"

"My breasts!" she said angrily.

"Oh, for Pete's—"

"You'd better take me home."

"All right," he said. "We'll get out at the next exit."

"I want to have the drink first," she said icily.

"All right."

"You didn't have to be so damn blunt!"

"I wasn't blunt. I was honest."

"That's the same thing. You make me feel like a slut."

"I'm sorry. I didn't intend that."

"Would you have asked your *wife* that the first time you took her out?"

"You're not my wife."

"I know. I'm just the girl with big breasts you picked up on the street. Well, I don't like being treated like a whore."

"Maggie, we'll—"

"Don't call me Maggie!"

"Maggie, we'll go dancing or to a movie. All right? However you want it."

"I want *you* to make the decisions. You're the man! I want you to decide."

"But you don't like my decisions," he said bewildered.

"You're the man," she repeated emphatically.

"All right. A drink first and then a movie. Okay?"

"Yes."

They drove in silence for a long while. When he turned off the parkway, they began looking for a roadhouse. "How about that one up ahead?" he said. "The Big Bear?"

"Have you ever been there?"

"No."

"Then it's a first."

"You're a first, too," he said.

"Am I?" she answered. And then in the candid way that still surprised him, she said, "You're not."

He pulled into the gravel parking lot alongside the restaurant. A small sign outside read: CLOSED MONDAYS.

"We're lucky," he said, and he led her to the front door.

As they entered, his eyes hastily swept the room, first flicking to the left where the diners sat, and then to the cocktail lounge which was to the right of the entrance. He took her elbow, feeling strange taking anyone's elbow but Eve's, and walked with her to the lounge. There were four round tables across from the bar. He steered her to the table at the far end, helped her off with her coat, and then held out a chair for her.

She wore a black dress with a square neck, and he noticed for the first time that she was wearing dangling red earrings, and he wished she were not. The men sitting at the bar had turned to look at her. One man nudged another gently as she leaned over to sit. Larry felt suddenly embarrassed. He sat opposite her, looking at her dress and at the shaded dividing cleft between her breasts where the square low neck ended. Her beauty was a terrifying thing. He was amazed that he could be sitting with a woman so beautiful, but the open admiration of the other men in the bar annoyed him. He realized abruptly that this was not a girl you could take to a place where there was the slightest possibility of being observed by anyone you knew. Because this girl

114

would definitely be observed. Again he thought, You see her. You see her instantly.

"What would you like to drink?" he asked.

"A martini," she said quickly.

"Have you ever drunk one?"

"No," she smiled.

"They're slightly potent. Maybe you ought to have a whisky sour or something."

"What are you going to have?"

"Whisky and soda," he said.

"I'll have that too."

"If you prefer—"

"I prefer what you prefer," she said.

He ordered the drinks. The waiter's eyes lingered on Margaret as he placed them on the table. She lifted the glass without hesitation and put it to her lips.

"Wait," Larry said.

"Am I doing something wrong?"

"Yes. You're forgetting to toast."

"Oh, good let's toast."

"Here's . . ." He paused, holding the glass aloft. "Here's to holding hands in the movies," he said, and he hoped the sarcasm didn't show too completely in his voice.

She laughed lightly. "I'll drink to that," she said, and she sipped at the whisky. Her eyes, he noticed, kept wandering to the bar and then dropping to the table top. It was as if she checked to see if she was being admired and then—having discovered that she was—was embarrassed either by the admiration or her necessity for checking it.

"How do you like it?" he asked.

"It tastes awful."

"After the third one you'll complain they left out the whisky."

"I'm stopping after this one. I'm getting dizzy already."

"You've only had a sip!"

"I didn't eat dinner," she said. "I was too excited about seeing you."

"I'm flattered."

She sipped at the drink. "It's beginning to taste better," she said, smiling. "You're nice. I thought you were only going to be smart."

"Thank you. You're nice too."

"I'm a bitch," she said, surprising him.

She fell suddenly silent. Sipping at the drink, her eyes grew pensive. Her lashes fluttered. She did not look at him. Whenever she put the drink down, her fingers twisted the wedding band on her opposite hand, and all the while her eyes were seriously pensive and her lashes fluttered. And then, suddenly, she looked up and said, "All right. Whatever you say. Whatever you want to do. That's what you want, isn't it?"

"I want to please you."

"I want whatever you want."

Their eyes locked. "Finish your drink," he said steadily.

"Finish yours."

"I already have," he said, reaching for the glass and draining it. "Let me pay the check."

The motel was no more than a half mile down the road from the Big Bear. He was delighted by its proximity and by the "Vacancy" neon which flashed out front. He turned the car into the driveway and then navigated the steep hill and pulled up before a small gray building marked "OFFICE."

"This shouldn't take long," he said.

She nodded but did not answer. She sat huddled on her side of the car, a frightened look on her face. He got out and walked to the office. A screen door had not yet been replaced by a storm door. Somewhere inside, a dog was barking furiously. He rang the bell. A voice called, "Just a minute." He listened to the footsteps and then the same voice shouting, "Hans! Keep quiet! Stop that, Hans!" The barking stopped momentarily and then started again when the man opened the door. He was a fat man in an undershirt. He had a round beaming face. The dog behind him was a German shepherd, jowls pulled back over sharp teeth, a deep, malicious rumble in his throat.

"Stop it, Hans!" the man said. "Can I help you, sir?"

"I'd like a cabin."

"There's just one left."

"How much?"

"Seven dollars. Want to come in and sign for it?"

Larry looked at the dog.

"He won't bother you," the fat man said.

Cautiously, Larry opened the screen door. He didn't like the man or his growling German shepherd. He didn't like the ugly slate gray of the office building.

"Do you want to see the cabin first?" the man asked.

"No, that's all right."

The dog sniffed at Larry's trouser leg and then went to lie under the table. The fat man opened a register.

"The missus with you?"

"Yes."

"Just sign it right there."

Larry looked at the page. Without hesitation, he wrote "Mr. and Mrs. Calder." In the space calling for an address, he wrote simply "New York, New York." The next and final space asked for his license-plate number. He began writing his own number, changed his mind, and twisted the digits around. He put down the pen, opened his wallet, and handed the fat man a five and two singles.

"It's the first cabin as you come in," the man said. "Towels and sheets was just changed in there. You need anything, just call me."

"Thank you," Larry said.

"Thank *you*," the fat man answered.

He was silent when he got back to the car. He swung around and headed for the first cabin, a concrete square with a bright red door.

"Any trouble?" Margaret asked.

"No."

"Who are we?"

"Mr. and Mrs. Calder."

"How do you do, Mr. Calder?"

"How do you do, Mrs. Calder?" he said, but he was not smiling.

They got out of the car. From the office, the owner yelled, "The door's open. Key's inside on the dresser. Leave it open when you go, will you?"

Then he had not fooled the owner at all. The man had only wanted his seven dollars. There had been no need to register falsely, probably no need to register at all. A practiced man would simply have winked, and there would have been immediate understanding. Feeling foolishly naïve, he opened the cabin door, flicked on the light, and allowed Margaret to enter the room.

Then he closed and locked the door.

The room was not at all unpleasant. The walls were a painted concrete. There was a large double bed with a bright yellow cover on it. There was a dresser, and a writing table, and a door that led to a small bathroom. There was a coat closet with wire hangers in it, and three windows with venetian blinds. A gray pay-radio rested on a small table.

Margaret stood just inside the door and looked at the bed.

"I wish . . ."

"What?" he asked. He took her coat and draped it over one of the chairs, and then threw his own over it unceremoniously.

"I wish it wasn't the first thing you saw," she said, staring at the bed.

"We can still leave," he said. "Or we can stay and just talk."

"No. It's all right." She went to the bed and sat on the edge of it. There was a peculiar resignation in her eyes. She sighed and then reluctantly lay back. Pulling her legs up onto the bed, she closed her eyes and said, "This is what you want, isn't it?"

"Doesn't what *you* want count at all?" He sat down beside her. He did not touch her. He sat watching her. She opened her eyes

117

and looked at him with mild surprise, as if first discovering him and the room they were in.

"Take off your lipstick," he said.

She shook her head.

"Take it off."

"No, if you want to kiss me, kiss me."

He brought his face very close to hers. Her eyes remained open, wide and brown, never leaving his face. He could smell the scent of her hair, the faint trace of perfume. He kept watching the cushion of her mouth, but he did not kiss her.

"You're very lovely," he said.

"Are you going to kiss me?"

He kissed her, and his lips clung to hers, clung to the adhesive lipstick for just a moment. And then he moved back from her and looked at her mouth, puzzled. "You don't know how to kiss," he said.

She shook her head.

"But . . ."

"Teach me," she said, and he wondered if this were the same gag she'd pulled with the drink and the holding of the glass. He kissed her again, lightly. She kept her lips firmly together, her mouth unmoving, accepting his kiss the way a mother or a sister would.

"Take off your lipstick" he said again.

"Why?"

"Because I'm going to kiss you hard, and I have to go home tonight."

She did not move. She stared at him in silent defiance. He reached for her bag, opened it, took out two tissues, and said, "Shall I do it?"

"No." She pulled the tissues from his hand and wiped her mouth. She rubbed the lipstick off most fiercely, and then she snapped her bag shut and lay back again.

"Now teach me," she said.

He took her chin in his hand. He leaned over her, his mouth an inch from her lips. "Open your mouth," he said.

She parted her lips. He kissed her and then said, "Suck in your breath. Give me something to kiss."

"Like this?" she asked, and pulled his mouth to hers.

"That's better."

"Again," she said. Her voice was very low. He kissed her again, and then drew away.

"You're doing much—"

"Kiss me," she said.

He kissed her again.

"Kiss me. Don't stop kissing me."

He pulled her to him, his mouth hard, his arms hard, feeling

118

a sudden spasm of desire as her body moved in against his. She was incredibly soft and pliant, and she moved into the closeness of his arms as if she had been there many times before, as if she knew every angle of his body and moved now to adjust her own body so that the bones, the warm flesh, the willing muscles clicked, locked into place with his, fit into place like the last piece of a long, long puzzle.

"Larry," she said.

"What?"

"You're getting me hot."

He had never heard a woman use that expression, and he felt something wildly alien stir within him. He seized her roughly, fiercely catching her mouth with his own. His hands found the zipper at the back of her dress and as the zipper lowered she said, "No," and then "No" again, and then he slid the dress from her shoulders and she wriggled to help him as he lowered it to her waist saying, "No, no," all the while. He unclasped her brassière and the globes of her breasts were free, and she said, "No, please, no," and he kissed her, and the flow of words stopped until his hands were on her breasts and then she said, "Oh, please, please, no, please, no," under his fingers, and suddenly her back arched and she pulled his head to her breasts and her hand tightened at the back of his neck, and he kissed her nipples and her throat, his hands covering her body, her body arching to every quivering touch of his hands, and she kept saying, "No, no," and then they were naked, their bodies still locked as if they had always been together, locked, and he was dizzy with the scent of her and the sight of her and the touch of her, and she said, "Do you have . . . I don't want a baby," and he said, "Yes, Maggie," and she said, "Yes, yes, yes," and then she sighed, "Oh, Larry."

And for him there was nothing in the world but her, nothing but the warmth of her surrounding him, gently cradling him, nothing else but the woman beneath him moaning; he was senseless, bodiless, mindless, soulless, she was all, she was everything, and he took her, took her with both hands, took her with honey overflowing both hands.

And for her there was nothing in the world but him, nothing but the warm thrust of invasion, penetration, deep, deep, nothing else but the man above her moaning; she was senseless, bodiless, mindless, soulless, he was all, he was everything, and she accepted, surrendered, gave, gave, with all, captured at last, held at last, overflowing.

They did not put it into the formal words until they had seen each other for a total of four times. He called her often between meetings, but they did not exchange the formal words until a cold night in December.

And then, spent, lying side by side in the room, watching the

119

coals of their cigarettes in the darkness, listening to the music from the pay-radio and the howl of the wind outside, he said simply, "I love you, Maggie."

And she said, "I love you."

And the words had been spoken, and now there was no return.

BOOK TWO

14

SHE wore the topaz earrings for the first time in January.

The earrings had belonged to her grandmother, who'd died long before Margaret was born. Her grandfather had kept the earrings and given them to Margaret several weeks before his own death. She had never worn them before. Up until the time he'd died, she had taken them out of their box almost every day, standing before the mirror and holding them to her ears, a saucy gleam in her brown eyes, just waiting for the day when she'd be old enough to wear them.

And then, with his death, all joy seemed to go out of the tear-drop-shaped earrings. She wrapped them carefully and put them away. They had been pressed into her hand by the man she called "Papa," and now Papa was dead, and suddenly the earrings had gone lifeless and she'd had no desire to wear them ever.

She wore them in January.

She wore black slacks, and a black sweater, and a short red car coat, the collar high against her cheek. And she wore the topaz earrings, and she hustled Patrick out of the house twenty minutes before the bus was scheduled to arrive. The weekend had been a very long one, and she looked forward to seeing Larry this morning, and she wanted to look very pretty. She told herself she was behaving like a silly adolescent girl, but nonetheless she hurried to the bus stop, and she was annoyed because she could not see his house, from there.

"It's cold, Mummy," Patrick said.

"Yes," she answered absently.

"Why'd we have to come so early?"

"The fresh air will do us good," she said.

"Mum?"

"Yes?"

"Do you love me?"

Startled, she looked down at her son. "Why . . ." It had never occurred to her that he wondered such things. She stared at him in slow understanding. "I love you very much, sweetheart," she said.

Patrick nodded. His hair was a pale wispy blond, the color of his mother's, but lacking the rich texture of her hair. His eyes were wide and brown, his mother's exactly, large now in a pale face as he stared up at her.

"Do you love Daddy?"

"Of course I love Daddy," she said.

"Very much?"

"Yes." She turned her eyes from his, embarrassed by their scrutiny. "Yes, very much."

"Honest?" he said.

"Yes, of course. Why?"

"Does he think you're pretty?"

"I suppose so."

"Doesn't he?"

"Why don't you ask *him*, Patrick?"

"I did."

His answer startled her. She looked at him again, feeling almost as if she were standing in the cold with a little stranger who asked personal questions and gave startling answers.

"What . . . what did Daddy say?" she asked.

"He said I was too young to be asking such things."

"What things?"

"I don't know," Patrick said, puzzled.

"Well, he meant . . ." She paused, wondering what he *had* meant. Too young to ask *what* things? To ask if a man thought his wife pretty? What kind of nonsense . . . ? "He meant . . . that . . . that a boy should always think his Mummy is pretty. That's what he meant, Patrick."

"But I do think you're pretty."

She hugged him to her and said, "I think you're pretty too."

"Pretty is for girls," Patrick said. "I'm handsome. That's what my honey tells me."

"Your honey?" Margaret said.

"Sure, Lucy. Lucy Hager. She's in my class. She's my honey."

"I didn't know that," Margaret said.

"Sure, everybody knows it. All the kids in the class. I chase her all around."

"You do?" Margaret said, stifling a laugh.

"You should see the way I clobber her. She loves it. That's 'cause she's my honey."

"I see."

"She's kind of pretty. But not so pretty as you," he said quickly.

"What does she look like?"

"I don't know. She's got pigtails. Is that what you call them? Where the hair is . . . you know . . ." He indicated braids with his hands.

"Yes, pigtails."

"That's what she's got. Her mother is pregnant."

"How do you know?"

"She told me. Lucy, you know. She said her father gave her mother a seed. It's in her mother's belly now. You should see her mother. She's fat as a horse."

122

Margaret burst out laughing.

"Well, what's so funny about that?" Patrick asked.

"Nothing, nothing. I—"

"There's Chris!" Patrick shouted.

She felt her heart quicken instantly. Purposely, she did not turn because she didn't want to seem too anxious to see him. She could hear Patrick shouting, could hear the answering shouts of Larry's son as the boys ran to join each other. And then, slowly, she turned, wanting to see the expression on his face when he first saw her.

The woman had black hair.

The hair was caught at the nape of her neck with a bright blue ribbon, and even from this distance her eyes were lovely, a clear sky blue. As she came closer, Margaret saw that the woman had a good nose, and a full mouth, and that she walked with certainty, her head erect, her shoulders back. And even though she wore faded dungarees and a heavy sweatshirt with the words PRATT INSTITUTE on it, Margaret could see that the woman's figure was trim and curved, and that her breasts beneath the shapeless garment were firm.

The woman was smiling. She walked directly to Margaret, extended her hand and said, "You couldn't be anyone but Margaret Gault. How do you do? I'm Eve Cole."

He held her to him, and he thought of the reality of her, amazed that he could be loved by her. In his eyes, she had miraculously become more than a woman, more than mere flesh and blood. He did not like to think of her as a symbol, but he was a symbol manipulator by trade—except during the exciting time when symbols became realities, when inked lines became walls, when pencil sketches became cypress panels and native stone—and in his mind she became Woman. Not this woman but every woman he had ever known or would want to know.

In the motel room, he clung to her, completely relaxed except for the urgent pressure of wanting her. He did not want her because she was close at last after a week of waiting; but he knew the ritual, knew he would have to release her to truly possess her, to undam the terrible urgent longing inside. She had kept him perched on the narrow edge of desire on the drive to the motel. She had caressed him and whispered to him gently, and then turned away from him to light a cigarette or change the station on the radio. And then she had returned to him, and her hands were gentle again and then fiercely demanding, and then again she left him, and his fingers trembled on the wheel.

Here at last, here alone at last, he released her gently. He helped her off with her coat, and she picked up her purse and then went into the bathroom, closing but not locking the door. He could hear the sink water running as he put the coin into the pay-radio and fiddled with the dial. He moved with complete familiarity in the small cabin. The room was furnished with absolute indifference to taste or lack of taste, concerning itself solely with essentials. The room was as basic as their need for each other. And in the room, the person who was Larry Cole did not think of interior decoration. The surroundings of the room, the furniture, the insipid paintings on the walls, were as meaningless as the furniture of life and of absolutely no importance to what he shared with Maggie.

How had he lived without her? he wondered. How had he possibly lived before this face had come to him, before this warm rich body had been delivered to him, before this wonderful creature, this marvelously live creature, had come to him to keen of love and life, had come to him with her promise of faraway places, had come to him with a gentle mouth and fierce hands to keen to him a song he once had known, a song that lingered half-remembered in the dim passages of his memory?

He took off his jacket and hung it in the closet, and then he pulled down his tie and placed the tie clasp on the dresser top together with his wallet, his car keys, his cigarettes and his loose change. Humming to the radio, he took off his shirt and his tee shirt, and then his shoes and socks. He walked about the cabin bare-chested and barefooted, pulling down the yellow chenille bedspread, pulling back the blankets, lighting a cigarette, which he would put out the moment she came to him.

When she emerged from the bathroom, the lipstick had been wiped from her mouth, her face was clean-scrubbed, the skin glowing, the brown eyes searchingly alert.

She still wore her dress and earrings, but he knew she had removed her stockings and undergarments, knew the back of her dress would be parted in a wide V where she had left the zipper lowered. There was a cool precision with which she approached the act of love each time, a methodical female skill to the way she torturously aroused him and then allowed him to possess her wildly and completely. She had, over the months, changed radically from the person he'd known that first night. He sometimes wondered about her reversal of seeming inexperience. Had her ignorance been only a pose, or had he truly released an untapped passion in this woman? He did not know. He knew only that each time they were together now, her eyes patiently refused to acknowledge her own overwhelming demands; cruelly woman-like, she seemed to savor his agony, scientifically manipulating touch and tongue, urging, beckoning, pressing assault, withdrawing only to counterattack—and then succumbing in warmly limp surrender, the absolute female again, sufferingly impaled, supple beneath a mercilessly battering rigidity, grasping at, locking in immensity, mounting in spasm after spasm of aching dissolution.

He watched her with tireless delight as she approached him now.

Anticipation arched in him like a suddenly drawn bow. His eyes coveted the fluid motion of her body, hip against thigh, the nuance of her hands, the veiled uncertainty of her face. Her dress, loosened by the lowered zipper, clung tenuously low to the high swell of her breasts. She sat beside him to remove her pumps, crossing her legs and pulling back the skirt of her dress so that it draped in carelessly loose concealment over the mound where her thighs joined.

He reached for her, but she smiled and playfully pulled away. She rose and walked to the dresser. He saw the expected V of white flesh against the black dress, swooping to the base of her spine. Casually unconcerned with his presence, she took a cigarette from the package and coolly lighted it. She shook out the match and put it in an ash tray. Then, barefooted, she padded back to the bed. She smiled gently, standing beside the bed, the cigarette in one hand.

"Tell me about Eve," she said.

He was sure she was joking. He pulled her to him, his head cushioned against her breasts. But she caught his hair with her free hand and gently drew his face from her body. Then she sat beside him on the edge of the bed. Drawing on the cigarette, she said again, "Tell me about Eve."

"Maggie . . ."

"I want to hear about her. I want to know how you met."

"Later."

"Now."

"I've been waiting all week for—"

"So have I," she said, and her eyes smoldered for just an instant and then turned strong with purpose. "Tell me about her."

"Maggie, don't—"

"How did you meet? Was it romantic?"

"How the hell do I know?" he said angrily, squashing out his cigarette in the ashtray beside the bed.

She handed him her cigarette. "Put this out, too," she said, and then immediately said again, "How did you meet Eve?"

She knew he thought the question strange. But their own meeting had been unreal, and she sought to bring reality to it now by comparing it with one of supposed substance. It was important to her that she know about his wife and how he'd met her. She knew her thus far only as the attractive brunette who'd brought Chris to the bus stop. Mrs. Cole. She knew her as the woman whose eyes she had avoided. She had given nothing of herself to this woman, and she hoped this woman would in turn give nothing to her. She had taken enough from her already, and she did not want more.

125

But even while feeling a perverse compassion for Eve, she could not dismiss from her mind the idea that Larry went home to this other woman each time he left her, and the thought stabbed deep with jealousy. Whether she enjoyed it or not, a competition was upon her. The claims of previous and prior ownership were now invalid, and in her own mind she ceased being the intruder: *Eve* was the other woman.

Stubbing out the second cigarette, Larry said, "I met her in a subway car. Is that what you want to know? The B.M.T. I was going to school."

"Pratt," she said. It was not a question. "She wears your school sweatshirt. She was wearing it at the bus stop yesterday."

"So *that's* what this is all about. You ran into Eve."

"With Pratt Institute across the front. Like a brand." It angered her that their relationship went so far back, that Eve had known him when he was still a student, that Time had so conspired to cheat Margaret Gault. He looked at her curiously and again reached for her. Bu she drew away and said, "No. How long ago was this . . . this subway romance?"

"Nineteen forty-three," he said.

"You remember the year very easily."

"Don't you remember when you first met Don?"

"Of course I remember. Tell me what happened."

"She slapped me," he said, grinning.

"You must have liked the slap," she said, annoyed by his grin.

"Not particularly. It was very embarrassing."

"She just slapped you? For no reason?"

"Oh, she had a reason, all right. She thought I was getting fresh with her."

"Were you?"

"No, but it was a crowded car, and *somebody* was, and when she turned around I was the first guy she saw. So I got it."

"Hard?"

"Damn hard. And shocking too. I didn't even know she was there until she slapped me. I hate crowded subway cars and all I was thinking of was fresh air. No, that's not true. I had an exam that day. I was also thinking about that."

"How old were you?"

"In nineteen forty-three? I must have been about eighteen."

"And Eve?"

"Just a kid."

"How old?"

"No more than fifteen. But a very developed—"

"You molested a fifteen year-old girl?"

"Wait a minute! I never touched her! Who said I—?"

"You know her *that* long?" The idea was becoming more and more painful. She tried to twist away from its painfulness, but she could not. He looked at her face and again tried to take her

126

into his arms, but she sat erect and unmoving. He lay back against the pillow and sighed heavily.

"Well, she slapped me," he said, "and then she huffed out of the car and that was that."

"When did you see her again?"

"In nineteen forty-six."

"And you remembered her?" she asked, astonished.

"Sure. How often do you get slapped in the subway?"

"I suppose so," she said dubiously. "Where was this?"

"At the Officers' Club."

"Did they have one in New York?"

"Not an official one; this was a thing sponsored by some women's organization. I think the Morgans donated the place to the Army and Navy. It was on East Thirty-seventh or Thirty-eighth. I'm not sure which. Right near Park Avenue, though, in the Murray Hill section."

"Isn't New York your home? Didn't you have anything better to do than go to the Officers' Club?"

"I was getting discharged at the time," Larry said. "Waiting at Dix. I came in for a weekend, and it occurred to me I'd never been down there. So I went. Just on impulse, that's all."

She smiled. "Do you do a lot of things on impulse?" she asked.

He took her hand and said, "I used to then. I was just a kid."

"How old, Larry?"

He wagged his head. "Twenty-one. And all decked out with my battle ribbons and my lieutenant's bar." He kissed her fingers. "You have nice hands. Did I ever tell you?"

"Were you a lieutenant?"

"Yes."

"That's very exciting. Don was a private. Or a pfc, I think. Is there a difference?"

"Sure."

"Don enlisted." She moved closer to him, making herself comfortable, and he put his arm around her waist.

"I wanted to enlist," he said. "My mother wouldn't let me. I wanted to join the Air Corps."

"Did you see any action?"

"Yes."

"Did you kill anyone?"

"Yes. At least I think so. It's hard to tell when everyone's shooting at once."

"Where were you?"

"The Pacific."

"Don was in the Pacific too," she said, surprised.

"Really? Where? Was he on Tarawa?"

"I don't know."

"In combat?"

"Oh, yes."

"Then he's killed his share, too."

"I don't know. He never talks about it."

"Lots of men don't."

They fell silent. She felt quite content all at once. She had forgotten how the conversation had started. She knew only that they'd been talking in a friendly, easy, intimate way. She pictured him as a lieutenant in his Army uniform, shooting at the enemy. And then she moved away from him suddenly.

"Eve," she said.

"What?"

"What happened at the Officers' Club?"

"Are we back to that?"

"Yes, we're back to that." Unfortunately, I'm only a woman, she thought, and "Curiosity" is the password of our secret sorority, and so we are back to that. And perhaps we will always be back to wondering what it was about Eve besides the accidents of time and place that made you choose her.

"All right," he said wearily. "I was there and she came in with an ensign. Her mother would have killed her if she'd known. Eve wasn't allowed to date servicemen."

"How *sweet*," Margaret said, hearing the nasty tone of her voice, and marveling at it, and despising it.

"Were you?"

"I was a baby during the war. I was only twelve when it started and almost sixteen when it ended. I never knew any servicemen except cousins."

"How old are you now?"

"Twenty-seven."

She was about to be amused. After what they had shared together, he did not even know her age. She was about to smile when he said, "Two years younger than Eve. She's twenty-nine," and then she was no longer amused.

"How old are you?" she asked.

"I'll be thirty-two in July."

"Don's thirty-two already."

"Remember how old thirty used to seem when we were in our teens?"

"It still seems old to me. Sometimes I wonder if I'll ever reach it."

"Are you in a hurry?"

"Hell, no."

He sat up and kissed her quickly and suddenly. "I like women who say hell," he told her.

"Does Eve?"

"Yes."

"Oh."

"You mean she does say hell?"

"Yes."

128

"That's what I thought. It could have meant . . . you know . . . does she like women who say hell."

"No."

"No, I didn't think you meant that."

"No."

They were silent again. She sat at the core of the silence, her lips pursed, smoldering. I won't ask him another thing, she thought. Not another thing. I don't care who they met or where or why. I don't give a damn, and I won't ask.

"What happened when she came in?" she asked.

"I recognized her, but she didn't seem to remember me. Looked straight at me and then went off dancing with her ensign. Later on, I asked her to dance. She's a good dancer, always was."

"What else does she do well?"

"Lots of things."

"Like what?"

"Look, you don't want to hear this. You're getting angry. I'd rather not tell it if you're—"

"I want to hear it, Larry."

"All right, I was dancing with her and I said, 'You don't remember me, do you?' and she said, 'Should I?' and I said, 'You slapped me on the B.M.T. in nineteen forty-three.' And then she remembered."

"What did she say?"

"She said, 'I'm surprised the government allows degenerates to become officers.'" He laughed with the memory. "I explained to her that I hadn't been the offender, though I certainly would have been if I'd known how pretty she was."

"God, what a line!"

"It wasn't a line."

"Then you meant it?"

"Well . . . well, yes, I did."

"You're such a damn—" She stopped. "Did she swallow the hook?"

"She . . . oh, hell what's the sense of this? I'm with *you*. Must we talk about Eve?"

"What happened?"

"Nothing happened. I asked her out, and that was the start of it. Let's not talk about it."

"You don't seem to mind very much. You've been talking about it for the past fifteen minutes."

"Look, you know she's my wife, don't you?"

"Of course I know it," she said sharply.

"Then you know that people don't get born married. They meet, and they go steady, and they get engaged, and things go through a natural progression, and then eventually they get married. So we went through the same natural progression and—" He grinned suddenly. "I don't know what the hell I'm talking about."

"You're talking about your wife, Eve."

"Let's talk about Don, shall we?"

"You love her very much, don't you?"

"Oh, for Pete's—"

"Why is it so painful for you to talk about her?"

"It isn't. I just can't see why—"

"Is she good in bed?"

"Excellent!" he answered quickly, angrily. "The next question is 'Is she better than me?' Go ahead. Ask it."

"I'd never ask that," Margaret said.

"Why not?"

Her voice was very low. "I'm afraid of the answer."

"Don't ever be afraid of anything, Maggie," he told her, and his voice was suddenly gentle. She looked at him a moment, rose suddenly, and walked away from the bed. She turned her back to him and stood by the dresser as if debating her next move. Then, without looking at him, she lowered the dress from both shoulders. It slid to her waist, catching at her hips. She pushed it over her hips, and then stepped out of it when it fell to the floor. Then she turned. He watched her as she walked to the bed.

"Do you know how much I love you?" she asked.

He did not answer.

"You'll know," she said. "Kiss me. Put your mouth on me."

He sat up and pulled her to him. She stood close to the edge of the bed, her hands at her sides, accepting his mouth.

"Touch me," she said. His hands moved over her body. She watched him with curiously calculating eyes. "We're strangers until now, aren't we?" she said. "Until this minute, we're strangers." And then she pushed him back onto the bed and her mouth descended fiercely, hungrily.

"Say it!" she said.

"I love you."

"Again."

"I love you."

"Oh, you," she said. "Again, you. Say it again, you, *you!*"

"I love you."

"Don't stop. Don't stop saying it. Tell me you love me. Tell me I'm all that matters."

"You're all that matters."

"Nothing else matters. Not her, not anything."

"Nothing else matters."

"No one, Larry. Nothing. Only me. Tell me you need me. Tell me you want me."

"I want you."

"Ohhh, yes. Yes. Yes. You, you, you, you. Tell me. Tell me. *Tell me!*"

130

15

Eve sat alone in the living room.

When the doorbell rang, she put down the socks she was darning and went to answer it. The clock in the kitchen read 10:45, and whereas she knew it was too early for him to be back, she hoped it might be Larry.

"Who's there?" she said.

"Me. Mrs. Garandi."

"Oh, Signora," she said, disappointed. "Just a moment."

She unlocked the door. Mrs. Garandi, holding open the storm door, a shawl thrown over her shoulders, said, "Eve, are you busy? Why don't you and Larry come over for some coffee? Arthur brought home a beautiful cake, and the three of us will never finish it alone."

"Larry's out," Eve said. "Why don't you come in a minute?"

"All right, but just for a minute." She closed the door behind her. Together they walked into the living room. The Signora looked curiously at the television screen and then sat opposite Eve.

"Come over anyway," she said. "It's right across the street. You'll be able to check on the kids."

"I've got darning to do," Eve said.

Mrs. Garandi nodded. Silently, she studied Eve. "Did Larry go to a lecture again?" she asked.

"No, not tonight. He's with a client. He delivered some sketches this week, and they're going to discuss them tonight."

"I see." Mrs. Garandi was silent again. "These lectures he goes to. Does he go alone?"

"Yes."

"Where are they?"

"At Pratt."

"Why don't you go with him?"

"They're for architects, and pretty technical from what Larry tells me. Besides, it's good for a man to get away from his wife once in a while, don't you think?"

"No. A man doesn't need to get away."

"Not even once in a while?"

"Not even *ever*. You should go with him."

"Someone's got to stay with the children."

"Get a sitter. And if the lectures don't interest you, meet him afterward. Go for a coffee together."

"Oh, that's silly," Eve said. "I trust him completely."

"Then why do you bring up the question of trust?"

"Well, you seemed to be imply—"

131

"Trust is only a word, Eve. Man-made. The things men conveniently make can just as conveniently be destroyed."

"I think it's a lot more than a word, Signora," Eve said.

Mrs. Garandi shrugged. "If my husband were alive, I wouldn't let him go wandering alone."

"Larry doesn't go wan—"

"I wouldn't let him go wandering," Mrs. Garandi said firmly.

Eve stared at her levelly. "Larry's not that kind of man," she said.

"He's a man. And a woman is a woman. And there's no such thing as *that* kind of man or *that* kind of woman. There are stronger things than the meaningless words we can invent, Eve. Are *you* so invulnerable?"

"Me?" Eve laughed. "I've never even looked at another man."

"I don't believe that."

"Oh, well, *looked*, yes. But I never once thought of—"

"Stop him from going to his lectures."

"I can't do that, Signora."

"Why not?"

"Because I trust him," Eve said simply. "If I stopped him going to Pratt, I'd have to stop him from going to the store for cigarettes. I'd have to begin distrusting him. And I don't want that."

"I would stop him."

"No." Eve shook her head. "Larry's not a cheat."

"Another word," Mrs. Garandi said. "Who's to say what and what isn't? Who's to say what's cheating? A man is a man, and a woman is a woman. That's life, and that's living, and I wouldn't let my man go off alone each week."

"Larry is satisfied," Eve said calmly.

"With everything? Or only with you?"

"I try to keep him happy."

"Then keep him home. Keep him happier."

"I do everything I know how to do. He is happy, Signora. Really he is. I don't know why you think he isn't."

"Eve, *carissima*, I don't think anything. I don't know. But marriage is a funny thing in America, and the American wife has in many ways stopped being a woman." Mrs. Garandi paused, and her eyes met Eve's. "Forgive me," she said. "I'm a foolish old woman. I only came to invite you for coffee."

"That's all right," Eve said, smiling.

"Eve?"

"Yes?"

"Keep him home."

And again Eve said, "I trust him," and to this there was no answer.

"Will you come over later?"

"Maybe."

"Not after eleven-thirty," Mrs. Garandi said. "Arthur has to work tomorrow."

"All right."

"Do you think Larry will be home by then?"

"I don't know. He's with Roger Altar—his client. If he's home, I'll bring him over."

"Please come." Mrs. Garandi said, and she left the house. Eve closed the door behind her. She went back into the living room and picked up the sock she had been darning. A television comic was laughing at his own humour. The house felt very still and empty. In the bedroom, one of the children mumbled something in his sleep.

I trust him, Eve thought. I love him.

It was strange that she loved him so much now, she supposed, because she hadn't even liked his looks that night so long ago at the Officers' Club. She'd always preferred light-eyed boys. Even the ensign she'd been with was green-eyed. And then when Larry'd reminded her of their first encounter, she couldn't look at him for the next five minutes without remembering again the shame she'd known that day on the subway. Even though she became convinced that she'd wrongly slapped him, he was nonetheless a reminder of what had been a terrible experience for her. She wanted to dislike him, and his looks supported her original premise. But she found herself succumbing to his warmth and honesty as they danced. Honesty. That, she supposed, was what had first appealed to her. He was honest. When he asked her out, she surprised herself by accepting. But she didn't particularly care for his looks.

The Harder apartment, on the morning after their first date, was in the customary coma of its Sunday lethargy. The building was on the corner of Eighty-ninth Street and Fifth Avenue, opposite the park. The dining nook faced the side street, and the apartment was on the third floor, so that Sunday churchgoers could easily be seen from the window. Mr. Harder's half of the table was covered with *The New York Times*. The twins had appropriated most of the remainder of the table for the Sunday comics. Cereal boxes, bowls, coffee, utensils, were somehow squeezed onto the table between the newspapers.

Mr. Harder staunchly believed that everyone in a family should eat at the same time. The table, he maintained, was an exchange board for the activities of the day, the one place where a family could catch up with itself. He relaxed his dictum only on Sunday mornings when everyone in the house seemed to drift into the dining nook at different hours. He imagined this had started when Eve began having Saturday-night dates. In any case, he felt that any regulation was strengthened by periodic lapses, and he did not mind the Sunday-morning disorder.

Mrs. Harder, wearing a dressing-gown over her nightgown,

looking as fresh as she always did in the morning, said, "That boy was very handsome, Eve."

Eve was still half asleep. She sat at the table in pajamas, and a strand of black hair hung over one eye. "You don't *really* think so, do you, Mama?" she said.

"I certainly do," Mrs. Harder said.

Mr. Harder, who was used to discussions about male strangers at the Sunday-morning breakfast table, put aside the *Times*, moved his platter of pancakes into a position of attack, and then looked across at Eve. He wanted to say something about her being a big girl now and wearing a robe to the breakfast table, but instead he said, "Who's this we're discussing?"

"Oh, a boy," Eve said disinterestedly.

"Larry," Mrs. Harder said.

"A new one, huh?"

Lois, bright-eyed and almost seven, said, "He's tall."

"How do you know?" Eve asked. "You were asleep when he called for me."

"I wasn't asleep," Lois said impishly. "I peeked."

"I peeked, too," Linda said. "He's nice, Eve. Do you think you'll marry him?"

"He hasn't asked me yet," Eve said breezily. "Is this coffee mine, Mama?"

"Evie has a boy friend," Lois chanted. "Evie has a boy friend, Evie—"

"Oh, stop it!" Eve said.

"Evie has a boy—"

"Mama, will you please ask this child to shut up!"

"Shut up, Lois," Linda said.

"Your sister is very sensitive about her gentlemen friends," Mr. Harder said, smiling. "Especially when they're attractive."

"I don't like you to say shut up, Linda," Mrs. Harder said. "That's a foul expression." Linda pulled a face and went back to the comics. "Aren't you going out with him again, Eve?" Mrs. Harder asked.

"I suppose so."

"When?"

"Next Saturday."

"He seemed like a very nice boy, Alex," Mrs. Harder said. "He used to be a captain."

"A lieutenant, Mama," Eve corrected.

"Yes, that's higher than a captain, isn't it? He just got discharged, Alex." She turned to her daughter. "That's right, isn't it?"

"Yes, that's right."

"A nice boy, Alex."

"They're all nice boys," Mr. Harder said without enthusiasm. "Is there any more syrup?"

134

"You should see him again, Eve," Mrs. Harder said pleasantly.

"Stop marrying the girl," Mr. Harder said. "Is there any more syrup?"

"Linda, get your father some syrup. In the cabinet."

"Why can't Lois ever get anything?" Linda asked. "Can I be a flower girl, Eve?"

"*May* I," Mrs. Harder corrected.

"May I, Eve?"

"When I get married," Eve said.

"Me, too?" Lois asked.

"You, too."

"He's very good looking," Mrs. Harder said, and Eve grimaced. "He is, Eve. Stop making such ridiculous faces. He's studying to be an architect, Alex."

"Who went out with him?" Mr. Harder wanted to know. "You or Eve?"

"I can see nothing wrong with taking an interest in my daughter's friends," Mrs. Harder said with a touch of royal dignity.

"I'm delighted he's so handsome and is going to be an architect, Patricia," Mr. Harder said in an attempt at irony which was difficult for a Sunday morning, "but will somebody please get me the syrup?"

"I'll get it," Linda said, rising.

"And then you can leave the comics and begin practicing," Mrs. Harder said.

"On *Sunday*?" Linda protested. "Gee whiz!"

"We spent eleven hundred dollars for that piano," Mrs. Harder said, "and someone is going to learn to play it."

"Well, why pick on me?" Linda asked. "Eve's got bigger fingers."

"You play very well, Lindy," Eve said. "You really shouldn't let your practicing go."

Linda put the syrup down in front of Mr. Harder and climbed onto Eve's lap. "Are you really going to marry him, Eve?" she asked.

"Oh, don't be silly, Poo. I hardly know him."

"Did you hear me play the 'Minute Waltz'?"

"No."

"It takes me more like an hour, but I'll play it if you like."

"I'd like to hear it," Eve said.

Linda went into the living room.

"This stinks," Lois said. "I hate it. When's she going to learn Boogie-Woogie?"

"Quiet," Mrs. Harder said.

Linda began playing. Mr. Harder started eating his pancakes, and then opened the *Times* again. "The new look," he said. "It's more like what you wore when I first met you, Patricia."

"I like it," Eve said.

"I'm against any style that hides a woman's legs," Mr. Harder said. "Incidentally, young lady, don't you think you should start wearing a robe to the breakfast table?"

"Larry Cole," Eve said, and again she grimaced. "I'll probably never see him again after next Saturday."

Mrs. Harder raised her eyebrows in something close to restrained displeasure, and from the living room Linda shouted, "Hey, are you listening?"

Inexplicably, she continued to see Larry. She still did not like the way he looked. Oh, he was all right, she supposed. In fact, when she invited him to her Freshman Tea at N.Y.U., some of the girls thought he was quite attractive and wanted to know if he'd pinned her yet. The idea was preposterous. Eve knew exactly what she expected her man to look like, and Larry Cole didn't fit the mental image at all.

Besides, he was fresh.

Not obnoxiously fresh, and perhaps not fresh at all, but certainly fast. Larry Cole, it became clear, did not believe there were any intermediate steps between necking and petting.

"Never sit on a boy's lap," Mrs. Harder had said.

Well, despite Mrs. Harder's mysterious proclamation, Eve had sat on a good many laps. She considered herself a knowledgeable young lady who was familiar with most of the approaches then in vogue. But Larry's speed amazed her. And what amazed her more was the rapidity with which she adjusted to his pace. Swept along by him, she began to look at him in a different light.

He was, she discovered, a remarkable person to be with. Everything he said or did seemed calculated to please her and no one else. He performed this feat effortlessly, and she imagined it was standard procedure with every girl he dated, but she nonetheless enjoyed the exclusiveness of being with him. She found herself refusing other dates, gradually whittling down the list of boys who called her, surprised but somehow pleased when she realized she had no desire to go out with anyone but Larry. It was then that they officially began going steady.

She did not know whether or not she loved him.

She liked him enormously. She looked for good in him and, looking, she found it. Unsatisfied, she enlarged upon his virtues so that in her eyes he became impulsive without being childish, discriminating but not intolerant, dedicated but not fanatic, comical but not foolish, polite but not deferential, talkative but not garrulous, serious but not solemn, stylish but not foppish, romantic but not—well, the poems for example.

He was the only boy she'd ever known who wrote poetry to her. She was later to discover that many boys wrote poems for girls, but up to the time she received Larry's first effort she'd thought it was something reserved for Byron or Shakespeare.

Mrs. Harder brought the letter up from the mailbox together

with the rest of the afternoon mail. It was a Saturday, and Eve was going over notes for a French class. Her bedroom was to the left of the kitchen, facing on Eighty-ninth. The window was open, and the curtains rustled in a mild spring breeze. Linda was murdering Beethoven in the living room. Lois was destroying the kitchen in an attempt to bake a cake. Both girls miraculously appeared in Eve's bedroom the moment Mrs. Harder handed her the letter.

"It's from Larry," her mother said.

"Larry?" and she felt an immediate sense of doom.

"What does he want?" Lois asked.

"Is he sick?" Linda asked.

"Mama, would you get them out of here, please?" Eve said.

"Come, girls," Mrs. Harder said.

"But what's in the letter?"

"Is it a love letter, Eve?"

"Evie got a love letter, Evie got a love letter . . ."

Mrs. Harder shooed the girls out and closed the bedroom door. In the living room, the piano started again. Eve opened the envelope. He had typed on graph paper. The back of the page was covered with a hasty floor plan, a rough elevation sketch, and penciled notes in Larry's own undecipherable shorthand. She realized he'd probably torn the page from his notebook impulsively and then typed on it. She read the poem. Then she read it again. And then she read it a third time:

EVE

> *You are truly Eve.*
> *I mean . . .*
> *Had you never been,*
> *Had I never seen*
> *Your face or known*
> *Your grace, there would*
> *For me*
> *Be no eve.*
>
> *No eve of things*
> *To come unended,*
> *No eve of splendid*
> *Things to come*
> *For us together*
> *Forever.*
>
> *You are truly Eve.*
> *I mean . . .*
> *The eve of wonder*
> *And surprise*

137

> *Is in your eyes.*
> *You are my eve,*
> *And, Eve, I love you.*

Quite suddenly, her eyes brimmed with tears.

She ran to the telephone to call him, and over Linda's merciless pounding she told him she loved him and that he was foolish to write a poem but that she loved the poem and she loved him—but even then she didn't know if she believed her own words.

Eventually, she went to bed with him. She waited until they were engaged because engagement seemed to condone intimacy, but actually it came naturally, the way everything in their relationship seemed to come naturally, unforced. Their marriage came the same way.

And on their wedding day, she sat alongside Larry on their way to Atlantic City, and she looked at him for the first time in a long time, really looked at him the way she might have looked at a stranger. They had bought at least a dozen magazines before boarding the train, and Larry began thumbing through them at once, surprisingly conversationless. She looked at him and realized with a start that she had married this man, that she was his wife, that she would live with him forever, that they had exchanged absurd vows, that they had entered an ironbound contract, and she didn't even like his looks!

She nearly panicked.

She did not want to be going on a honeymoon. She did not want to wake up in the morning to find him beside her. She had been to bed with him spasmodically for perhaps six months, but she suddenly felt like a terrified virgin, suddenly felt she would be horrified by the sight of him in his pajamas brushing his teeth. Or did he sleep in his underwear? Good Lord, suppose he slept in his underwear?

She glanced down at the magazine in his hands. He was still reading a paragraph he'd begun a half hour ago, the lead to an article titled "Have You Chosen a Burial Plot?" She began chuckling silently, her fear evaporating. It would be all right. This was Larry, and he was just as frightened as she. It would be all right. She touched his sleeve, and he turned to her and smiled, and she returned the smile gently.

She did not really fall in love with Larry Cole until after Chris was born. She supposed she had loved him all this while, but now she fell hopelessly in love with her own husband. She felt somehow ridiculous. She was a wife and a mother now, and it was a little late to be getting foolishly romantic. But it was then that her love flowered, and then that her true relationship with him began.

Now, eight years after they had taken the marriage vows, five years after Chris had been born, she sat alone in the living room

138

and thought of how empty the house seemed without him. She wanted him to be there. She wanted to neck with him, no sex, just necking, the way they'd exchanged kisses when she was still a college girl and he was a student at Pratt. Romance had a way of going out of living. And one day you probably woke up as an old old lady who thought back to the days when necking was fun, when a kiss was the most exciting thing in the world.

What had Mrs. Garandi been trying to say?

She knew, but she would not accept the thought. She suddenly wanted to call Larry, tell him to come home early so that she could neck with him. She went into the bedroom, looked up Altar's number, and dialed it. Then, while the phone began ringing on the other end, she slammed down the receiver.

Why, he'll think I'm checking on him! she thought.

But why should I be checking, what is there to check? I trust him, I trust him.

She began trembling. She did not want to be alone in the house. The house was too still and too empty. She put on her coat, and then went across the street to the Garandis, hoping Larry would come back from his visit with Altar early.

There was an eagle in the sketches. A wild, soaring eagle.

Altar studied them, and he felt the excitement of creation, and then he felt wild elation, and then a new surge of excitement as he shared vicariously in the creation. This was a house! This was really a house!

"Is it good?" the girl with him asked.

"Baby, go wash your face or something," he told her.

"I only asked a question."

"It's magnificent!" he said, and he scooped up the sketches and went into his study and began dialing Larry's home number.

He wanted to tell Larry that this was it. He wanted to tell him he appreciated this, shared it, that it made him feel like doing something, like running, like flying! He wanted to tell Larry he was a craftsman, and an artist, and a creator, and he wanted to tell him to hold onto whatever he had, hold onto it tight because it was a rare thing. He wished Larry were there so that he could clasp his hand and slam him on the back and buy him a drink and laugh with him and sing with him because he had it, by God he had it!

The phone kept ringing.

Altar waited impatiently. He let the phone ring for a long while, and then he hung up.

Eve, across the street at the Garandis, ate Arthur's cake and drank Mary's coffee, and listened to the Signora tell a story about the old country. Altar's call woke up David, who sat in his wet pajamas in his crib and blinked at the darkness. But that was all it did.

139

And even David fell asleep again when the phone stopped ringing.

16

THE BUILDER'S name was Frank Di Labbia.

"I'm Italian," he said, "and proud of it," and Roger Altar instantly doubted his pride.

They sat in the rustic dining room of the rustic, exurban inn, the timbers exposed in the old ceiling, the stone fireplace crackling with a roaring fire, the Revolutionary War relics scattered about the room: the huge black kettles, the butter churns, the foot warmers, the pewter candlesticks. The planks in the floor were wide and hand-pegged, polished with Butcher's wax so that they gleamed as they never had for General Washington. There was a gray wintry afternoon pushing at the leaded casements, and there were lighted candles on each table adding to the cherry glow of the fire. Carefully coifed, carefully windblown women in leather car coats sat over their luncheon salads and sipped vodka martinis. Outside the rustic inn, the foreign cars and the American cars mingled in allied camaraderie: the MG's and the Corvettes and the Volkswagens and the station wagons with heavy-duty snow tires.

The builder was tall and dark and wide-shouldered and handsome in an outdoor, windburned way. Thick black hair rose wildly from a well-defined widow's peak on his high forehead. He wore a bulky, expensive woolen sports shirt open at the throat, and a cashmere sports jacket with leather elbow patches, and dark gray flannel slacks imported from England and purchased on Madison Avenue. His face was a strong face, square with a black mustache on the upper lip.

His eyes were bright and brown, and his hands were thick builder's hands curling with thick builder's hair, but the fingernails were manicured. Altar studied him and wondered whom he was playing. He decided it was a young Clark Gable in an old movie. He even had Gable's trick of quirking mouth and eyebrows simultaneously, as if he were secretly amused by a cosmic joke too rarefied for the rat pack to appreciate.

There was the pleasant hum of alcohol-stimulated luncheon chatter behind Di Labbia, the pleasant, pretty hum of pleasant, pretty women sitting in leather car coats sipping tasteless vodka martinis, their pretty, manicured fingers curled around frosted glasses in which lemon peel bow ties floated. Di Labbia's voice, firmly assertive with a frank Connecticut twang, cut through the hum like an All-American fullback going for twenty yards against the freshman team.

"My brother changed his name," Di Labbia said. "From honest Mike Di Labbia to meaningless Mike Libby. My name is still Di Labbia, and it'll always be Di Labbia, and I'm proud of the fact that I'm a Wop."

Then why do you derogatively call yourself a Wop, Altar wondered.

"When I first came into this area," Di Labbia went on, "the people here had a stereotype of what Italians should be. A Wop was the man who came to clean out the overflowing septic tank. He had dirt under his fingernails, and all he did was eat starchy foods, propagate, and add a gratuitous vowel to the end of every word. I taught the people here a new kind of Wop. I gave them quality. Do you see what I'm driving at?"

"No, I don't," Larry said frankly.

He had been strangely quiet, and Altar watched him now, disturbed by his lack of enthusiasm. He had met with the same indifferent acceptance when he'd told Larry how much he liked the new sketches. He could not quite understand it. For if Di Labbia were laughing secretly at a vast comedy, Larry Cole seemed to be brooding secretly about a universal truth. Or was the preoccupation only feigned? Was the withdrawal phony, or did Larry really have something important and profound on his mind, something more pertinent than a silly house for a silly writer?

Altar didn't know. He knew only that Larry, who had never shown very much of himself, was now presenting only a thin surface veneer, a falsely interested eye, a falsely attentive ear.

He should not have expected more from Larry. His ten per cent was buying an architect, not a friend, and he honestly didn't know if he even wanted Larry for a friend. But the building of this house was an important thing to Altar, an achievement he could not have accurately described if he'd tried, and he hated his own enthusiasm to be dampened by an uninterested architect.

"I beg your pardon," Di Labbia said.

"I said I don't know what you're driving at," Larry answered.

There was not harshness in his voice; Altar could not claim that. But there was a cold indifference, a feeling that Di Labbia didn't count at all to this young man who sat opposite him at the table. Sitting in the rustic inn, Larry Cole had become a hard-headed businessman intent on closing a deal and closing it fast. And Altar wondered which school of architecture had taught him to appraise a deal so ruthlessly.

"I'm only saying this," Di Labbia said, quirking his eyebrows, smiling secretly. "Every house I build up here is *my* house. Mine." He squinted his eyes heroically.

Larry didn't seem frightened or even mildly impressed. Like a

141

savage listening to the hellfire threats of a visiting missionary, Larry sat with calm calculation in his eyes.

"I give quality," Di Labbia said. "When I build a house, it's mine, and you get a dollar and two cents of value for every dollar you spend. That's what makes it a Di Labbia house."

"I should imagine you'd lose money that way," Larry said dryly.

"I'm doing fine, thanks," Di Labbia answered, suddenly defensive. "Don't worry about me."

"I'm not," Larry assured him. "What did you mean when you said *your* house?"

"*My* house," Di Labbia repeated. "How much simpler can I state it? I build it, it's my house. Mr. Altar is moving into our community. A year from now, you've vanished into the wood-work. If the house is no good, does he come screaming to you? No, sir. It's me he calls. So it's my house. I stand behind it."

The guarantee did not seem to impress Larry. "Your bid is very low, Mr. Di Labbia," he said. "I think you'll lose money on this house if you stick to your bid."

"Let me worry about that."

"Unfortunately, *I* have to worry about it, too. Understand me, Mr. Di Labbia. If you want to lose money, that's your business. But I don't want my client slapped with an 'extra' every time he blows his nose. If you plan on killing us with extras, I can take a higher bid from a competitive contractor and wind up cheaper in the long run."

"I don't plan on killing anybody with extras," Di Labbia said. "My bid stands."

"And I tell you honestly that it's too low."

"And I tell you that I'll build it for what I bid."

"You've seen the heating layout? And the electrical scheme? And the amount of Thermopane? And the special-order glass doors?"

"I've seen them."

"Your bid still stands?"

"It does."

"You know, of course, that I'll be up here once a week to inspect the job. If I see something being done contrary to my plans or specs, you'll have to rip it out and do it over again."

"I've worked with architects before," Di Labbia said.

"Then you must know," Larry said flatly, "that an architect considers the house *his*, and not the builder's."

"You'll be satisfied," Di Labbia said.

"Not if you suddenly decide something in the plans doesn't agree with your aesthetic taste. Not if you decide this house is *yours*."

"I had the impression this was *my* house," Altar said.

142

"That's just my point," Di Labbia said. "This is the man who'll live in it. He'll be satisfied."

"Mr. Di Labbia," Larry said, "an architect's job is to protect his client against being satisfied too easily. It's also to see that the house he designed is built as he designed it. I have every respect for your reputation and your honesty. But I consider you a bugler playing Taps, and that's all. The materials you work with are your bugle, but I wrote Taps, and I want it played the way I wrote it. I don't want you to ad lib your way through it."

"I don't need parables, Mr. Cole."

"I'm stating a simple fact. In this act of creation we are about to commit, there's room for only one creator. Me."

"I understand. But there are bad buglers and good buglers."

"Sure. And in this act of commerce we're about to commit, I'm telling you now, flatly and honestly, that if you stick to your bid and build this house under my supervision according to my plans and specs, you'll lose money."

"I'll take that chance."

"Why?" Larry asked.

"I'm a Wop," Di Labbia said. "I started by digging ditches. I don't dig them any more. I build houses. I build damn fine houses, and I'm proud of each and every one of them. I'm not a successful writer or a creative architect, but I think I'm accomplishing something. I like this community and I'm helping to build it. I build houses and I build roads and I build stores, and that's something to me. I'm a *builder*. Frank Di Labbia, Builder. That's what it says on my stationery. Builder, not contractor. And maybe you think I'm only a bugler, Mr. Cole, but without the bugler you don't get your goddamn song played, and that's the God's honest truth."

"Okay," Larry said.

"Okay. I'll build this house the way you designed it, but it'll still be *my* house because *my* hands are putting it up. And if you've got any kicks about how it's being built, you just let me know. Maybe a contractor wouldn't worry about it, but a builder does. And I'm a *builder*."

"When you find out how much money you're losing, don't weep," Larry said, grinning.

"I never weep except in church," Di Labbia answered.

"I think you can build the house."

"I know I can."

"Then we've got a deal."

"Good."

"Provided Mr. Altar agrees."

"I agree," Altar said, somewhat bewildered.

"Good," Di Labbia repeated. "Let's drink to it, shall we?"

They ordered a round and consumed it. Then they put on their coats and all shook hands outside the rustic exurban inn where

143

the foreign cars mingled with the American infidels. Di Labbia climbed into a Ford and shoved off. Larry and Altar got into the convertible.

"What do you think?" Altar asked.

"I think he'll do a fine job."

"Then why were you so rough on him?"

"Was I?"

"You know you were." Altar started the car and let the engine idle. The exhaled breaths of the two men fogged the windshield and Altar reached over to mop it with a gloved hand.

"I wanted to know why his bid was so low," Larry said. "I checked him with some architects up this way, so I knew he was honest. But why the low bid? If he bid so low out of stupidity, he's not the man to build our house."

"Do you think he's stupid?"

"No. I think he really wants to build it."

"Why?"

"Because it's something different from the pap he's been putting up. He wants the challenge, he likes it. Or maybe he just wants the distinction of having built Roger Altar's house. How do I know? But he wants to build it. He'll lose five grand, but he'll still build it."

Altar nodded and pulled the car out of the parking lot. He hesitated before entering the main road, executed his turn, and then stepped on the accelerator.

"Do you like this house, Larry?" he asked.

"Of course I do."

"You don't seem to. It doesn't seem very important to you."

"It is."

"I don't sense that."

"It's a good house, Altar, and I'm proud of it. Hell, are you excited about a book three weeks after it leaves the typewriter?"

"It left the typewriter *last* week, you know."

"Which? The new book?"

"Yes. I'm rereading it tonight. And then I'll forget about it until the day before publication. That's when I'll begin dying. Slowly."

"What do you mean?"

"Waiting for those reviews."

"Are they that important?"

"It depends on what you want, I suppose."

"What do you want, Altar?"

"Nothing. Nothing."

He fell silent. He drove with his eyes on the road, not looking at Larry.

"I die," he said suddenly. "I'm like the kid on Christmas Eve. I can't eat, I can't sleep, I can't even think. I'm just waiting for Christmas morning." He laughed a short, sardonic laugh. "The

144

trouble is I've opened all the presents already. I've had the big magazine sale, and the book club, and the movie deal all before publication. There's only one present left to open. And that always turns out to be the coal you're promised if you're a bad little boy. Argh, the hell with it. I don't even like to think about it. I get depressed thinking about it."

"Your readers like you," Larry said.

"Sure. They like Dick Tracy, too. But will your great-great-grandchildren be reading him?"

"You can't expect immortality, Altar."

"I don't. Honestly. I'm not that egotistical. I don't want much at all."

"What *do* you want?"

"I want some good reviewer, just once, to say that I'm a writer, that's all." He paused. "I try, Larry. I really try like hell!"

"You succeed."

"Oh, sure, I succeed. Jesus, do I succeed! But sometimes I wonder about success. What good is it if you don't feel you're doing something important?" He shook his head. "Don't you see? Who wants to be kept by a bitch like success? I want to be contributing something, giving. I can't just take all the time." He shook his head. "The hell with them. It's just . . . well, you hang your clean wash on the line and they throw mud at it. It takes guts to hang up your underwear. When they . . . the hell with it. The hell with it. What do *you* want, Larry?"

"Me?" Larry grinned. "I don't know."

The heater had begun to throw its warmth into the car. Both men had unbuttoned their overcoats and lighted cigarettes. They both seemed completely relaxed, like two old friends driving home after a day's hunting. Larry with his knees propped up against the dashboard, Altar slumped idly behind the wheel. Oddly, they were not old friends. Nor was either sure they were *new* friends. Yet, with the heater spreading its warmth around them, with the barren gray countryside blurring past outside, there was a mood of relaxed friendliness in the automobile. And each man recognized the mood and allowed it to claim him completely.

"Every man has to want something," Altar said.

"I guess I want too much."

"What's that, Larry?"

"I want to be happy."

"Ahhh," Altar said.

"Don't you?"

"Sure."

"So. That's all. Just to be happy."

"How do you just 'be happy'?"

"I'm not sure I know."

They fell silent. The automobile hummed through the countryside. A boy rode past on a bicycle and waved at the car. Altar waved back.

"Have . . . have you ever—" Larry cut himself off.

"Ever what?"

"Ever been in love?" he said, turning to face Altar.

"It depends on what you mean by love."

"You know what I mean by love."

"If you mean have I ever known a woman who was beautiful and passionate, yes."

"Well, more than that. I meant . . ."

"If you mean have I ever known a woman who was knowledgeable but ignorant, yielding but obstinate, sensible but illogical . . ."

"Yes, something like that."

"If you mean have I wanted her despite her shortcomings, or because of them; if you mean, Larry, has a woman ever made me *forget* myself and yet *become* myself . . ."

"Yes," Larry said, "yes."

"Then, no. I've never been in love." He paused. "I'm sorry. I wasn't building to a climactic letdown. I'd like to feel that way about some woman, but I don't. Do *you*?" He touched Larry's arm quickly. "Never mind, don't tell me. I don't want to know."

Larry hesitated. Then he said, "Jesus, Altar, I'm all mixed up. I feel like a dozen phony people. Do you ever feel that way?"

"Sometimes."

"I've got a closetful of manufacturer's labels. Architect, Husband, Father, Son, Striver, Brooder, Man! I sew the labels into my clothes, but the suits never fit me. Underneath all the crap, there's *me*! And I'm never really me, never the Larry Cole I want to be until I'm with—" He cut himself off, suddenly wary.

"Sure," Altar said, "and then you fly, don't you? Then you're bigger and stronger and handsomer and wittier, aren't you? Then you can ride your goddamn white charger against the black knight! Then you can storm the enemy bastions!"

"Are you playing with me, Altar?"

"I never kid a man who's serious," Altar said. "I thought you knew me better than that."

"I guess it's . . . I don't know what's real or true any more. What happens when values shift, Altar? What happens when all your life you've believed in honor and trust and decency and all at once they've become labels, too? How can you tell right from wrong if wrong suddenly seems right? What do you do, Altar?"

"I don't know," Altar said. He paused. "Is this why the house seems unimportant to you now?"

Larry did not answer.

"Whatever you do, don't lose your head," Altar advised. "You didn't invent infidelity."

Again Larry did not answer.

146

Altar sighed and turned on the radio.

In his apartment that night, he took the box containing the manuscript from his desk.

THE FALL OF A STONE
by
Roger Altar

The title pleased him. He had typed it, together with his by-line, on a small slip of paper which he'd then Scotch-taped to the lid of the box. Fondly, he lifted the lid now. Then he sat down with the manuscript in his lap. A bottle of Scotch and a box of cigars were on the coffee table before the couch. He propped up his feet on the table and began reading the book from the beginning.

He liked to read his own work. He was, he supposed, his own favorite author. When reading himself, there was always total communication. The perfect author's foil, he wept when he was supposed to weep, reacted indignantly when he was supposed to, laughed at funny lines, reeled back in shock at surprise chapter endings. It was wonderful to be so understood and so understanding. He made several corrections as he went along, but these were mostly the corrections of typos. He considered himself a craftsman, and he would not have typed "The End" onto the last page had his major revisions not already been completed. The corrections he made now lessened in no degree the pleasure he experienced as he read.

When he finished the book at eleven-thirty that night, he tenderly placed it back into the empty typewriter-paper box and then put the lid on it again. He felt intense relief and immense gratification, but he also felt a little empty. Tomorrow he would deliver the novel to his agent. Tonight he felt a little empty. He would continue to feel that way until the approval came: approval from his agent, and then his publisher, and then the others, all the others.

He sat in the quiet apartment for perhaps ten minutes. He sipped at his Scotch, and he puffed at his cigar, and he wondered what to do next.

Then he went to the telephone and called a girl.

17

THE NEXT name on Eve's list was Betty Anders.

She didn't know Felix Anders very well, and her conversational acquaintance with Betty was hardly the stuff of which lifelong friendships are made. But she figured that every good party needed an extrovert, an uninhibited male or female who would supply the spark of revelry, and Betty Anders was perhaps the most uninhibited female she knew. Or, at any rate, the loudest.

Of course, Felix had once asked Larry to work out a landscape plan for him—a task Larry had never even started—and she wondered if Felix's presence would make him uncomfortable. She decided it would not, and dialed Betty's number.

"Hello?" the booming voice asked.

"Betty?"

"Yes, who's this?"

"Eve Cole."

"Hello. Just a second, Eve."

Eve heard the telephone clatter to a hard surface, and then she heard Betty shouting something, and then shouting something else, and then she heard someone crying and then the phone was picked up again.

"That little bastard," Betty said. "He can't let his sister play in peace. How are you, Eve?"

"Fine. And you?"

"Exhausted. With Felix after me at night, and his monsters after me all day long, I think I'll wind up in a nut house."

Eve laughed in delighted phoniness and said, "Why don't you come over to our place next Saturday night and let your hair down? We're having a little party."

"I can use a party," Betty said. "February depresses the hell out of me. I can use a good stiff drunk."

"We'll have a lot of good stiff drunks here," Eve said.

"You're a bigger slob than I am," Betty answered, chuckling.

"What?" Eve said, puzzled for a moment. "Oh. Oh, I didn't—"

"Let me look at the calendar, Eve. Which Saturday is that?"

"The ninth. Next week."

"I'll ask Felix. He doesn't like to leave the kids with a sitter. If his mother'll come out, we'll be there. Can I call you tomorrow?"

"Sure. If I'm not here, just give the message to Larry."

"Fine. How can you stand living with a man who's home all the time?"

"Well, you get used to it."

"If Felix were home, I'd be flat on my back all day long. That man—"

"I hope you can make it, Betty," Eve interrupted.

"I'll try my damnedest. I wasn't kidding about getting fried."

"You'll have all the ingredients."

"It only takes three and I'm flying."

"All right, call me, will you?"

"First thing tomorrow. I'd better hang up. That bastard is

148

after her again." There was a sudden click on the line. Eve hung up, smiling to herself.

Actually, she was very pleased with the way the party was taking shape. The idea had come to her impulsively. With Larry in the city for the afternoon, she had made out her list and then begun her calls, more and more excited by the idea. There was, after all, nothing more depressing than a winter in Pinecrest Manor and a party would do a lot toward dispelling the gloom.

Never did the development seem more like a giant apartment house than in the winter time. Then, the individual homes became cubicles in a brick and concrete structure, cubicles separated by thirty feet of browning grass. Wrapped in seeming seclusion, they defied sameness, turned in upon themselves while belching smoke from their identical chimneys. We are alone, the houses seemed to say. We are a brave family unit facing the winter, and we like it this way. But spring gave the lie to the declaration. In the spring, Pinecrest Manor anxiously burst outdoors, where it pursued the favorite sport of all developments: invasion of privacy.

The winter gloom, then, provided Eve with the good reason for her party. The real reason was another thing again.

She would not admit the real reason even to herself. She knew only that Larry was behaving strangely, that something was crumbling the solidity of their marriage. And so, intuitively, she was utilizing the magnetic pull of a man's home, planning a party with the man and his home as its nucleus. She honestly did not know what the party would accomplish. She hoped only to surround Larry with people he liked in a setting which was familiar and comfortable. She hoped only to remind her husband of what they shared together.

And so she went down her list and made her plans.

There was only one other couple's name on the list. She had debated adding them because she hardly knew the girl at all, and she didn't even know the husband to talk to. But the girl, no matter what one's personal taste preferred, did have a vibrant sort of beauty, and Eve figured it wouldn't hurt to have someone decorative around. It would keep the women on their toes, make the men more gallant, and the living room more attractive.

She put a small check next to Betty Anders' name, and then thumbed through the telephone directory looking for *Gault, Donald*.

When the telephone rang, she felt a faint stab of panic because she thought it might be he again, would he never stop calling, would it go on and on forever, would the voice say "Margaret?" and would she say "You!" and would the interminable argument begin again, the pleading, the begging, would it never never end?

And then she remembered that Larry had gone into the city to deliver his Puerto Rican recommendations to Baxter, and she smiled because she was suddenly certain it was Larry calling. She rushed downstairs excitedly and snatched the receiver from the cradle.

"Hello?" she said.

"Margaret?" the woman's voice asked.

"Oh," she said.

"Is this Margaret Gault?"

"Yes. I'm sorry. I was expecting someone else."

"You sound disappointed," the woman said.

Margaret's eyes glowed secretly. "I am."

"Then perhaps *I* should do the apologizing," the woman said. "This is Eve Cole."

She knew instant pulverizing shock. She froze and then backed against the counter, aware that the receiver was shaking in her fist. She could only think, She knows, she knows, and then wonder in horror why Larry had not phoned to warn her.

"Wh . . . what is it?" she asked. She could barely speak. The phone continued to shake in her fist. She was afraid it would slam into her teeth, afraid she would faint. What could she say to this woman? What, oh, God, what could she say when Eve Cole accused her?

"Are you all right?" Eve asked. "Is something the—"

"I'm all right. What is it?"

She was covered with sweat now, a cold sweat that seeped from every pore. She could feel her knees going weak. Uncontrollably, she continued trembling. Say it, she thought. Get it over with!

"We're having a party at our house next Saturday night," Eve said. "We thought you and Don might like to come."

"A party?" she asked incredulously.

"Yes, a party. Margaret . . . are you . . . are you sure nothing's the matter?"

She wanted to laugh hysterically. Intense relief flooded her, and the overwhelming gladness.

"What . . . what night did you say?"

"Saturday. The ninth."

"I'll have to ask him," she said absently. "If it's all right for us to come."

"Don?"

"Yes," she said quickly. "Yes, Don."

"Will you let me know? We'd love to have you."

"I'd love to come," Margaret said. "I'd love to see your house."

She was regaining her composure, and with it her sense of immediate danger. Eve had undoubtedly extended this invitation without consulting Larry. She was tempted to accept, but she knew Larry would be displeased. It would, certainly, be the stupidest sort of risk. But still, the idea appealed to her, and she restrained herself from accepting, remembering that her behavior of a few moments before must have seemed very odd to Eve.

"I must have sounded idiotic when I answered the phone," she said carefully. "I was sleeping and you woke me."

"Oh, then I *am* sorry," Eve said. "Forgive me for waking you."

"I had to get up anyway," Margaret said. "To answer the phone."

Eve laughed. "That's one of Larry's favorite gags."

There was a slight pause. "Larry?" Margaret asked.

"My husband."

"Oh, yes."

"You two met," Eve said. "At the bus stop or the delicatessen, or somewhere. He was crowing like a rooster when he came home. You'd think he'd never spoken to a woman in his life."

Margaret laughed a forced, light laugh. "Mine is the same," she said. "They're all such little boys."

"I think you're the only reason he *keeps* taking Chris to the bus stop," Eve said, laughing genuinely.

"Really?" Margaret asked, feigning surprise and innocence, hating the game she'd been forced to play, not wanting to talk to Eve, not wanting anything from this woman. Don't give me anything, please, please, don't. "Oh, you're joking. You make me feel terribly embarrassed."

"I'm joking, of course," Eve said. "Margaret, do try to come to the party, won't you? We'd like to meet your husband, and there'll be a nice crowd. It'll be fun."

"I'll try," Margaret said. "I'll call you."

"Do you have the number?"

She almost said yes, she almost trapped herself into saying yes. She knew the number by heart, could reel it off a hundred years from now if Satan asked for it, but to this other woman she said, "No. Would you let me have it, please?" and she wrote it down as if she'd never heard it before, never known it. And then she promised she'd call tomorrow and then she said goodbye.

She sat down, and for the first time since the thing had started she felt like a bitch, a dirty little bitch.

We're all bitches, she thought. We have to be bitches to get the things we want and need. I need him. I need him very much, and if I have to be a bitch to keep him, then I'll be one. I didn't call her, she called me. I'm a bitch, but I didn't ask to be one. I *have* to be one. I couldn't stop being this way unless I died, and I'd die if I lost him. I'm not a bitch for taking what I need. I'm not a bitch for wanting him. I'm not a bitch.

I'm a bitch, she thought. I'm a dirty little bitch.

"No!" Hank shouted. "Be careful! You're crossing your . . . watch your poles! Pull them back! Get your . . ."

Arms flailing, poles wildly gyrating, knees together, toes turned in, skis crossing, Linda Harder came swiftly down the slope, a

151

wehrmacht in ski pants and bright red sweater. Bending from the waist, powerless to stop her descent as the crossed skis carried her, she pulled up the poles, twin pikes ready to pierce the enemy's breast.

"Linda, you're . . ."

Hank gritted his teeth. Helplessly, he stood at the bottom of the slope, trusting to God that . . .

"Linda!"

Over she went, the tip of her left ski digging up a furrow of snow, pitching forward headfirst, the poles rotating like the arms of a windmill. She landed in a welter of arms and legs and wood and bright red confusion. Hank dug in his poles and herringboned to the tangle. Quickly, he knelt beside her.

"Are you all right?"

Linda nodded. Her sweater and face were covered with snow. Her black hair hung on her forehead, speckled with crystalline white.

"No legs broken?"

She nodded again.

"Let me help you up." He rammed his poles into the snow, moved behind her and lifted. Unsteadily, Linda got to her feet, digging her poles into the fresh powder. "What did I do wrong?" she asked.

"Well," Hank said judiciously, "that's a little difficult to answer. Where do you want me to begin?"

"Was I that awful?"

"No, no, you were fine. Except, Linda, a snowplow was designed to *stop* you, see?"

"I *wanted* it to stop me. It just didn't."

"You didn't edge your skis in. That's why they crossed. Also, watch your poles. They're dangerous weapons the way you use them."

"I love this," Linda said suddenly.

She threw her head back and sucked in air. It was a sparkling cold day at Bear Mountain. There had been fresh snow the night before, and the powder was crisp when the skis bit into the slope. The sky was a flawless blue, the snow a blinding white. Hank, a thin boy in street clothes, looked magnificent in his bulky ski garments.

"Want to try it again?" Hank asked.

"Yes. But when can I use the tow?"

"After you've learned to come down."

"I have to *climb* up again?" Linda asked plaintively.

"Yep."

"What do you call the thing?"

"The herringbone."

"Okay." She sighed. "Let's go." She started up the slope, Hank behind her.

"Edge in," he said. "Otherwise the same thing'll happen backwards. Linda, edge in! Linda, you're . . ."

The poles came up again. Slowly, Linda began to slide backward, on a collision course toward Hank. He braced himself.

"Hank!" she shouted. "I can't stop!"

"You will," he said, and she struck him, and they tumbled into the snow together. Her left ski came up, narrowly missing his head. Hank's right boot, released by the awkward pressure, snapped out of the safety binding.

"I fell again," Linda said, and Hank began laughing. "Well, you idiot, it isn't funny," she said. She blew snow from her lips. "If you taught me properly—"

"You know something?" he interrupted.

"What?"

"I love you."

She blinked. "You do?"

"Yes."

She sat with her knees up, her skis awkwardly akimbo, the poles dangling from their straps at her wrists.

"Well," she said. "I love you, too."

He pushed her down onto the snow. He was kissing her when her skis slid out from under her. "Hank!" she screamed, and he captured her and pinned her and kissed her again, and a skier flashing down the slope shouted, "Hey! Cut it out!"

18

FELIX ANDERS was man who thought he was well dressed because he wore a carnation in the buttonhole of a Robert Hall suit.

Every morning, as Felix Anders waited for the train with his copy of the *Daily News* tucked under his arm, he surveyed the platform with a faintly bored air. There was something demeaning about having to wait for a train, and Felix Anders allowed his displeasure to show in his stance and in the set of his Lincolnesque face.

He was a tall man with straight brown hair and green eyes. The green eyes added to his expression of untouchable aloofness. He had a massive craggy nose and a lean lantern jaw, and he looked around him as if he had just delivered the Emancipation Proclamation to a horde of ignorant slaves who didn't understand English.

Felix Anders was a butcher.

He owned a small market on Sixty-third Street and Lexington Avenue, and he cut meat for the major part of his waking day.

But even in his blood-stained apron, Felix managed to look disinterested and bored. In his mind's eye, standing outside of his body and slightly to the left of it, Felix did not look like a butcher in his butcher's apron. He looked, instead, like a noted brain surgeon who had just performed a delicate operation. And when Felix discussed veal cutlets with female customers, he exuded the distant charm of the brain surgeon pulling off his rubber gloves after passing on the job of suturing to an assistant.

Felix was, he knew, poised, charming, bored, aloof, secretive, superior and intelligently cunning.

On Tuesday morning, as Felix waited to board the train, he noticed Larry Cole standing on the platform. He knew that he had been invited to a party at Cole's house for this Saturday night, but he also remembered that he'd once asked Cole to work out a landscape plan, and Cole had said, "Sure, as soon as I get a chance," and then never delivered it. Felix Anders did not take such treatment lightly.

He would, on Saturday night, go to Cole's house and drink his liquor and eat his food, but that didn't mean he had to say hello to him on a station platform. He busied himself with watching the tracks for the approaching 8:07. A slim redheaded girl with an overnight bag stood alongside Felix, staring down the length of track. Munificently, Felix glanced at her, and then turned away to tug at his glove. When the train pulled into the station, Felix allowed the redhead to mount the steps before him, glancing magnanimously at her legs when the skirt rode up over her nylons as she climbed the steps. He then politely shouldered a fellow commuter aside and, *Daily News* tucked securely under left arm, went into the car and found himself a seat near the rear. He was lighting a Parliament when Larry Cole came into the car, looked around for a moment, and then walked back to sit beside him.

Felix very rarely said hello to anyone first. He waited.

"Hi," Larry said. "Haven't seen you in a long time."

"Well, you know," Felix answered. "Busy, busy."

"Oh, sure. I understand you're coming over to our place this Saturday night."

"Is that right?" Felix asked.

"Didn't Betty tell you?"

"Must have slipped her mind."

"Well, you are," Larry said.

"My pleasure," Felix answered. "Cigarette?" He extended the package to Larry.

"Thanks, I'll have one of my own."

"These cost a few cents more," Felix said, even before he saw Larry's cigarettes, "but they're worth it."

"I guess you get into the habit of smoking one brand, and that's it," Larry said, shaking a cigarette free and lighting it.

"Oh, indubitably," Felix said, and then translated it for Larry. "Without doubt, without doubt."

"Not too crowded this morning," Larry said.

"It hasn't been too bad lately," Felix said. "They've added several cars. Of course, you don't have to do this very often, anyway. I imagine it's immaterial to you."

"Well, I like a seat no matter how few times I go in."

They were silent for a few moments.

"Something important?" Felix asked. "In the city?"

"The firm that sent me to Puerto Rico," Larry said. "I told you about that, didn't I? On the train, in fact, I think it was."

"Yes, I seem to recall," Felix said, remembering instantly.

"They want to see me again."

"What about?"

"I don't know. Probably the recommendations I made. They're probably ready to start work on the scheme."

"Must be interesting work," Felix said. "Designing the buildings, and the grounds, and the . . . landscaping."

"Oh, yes, it certainly is. I love it."

Felix cleared his throat. "I hear you're designing a house for Roger Altar."

"Designed already," Larry said. "We'll be pouring the foundation as soon as the snow is gone."

"Why would you want to design a house for him?"

"What?" Larry said. "I'm sorry, I don't think I heard you corr—"

Clearly and emphatically, Felix said, "Why would you want to design a house for him?"

"Yes, that's what I thought you . . ." Larry paused. "Well, why not?"

"I'm only a butcher, you understand," Felix said, making it sound as if he were saying, "I'm only a noted brain surgeon, you understand." He raised his eyebrows. "But do you think Altar is a good writer?"

"Yes," Larry said.

"Well, I'm only a butcher."

Both men fell silent again.

"But," Felix went on at last, "I think he stinks, if you'll excuse the plain English."

"Every man's entitled to his opinion," Larry said, shrugging.

"Certainly. I prefer the purists myself."

"Like who?"

"Like James Jones," Felix said. He paused. "Will you be seeing Altar again soon?"

"I imagine so."

"Tell him I don't like his books, would you? Tell him for me. Tell him Felix Anders thinks he stinks. Do me that favor."

"I'll introduce you. I'm sure you'd rather tell him yourself."

"No need to do that," Felix said. "Just pass my message on." He paused. "How much does he get for each of those books?" Felix asked.

"I don't know."

"A good chunk, I'll bet."

"Oh, indubitably," Larry said. "Without doubt, without doubt."

"Stealing," Felix said, and then let the matter drop. "This party Saturday night?"

"Yes?"

"A lot of people?"

"Thirteen, I think."

"Anyone I know?"

"All from the development," Larry said. "I'm sure you'll know some of them."

Felix seemed to be debating whether or not it was worth while continuing the conversation. At last, he made up his mind, opened the *Daily News*, and said to Larry, "Do you want a part of this paper?"

"Thanks," Larry said. "I'll just sit and smoke."

Felix shrugged his shoulders and turned to Dick Tracy.

There was a tray of pencils on Harry Baxter's desk. Not all of the pencils in the tray were sharpened, the way an idle executive's pencils are always sharpened in readiness for the next master stroke. Some of the pencils were stubs. All of them had been chewed so that their yellow stems were ragged and splintery. Larry glanced at them and knew at once that Baxter was a working-man.

A ludicrous figure in pencil-striped trousers and white shirt, Baxter rose the moment Larry entered the office. His tie was pulled down, the shirt sleeves rolled up to reveal thick arms. He crossed the room with his hand extended, and he took Larry's fingers in a firm grip.

"Did you drive in?" he asked.

"No, I took the train, Mr. Baxter."

"Call me Harry. Please." Baxter smiled. "I was just going to have some coffee. Will you join me?"

"I'd love some."

"Cream? Sugar?"

"A little cream, and two sugars."

Baxter went to the intercom on his desk and flipped a toggle. "Nancy, some coffee, please," he said. "Make mine the usual, and another with two sugars and a little cream."

"Yes, Mr. Baxter," a pert female voice answered.

"Do you want anything to eat, Larry?"

"I don't think so."

"Have something. Nancy?"

156

"Yes, sir."

"Some English muffins, too."

"Yes, sir."

He flicked off the toggle and walked back to Larry. "How's the Altar house going?"

"We've got a builder," Larry said. "A fellow named Di Labbia. Do you know him?"

"Yes. He's honest. He'll build you a tight house."

"That's what I figured."

"Have you broken ground yet?"

"This week, I hope. As soon as we get rid of this snow."

"I take it Altar is pleased with the design."

"Yes."

"I didn't expect otherwise." Baxter paused a moment, thinking. "This Di Labbia's good. We used him on a bank in Westport. He's fast, and he's proud of his work. You don't find many craftsmen nowadays who are. I admire men who take pride in their work, Larry. This is your product, and if it's good, you've every reason to crow about it. Do you follow me?"

"Yes."

"All right. Di Labbia's fast. If he pours sometime this month, you should have your house by the fall. Ready for occupancy."

"I was figuring on December."

"Not with Di Labbia, believe me. Unless you've got a lot of special-order stuff."

"Some big sheets of Thermopane, but I've been promised four months delivery on that. And some sliding glass doors from California. I'm not so sure on those."

"Slipwell?"

"Yes."

"A good outfit. You should have six months delivery at the outside. I suggest you get Di Labbia to order them right away." Baxter began ticking off months on his fingers. "March, April, May, June, July, August . . . There, you'll have your doors by August if you order now. I can help you on that, if you like. We've used Slipwell before. On really big orders. I might be able to pressure them."

"I'd appreciate it," Larry said.

Baxter jotted a reminder onto his memo pad. "Will there be an enclosure problem without those doors?"

"I don't think so. We won't have to worry about heat because they'll be working during the summer. And tar paper should keep out the elements."

"Your house'll be ready in September. I guarantee it."

Larry laughed.

"Don't laugh," Baxter said. "You don't know Di Labbia. The man's a demon on the job. Perhaps you met him over a cocktail where he looks like something out of *The Barretts of Wimpole*

157

Street, but have you ever seen him with a hammer in his hands?
He works like ten men, and he demands the same performance
from his crew. This is a real builder. You don't find them like
him any more."

"He underbid by about five thousand," Larry said.

"Perhaps not. He's thorough, but fast. He doesn't get into those
costly months of men piddling around doing nothing. When his
men are on the job, there's work to be done. He sees to it that
they do it, and then gets them out quick. Larry, he's a businessman. He knows the mortgage holding company will give him a
quarter of his money at roofing and rough enclosure, and
another quarter when his brown plastering is done. He gets his
next payment when he's fully plastered and has his heating unit
completed. His final payment doesn't come until C. of O. So why
should he fool around? He wants to build and get out. If he bid
five thousand lower than the next closest bid, it's because he can
damn well *do* it for five thousand lower. He's organized and
smart. I tell you Altar will move into that house in September.
I know Di Labbia."

"Okay," Larry said, smiling. "I'll take your word for it."

"I'm not just making talk about Di Labbia," Baxter said. "I'm
a businessman myself. You may remember my telling you that."

"I remember."

"I'm lucky because I'm in a business I like, and also because
I feel it's a worth-while one. Suppose, for example, that I made
ten million dollars a year manufacturing plastic practical jokes?
I'd feel like a pimp."

Larry burst out laughing.

"He laughs," Baxter said. "There are men who do that for a
living, Larry. When they die, they've left a plastic practical-joke
empire built on Japanese labor. Maybe some Japanese factory
town will erect a statue to the beloved departed benefactor. I
doubt it. We're dealing in essentials, you and I, basics. Architecture is a noble profession, and I'm proud to be a part of it. But
at the same time, it's my livelihood, and I'm forced to look at it
cold-bloodedly every now and then. Which is why I'm concerned
with when Di Labbia finishes that house. I'm not at all interested
in Di Labbia, and even less interested in Roger Altar. I'm
interested in *you*."

"Me? I don't understand."

"Your direction, your goals. Are you happy doing private
residential work? Because if you are, I've no right to interfere.
But the job you turned in on the Puerto Rican development was
superb. Building will begin as soon as we've completed the
scheme. I was going to ask you to do that for us, but something
else has come along. Larry, I'd be interested in knowing—"

There was a discreet knock on the door.

"Come in," Baxter said.

The door opened, and a tall brunette came into the room carrying a tray upon which were the coffee cups and the English muffins.

"Ah, Nancy," Baxter said. "Just put it down anywhere on my desk."

Nancy moved aside some papers, slid some tile samples to the corner of the desk, and then put down the tray.

"Mr. Fandella called about five minutes ago," she said. "I told him you were in conference. He asked that you call him sometime this afternoon."

"Thank you."

"You still don't want to take any calls?"

"Not until Mr. Cole leaves."

Nancy smiled at Larry and then walked out of the room. She was a very attractive girl who walked with certain knowledge of her quiet good looks.

When she was gone, Baxter said, "I like to surround myself with pretty people. It's absurd, I know, but I have to look at my staff for from eight to sixteen hours a day. Take your coffee." He handed Larry a cup and then picked up his own cup of black coffee. "Toasted English? There's some jam here."

"Thanks," Larry said. He walked to the desk, picked up one of the muffins and spread it with jam.

"Eloise objected at first. She didn't see why every secretary or receptionist I hired had to be pretty. I explained to her that it was all her fault."

"How so?"

"She'd set such a high aesthetic standard at home that she'd spoiled me!" Baxter began chuckling. "She's an angel, that woman. I love her." He chuckled again. "She's used to pretty girls around the office now. In fact, I think it pleases her. It's completely unfair to plain people, I know, and *I'm* certainly no paragon of beauty. But I like what it does for the office. It's American to be beautiful. Does that make any sense? I think of America as strong bodies and straight legs and good teeth and suntans and quiet beauty. Not the Hollywood junk. So I feel more like a working American in an office which employs pretty girls as file clerks. My weakness," Baxter said, smiling and shrugging. "Quiet beauty."

Larry nodded and said nothing, but he thought of Maggie's shrieking loveliness.

"About you," Baxter said, spreading jam on one of the muffin halves. "What were your impressions of Hebbery?"

"He seemed like a nice person and a competent architect."

"Are you reluctant to talk about him?"

Larry smiled. "To his employer? Yes."

"He's a good man within his own sphere," Baxter said. "He's

159

in no danger of losing his job with us no matter what you say. Now, what did you think of him?"

"I imagine he was an honor student in a Connecticut high school," Larry said. "He probably went on to Harvard, where he became a member of the chess team in his freshman year." He thought for a moment. "He made Junior Phi Beta Kappa, and graduated *cum laude*." Again he stopped, thinking, and then he nodded, his impression complete, and the words flowed from his mouth. "He doesn't wear his Phi Bete key because he doesn't like to show off, except at school functions where he feels it's important. Actually, he always feels it's important and will look back upon having made Phi Bete in his Junior year as one of the *real* achievements in his life. He copped a straight A average in every theory course he ever took, and excelled in draftsmanship. His planning problems were always turned in a week before the instructor's deadline, spotlessly submitted, with no erasures. He should have gotten A's but he didn't because his spotless, exquisitely executed drawings somehow lacked imagination."

"Go on," Baxter said.

"He talks too much about how much he likes Puerto Rico. I think he really hates it. His wife certainly hates it. In early November, she was asking about Christmas in New York. But he filled me in beautifully on the problems I was to study, and he had the decency and good sense to know I'd work them out my own way in my own time. He was a cordial and gracious guide and host to us, but I wish his Spanish didn't rely so heavily upon the single word *bueno*. That's all I think about Frank Hebbery."

Baxter nodded thoughtfully. Silently, he worded his next question, and then said, "What do you consider the architectural dangers of an unplanned but expanding community?"

"In brief? I'd say deterioration and obsolescence."

"Have you ever done any city planning, Larry?"

"I began a job for a Long Island town but had to quit when they couldn't appropriate the necessary funds."

"Then you know what it entails?"

"Yes. I assume we're discussing modern city planning and not the outmoded concept of the city beautiful?"

"That's right."

"Well, it's a two-part project. The first part, and easily the most important, would be the study of sociological and economic data."

"Such as what?"

"Population growth, industrial potential, natural resources, transportation facilities . . ."

Baxter nodded.

"And then, of course," Larry said, "would come the actual physical planning of the environment."

"By which you mean?"

"The physical structure. Details like how far a building will be set back from a road."

"How long do you suppose it would take to work out a master plan for a place the size of Puerto Rico?"

"For the entire island, do you mean?"

"Yes."

Larry was silently thoughtful. After a long while, he said, "Five years."

"Oh, surely it could be done in much less time than that," Baxter said.

"Not if it's to be done well," Larry answered. "Generic planning can't be done overnight. An island-wide project would entail a study of each of your major cities with a view toward urban renewal or redevelopment. You'd have to plan *new* cities wherever the need is indicated, find ideal locations for residential growth and recreational spaces, industrial parks. You'd have to study your existing roads and then consult with highway engineers as part of the overall scheme of relating new transportation patterns with natural resources. And in addition to your master plan, you'd need a detailed study of at least one area. I don't see how all that can be accomplished in less than five years."

"Neither do I," Baxter said promptly, and Larry realized he'd passed through a trap unharmed. "Do you think Hebbery is the man to handle such a development project?"

"No," Larry answered without hesitation. "Why?"

"Because Baxter and Baxter has been asked to do the job."

"Planning the island?"

"Planning all of it," Baxter said, his eyes glowing. "You know what Sert's done on a limited scale in Cuba and South America. Well, we've got an entire island to change from dirt and filth and disorganized growth to beauty and cleanliness and directed expansion! My God, where's the challenge of planning Great Neck when you compare it to this? Can you visualize that island fifty years from now? Can you visualize what five years of intense planning can do for it?"

"It can make it a dream island," Larry said.

"A *reality*, Larry." He paused. "Will you be my assistant?"

All he could register for a moment was complete shock. Speechless, he stared at Baxter.

"Not an errand boy and bottle washer," Baxter said. "A real assistant to work with me on every phase of the study and plan. What do you say?"

"I haven't caught my breath yet!"

"Then catch it. I'm going down in September to enlarge the field office. I'm taking some of the New York staff with me. I'd like you and your family to come along."

Sudden doubt crossed Larry's face.

"What's the trouble?" Baxter asked.

"Nothing. I'm . . . I'm flattered and . . . and overwhelmed. I . . ."

"You shouldn't be. I think you're talented and imaginative and blessed with foresight. You should have won first prize in 1952, and I'm offering you first prize now. The opportunity to accept an architectural challenge of scope and magnitude. Or would you prefer the obscurity of residential design for the rest of your life?"

"No, but . . ." Larry paused. "I'll have to think about it."

Baxter looked at him curiously. "I didn't imagine I'd meet with any difficulty," he said. "I honestly thought you'd leap at the opportunity. Must I convince you?"

"It's not that. I . . ."

"Larry, this will be just about the most highly publicized architectural venture of the century. Succeed with this, and your name goes into the architectural primers, I can guarantee that. And if you're thinking in terms of money, the job is worth a small fortune to us. You'll be paid regally."

"But it would mean leaving New York for five years."

"Certainly. But your wife and family would go with you."

"Yes, but . . ."

"Five years is a short time to invest in a sure future, Larry."

"I'll have to think about it," Larry said.

Baxter seemed more puzzled. He stared at Larry uncomprehendingly. "I want you along," Baxter said. "If I can't have you, I'll handle it myself with whatever help my staff can give me. Do you know what I'm saying?"

"I'm not sure."

"I'm saying that as far as I'm concerned, the job is open until the day I get on that plane in September."

"I appreciate that," Larry said.

"But I hope you'll call me tomorrow to say you're coming along."

"I wish I could say it right now," Larry said. "But I'll have to think about it. September, you said?"

"September. Talk it over with Eve. Make sure it's what you want."

"It sounds like everything I ever wanted," Larry said.

There was a curious sadness in his voice. For a moment he seemed terribly troubled and unsure, so much so that Baxter almost reached out to lay a reassuring hand on his shoulder.

"Think about it," Baxter said gently. "Talk it over with Eve."

He did not talk it over with Eve.

He did not even mention the proposal to her. He knew exactly what her reaction would be. Grab it, she would say. Take it, fly with it, soar with it! This was the golden chance, the dream offer, the jackpot tied with a bright silver ribbon!

He could visualize himself in Puerto Rico, a different Puerto

162

Rico this time; not a tourist's island, but a place to live and work.

In Puerto Rico, he was the handsome *Americano*. He was the respected architect who had come with a solution to the people's problems. He was the hero who had come to liberate the land from filth. He would wear white ducks and he would get deeply tanned, and his eyes would be very dark, and there would be understanding intelligence in those dark eyes. They would have a house, he and Eve and the kids, and perhaps there would be a banana tree in the back yard, and wild orchids growing, and he could set up the drawing board there after a day of conferences and doodle with ideas as the afternoon lengthened into purple dusk.

He would come inside then, his white shirt open at the throat, the sleeves rolled up onto his forearms against his deep tan. He and Eve would sit on the screened terrace and sip their rum drinks or their gin drinks; there would be bird sounds in the garden and perhaps, in the distance, the steady thrum of guitars. They would have a quiet dinner served to them by native help, and then they might go for a walk under crisp Puerto Rican starlight, say hello to people in Spanish, or chat a bit about the rainy season.

Or perhaps they would drive out into the country and stop for roast pork, watching the pig turning on the spit, a glistening burnished brown, the fats dripping onto the charcoal fire, the fire spitting angrily as the meat rotated. They would eat their pork and drink wine, and when they went home they would make love. They would make love the way they used to. In Puerto Rico, everything would be all right between them again.

And during the day, there would be the challenge.

The study, the steady compilation of facts and figures, the tentative stabs at solving the problem, the firmer thrusts, the solidified ideas, the problem slowly succumbing to creative onslaught, and finally the plan. He could almost see the plan on paper. He could visualize the island years from now, when the plan had left paper and become reality. Fifty years, a hundred years, a thing of form and beauty on an azure sea. He could see himself walking through the streets and thinking, I helped create this.

The dream was within reach. All he had to do was grab it.

But there was Maggie.

He had told Altar that all he wanted was to be happy. He did not think he was lying to himself at the time. But now, with everything he desired being offered to him, he began to wonder seriously about his own goals.

Sitting behind his drawing board in the third bedroom of his development house in Pinecrest Manor, he asked himself, What the hell do I want out of life?

I want to be happy, of course, but that's pure rubbish. Everyone wants to be happy. You can probably be happy dead as well as alive. Life is not a prerequisite for happiness. The dead sleep

163

exceedingly well, with no problems whatever, and they are no doubt deliriously happy. But they are also dead, and I'm concerned with what I want out of life.

All right then, I want to be famous.

That's reasonable, an attempt to dissect this thing called happiness. Everybody wants fame, or at least recognition. And, like all human beings, I want to feel I'm different, unique. I want identity. I want to know I'm unique and loved for my very uniqueness. I want to know that I'm a very complex, very individualized, very important person. I want to be me. This is my fame, and this is what I want. But I also want fortune.

I want to be rich.

Maybe everyone doesn't want to be rich, but I do. I need money. I like money. It's good. Not because it's crisp and green, but only because it buys things. And buying things helps me to realize myself. A look down the price column of a menu destroys a little of my ego, and am I not a cipher, a less-than-cipher, a zero when I have lost that?

I want money, he thought, lots of it; and I want respect.

Respect as a man, as an architect, as a human being with dignity. And this too, like fame and fortune, isolates me as an individual. Being alive is simply being myself, and being myself is happiness.

I want Maggie, he thought.

I want her because when I'm with her I'm completely and indisputably *me*.

But how much do I want her? If I could have Maggie alone, would I be willing to ignore fame, fortune and respect—all of which are being offered to me—and be content with what she is and with what she brings to me? Am I willing to sacrifice one identity on the altar of a second identity? And which is the true image?

Are there two Larry Coles, and which one do I want to be? How can I possibly think of refusing Baxter's proposal? Four months ago, five months ago, before I knew her, I would have accepted it instantly. And now a casual exercise—was it *ever* a casual exercise—has become an indestructible bond. I cannot leave her. I cannot go to Puerto Rico and be away from her for five years. I cannot.

I've found myself, he thought, but the person I found is lost.

19

Eve could not have asked for a more beautiful party night.

The temperature had hovered in the low forties all day long, dipping to thirty-three degrees along about seven o'clock when she and Larry were dressing the children for bed. It was bitingly cold outside, but stars had appeared in a cloudless black sky and a brilliant moon tinted the snow-banked streets and the plants and the houses with silver. The sharp tang of the cold was a thing to savor, but the warm glow of the houses beckoned one indoors again. It was a wonderful night for a party, and when Eve left Larry with the children to read them their story, she was humming contentedly.

He joined her ten minutes later as she was pulling on her nylons. Sitting on the edge of the bed, she looked over her shoulder when he came into the room.

"Are they in?"

"Yep."

"Good."

"Do you want a drink before the horde arrives?"

"Let's dress first," Eve said. "I think this is going to be a good party, don't you?"

"Yes, I think so."

"Don't you have to shave?"

"I did. Before dinner."

"That's right. Let me feel." He went to her, and she rubbed her palm over his cheek. "Oh, a nice smooth one tonight."

"Is it really? I couldn't tell with that damn fluorescent bulb on the blink again."

She fastened her stockings to her black garter belt and then rose, slipped off her robe, and walked around the room humming, busily collecting the clothes she would wear. Larry went to the dresser, and she was aware of his eyes upon her.

"I'm putting on a little weight," she said.

"You look fine to me."

"Men," she said vaguely. She went to the closet, took a black cocktail dress from a hanger and put it carefully on the bed. "Do you love me?" she asked suddenly.

"Of course I love you," he said.

"Has something been on your mind?"

"No."

"Are you sure?"

"Yes, I'm sure."

"You seem . . . I don't know . . . distant. I'm not used to your being this way."

165

"I'm sorry. I guess I'm concerned about the Altar house."

"But you're not anticipating trouble, are you?"

"No. I'm just anxious for construction to begin."

"Well, it will soon," Eve said. She paused and then added, "You haven't been very sexy lately."

"I know."

"Okay," she said.

She took her good bra from her dresser drawer, changed into it, and then went to the bed. Picking up the low-cut dress, she slipped it over her head and then smoothed it past her hips. She turned her head to examine her stocking seams. "Just haven't felt like it? Or what?"

"Just haven't thought much about it," Larry said.

"*Is* something wrong?" she asked.

"No, nothing at all. I'm sorry I've been withdrawn, Eve, but I always get that way when I'm working."

"Never like this," Eve said.

"Well, I'm sorry."

His voice had grown suddenly sharp. She looked at him and said, "I don't want to start an argument."

"Neither do I."

"Good. Let's not. I'm only trying to find out why you've . . . you've cut yourself off from me. What is it, Larry? Where have you been for the past four months?"

"What do you mean?"

"Where have you been? Where are you? You're not here, that's for sure. Where are you?"

He went to her suddenly and lifted her chin. "Hey, come on," he said, "don't be silly. You look as if you're ready to cry. We're having a party, remember?"

She nodded and then put her arms around his waist and buried her head in his shoulder. "I bought mascara," she said.

"What for?"

She shrugged. "And pancake, too."

"You don't need that crap."

"Do you think I'm pretty?"

"Yes. You're very pretty."

"Do you love me?"

"Of course I love you."

"Larry?"

"Yes?"

"Will you make love to me later? When everybody goes home?"

"Yes."

"Kiss me now before I put on my lipstick."

He kissed her and she clung to him, and he said gently, "You'd better hurry. They'll be here soon."

"All right," she answered, smiling.

She kissed him again and then walked down the corridor to the bathroom.

The Ramsays were the first to arrive. Larry greeted them at the front door.

"Hi," he said. "Beautiful night, isn't it?"

"Better bring in the brass monkeys," Ramsey said.

Larry laughed. Closing the door, he said, "Let me have your coats." He took Ramsey's and then his wife's. Doris was wearing a blue woolen dress, her hair clipped short. She was an unattractive woman except for her mouth, a loose-lipped, sensually inviting mouth in an otherwise plain face. Ramsey, on the other hand, had no physical saving grace. He was possibly the ugliest man Larry had ever known. They'd met at a Pinecrest Manor beer party, and it had taken an effort on Larry's part to prevent a snap judgment of character based on Ramsey's looks.

"What are you drinking?" he asked.

"Scotch and water," Ramsey said.

"The same for me," Doris added, and Larry hoped there would not be too many Scotch drinkers tonight. He had bought more rye on the assumption that most of his guests would prefer that. They followed him to the makeshift bar in the kitchen.

"Nice wallpaper in here," Doris said. "I'll bet it was well over the allowance."

"Ten cents over, I think," Larry said.

"If that's mine," Ramsey said, "just put a drop of water in it." The doorbell rang. "Finish the drinks," he said. "I'll answer it." He walked to the door, opened it, grinned at Felix Anders and said, "My, my, they let all sorts of people into these parties, don't they?"

"Hello, Paul," Felix said, and the men shook hands. Larry came to the door, handed Ramsey his drink and then said, "Hi, Felix, Betty. Here, let me take your coats."

"You'll never get them in that hall closet," Ramsey said. "You'd better start using the bed."

"Come on, Larry," Betty said, winking. "Let's use the bed."

Eve came into the living room. "Hi, everybody!" she said. "Come on in. Sit down." They moved out of the entrance corridor and into the living room, sitting with the stiffness of early arrivers, waiting for the ice to break.

"I'll have gin and ginger ale, Larry," Betty said.

"Gin and ginger ale?" Ramsey asked. "What the hell kind of a drink is that?"

"It's called a Gin Buck," Betty said. "It's perfectly legitimate."

"Then it must be dull as hell," Ramsey said.

"Can I help you with the drinks, Larry?" Felix asked, following him into the kitchen.

"Eve, honey," Ramsey said, "if your husband wasn't in the

167

house I'd tell you exactly how much I like that low-cut dress."

"Tell her anyway," Betty said. "There's nothing a woman likes more."

"You look lovely, too, doll."

"Second fiddle," Betty said. "Larry, is that juice coming?"

"In a minute," Larry called from the kitchen.

The doorbell rang again. Eve went to answer it. "Mary, Arthur," she said. Turning to the living room and her other guests, she said, "It's the Garandis. Hello, Signora," she added warmly. "Come in."

In her best prehistoric mother turtle manner, Mary Garandi, the Signora's daughter-in-law, said, "Looked like there was a party here, so we decided to come over."

"Good evening, Eve," Arthur Garandi said stiffly, palely, blondly.

"Coats in the bedroom, please," Eve said. "Give me your orders and I'll have drinks ready when you return."

"Do you have any Scotch?" the Signora asked.

"Yes."

"Scotch and soda, Eve."

"Fine. You know where the bedroom is, don't you? I'll introduce you when you get back. What are you drinking, Arthur and Mary?"

"Anything," they chimed together as they walked to the bedroom.

There was a knock at the kitchen door.

"Who the hell . . . ?" Larry said, and went to open it.

"Good morning," Max Levy said, popping his red head around the door jamb, bugging his blue eyes. "I represent Collections, Incorporated. About that delinquent payment on your automo—"

"Come in, idiot," Larry said, grinning. "Where's Fran?"

"Here I am," Fran Levy said. She was a tiny girl with brown hair and brown eyes. She came into the kitchen after Max, wagging her head. "He insisted we make a grand entrance through the side door. He threatened to divorce me if I didn't come with him."

"Throw your coats in the bedroom," Larry said, "and I'll mix you some sauce. What'll it be?"

"Scotch," Max said. "A water glass full. And I won't bother you for the rest of the night."

"Fran?"

"Rye and water."

"I love you," he said. "Do you two know Felix Anders? Felix, this is Fran and Max Levy."

"How do you do?" Felix said, taking Max's hand. He nodded at Fran. Felix never shook hands with women.

168

"Fran, Max," Eve said, coming into the kitchen. "How'd you get in?"

"Hiya, honey," Max said, kissing Eve on the cheek. "Down the chimney. How else does Santa arrive?"

"Put your coats away. Watch out for the traffic," Eve said. "Larry, is Betty's drink ready?"

"Oh, God, did I forget to bring it to her?"

"Which is it?" Felix asked. "I'll take it out."

"Your husband loves me, Eve," Fran said. "He just said so."

"Yeah? How come?" Eve asked.

"She drinks rye," Larry said. Fran laughed and followed Max to the bedroom. Felix took his wife's drink into the living room. Alone in the kitchen with Larry, Eve said, "You love me, too?"

"Sure."

"How much?"

"The world."

"Baloney. The Signora wants Scotch and soda. Mary and Arthur want anything."

"We'll give them rye. The Scotch is getting too big a play."

"Okay. Remember your promise?"

"Sure, I do."

"I'm pretty shameless, huh?" Eve said.

"It's attractive," Larry said. "You should get that way more often."

"You sound like yourself. I'm beginning to like you again. Do I get a drink, or doesn't the hostess count?"

In the bedroom, Max Levy said, "They look like a bunch of stiffs."

"Larry and Eve aren't," Fran whispered.

"No, but the rest seem to be. I'll bet we'll be talking about crab grass within ten minutes."

Fran burst out laughing. Together, they went into the living room.

"The only way to beat crab grass," Arthur Garandi was saying, "is to pull it out by the roots. That's the only way."

"There are some effective chemicals on the market," Felix said.

"By the roots," Arthur insisted. "It's like cockroaches. The only way to kill them is to step on them. Well, it's the same way with crab grass."

"Stop talking about cockroaches," Mary Garandi said. "Everybody'll think we got them."

"Who's got cockroaches?" Max asked, coming from the bedroom with an imaginary spray gun and a hunter's gleam in his eyes.

"Oh, my God, you see!" Mary said.

"You got cockroaches, little lady?" Max asked.

"No, no!"

"I'm Max Levy, Cockroach Killer. This is my assistant, Fran."

169

"Hi," Fran said.

"My wife Betty," Felix said, handling the introductions. "Paul and Doris Ramsey. Arthur and Mary Garandi, and Mrs. Garandi."

"You have *two* wives, Arthur?" Max asked.

"No, she's my mother," Arthur said.

"Your mother indeed! This young lady? Preposterous!"

"Him I like," the Signora said.

"*You* I like," Max said, bowing. "Let's get crocked together."

"Together or alone," the Signora said, "*that* is the general idea."

"You're Italian," Max said.

"With a name like Garandi, how did you guess?"

"It's not the name. I like Italians. I was in Italy during the war. They called me The Flying Jew."

"Who did?"

"The Italians."

"Why?"

"Because I was a flying Jew," Max said, shrugging.

The doorbell rang, and Eve went to answer it.

"Excuse me, plizz," Murray Porter said in a thick feigned dialect. "This is maybe Temple Emmanuel?"

The Porters had arrived. The party was ready to start.

The more they drank, it seemed to Larry, the more obnoxious they got. And the more obnoxious they got, the more they drank. And to blot them out, he drank with them.

He had lost count of how many drinks he'd had. There was music coming from the living room, but no one was dancing. In Pinecrest Manor no one danced at house parties; dancing was reserved for the yearly beer parties. There was the sound of loud laughter, oh how these sturdy goddamn rafters rang with laughter, and the sound of loud conversation, and a feeling of too many people in too small a house. He stood alone by the kitchen sink, holding a glass, and he thought, This is a rotten party. Maggie, this is a rotten party, and I should have let you come.

When the Signora walked into the kitchen, he looked up but he did not say hello. She studied him for a moment.

"Any more Scotch?" she asked.

"Sure," Larry said. He picked up the bottle, held it up to the light, took her glass, and poured. "Water, soda? I forget."

"Soda."

He poured from the open bottle on the sink, and then handed her the glass. "Lousy party, ain't it?" he said.

"It's a good party."

"If I wasn't the host, I'd leave," Larry said. "I may leave anyway."

"Where would you go?" the Signora asked.

"There's lots of places to go, Signora," he told her. "Lots of places."

"To a lecture?" she asked.

He looked up suddenly. As drunk as he was, his eyes narrowed and he studied her suspiciously. "Why would I want to go to a lecture?"

"You like lectures, don't you?"

"Sure, I do."

"I do, too. Maybe I'll go with you some night."

"They're very technical," Larry said. "Even Eve doesn't come."

"Of course," the Signora said. "Besides, I'm very rarely free. I've been baby sitting. It passes the time, I get paid for it, and it's right in the neighborhood."

"That's good, Signora. That's very good."

"I baby sit for Margaret Gault quite often," the Signora said.

Larry looked up. Mrs. Garandi was studying him with expressionless brown eyes. He looked at the white-haired woman, the patrician face set incongruously upon the thick body. The eyes were blank, but the mouth was sad.

"She goes out a lot," the Signora said, "and I sit for her."

"That's nice," Larry said carefully.

"Do you think she goes to . . . lectures?"

"I don't know where she goes," Larry said, "and I don't much care." In his drunkenness, he wondered why Maggie had never mentioned that the Signora sat for her. Couldn't she see the danger in that? Didn't she realize the old lady lived right across the street, could observe his comings and goings and relate them to Maggie's?

"She's a beautiful woman," the Signora said.

"Beauty's only skin deep. You don't have to be happy just 'cause you've got beauty. Didn't you know that?"

"Is she happy?"

"How do I know?"

"Are *you* happy?"

"I'm very happy. Whisky makes the whole world happy. Have another drink, Signora."

"Why don't you get out, Larry?"

"Out where?"

"Out of Pinecrest Manor. This isn't the place for you. This is no good for you."

"I like it here."

"Do you love Eve?"

"Sure, I love Eve."

"Then get out."

"I can't go anyplace else."

"Why not?"

"I can't, that's all."

"Why not?"

"Signora," Larry said drunkenly, "life is a pretty complicated thing, you know? It doesn't work the way you figured it was gonna. It just goes along its own merry goddamn way and you call the plays as they come. That's what, Signora."

"Get out of Pinecrest Manor. Go someplace else."

"Is it gonna be any different anyplace else?" Larry asked. "Where's the pot of gold, Signora? Where the hell is the pot of gold? I can't even find the goddamn rainbow!"

"Margaret Gault isn't the pot of gold," the Signora said, and he looked at her long and hard, and neither spoke for a long time.

Then he said, "Signora, I like you a hell of a lot. You've got it all over that creepy son of yours and his Minnie Mouse wife. Only one thing, Signora. Mind your own business."

"I like you, Larry," she said. "I always have. I'm trying to help you."

"There isn't nobody who's going to help me but me myself," he said.

"How?"

"I'll figure it out. I'll cross the bridges when I come to them. If there's no bridges, I'll design some. I'm an architect, ain't I? Am I not?"

"You are."

"Sure, I am. A big architect! You can tell just by looking at my house, can't you? My magnificent palace! But then this is everybody's palace, ain't it, Signora? This nice lovely Pinecrest Manor with the fresh air for the kids and the patios where you drink gin and talk about lawns and clean living? The dream palace with the spotless lawn, no crab grass, Signora, it is absolutely essential that there be no crab grass. You know something?"

"What?"

"Who *cares* about crab grass?"

The Signora smiled.

"Who gives a damn if crab grass devours the whole lawn or the entire development or even the world? I don't give a damn about it, and I don't think anybody else really does either. But they've learned that their sixty-by-a-hundred coffin has to be a *green* coffin. If it isn't, some son of a bitch up the street will report you to the Civic Association for spoiling the looks of the goddamn cemetery, pardon the language."

"Larry, if you . . ."

"They don't care, Signora. Here they are in the country, why should they care? Here's the big dream. The corner plot, and the white house with the pink shutters, and the entrance hall, and that washing machine humming in the basement, and that one-year's-free service contract for that oil burner humming in the basement, and that slate patio in the back yard, and that new garage going up with its Building Permit tacked to the door.

Here's the big dream, who cares if we ate beans and bread crusts for the first fifteen years of our married lives?

"Signora, here are all these people in the idyllic little collections of crackerboxes with the pastoral-sounding names dreamed up by copywriters in Madison Avenue offices who live in the heart of the big, dirty, no-fresh-air city. Maplebrook Acres! Or Hillside Knolls! Or Four River Birches! Here they are ready to start living that big fat American dream! But when the hell does the living start?

"When is there time, after that crab grass has been picked, and that storm replaced by a screen, and that Boxer walked, and that newest shrub planted, and the fence put up, and the gable painted, and the patio built, and the lawn mowed and fertilized and limed and edged, and the slide-upon and the swing erected, and the rubber swimming pool inflated and filled, and the automatic sprinkler set on the lawn, and the forsythia cut back, and the asphalt tile put into the basement—when is there time to sit on that new patio and have that lousy gin-tonic you're thirsting for? When is there time to live?"

"There's time to live, Larry," the Signora said.

"Oh, sure, there's time. We have fun at our gleeful out-door barbecues, don't we, where the flying sparks almost burn down the whole damn development, and where every scroungy hound in the neighborhood comes around to snatch some beef, and where the hamburgers are burned and where your identical neighbor who is just as old as you are and who has just as many kids as you have and who earns as much money as you do and who is at that very moment in his identical back yard having the same identical barbecue yells over, 'Hi, there, neighbor! Having a little outdoor barbecue?'

"Sure, there's time. Don't we have fun at our indoor and out-door ingrown versions of the cocktail party? Where every neighbor brings his own bottle, and where we've all chipped in for stale potato chips and the keg of beer upon which the matriarchs get so crocked they can't walk? We have fun at those, don't we? We laugh loud as hell, don't we? Laugh, laugh, oh, how these sturdy rafters ring with the laughter of the identical people who live in the identical houses.

"JESUS, SIGNORA, THEY'RE DEAD!

"They've got their stupid dream, but the dream really has *them*! And one day all these silly sons of bitches will wake up and realize they're living in a cemetery for young people, and that they all dropped dead the day they took title to their**!! *All brick four bedroom entrance hall separate dining room wall ovens all G.E. appliances spacious plot walking distance church and shopping center bus to school and station fifty minutes New York City*!!** coffins!

"They'll realize their dreams are dead, too. They're only young

173

dead men living with old dead dreams. And do you know how they'll solve it, Signora? Do you know how they'll accomplish the resurrection?"

"How, Larry?"

"By moving into another development! A split-level development this time. A house that costs twenty thousand instead of fifteen-four-ninety on the same goddamn sixty-by-a-hundred plot with the identical neighbors all over again!"

"If you hate it so much, why don't you get out?"

"Because I can't, Signora. I'm trapped. God help me, I'm trapped. You know what I want? I want golden bridges, big golden bridges spanning sapphire waters! I want to gallop over them in ruby chariots, but I'm trapped, I'm trapped."

He poured more rye into his glass.

"Go easy, Larry."

"I'm all right."

"Why don't you go to Eve?"

"Why doesn't Eve come to me?"

"Larry, Larry, you're so unhappy."

"I'm happy as hell. Don't tell me I'm unhappy."

"Do you want to come in the other room?"

"I want to stay here by the sink," Larry said. "Leave me alone, Signora. I want to go down the drain."

"Larry . . ."

"Leave me alone!"

In the living room, Felix Anders was talking to Phyllis Porter. Phyllis was a brunette with green eyes and a good figure. She had a pert Irish nose and an Irish sort of mouth, puckering, with good white teeth behind it. Her husband, Murray, was telling a garment-center joke to the Garandis and Eve and Fran.

"Of course," Felix said, "a man has dreams, too. A man doesn't always want to be a butcher."

Phyllis, having consumed a good deal of alcohol, listening to Frank Sinatra singing his *Wee Small Hours* album, hearing the gentle hum of conversation all around her, feeling motherly and womanly and understanding to all mankind and to all men in particular, said, "What's your dream, Felix?"

"It's a big dream," Felix said. "For a butcher, anyway."

"Butchers can dream the same as candlestick makers," Phyllis said philosophically. "What was Marty if not a butcher. Didn't he dream? Of course he dreamed. What's your big dream, Felix baby?"

"My dream is to make people happy," Felix said. He paused dramatically. "Does that make sense to you, Phyllis?"

"Sure it does. Who you want to make happy, Felix?"

"Everybody," Felix said. He was still holding the first drink that had been given to him that evening. He was not drunk and

174

had no intention of getting drunk or even slightly high. "Everybody," he repeated. "You."

"Me?" Phyllis grinned lopsidedly. "How would you make me happy?"

"How do you think?"

"I d'know. You tell me."

"What would you like?"

"Right now?"

"Right now."

"I'd like to go to bed," Phyllis said. "I mean, to sleep."

"So would I."

"You've got things on your mind," Phyllis said slyly. "Little Felix the cat has things on his mind."

"Nothing. Just to make people happy."

"You can't make me happy, Felix." Phyllis shook her head solemnly. "I'm happy already."

"You see?" Murray said, delivering his dialect punch line. "Everybody's cutting corduroy, we had to cut voile?"

"I think I hear David," Eve said. "Excuse me."

Larry had taken off his shoes, and he leaned against the sink and looked into the bottom of his glass. It was almost one o'clock, and he wondered when Eve would serve coffee and cake, wondered when all these people would go back to their own houses. The Signora had gone into the bathroom, and he stood alone in the kitchen, holding up the sink and listening to the saddest music in the world and hearing the happiest, gayest voices in the world and hearing above those the ring of the telephone.

"Telephone," he said.

No one answered. He put down his glass, shoved himself off the sink and went into the corridor leading to the bedroom. The light in the boys' room was on, and he could see Eve leaning over David's crib, talking to him soothingly. The telephone kept ringing.

"Nobody going to answer that?" Ramsey shouted from the living room.

"I'm getting it," Larry said to Ramsey. "I'm coming, I'm coming," he said to the telephone, and then he picked up the receiver.

"Hello," he said.

"Hi."

David was crying without reason, the way only a small child can cry when awakened by strange voices in the middle of the night, crying without fear, without sadness, simply crying uncontrollably.

Eve said, "Don't cry, baby, Mommy is here. Now don't cry, baby. Please don't cry."

David would not stop. She held him close to her breast, the way she had done when he was an infant, and he sobbed his misery against the naked flesh above the low-cut neckline.

"Please, darling. Come now, darling. Don't cry. Mommy's here," she said soothingly, over and over again. "Don't cry. Don't cry, darling."

He stood quite still by the telephone. He had not expected her voice. In the darkness of the bedroom, with the laughter coming from the next room, her voice sounded calm and warm and loving.

"Where are you?" he asked.

"Home."

"Him?"

"Upstairs. Asleep. I had to call you. Can you talk?"

"No."

"Are you drunk?"

"Yes."

"I'll talk. You listen. Do you love me?"

"Yes."

"Why are you drunk?"

"Because I love you."

"I miss you, Larry. I miss you so much. It's torture to know that you're there having a good time."

"Please!"

"Is it bad?"

"Yes."

"Very bad?"

"Yes."

"I'm glad. I want you to be miserable without me. I want you to miss me as much as I miss you."

"I do. Maggie, what are we going to do?"

"About what?"

"I don't know."

"About what, darling?"

"About the world," he said.

"The world?" She began giggling. "Honey, you're drunk! You sound adorable! Oh, I wish I could hug you."

"Honey, what're we gonna do about the world?" Larry asked again.

"We'll let the world worry about itself," she said. "Let's just worry about each other."

"All right. But what about Puerto Rico?"

"What about it?"

"I don't know. What about it?"

"Larry, I don't understand you."

"It's poor and dirty," he said. "It could be clean. I can make it clean."

176

"Yes, darling." She giggled again. "Oh, God, are you drunk! Oh, I could kiss you." He heard a smack against the mouthpiece. "Did you get that? I kissed you. Did you get it, darling?"

"Yes."

"Will you get drunk with me sometime? I want you drunk."

"Yes."

"When?"

"Tomorrow morning. We'll get drunk for breakfast."

She giggled again, her voice close to his ear, her giggle very warm and very intimate.

"I love you," he said.

"Again," she whispered. "Again."

"I love you."

"Don't cry, David. There are people here, honey. You don't want them to think you're a baby, do you?"

"Where's Daddy?" David asked, sobbing.

"Outside. Do you want him?"

"Yes," David said, nodding, sobbing.

Eve went to the door frame.

"Larry!" she called. "Will you come here a minute, please?"

"I'll get him," Ramsey shouted from the living room. "He's on the phone." Ramsey got to his feet and walked to the bedroom. Leaning in the doorway, he said, "Hey!"

Larry turned from the phone, saw Ramsey, and then turned back to the mouthpiece. "Who did you want?" he asked.

"I want *you*," Maggie answered.

"I'm sorry," Larry said. "I think you've got the wrong number."

"I've got the right number, darling," she said.

"I'm sorry," Larry said, "there's nobody here by that name."

"Call me tomorrow," she said.

"Yes."

"I love you."

"That's quite all right, sir," Larry said. "I feel the same way. Good night."

"Good night, my darling."

He hung up. He turned to Ramsey. "Wrong number," he explained.

"Your wife wants you," Ramsey said.

He walked past him and into the corridor, hearing Betty singing with Doris in the living room, seeing Felix off in the corner talking to Phyllis, hearing Murray telling a dialect joke to the Signora, watching Max using his hands to describe flight to the Garandis, seeing Fran stagger out of the living room toward the kitchen bar, her empty glass in hand. He walked past the living room and down the corridor to the boys' room, and then into the room.

"You'd better talk to him," Eve said frostily. "If you're not too stinking drunk."

"What's the matter with him?" Larry asked.

"Nothing," Eve said. "His father is a fool, that's all."

"What's the matter with *you*?"

"Nothing at all. I'm going to make some coffee. You can use a gallon or two."

Larry walked to the crib. "What's the matter, Chris?" he asked.

"I'm David."

"Well, what's the matter?"

"I di'n wet the bed."

"Well, who said you did?"

"Nobody."

"All right, so what's the matter?"

"Nothing," David said.

"I'll make the coffee," Eve said. She paused in the doorway. "Who was that on the phone?"

"Altar," Larry said. Eve left the room.

"Mommy's angry," David said. "Why?"

"I don't know. Women get angry."

"She said you were drunk."

"I am."

"What's drunk?"

"What's sober?" Larry asked the wall. "Can't you get back to sleep now?"

"Sure. I di'n wet the bed."

"That's a good boy."

"I'm never going to wet the bed again. Then I can go to school with Chris."

"Sure."

"Can't I?"

"Sure."

"I'm going to be like Chris when I'm bigger."

"That's good," Larry said. "Lie down, son. I'll cover you."

"And when I'm really big, I'll be a daddy like you. You're a good daddy. You're the nicest daddy in New York."

"Thank you, son," Larry said. He kissed David on the cheek.

"Me," David said. "I want to kiss you."

He kissed Larry, and Larry suddenly clasped his son to him, holding him fiercely close.

"Good night, son," he said. "Good night."

"Good night, Dad."

He flicked out the light and went out of the bedroom and past the bathroom and through the kitchen where Eve stood at the stove with the coffeepot and through the entrance hallway and then out the front door and onto the stoop. He walked down the front steps and down the path and he turned left at the sidewalk and then simply walked up the block, feeling the sudden cold, realizing all at once that he was in his stocking feet, not giving a damn, walking faster and faster and thinking only, I've got to get away, and not knowing from what he had to get away.

The development was closed for the night, the sidewalks pulled in, the eyes of the houses shut, the houses standing uniform and silent behind their lawn moats, the telephone poles stiff and unbending, the telephone wires zooming off into the distance, the sky a solid black slammed with stars and a storybook moon.

He walked alone on the silent streets, walked with a rushing, headlong pace, breathing hard, *away*, *away*, not thinking of where he was going and then suddenly knowing where he was going and stopping dead in his tracks. He was heading for Maggie's house.

His arms fell to his sides. His head drooped, and he stood in the center of the sidewalk, limp within his body frame, shaking his head slowly and meaninglessly, thinking. What's happening to me? What's happening to my life?

He felt an enormous sadness. He knew he would not cry, but there were tears behind his eyes, silent tears that wept without moisture. The sadness was heavy, a burden that pressed on his shoulders and head, filling his chest and his eyes and his hands. He stood alone, unmoving, his stockinged feet against the pavement in the brilliant moonlight. There was no wind. The world was silent. He was alone in a silent world, alone and sad, and unable to think, able only to feel this enormous sadness.

The car pulled up alongside him. The front door opened.

"Get in," a voice said.

He stood silent for another moment. With great effort, he turned and walked to the car. He climbed onto the front seat alongside the driver.

"Close the door," the voice said.

He closed the door.

"Not that I much give a damn," the voice said, "but are you all right?"

"I'm fine," Larry answered.

The car was in motion now. The houses outside fell by in regular monotony.

"You're not very smart," the voice said. "Even a butcher knows that."

"I'm smart as hell."

"Why'd you walk out on your own party?"

"I wanted to. Who the hell are you?"

"Felix Anders."

"Go to hell, Felix. Who asked you to come after me?"

"Eve did."

"Hero. Big hero butcher who reads the *Daily News*."

"We can't all be smart architects who read the *Times*." Felix paused. "We're going to a little ride. To clear your head."

"My head's clear."

"Your head's all ass backwards."

"My, my, the butcher curses. The butler-butcher curses. The neat superior—"

"I can't stand amateurs," Felix said. "If you're going to play the game, play it right."

"What are you talking about?"

"Walking out of your own party is a stupid kid stunt."

"I don't know what you're talking about."

"What is she?" Felix asked. "A blonde or a brunette?"

"What is who?" Larry asked shrewdly.

"It's too late to get smart," Felix said. "You showed all the signs tonight. Don't get smart when I'm trying to help you."

"I don't need your help."

"Eve's a shrewd cookie. You keep on—"

"I don't like that," Larry said. "Eve's my wife—"

"And you love her," Felix said dryly. "I know."

"Damn right, I love her."

"Love's got nothing to do with it."

"Love's got everything to do with everything," Larry said. "That's how much you know, butcher."

"I don't know anything at all," Felix said slyly. "I'm just a butcher. But if you're going to play the game, play it right."

"What game were you playing in the corner with Phyllis Porter? Footsie?"

"Someday I'll explain life to you."

"A game! What the hell do you know?"

"Nothing. I'm a butcher."

"Stop telling everybody you're a butcher. They'll begin believing you."

"Where were you headed just now?"

"No place."

"I hope you're not playing close to home," Felix said. Larry did not answer. "There's an old proverb: never spit where you eat. You might remember it."

"Felix Anders, proverb maker," Larry said.

"You ready to go back?"

"I was ready long before the lecture started."

"In one ear and out the other," Felix said. "I'll talk to you sometime. When you're sober. Let me handle this when we get back to the house."

"What's there to handle?"

"You don't know how close to the brink you are," Felix said. "I don't even know why I'm bothering to help you."

"Who needs your help? I don't even think I like you."

"I don't like you, either. You think you're superior because you're an architect. I'm a butcher, and I know more about life than you'll ever know."

180

"Sure."

"Sure. Every butcher does. Life is just a big piece of meat. There's your house. Let me handle this." He pulled the car to the curb. "Sit where you are," he said. "I'll come around and help you out of the car."

"I can walk."

"I know you can. Sit where you are." He walked around to Larry's side and opened the door. "Put your arm around my shoulders. Let me do all the talking. Just follow my lead."

He seized Larry's arm and swung it over his shoulder. Together, they swayed up the front walk. Eve was waiting at the door.

"Is he all right?" she asked.

"Just too much to drink," Felix said. "He felt sick, had to get some air. I think we're going to need the bathroom."

Eve looked at her husband with mingled sympathy and disgust. Larry smiled blandly. He and Felix went into the house and past the coffee drinkers at the kitchen table. Eve followed them to the bathroom. As Felix closed the door, she said, "I'll have coffee waiting for him."

With the door locked, Felix said, "Make noises. I'll get the water going."

"This is a little foolish, isn't it?" Larry asked.

"Protection. You're in trouble, mister. I suggest you lay your wife the moment everyone leaves."

"That's none of your goddamned business," Larry said heatedly.

"Isn't it?" Felix smiled a knowing, superior smile. "Architect, you just joined an international fraternity." He turned on the water tap. "Make sick noises," he said. "Make a lot of sick noises."

The house was very still.

The guests had all departed, and he and Eve lay side by side in the silent bed in the silent bedroom. She lay quietly tense, and he could feel anger coming from her like electricity before a summer storm.

"It was a lousy party," he whispered.

"It was the most horrible party I've ever been to in my life," Eve said tightly.

"Thirteen people. You should never give a party with thirteen people."

Eve did not comment. He reached over for her.

"Don't touch me!"

"What's the matter?"

"Just keep your hands off me!"

"Is it my fault it was a lousy party?"

"It was lousy and boring and loud and horrible and nothing

181

at all like what I thought it would be," Eve said. "But I stayed."

"Well . . ."

"And you walked out. And that's the big difference, Larry. You walked out."

There was a long silence in the bedroom.

"Good night," Eve said at last.

20

HE SOUGHT out Felix Anders for two reasons, one of which was realized, the other of which was totally unconscious.

Primarily, he wanted to hear more from Felix about this "international fraternity." He wanted to assure himself that what he shared with Maggie was not a run-of-the-mill gutter alliance. He had always liked Van Gogh until mass-production techniques put a Van Gogh print into every lower-middle-class living room. He did not wish to believe a love like his was hanging in living rooms across the face of America. He wanted to know that he and Maggie were different. This was his prime reason and his good reason for seeking out Felix.

Unconsciously, he needed a confidant.

He could not discuss with Eve the conflict which was uppermost in his mind, nor could he very well confide in Maggie the doubts and uncertainties which plagued him. Felix had come along with a hint of vast knowledge. He did not know Felix very well. Indeed, the Felix who'd picked him up didn't seem at all like the Felix he knew even slightly. And he didn't particularly like *either* Felix. But he looked for him on the Sunday morning after the party; and perhaps he'd been looking long before he found him.

Felix was in his garage oiling a hand saw. Larry hesitated on the sidewalk a moment, and then walked up the concrete driveway strip.

"Morning," he said.

Felix looked up. He did not smile. He wore an old Army Eisenhower jacket over a green sweater. His eyes looked very green and very clear.

"Good morning," he said. He oiled the saw with meticulous care, rubbing the oil in, wiping away the red smear of rust.

"I guess I was pretty loaded last night," Larry said.

"We all get high sometimes," Felix answered.

"You didn't."

"I don't need alcoholic stimulation to enjoy myself."

The men were silent. Felix wiped oil from the saw.

"I wanted to thank you," Larry said.

"Don't mention it."

"You were right about Eve's being angry. She was."

Felix gave the saw a last wipe, hung it on the garage wall, and took down a hand scythe. "Amazing the way rust collects," he said.

"I'd like to talk to you sometime," Larry said. "About some of the things you said last night."

"I'll give you a piece of gratuitous advice," Felix said, squirting oil onto the scythe blade.

"Yes?"

"Never confide in strangers."

"Are *we* strangers?"

"Yes," Felix said, and he wiped rust from the blade.

It was Lincoln's birthday, and Larry walked past Felix's house hoping he'd be home from work. He found Felix washing his car. He walked over to him and said, "No work today?"

"We switch the holidays," Felix said. "My partner and me. He's got Washington's birthday."

"Washing the car?"

"Just about finished. Looks good for an old shebang, doesn't it?"

"I thought you might like to take a walk up to the center."

"What for?"

"Cup of coffee."

"All right," Felix said. "Let me check with Betty."

He went into the house. When he came out, he was pulling his Eisenhower jacket over his sports shirt. "Let's go," he said.

They walked silently. The day was mild and blue, warm for February.

"What's on your mind?" Felix asked.

"A cup of coffee."

"You walked over here to get me to come for a cup of coffee, is that right?"

"That's right."

"Okay," Felix said.

"You said you'd talk to me sometime. When I'm sober. I'm sober now."

"What do you want to talk about?"

"*You* made the offer," Larry said.

Felix nodded. "Are you playing around with some dame?"

"Maybe. Are you?"

"Definitely not," Felix said.

"You are. I know you are."

"You know nothing," Felix said. "Why are you talking to me?"

"Because you're the only person I *can* talk to," Larry said honestly.

"The only person you should talk to is yourself. And your blonde." Felix paused. "I use that figuratively. She may be a redhead."

Larry said nothing.

"By your silence, I gather she's a blonde."

Larry still said nothing.

"It doesn't matter what she is," Felix said airily. "Have we finished talking?"

"What makes you think Eve is suspicious?"

"I only think she's on the edge of suspicion. Unexplained behavior is always suspicious. Learn the secret. Consistent behavior at home, inconsistent behavior the moment you leave the house."

"I don't understand."

"Never meet on the same street twice," Felix said. "Don't call from the same phone booth, don't go to the same motel, the same restaurant, or the same anything. Be inconsistent. A habit pattern is likely to attract attention, and attention is dangerous."

"I thought you weren't—"

"I'm not," Felix said. "I'm a student of human nature. I keep my eyes open."

"Sure," Larry said. "Listen, if we're going to talk at all, let's lay our cards on the table, shall we?"

"Why?"

"Because that's the only way I can talk."

"Then let's not talk," Felix said.

Sitting next to Felix on the train that Wednesday on his way to meet Altar, Larry wasn't thinking of the bathroom fixtures the writer would select that day. He wasn't thinking of the necessity for early selection and early ordering in these times of interminable waits for equipment. He was thinking of what Felix had said to him the day before.

"Your own behavior wasn't exactly consistent," he said.

"Wasn't it?" Felix asked, opening the *Daily News*. "Do you want a part of this paper?"

"No, thanks. At the party, I mean."

"How was I inconsistent?"

"Your play for Phyllis Porter."

"How do you know I don't do that at every party? How do you know I don't single out one woman, make inexpert sex talk with her, and then go home to lay my wife silly? How do you know Betty isn't conditioned to all this and considers it harmless?"

"I don't."

184

"Then don't say my behavior is inconsistent. Your own behavior needs careful watching."

"I don't think Eve is suspicious. There's really no danger."

"Overconfidence is the biggest danger," Felix said. "Does your blonde ever call you at home?"

"Sometimes."

"That's careless. Do you call her when her husband is home?"

"Sometimes."

"She *is* married then?"

"Yes, she's married."

"You shouldn't call when he's home. Do you check the car after she gets out? No lipsticked butts, no earrings, no gloves, no stray blonde hair or blonde bobby pins? Eve's got black hair, remember."

"I'm very careful."

"Because all that's necessary is a shred of suspicion, and then the game's up. Then you haven't got a wife any more, you've got the New York branch of the F.B.I."

"Well, I've been very careful," Larry said. "Besides, she's careful too."

"Never mind how careful *she* is. You can't trust her."

"Why not?"

"Because you can't trust any woman. The minute they enter an affair, they get emotionally involved. Once they start *feeling*, they stop *thinking*." Felix paused, folded his newspaper, and turned his green eyes full on Larry, searchingly. "I hope *you're* not emotionally involved."

"I—" Larry stopped.

"I hope not," Felix said. "A woman is a woman, and they're all exactly the same after the first few months. Never forget that. The hardest part of any affair is getting out of it when you've had enough."

"I don't believe all women are the same," Larry said.

"Then you don't know women."

"I don't claim to be an expert."

"They're all the same. If you've had her, somebody before you has had her. No matter what she says, you're not the first. And if, by a holy miracle you happen to be, you're certainly not going to be the last. You can bet your eyes on that."

"I don't believe she . . . well, I really don't know. But it doesn't matter, in any case."

"It *does* matter," Felix said. "I can see you getting angry just thinking of the possibility. You're too involved with her. Pull out now."

"I don't want to."

"Why not?"

He hesitated for a moment, finding it difficult to say the words to Felix. Then he said, "Because I love her."

"Sure," Felix said. "If you didn't love her, what would be the sense?"

"I don't follow you."

"Love them all. One at a time, or all together. Love makes the world go round."

"How can you love more than one person at the same time?"

"You love your wife, don't you?"

"Yes."

"And don't you love your blonde?"

"Yes."

"So? There you are."

"That's different."

"How?" Felix shrugged. "A woman is a woman."

"Well, I look at it differently."

"Only because you've still got the glow. Well, good. Without the glow, there's nothing. But it'll wear off, you'll see. Your blonde'll be just another wife then. That's the time to get rid of her and start looking for a redhead."

"I don't think so."

"And if you imagine you'll have to look far, you're crazy," Felix said. "Do you know what America is?"

"What?"

"It's a big soapy dishpan of boredom. That's the truth. And no husband can understand that soapy dishpan. And a woman can't explain it to another woman because they've all got their hands in that same soapy boredom. So all a man has to be is understanding. *Yes, baby, I know, I know, you've got a miserable life, here're some flowers, here's some perfume, here's 'I love you,' take off your pants*. Bang!"

He watched Felix, fascinated. Felix was beginning to loosen up, and as his mind loosened, his body also relaxed so that he began shedding his stiff formality, becoming another person before Larry's eyes.

"Do you think you're an outstanding lover?" Felix asked. "You're not a movie star, are you? Not Rock Hudson or Cary Grant?"

"No."

"You're just an ordinary guy, am I right?"

"I suppose so."

"All right. What makes you think your blonde wouldn't be fooling around with another ordinary guy if you hadn't come along?"

"I don't know."

"Believe me, you're not the first, and you won't be the last. It's a big procession, an American Marching Society. From bed to bed to bed, they march. March, march, march! And everybody looks the other way and pretends not to see the parade. Half the people in the world are out there keeping time to the music, and the other half are itching to march, too, but they haven't got the guts. And do you know who's leading the procession?"

"Who?"

"A woman."

"You don't think much of women, do you?"

"I love every last one of them. But I wouldn't trust any of them as far as I can throw the Empire State Building. There isn't a woman alive whose shoes can't be placed under some man's bed."

"There are," Larry said.

"Who? Your blonde, whatever her name is?" Felix paused. "She *is* a blonde, isn't she?"

"Yes."

"Sure. Her?"

"I don't know."

"Your wife? Eve?"

"I don't think Eve would," Larry said firmly.

"Want me to try?"

"No."

Felix smiled in a very superior way, and Larry wanted to hit him all at once. He wondered why he was talking to a schizophrenic jerk like Felix, especially when he didn't like either of the man's personalities: the butler-butcher who looked at the world with secret eyes, or the cynical boudoir philosopher who imparted vast sexual wisdom to a small chosen audience.

"They're all the same," Felix said. "They want romance. There's nothing romantic about changing diapers. And there's nothing romantic about the unshaved man they see in the bathroom in his pajamas. Once in a while this man will do something heroic. The rest of the time he's just that tired old unromantic husband. He's the comfortable living-room sofa. You, me, we're furniture in our own homes. But if we go next door, ahhh! Next door, we're heroes!"

"I think Eve loves me," Larry said.

"Of course she loves you! Who said she didn't? But you're still that living-room sofa. If the right man-next-door comes along, she can fall as easily as any woman in the world. One night she'll be ripe, and once she takes the first step in her own mind, she's on the way to joining the Marching Society."

"Not Eve."

"Who then? Your blonde?"

"Not her, either."

"All married women are the same. You said she was married, didn't you?"

"Yes."

"Sure. Any kids?"

"One."

"A boy or a girl?"

Larry grew suddenly cautious. It occurred to him that he had

187

admitted far too much about himself while Felix spoke only in vague, philosophical abstracts. "What difference does it make?" he said.

"Then she *does* live in the neighborhood?"

"I didn't say that."

"Why are you clamming up if she isn't someone I might recognize?"

"I'm not clamming up. She's got a little girl."

"You said that too fast. She's really got a little boy."

"Draw your own conclusions."

"Sure. You've got a married blonde in the neighborhood, and she's got a son. How'd you meet?"

"None of your business."

"You're crazy if you're playing close to home. Nobody with any sense plays close to home."

"Then I'm safe," Larry said, annoyed. "If nobody does it, it's not expected and not looked for."

"It's *always* looked for," Felix replied. "Every woman in the world is just itching to sink her teeth into some other woman's juicy bit of homegrown gossip. It makes her own running around seem more pure. Look, count up the shopping trips, and the visits to the doctor, and the bridge-club meetings, and the sewing-club meetings, and the out-of-town girl-friends who have to be met in New York, and the dental appointments, and the dancing classes, and the adult-education routine—do you know where half of these women *really* are?"

"Where?"

"In bed. Any hour of the day. Morning, noon or night. With the husband, it has to be at night, it has to be dark on clean sheets, with candlesticks on the dresser and a bucket of iced champagne near the bed. With the man next door, it can be in broad daylight in a smelly barn on dirty straw, and it's romantic."

Larry smiled.

"Romance," Felix said. "They're all looking for romance because they've learned it from books and movies. And what can be more romantic than a man who's willing to risk your husband's shotgun to have you? Jesus, you must be the sexiest thing on wheels! This is romance. This is what Mrs. America wants. Do you know what she's got?"

"What?"

"She's got a stranger on top of her. And the only exciting thing about this guy is that he *is* a stranger. She'll do anything for this stranger. Things she wouldn't dream of doing with her husband, she'll do with this stranger. Why? Because she doesn't own him and he makes her twitch. She's got to have him. Every other woman in the world is her enemy. She tells herself she's in love, and she's willing to risk her home, her happiness, her pride, everything, just to be with this stranger who fills her once a week.

The romance seekers. They're everywhere, ready to fall in love at the drop of a hat. Anyplace you've got a housewife, you've also got a potential mistress for a stranger."

"*Your* wife, too?" Larry asked.

"Betty'd like nothing better than to roll in the hay with a stranger. She'd be good for him, too. And he'd be great for her. I wish she'd get herself somebody."

"Why?" Larry asked. "To ease your own conscience?"

"Who me? My conscience is clear. I'm a respectable butcher."

"But the rest of us are all animals, huh, Felix?"

"*Aren't* we all?" Felix asked, smiling.

The walls were down, and now Felix would talk.

And now, beginning to know the man at last, Larry suspected he'd wanted to unload his mind from the very beginning. They sat side by side in the bar at the shopping center. Darkness pressed at the plate-glass window, and they spoke in whispers, like two old friends discussing family trouble.

"Larry," Felix said, "there's nothing like it. I know just how you feel. You're in love, and there's nothing like it."

"Have you ever been in love?"

"I'm always in love," Felix said. "If I wasn't in love, I'd be dead. Jesus, Larry, I'm a *butcher*!"

He looked at Felix, and he thought Felix is a butcher and he doesn't like being a butcher or living in Pinecrest Manor with a wife who's too loud no matter how cute she is. And so he plays around. This is the only excitement in the life of Felix Anders: the meeting, the discovery, the conquest, the retreat, the further conquests. There are no real worlds left for Felix Anders to conquer, no worlds left for the butchers of America; there are only women.

So this is the real profession of Felix Anders.

He is poised, charming, bored, aloof, secretive, superior and intelligently cunning. He is a discoverer and an explorer and a conqueror. There are worlds of lonely housewives, and Felix is a master at his profession, which is the conquest of these women.

Am I like Felix Anders?

"Love, Larry," he said. "That look in their eyes, the look that's for you alone. Sweet, sweet. Ahhhh, you become alive again, do you know? Women are so goddamn sweet. There's this model I'm dropping now. Not cheesecake, fashion. Pretty as a picture. Long black hair, brown eyes, a high-class model's walk. Do you know how models walk?"

"Yes."

"She came into the shop one day with this sweet sweet smile on her face, and she asked for fourteen pounds of eye round. I explained to her that a rib roast would be better if she was planning on so big a party. We got to talking. I'm just a butcher. I

189

start with meat, and from meat I go to other things. We got to talking about parties. She said she liked small parties better than big parties. I said I liked small parties, too. That was the beginning. And now, after three months, it's almost the end."

"Is she married?" Larry asked.

"Oh, certainly. Her husband is a salesman. He sells steel. He's away two weeks out of every three. I was seeing more of her than I saw of Betty. She's the sweetest thing alive, and she loves me, and I used to love her. But that's all over now. I only want to get her off my back now."

He talks differently, Larry thought, when he is Felix Anders, Conqueror.

He warned me not to confide, but he's confiding in me, telling me everything, explaining Felix Anders, Conqueror. The other Felix is only the mask. The Felix Anders who stands coolly distant on a station platform is not this man in armor. He is only the mask donned for society. Betty and the children are part of that mask. But this Felix Anders is a hero. This Felix Anders was born two thousand years too late. He should be wearing a beard, and a plumed hat, and a sword. He should be laying his way across France, barmaid by barmaid.

"I never kid myself, Larry," Felix said. "I always recognize that moment when it's over. I always know when I'm falling out of love."

"It seems to me you're never really *in* love," Larry said.

"What's love?" Felix asked. "Do you know?"

"I'm not sure."

"Then how can you say I'm never in love?"

"Love is mutual and equal pleasure, I suppose," Larry said. "But whose pleasure comes first?"

"It has to be equal," Larry said. "In fact, the other person's pleasure might even be more important to you than your own."

"There's the mistake," Felix said. "*My* pleasure comes first. A woman is a woman, and I never forget that. When I start forgetting it, I always ask myself, 'How would you like to be married to this girl? Do you think it'd be any different from being married to Betty?' And I always get the same answer."

"And what's that?"

"No."

"Well . . . I sometimes wonder what it would be like. Being married to her."

"Get it out of your mind. You're crazy."

"Maybe I am, Felix. All I know is that this isn't the kind of stuff you've been talking about. This isn't just another streetcar. This is it."

"It?" Felix laughed. "What's *it*?"

"This. What I have. What she has. What we've got together. This is it."

"It'll pass," Felix said. "This, too, shall pass."

"I hope not."

"You're stupid. If you were smart, you'd pull out right this minute. You'd go to that phone and call her and say, 'Goodbye, Blondie, it's been swell.' That's what you'd do."

"I can't. I love her."

"Everything about her?"

"No. Not everything."

"What does she look like?"

"She's the most beautiful girl I've ever known."

"Oh, brother!" Felix said.

"I'm talking objectively. Wherever we go, men look at her. You can't miss her, Felix. It embarrasses me sometimes."

"They smell it on her. They smell ripeness."

"No, that's not it. She's beautiful."

"All right, she's beautiful. What *don't* you like about her?"

"A lot of things."

"Do they bother you? Would you like to change them?"

"Yes."

"Brother, pull out now. Take my advice. You're heading for a lot of trouble."

"No," Larry said. He shook his head. "I can't."

In the finished basement of Felix Anders' house, they talked. It was the end of February, and they knew each other well enough to talk easily, but with no real friendship between them. Larry had told Eve he'd wanted a look at the finished basement about which he'd heard so much. He'd planned to walk up to the center with Felix, but Betty had gone to a movie with a neighbor, and so they sat downstairs and smoked and talked without friendship in a friendly manner.

"You know the old gag," Felix said. "It's the same as that."

"Which gag?"

"This fellow comes home to his wife, and he's undressing, and there's a big lipstick imprint on his undershorts. A big red pair of lips! Well, his wife sees it, points to it, and shouts, 'There's lipstick on your undershorts!' The fellow looks down at it. Then he looks up at his wife. Then, with a surprised look on his face, he says, 'Hey, how 'bout that?'"

Larry burst out laughing, and Felix chuckled at his own joke.

"It's just what I was telling you," he said. "Bluff it through. There's only one person in your house who knows the truth, and that's you. Your wife is only guessing. Even if someone actually *sees* you with Blondie, your wife won't want to believe it. If you know you've been seen, come home and beat her to the punch. *Tell her first.* Tell her you ran into an old high-school chum and bought her a drink, and she's married now and has four kids and lives in Richmond Hills with her dentist husband. Lie your way out of it. The bigger the lie, the better. The only thing you can't lie your way out of is actually being caught right in that bed. And that practically never happens."

"I don't like lying," Larry said. "I'll never enjoy that part of it."

"It's a necessity, part of the game. What can you do? You've *got* to lie. For example, suppose you come home some night smelling of perfume."

"She doesn't wear perfume any more."

"Some night she'll wear it, believe me. She'll want to send you home stinking of her, just to make you squirm, just to show your wife that *she* owns you too. Believe me, Larry, she'll do it. Especially if her husband's not home. Then she can pour the stuff on without having to explain why she's wearing Tabu to a civic association meeting. Does he work nights?"

"No."

"What is he? A white-collar worker? No? A factory worker? It doesn't matter. Some night he'll be out, and she'll climb into that car reeking of perfume. 'I just didn't think,' she'll say. Ha!"

"How can I lie my way out of perfume?"

"Oh, simple. On the way home, stop off at a drugstore and buy a bottle for Eve. Tell her the salesgirl, stupid idiot, offered you a sniff and then spilled it accidentally on your shirt front."

"I see."

"If you get lipstick on your handkerchief, throw it out."

"She takes her lipstick off."

"Some night she'll smear it on as thick as warpaint. Especially if her husband isn't home. He works nights, did you say?"

"No. No, he doesn't."

"But he's a factory worker?"

"Yes."

"Sure," Felix answered. "She'll get lipstick on you because she'll be getting tired of hiding. Isn't her love as real as Eve's? Why should *she* have to hide it? She's a woman, Larry, a woman! And they're all the same. I try to carry a clean shirt in the trunk of my car. Sometimes it comes in handy. Has she marked you yet?"

"What?"

"Marked you? Bitten you? Sent you home bruised for your wife to see?"

"No."

"She will. It's another way of claiming you. If you want to keep her, Larry, you've got to be careful for both of you. For your own protection."

"She isn't like that," Larry said.

"She will be. Look, you've got this beautiful blonde who lives right here in this development, right?"

"Well . . ."

192

"She's married, and she's got a young son. That's what you said, wasn't it?"

Larry shrugged.

"Her husband's a factory worker! And you're an architect, probably the best thing that ever happened to her. She wants you. She's going to do everything in her power to get you. Watch out."

"You've got it all wrong."

"Have I? Women are women. And I know women."

"Well, I think you've got *this* woman wrong."

"Have I? I know this woman pretty well."

"Sure, sure," Larry said, smiling.

"I can even tell you her name," Felix said.

The smile dropped from Larry's face. He sat speechless, but Felix wasn't waiting for an answer.

"Margaret Gault," Felix said, grinning.

21

MARCH came in like a daisy.

White with mild snow flurries that touched the pavement, lingered gently kissing, and then were gone. Yellow with unexpected, unseasonably bright sunshine that seemed anomalous without forsythias in bloom. Green with anxious bulbs pushing their way through frozen soil. In the city, people shed their overcoats and walked with a jaunty perkiness in their step. It had been a short winter and a mild one, and soon it would be spring.

When the telephone rang, Roger Altar was in the shower. He mumbled something about it never failing, wrapped a towel around his waist, and then went dripping into the room which served as his office. Viciously he snapped the receiver from its cradle, and viciously he said, "Hello?"

"Rog?"

"Who's this?"

"Bert."

"What the hell do you want, Bert?"

"Nice greeting."

Bert Dannerdorf was Altar's agent, a small man with bright brown eyes and a stable of successful writers. Altar was number-two horse in the stable, number-one horse being a mystery writer who outsold even Hemingway.

Dannerdorf was a good agent in that he spoke, ate, drank and slept with editors and publishers. He talked of his clients while he was eating and drinking and perhaps even when he was sleeping. There was a time when Bert had been a sideshow barker at the

World's Fair. He was no longer selling Tanya the Snake Girl but he was still giving his spiel. Broken down, his spiel said, "My writers are the best in the world," and Bert never let you forget it.

He particularly reminded you of it when you were ready to purchase a property. When that moment came, Dannerdorf became the meanest, shrewdest, toughest son of a bitch in the United States. Even if his client were a run-down Western writer who lived in a Wyoming shack, when it came time to close that deal Bert acted as if the man were—at that very moment, in the dust-swept Wyoming shack—preparing his acceptance speech for the Nobel Prize.

Roger Altar didn't particularly care for business. Bert Dannerdorf thrived on it. Like Jack Spratt and his wife, they made a formidable pair.

"What the hell do you want, Bert?" Altar said. "I was in the shower."

"Dry off, and I'll call you back later."

"Call me back, my ass. The floor's soaking wet already."

"It's nothing important anyway," Bert said.

"What is it?"

"That assignment of copyright."

"What assignment of copyright?"

"You know. On 'The Mouse Trap.' That short-short you had in *Esquire*?"

"Well, what about it?" Altar asked impatiently, watching the spreading puddle at his feet.

"Nothing. We just got the assignment of copyright. In case we ever want to use it in a collection or something."

"Great!" Altar said. "Call me sometime when I'm in bed with a girl and tell me I misplaced a comma. Do that, Bert."

"Well, I'll be talking to you," Bert said, chuckling. He seemed ready to hang up. "Oh, yes, there was one other thing," he said.

"What?" Altar asked wearily.

In a rush, unable to hold it back any longer, Bert said, "We just sold serial rights to *The Fall of a Stone* for fifty thousand dollars!"

"What!" Altar said.

"To *Good House*. A five-part serial. How does that sound? You glad I got you out of the shower?"

"Yeah, I'll say."

"Okay. Who's the best literary agent in America?"

"William Morris," Altar answered.

"Screw you," Bert said. "They offered forty, and I jacked them up to fifty. That's agenting."

"Agenting is getting an assignment of copyright on 'The Mouse Trap,'" Altar said. "That's *real* agenting."

"No gratitude," Bert said jokingly. "Picked him up out of the gutter. Aw, no gratitude."

194

"I love you," Altar said. "Send the check."

"It's good news, isn't it, Rog? Seriously."

"It's great news. Good work, Bert."

"Any trouble on this check tax-wise? They're paying it in two installments, but both'll be this year."

"So what can we do?"

"I can deposit part of it for you."

"That's illegal," Altar said.

"You're so legal?"

"I'm legal. I don't want to be writing from Cell 21."

"Okay. Go write another book. I want a new Cadillac."

"How long a book?"

"Three hundred, four hundred pages."

"When do you want it?"

"Tonight too early?" Bert asked.

"No, fine," Altar said, "but first I want to finish my shower."

Bert chuckled, and Altar chuckled, both men captured in the glowing camaraderie of just having made fifty thousand simoleons. At last they said goodbye, and Altar hung up.

He stood looking at the cradled receiver for a few moments, and then he stood looking at the puddle of water on the floor. In an exciting instant of sudden awareness, he thought, It's started!

And then he went into the bathroom to finish his shower.

With the weather changing around them, they felt the need for more time together, more time to share. They had known autumn, and then winter, and now spring was rushing up to greet them, and they wanted to hold it close.

He told Eve that Altar wanted a sudden change in the plans, a change which might prove difficult now that the foundation had been poured. Allegedly, he was to meet Altar in the city for dinner and then thrash out the problem until it was solved—even if it took all night. Maggie told Don she was going to a dinner-baby shower in Brooklyn, and that she would not be home until very late. He'd offered to drive her, but she saw no need to pay for a baby sitter, especially when all the girls were meeting at the house of a girl in the next development who would drive them all to Brooklyn.

They met at five-thirty.

It was one of those days. It was just one of those days. The air was mild and balmy, and you wanted to say hello to strangers. You wanted to find a place where you could pick wild flowers. You wanted to kiss the air. It was just one of those days.

They had called Pat, the motel owner, and asked him to save a cabin for them, and he'd promised he would. It was only five-thirty, and the evening and the night were ahead of them. He was wearing a dark-blue suit with no topcoat, it was that mild, and she wore a red dress with a scoop neckline and cap sleeves, simulated ruby earrings on her ears. She looked quite beautiful and he felt very handsome in his blue suit. They felt as if they were really going out. It was strange, but this Tuesday night had the air of an occasion.

They ate at a small place with a pond and swans. There was candlelight at the table, and he ordered martinis first, with *olives* please, and the waiter brought them martinis with lemon peels, please. When they repeated their request for olives, he brought them a soup bowl full of olives. They each put four into their drinks and then ordered steaks and a bottle of Burgundy.

She did not do justice to the meal. She confessed later that she'd had a bite with Don before leaving the house; it was bad enough she'd rushed out like that, the least she could do was have dinner waiting for him when he got home from work. But she watched Larry eating, and she sipped at the Burgundy, and the color of the wine caught the color of her mouth and the glowing red of the earrings so that he leaned over the table once and kissed her fleetingly. They talked about everything they'd done that week, like a husband and wife who've been separated and have hundreds of stories to relate.

They talked and drank and smoked, and they watched dusk fingering the pond, watched the swans' white down turn blue-purple smoky as the late sun faded. When they finished their meal, they walked around the pond to the car. A piano was going in the cocktail lounge, and they listened to "I'll Remember April." Neither spoke. He walked with his arm around her; she with her head on his shoulder.

They did not see the yellow Buick which pulled out behind them when they left the restaurant.

On the way to the motel, she remembered that she'd promised to call Don when she got to Brooklyn. They drove until they spotted a small roadhouse with the round telephone plaque outside. The place was one of those which never seem to do any business. The dining room was off to the left, dim except for a small light burning over a separate entrance door at the far end. There were no diners in the room. The telephone booth was set against the wall near the swinging doors to the kitchen. Maggie squeezed his hand and walked toward the booth; Larry went into the bar to get a package of cigarettes from the machine there. The bar was empty, except for the bartender. When he got his cigarettes, he sat at the bar, his back to it. Through the windows, he saw a yellow Buick pull off the road and then cut in to park alongside the dining room.

He sat for a few moments, noticed the juke box, went over to it, and studied the selections. He wondered if he should play a record while Maggie was talking to Don. Well, she was supposed to be at a shower. Surely girls at a shower could play music. He made his selection and went back to the stool.

"Help you, sir?" the bartender asked.

"No, thanks," he said.

He opened the package of cigarettes, lighted one, and blew out a great cloud of smoke. Sitting and smoking, he listened to the record. When it ended, he put another coin in the juke and made another selection. It did not occur to him until the second record had spun through that Maggie was taking an inordinately long time in the phone booth. His first thought was that Don was giving her static. Figuring she could use some moral support, he stubbed out his cigarette and started for the dining room.

The boy was no older than nineteen.

He wore khaki trousers and a sports shirt. The door to the phone booth was open, and the boy was leaning into the opening.

The boy said, "Margaret, all I want . . ."

Larry quickened his step.

Maggie was sitting in the booth motionless. Her purse was in her lap, and her hands were clasped over the purse. She was looking at the floor of the booth, not raising her eyes to meet the gaze of the muscular young man who stood hulking over her. Larry walked directly to the booth.

"Did you want something, Bud?" he asked.

The boy did not turn. Without looking at Larry, he said, "Shove off."

He was as tall as Larry, heavier, with bright red hair, huge arms, and a barrel chest. He stood with his broad back to Larry, his arms widespread, a palm against each side of the booth as he leaned into the opening. Completely ignoring Larry, he said, "All I want you to tell me is—"

"The lady's with me," Larry said. "Get away from her."

The boy turned. His eyes flicked Larry in a fast appraisal. "You can go to hell," he said. "I've been waiting a long time to—" and Larry hit him.

He hit him quite suddenly, almost before he knew what he was doing. He brought up his left fist and threw it forward in a short sharp furious jab that caught the boy on the point of his chin and sent him staggering from the booth to collide with the wall.

The boy pushed himself from the wall, cocked his fists, took a step forward, and said, "Okay, mister. You asked for it." And then he lunged at Larry.

He first blow caught Larry on the side of his face, and he felt shocking pain as he backed away. The second punch hit him in the gut, as painful as the first, but with a dangerous accompanying effect. The second punch brought instant rage to Larry's throat and eyes. In the space of three seconds, all of his war training came back to him. He planted his feet solidly, balanced himself, and curled his fists into hard, tight, destructive weapons. He knew that if this boy threw another punch at him, he would

197

kill him. He would strike at his Adam's apple and kill him. His fists balled, he waited for the boy's attack.

The boy hesitated in mid-stride.

"Come on," Larry said. There was barely controlled fury in his voice. His body strained forward as he waited. His eyes were unblinking, cold with menace. Perhaps the boy saw what was in Larry's eyes. The attack did not come. Instead, the boy lowered his hands.

"Come on!" Larry said.

The boy did not move. Fear mingled with shame on his face, and then his shoulders seemed to collapse in total defeat. "All right!" he said, seemingly on the verge of tears, but he did not move. "All right, it's over. All right, all right, it's over," and still he did not move.

Larry waited. The boy's embarrassment and defeat made him curiously sad. There seemed to be countless things the boy wanted to say, but he only kept repeating senselessly, "All right, it's over; all right, it's over," and then he turned abruptly and ran for the door at the far end of the room. The door slammed shut behind him. The room was still. Larry turned to the booth where Maggie sat motionless.

"Are you all right?" he asked.

Maggie nodded, but she did not look at him. Outside, an automobile started. Tires grasped shriekingly at gravel.

"Come," he said gently. He took her hand and led her out of the booth. The yellow Buick was gone when they got outside.

In the car, he asked, "What happened?"

She was sitting silently close to him while he drove, her hands clasped over her purse. "He came in the side door after I was talking a while," she said. "He waited until I was finished, and then he wouldn't let me out of the booth. Did he hurt you?"

"No. What did he want?"

"If you're bruised, you'll have to explain it to—"

"What did he want?"

"The same thing they all want," Maggie said softly.

"All? How often does this kind of thing happen?"

"Often enough. Forget it, Larry, please. You were very sweet and foolish, and I appreciate it. But please forget it. I'm used to it."

"Used to what?" He felt extremely naïve all at once, and yet the idea of other men approaching her had never occurred to him. "Men annoying you?"

"Yes. Men annoying me."

"But why should—"

"Why do you think?" she asked. "Larry, can we please drop this? I'm sorry, but it's very upsetting. Every time it happens, I get—"

"You sound as if you're approached ten times a day!"

"I am."

"By whom? Which men?"

"Any men. All men. Men, Larry. Men!" She paused and then said, "Oh, Larry, forget it, please. What difference does it make? I'm what I am. Sometimes I wish I were ugly. Sometimes I hate my face and my smile and my hips and my breasts, these damn—" She shook her head. "Forget it. I'm used to it by now. Men are men, and they want what they want."

"Does that include me?" he asked.

"I *love* you," she said simply.

"You didn't always."

"No. And you also saw what you wanted and asked for it, didn't you?"

"And *got* it," Larry said.

"The rest don't."

"How do I know that?"

"Oh, please don't sound like a suspicious husband. You're the only one, believe me. Everyone else looks and tries to touch, but you're the only one who—"

"How'd that boy know your name?" Larry asked abruptly.

"He didn't."

"He did. He called you 'Margaret.' I heard him."

"He probably heard me say 'This is Margaret' when I started speaking to Don."

"You said he came in after you were talking a while. How could he have heard the beginning of the conversation?"

"No, he came in while I was dialing."

"You know him, don't you?" Larry said.

"No."

"Who is he?"

"I never saw him before in my life."

"Who is he, Maggie?"

"I don't know."

"You do know. Why are you lying to me?"

"Stop it, Larry. Please."

"I want to know."

"What gives you the right to know?"

"I thought you loved me."

"I do," she said.

"Then that's my right."

"And when you know? What then? Goodbye, Maggie?"

"Why? Is the truth so terrible?"

"The truth is always terrible. You're upset because men make *passes* at me. What happens when you find out—"

". . . that I'm not the only one? That the boy I hit has been—"

"He hasn't!"

"Then what is it? What are you hiding?"

She moved away from him to the opposite side of the car. Her lashes fluttered, and she seemed nervous and confused all at once, and he wanted to take her into his arms and comfort her. She lighted a cigarette inexpertly, blew out a puff of smoke, and then pulled her legs up under her on the seat, her skirt pulling back slightly over a nylon-sleek knee. Desire came full upon him in that moment. In that moment he did not want to hear her, he only wanted to hold her. And seeing his eyes, she said, "Go ahead, touch me. See if I'm real."

"Maggie . . ."

"If it annoys you, it annoys me more. I don't like it, not one damn bit. But don't blame other men for making the same assumption you made, and still make. And don't blame me."

"Tell me about the boy," he said.

"Sure." She sighed heavily. "In July . . ."

She was starting a story. She had said "In July" like "Once upon a time," and he knew from the first two words that the story would be extremely painful to her. He kept his hands tight on the wheel and his eyes riveted to the road ahead.

"Don came home one day. He had a chance to become a foreman. The factory wanted to send him to school in Detroit." She spoke as if by rote, as if she had gone over these words in her mind until they were bare of all emotion, all meaning. "He didn't want to go unless I said it was all right. I let him go. A woman shouldn't stand in her husband's way. He left. Right after the Fourth. It was a very hot Fourth, Larry. Do you remember?"

He did not answer. He was hearing the pain in her voice, and he wanted to tell her to stop, but he could not.

"It was a very hot Fourth," she repeated. "A hot summer, too. I can remember, just standing still I would sweat. I sweat very easily. I took a lot of baths. I like baths. I always . . ." She stopped and sighed again. "But that summer, in July . . ."

She had not really begun the story yet. She was back to the beginning again, back to the words "In July." He glanced at the speedometer and had the strangest feeling that the sands were running out all at once, that this would be the last car ride, and the last words he ever heard from her.

"I was very lonely. I told you that the first time in your car. Before you asked me out, I told you that. After Don'd been gone only a week, I was lonely. Patrick was with my mother at Montauk Point. I was alone. Things hadn't been going right with Don, there'd been a boat ride in June . . . and . . . and maybe they've never gone right between him and me, and maybe they never will. I don't know, Larry, but I missed him. And . . . and it was a very hot summer. Larry, do I have to tell you this?"

"Not if you don't want to."

"I don't want to."

"All right."

"But you have to know, don't you? Men always have to

200

know. You have to be certain the *aroma* isn't on me." A bitterness had crept into her voice. For a moment he had the odd feeling she was no longer addressing him but some unknown specter. "All right," she said wearily. "I was sitting outside one day, on the front stoop."

"You don't have to tell me."

"On the front stoop," she said. "The streets were very quiet, even all the children seemed to have disappeared, and all the women. I don't know. I had the feeling I was the last person alive on earth. I was wearing shorts and a halter, it was so hot, Larry, I wasn't trying to show off my body or anything, honestly, I *hate* to wear a bathing suit, I detest hungry eyes on me, I *abhor* it! I wore shorts and a halter because it was so hot, that's all, only because it was so hot. And I wouldn't have been sitting on the front stoop if there'd been any shade in the back yard. Do you believe me?"

"Why shouldn't I?"

"I don't want you to think I was asking for anything. I never do, and I wasn't then. I was sitting on my own front stoop, that's all. I had my arms wrapped around my knees, and I had my hair back with a little ribbon to keep it off my face because it was so hot. The streets were empty and hot. And then a truck came around the corner."

She caught her breath sharply.

"I don't know if I can explain it. It was like feeling there was another survivor after an atom-bomb attack, another human being, do you know what I mean?"

"Yes."

"The truck slowed down when it passed the house. There was a young boy behind the wheel."

"Him?"

"Yes. Him." She paused. "He smiled at me . . . and I smiled back. That was all. I swear to God, there was no more than that. He smiled, and it was a hot summer day, and I was lonely, and so I smiled back. That's all, Larry, nothing more. He looked at me, and at the house, and then the truck went down the street, and that was the end of it. For then."

"What happened?"

"He came back."

"When?"

"The next night. I was ironing in the living room, and there was a knock on the door. I went to the door and opened it, and he was standing there. He said, 'Hello. Can I have a drink of water?' She shrugged slightly as if once again faced with the simple inevitability of the boy's request. "I got him a glass of water."

"Go ahead."

201

Her voice was very low now. He had to strain to hear it, a whisper in the tight silence of the automobile.

"His name was Buck. Buck what, I don't know. I never asked. I never want to know. Ever. I wish I didn't even know his first name. I wish I'd never seen him, never smiled at him, never let him into my house."

She stopped talking, and again he waited, and at last she sighed and went on.

"He stayed a while. We sat in the living room. I ironed, and he talked to me. He was driving the truck for his father. They carted top soil for developers. They . . ."

"Get to it, Maggie!"

"He kissed me."

She glanced at Larry quickly. His eyes were on the road.

"Before he left. We were standing at the door, and I was saying good night, and suddenly he grabbed me. He was trembling all over, like a baby. He . . . he kissed me."

"Did you kiss him back?"

"No. I didn't know how to kiss before I met you. You know that." She paused. "I didn't want him to kiss me, but I couldn't stop him. Finally, he left."

The car went silent. Larry felt instant relief. He turned to her and said, "Is that what was so terri—"

"There's more."

His hands tightened on the wheel. The long silence before she spoke again seemed interminable.

"I . . . I got ready for bed after he was gone. I was in bed when the phone rang. It was him. He said he was coming over. I told him I was in bed. He said he was coming over. I told him he was crazy, that I'd call the police. He said he was coming over. I didn't know what to do. It was late by this time, midnight at least, maybe later. I couldn't disturb any of my neighbors, I was all alone in the house, Don in Detroit, Patrick with his grandmother. I didn't know what to do."

"Why *didn't* you call the police?"

"And let it become the talk of the development? How could I? I locked all the doors instead. Every single one. Then I took some sleeping pills and I—"

"Sleeping pills! When you knew he was on his way? For Christ's sake, why'd you—"

"I wanted to sleep! I couldn't think of anything else to do, I was so frightened. Larry, I couldn't *think* of anything else. I . . . I took two pills. I keep them. My doctor says it's all right. Sometimes I can't sleep."

"Go ahead," he said tightly, frowning.

"I was almost asleep when I heard his car pull up. The yellow Buick. He got out and came to the front door and rang, but I didn't get out of bed. I was half drugged, anyway. I couldn't

202

have got up if I'd wanted to. He tried the front door and then he rang the bell again, and then I thought he went away. I didn't know he was walking around to the back on the grass. I didn't realize that. Until I heard him try the kitchen door. And then I heard the door *open*!

"I couldn't understand it! I thought I'd locked every door, but he had got into the house. He called 'Margaret' from downstairs, and I lay in bed unable to move, half drugged. I was naked, Larry, it was so hot in the room, there was something wrong with the air conditioner. I tried to fight sleep. I don't remember him coming upstairs, I don't remember him getting into bed with me. I only remember him grabbing me and kissing my closed eyes and my breasts and—"

"For Christ's sake, stop it!"

". . . kissing me everywhere, everywhere, and then I began to wake up, began to come out of it a little, and I tried to fight him but it was too late by then, too late."

Caustically, Larry said, "How was it?"

"It was horrible, a horrible nightmare. It was a rape, Larry, don't you understand that?"

"No, I don't understand it. Why'd you take those pills?"

"To escape him!"

"How'd you forget to lock an entrance door?"

"I forgot!"

"Did he tell you he loved you?"

"Yes."

"And did you tell him you loved him?"

"No! I've never told that to anyone but my grandfather and you!"

"You're lying."

"I'm not lying, I'm not, do you think I wanted to tell you this, you asked me to, do you think I enjoyed what he did to me, do you think I enjoyed getting *raped*, damnit, do you think it was fun?"

"Why'd you leave the door open?"

"I thought it was locked."

"A goddamn door is either locked or it isn't! You *wanted* him to get into that house!"

"No, no, I didn't."

"You wanted him to find you. That's why you took the pills, so that you couldn't fight him, couldn't resist him!"

"No, no!"

"You went through all the motions—"

"Stop it, stop it!"

". . . but you wanted him to take you. Goddamnit, Maggie, you wanted to be—"

"*All right!*" she screamed. "I wanted to be raped. I was a bitch in heat, all right? The stink of it was on me, all right? It went out to all men everywhere, it filled their nostrils, it suffocated them with the stink of my hunger, all right? I wanted him, I wanted him, *I wanted him!*"

"You're a whore," he said, and without taking his eyes from the road, he lashed out at her in a backhanded slap which caught her on the side of her face and sent her reeling back against the seat.

"You fool," she said.

"Shut up!"

"You damn stupid fool, you damn idiot. Don't you know you're still the first man, no matter what happened? Don't you know you're the *only* man? Oh, you stupid, stupid . . ."

She began crying suddenly and fitfully. He had never seen her cry before, and the sight amazed him. Her misery was complete, the fullest misery he had ever seen on the face of a woman. It was as if, secure in the beauty of her face, she could allow it to crumble completely, allow it to dissolve without mercy, permit it to twist in uncontrollable sorrow.

"Cut it out," he said.

"I've . . . lost . . . you."

"Cut it out!"

"I've lost you! I've lost you!"

She moved suddenly toward him, a surprisingly swift motion, throwing herself into his arms so that he was forced to take one hand from the wheel to support the sudden weight of her body. The car swerved out of control for an instant, and then he recaptured the wheel, and her head was on his chest, and she was still weeping bitterly, gasping for breath.

"Tell me it doesn't matter," she said.

Doesn't it matter? he asked himself. Doesn't it matter that she's been had, didn't I suspect it in the beginning, be honest, wasn't it this about her which attracted me to her in the first place, didn't I *know* she could be had?

"Tell me you still love me," she said.

Love you? he thought. Do I love you? I'm mad as hell, I could kill that son of a bitch if he was here, I could kill him, I've turned into a fine man, a fine upstanding citizen, I hit young kids and defenseless women, the hero, the great god Cole! But do I love you? Where's the *end* of this, Maggie? Where the hell was the beginning? When do we ever start knowing each other, when do we ever progress beyond strangers in the straw, or should we, *should we*? I'm angry, and all right it's juvenile! I'm angry, and maybe it's a throwback to my first concept of womanhood, the mother's tit, the pure symbol of lily-white virginal security, but I'm still angry, and where the hell does it all lead, where does it end? If the redheaded kid had you, and if I had you, how many others can have you and will have you, goddamnit Felix Anders is right, Felix Anders is the sage of the century!

"Tell me," she said. "Please. Please."

Or maybe I want out, he thought. Maybe I've never loved her, maybe it always was biology and always will be biology, is that all life amounts to, is that all love amounts to, am I in love with Maggie or am I a statistic in the Kinsey Report?

"Tell me," she pleaded. "Tell me."

Sure, he thought, I'll tell you. I'll tell you it's over, Maggie, finished. It's over because I can't understand it any more, it's too complicated, too involved, it's strangling me, Maggie, I can't breathe! I know you all these months, and I haven't begun to know you, and I'm angry and I'm sad and I want to cry and I want to fight, and I love you, I don't know how you can do these things to me, how you can rip me up with a dagger, cut out my guts, leave me bleeding and crying and still loving you, still knowing I can't live without you, still wanting you and needing you, goddamnit why do I need you so much, Maggie, why do I need you, you slut, you bitch, you animal, I love you, I love you.

She sat up suddenly, as if by intuition, as if she had read his thoughts and knew his mind. She yanked the wheel sharply to the right, and the car bumped over the shallow concrete rim at the side of the road, and then rolled to a stop on the grass.

He began to shake his head, but she brought her mouth very close to his lips, and her eyes glowed in the darkness, and she said, "Love me, Larry. Now!"

And he seized her to him roughly.

22

LAWN talk was in the air. You could smell it. It was not yet April, but lawn talk was just ready to burst from everyone's mouth.

Felix Anders sucked secretly at the late March air.

The forsythias, encouraged by the mild weather, were banked in yellow fury around the six-room ranch he called his home. The emaciated tree on the front lawn was beginning to bud. White billowy clouds hung in the fair blue sky. Felix Anders sucked at the air, looking very much like a man who'd just returned home after the twelve o'clock Mass. He had, in fact, just come back from church. Felix considered himself a devout Catholic even though he did not believe in confession or birth control. He had made his peace with his faith, and he never ate meat on Fridays, nor did he ever miss Sunday Mass.

On this Sunday in late March he secretly sucked the balmy air into his lungs.

The model was behind Felix now. The parting had truly been

a sorrowful one, worthy of a major film by a major movie company, complete with that last long heart-rending sigh, oozing with the terrible bittersweet knowledge of star-crossed impossibility. He could see the final scene now, almost as if it were already in the can and waiting for national distribution. The limpid eyes meeting, the unspoken words *I'll Always Love You*. Pause. *Even Though This Can Never Be*. Double pause.

The model steps sorrowfully out of the Oldsmobile Felix Anders owns. For a moment her thigh winks at him, and he remembers again the finite pleasures of her body, the infinite treasures of her mind, remembers for only a fleeting instant. She walks away from him then, out of his life. He watches her sadly. He waves. Music up and under.

Felix sets the Oldsmobile in motion. He drives down a Cinemascope road lined with tall poplars into a Technicolor sunset. The words THE END, written on the wind, superimpose themselves over the car as it moves into the distance, farther, farther, farther, and is gone.

THE END
The End
The end
The end
The end

It was over.

Felix, the suburban father still wearing his blue Sunday Mass suit, walked the length of his property holding the hand of his three-year-old son Bruce. He scrutinized the length and breadth of his seventy-by-a-hundred corner plot with the uncompromising eye of a patroon. He could feel spring pulsing in the air, rushing through his blood, singing in his veins. Felix Anders was ready for love again. Patroon-like, he studied his real estate.

"Brucie," he said quietly, "spring is coming."

Brucie, who was walking at the moment with a full diaper, nodded and repeated, "Sp'ing."

"Stop beating your sister, Brucie," Felix said. "Love her. Spring is coming."

"Love," Brucie repeated.

The development seemed alive again after the siege of winter. All around him Felix could see people putting in shrubs and plants, people liming, giving their lawns a pre-seasonal mowing, putting up screens, painting fences. With faint superiority, he looked about him. He glanced at the women only briefly. Everyone in the development knew that Felix Anders was a reticently cold gentleman who was devoted to his explosive wife. Nothing in Felix's glance contradicted this supposition. God, they look sweet, he thought. No more winter coats now, only sweaters and slacks, nice round little backsides and nice rounded breasts. God, women are sweet!

Across the street, behind the Cape Cod, he could see Don Gault working with a shovel. Felix looked in both directions before he crossed the street, somewhat disdainfully, as if he knew no vehicle would have the audacity to run him down. He walked past the Gault garage and then onto the grass to where Don was digging outside the kitchen windows. He did not say hello. Felix very rarely said hello first.

"Hi, Felix," Don said, wielding the shovel.

It amused Felix that Larry Cole was having an affair with Don's wife. It amused him greatly that a Tarzan-muscled he-man like Don Gault had a wife who was running around. It was with remarkable restraint that Felix did not burst out laughing in Don's face.

"Hello there, Gault," he said. "Digging a garden?"

"No," Don said. "I'm putting in a patio." He rested the shovel against his hip, and then wiped sweat from his forehead. "It sure is hot for March, isn't it?" he said.

"Very unseasonable weather," Felix agreed. "A concrete patio?"

"No, bricks. I'm going to lay a bed of sand, and then set the bricks in it."

"I see," Felix said.

The situation was rather hilarious. Felix hummed with the secret hilarity of it. He could not think of a more enjoyable situation than discussing patios with Don Gault when he knew Margaret Gault was running around with Larry. The entire concept was almost too comical to contain.

Don put the shovel down and reached into his pants pocket. Pulling out a package of cigarettes, he said, "Smoke?"

"Thank you," Felix said. "I'm trying to cut down."

"Live it up a little," Don said. "Go ahead, have one."

"No, thank you," Felix repeated. "It's my only weakness, and I'm really trying to cut down."

"It takes a lot of will power," Don said. "The temptation is always there. Does your wife smoke?"

"Yes."

"Mine does, too. Not a lot, but there are always cigarettes in the house. It's a great temptation."

"Yes, I know what you mean," Felix said. He thought about temptation, and he thought about Don Gault's wife, and he had trouble keeping a straight face. He felt somewhat like God. The thought gave him no religious qualms. Today, on this day so close to spring, with his secret knowledge humming within him, talking to Don Gault, he felt somewhat like God.

"How *is* Margaret?" he asked kindly.

"Oh, just fine," Don said. "Same as ever."

"And Patrick?"

"Fine," Don said. "You don't mind if I smoke, do you?"

"No, no," Felix answered, "go right ahead."

Don lighted the cigarette and returned the package to his pocket. "You ought to learn to relax, Felix," he said. He did not say it unkindly, but immediately afterward he added, "Don't take offense."

"No offense," Felix said, smiling benignly.

"You always seem so . . . tense."

"I'm not tense at all."

"Well, dignified then. That's what I mean."

Felix smiled. "I don't see anything wrong with maintaining a little dignity, Don."

"I didn't mean that," Don said. He picked up the shovel. "You should live it up more. Get to know people. You're a hard guy to get to know."

"Really?" Felix asked. He smiled pleasantly. "Well, my life's an open book, Don. I'm a butcher. I work in Manhattan. I live right here in Pinecrest Manor with the most wonderful woman in the world, and three adorable kids. I'm a happy man." He paused. "Maybe I am a little quiet and introspective sometimes. Perhaps I think about things too much. But I'm sorry I give the impression of being difficult to know."

"Well, maybe I was mistaken."

"I guess a man like me becomes so involved with his own family that he forgets about his neighbors. I'm certainly sorry if I gave you the wrong impression."

"No, no, forget it," Don said. "Please, forget it." He drew in on his cigarette. "How's Betty?"

"Fine, thank you."

"The kids?" Don asked, looking down at Brucie and tousling his hair.

"All in fine shape," Felix said.

"Good, good."

Both men were silent for a while. Don smoked his cigarette, and Felix hummed secretly with his silent knowledge. Don didn't seem too anxious to get back to work.

"Where's Margaret now?" Felix asked.

"Inside. Napping." Don shrugged. "Lazy Sunday."

"Sleeps a lot, does she?"

"Catches a nap every now and then. You know how women are."

"Certainly." Felix smiled. "Tired, is she?"

"Not tired, just . . . you know. A little sleepy, I guess. You know."

"Sure."

They stood silently for another few moments. At last Felix

said, "Well, I guess I'll be strolling along. Let you get back to digging up that grass.".

"I'll see you," Don said. He stepped on his cigarette and then pushed the point of his shovel into the earth.

"Shobel digger," Brucie said.

"Yes," Felix answered. "Shobel digger." Turn the earth, Don, he thought as he walked away. Don't let any grass grow under your feet. Your sweet wife sure as hell isn't letting any grow under hers.

He almost burst out laughing.

God, it was good to be alive. God, it was wonderful!

"Do you know why she sleeps so much, Brucie?" he asked his son.

"S'eep?" Brucie said.

"Yes, seep. Do you know why?"

"Why?" Brucie asked, annoyed by the diaper, not having the faintest idea what his father was talking about, but humoring him anyway.

"Because when she sleeps, my son, she escapes. She flies to the arms of her lover. That's why. Love. Be a lover, son. When you grow up, love them all."

"Okay," Brucie said, nodding, still not understanding a word his father was saying.

Felix Anders was ready.

He walked the streets of Pinecrest Manor, and he nodded politely to all the busy busy men, and he glanced only briefly at the sweet women in their sweet slacks and sweaters, so rounded, so sweet. He was ready.

When he saw the dark-haired girl, he didn't recognize her at first. She was wearing tapered black slacks, and she was bent over digging into the earth at the front of the house, the black hair hanging girlishly over one eye. She looked very feminine and inexpert and Felix thought, How goddamned sweet women are.

She tossed her hair back then, lifting her head in a youthful, impatient movement, whipping the long black hair back over her shoulder. She was wearing a sweater, and her breasts were gently cradled by the wool, sweet, sweet.

"Oh, hi, Felix," she said. "Taking a little stroll?"

He walked over to her, holding his son's hand. "Out for my constitutional," he said. "What are you doing, Eve?"

"Oh, trying to get something to grow," Eve said. "I've never seen earth as stubborn as Pinecrest Manor's, have you?"

"No," Felix said. He kept watching Eve. There was a faintly bored smile on his mouth, a flicker of awakening intelligence in his green eyes. "You have to work it," he said. He kept watching her. "If you work it, it'll yield."

Smiling, he watched her.

The sweat rolled down Don's muscular arms, staining the handle of the shovel. He worked in old Army fatigue trousers and a khaki undershirt. The sun, so strong for March, beat down on his wide muscular back as he dug into the earth with his spade. There was an oppressively rich aroma to the freshly turned soil.

The memory did not come to him in an instant flash. He supposed later that the memory had been creeping up on him all the while he worked, and that the bird call had simply been the final triggering element to a long line of preceding elements—the Army costume, the hot sun, the smell of earth. He was using the spade with muscular force, pushing the point into the grass sod, shoving at it with the arch of his foot, digging deep, turning the shovel with a powerful wrist motion, getting under the sod and lifting it. He did not want to destroy good grass. He could use the sod to fill in patches on the front lawn. He could feel perspiration on his back and in his armpits and across his forehead, but it felt good to be out working with his hands. Foot by foot, he had measured out the proposed patio, indicated its boundaries with string, and then had begun digging. And all the while he dug, the memory of the island grew stronger and stronger, the rich fetid smell of the earth, the hot sun, the sweat, and then the bird call triggered it.

The leaves had been wet that day, despite the heat of the sun. It was impossible to move through the jungle without getting soaked to the skin. It was hard to breathe in the jungle. The air was dense and still, crowded with the exhalation of growing things, crowded in a tight, hot, timeless green prison. He moved through the jungle alone. He knew the rest of the men in his company were spread out in a wide arc working its way across the face of the island in a mopping-up operation. But if a man moved five feet away from you into the foliage, you could no longer see him. And so, though he knew he was part of a team, he felt alone.

He did not want to use his machete. If he ran across any Japs, he wanted his rifle in his hands where he could fire it instantly. He did not want to be caught swinging a machete by any god-damned Gook. He wanted to be ready. And so he moved cautiously, the machete speared through his belt to the right of the grenades. He wore no pack. He wore jungle issue gear and a netted helmet, and the sweat ran down the sides of his square face, trickled from his strong jaw onto his neck. The stock and barrel of the Browning automatic were moist with jungle sweat. He kept his finger inside the trigger guard, ready to fire. He did not want to be ambushed.

When he came upon the Jap, he was quite surprised.

He would have fired instantly if the Jap had burst from the jungle swinging a sword or leveling a rifle. But he had stumbled upon the enemy completely unaware; perhaps he should have fired the moment he saw him anyway, but he did not.

The Jap was an officer.

He knew that the moment he saw the Samurai sword in his belt and the insignia of his rank on the lapels of his blouse. He could not read the rank, but he knew that no enlisted Japanese soldier wore such insignia. The man was sitting against the trunk of a tree smoking. He carried no rifle. There was a pistol hanging in a holster on his belt. That, and the long Samurai sword. Nothing else.

He had not heard Don. He sat smoking leisurely under the tree, as if the island had not been exposed to bombing and shelling for the past four days, as if a Marine assault wave had not stormed the underwater barbed wire and the concrete pillboxes on the slopes facing the sea, as if the Army had not swarmed ashore and driven the enemy back across the island, as if the simplest mopping-up exercise were not now in operation.

He sat smoking casually. He might have been sitting on an outdoor terrace somewhere in Fukuoko, listening to a woman play a Japanese stringed instrument, watching the sun sink, watching the mountains of his homeland turn purple with dusk. He seemed completely unconcerned with the war, with the island, with the uniform he was wearing. For an instant suspended in time, Don had the strangest urge to walk to the man, sit down beside him, and share a smoke with him. And then the absurdity of the whim struck him. He felt the hackles at the back of his neck rising, felt his scalp begin to prickle beneath the netted helmet.

The Japanese officer looked up.

His eyes locked with Don's. He made no move for either the pistol or the sword. He sat beneath the tree with the thin cigarette curling smoke up past his face. The face was bearded and browned. The cheekbones were high, and the nose was flat, the eyebrows thick and black over hooded Oriental eyes. The man smiled. A gold tooth flashed in the corner of his mouth.

"Ah," he said in English. "At last."

His use of English startled Don. He knew the man was an officer, but he had not expected him to use English, and his knowledge of the language made him seem less the enemy.

"Don't move," Don said.

The man was still smiling. "I won't," he answered. "I've been waiting for you." His English was very good. He had probably been educated in the States, Don thought, and this too lessened the concept of enemy.

"Get up," Don said.

The officer rose. He was very small. He didn't seem more than a boy. It was difficult to judge his age. Don knew an officer couldn't be too young, but the man nonetheless had the stature of a boy, and would have seemed adolescent were it not for the thick black beard and the Oriental eyes—somehow aged, somehow ancient.

"Drop your belt," Don said. "Quick."

The officer continued smiling. He unclasped his belt. The holster, pistol, sword and scabbard fell soundlessly to the jungle floor, cushioned by the lush green mat.

"And now?" the officer asked.

"Hands up," Don said, and immediately wondered if he'd made a mistake, wondered if the Jap were holding primed grenades under his arms, tucked pinless into his armpits.

"You're not going to take a prisoner, are you?"

"Hands up!" Don shouted, still worried about the grenades, but more afraid that the Jap would leap at him. He was sweating heavily now. The sweat was cold. He could feel his fingers trembling inside the trigger guard of the piece.

The officer raised his hands. "Didn't they tell you about taking prisoners?" he asked.

"Shut up," Don said.

The man continued smiling. "I was waiting for you," he said, "because I want to die."

"You shut up," Don said. "Come on, we gotta . . . we gotta move back."

"I want you to shoot me," the officer said.

"Never mind what you want. Come on." He jerked up the BAR. "Come on."

"No," the officer answered, still smiling.

They were separated by five feet of jungle vegetation. They stood opposite each other, and Don swallowed the tight dryness in his throat, and then the bird began shrieking somewhere in the trees, a crazy discordant shriek, CAW-CAW-EEEEEE! EEEEE-CAW! EEEEE-CAW! The jungle reverberated with the terrible music of the bird.

"Come on," Don said.

"Shoot me," the officer said, smiling.

"I ain't gonna—"

"Shoot me, you Yank bastard," the Jap said.

"Look. Look, I gotta take you back to—"

"Shoot me, Yank warmongering bastard. Shoot me!"

The bird continued to shriek. EEE-CAW! EEE-CAW! Except for the bird, the jungle was still. The officer continued smiling. He continued watching Don and talking to him, and smiling while the bird shrieked and shrieked. The BAR was getting heavy. Don's hand was wet on the barrel.

"Come, Yankee son of a bitch, shoot me. Shoot me, you dirty Yank bastard!"

Don swallowed again. He could feel the cords on his neck standing out, could feel his heart drumming in his chest. He was drenched now, soaked, standing with a lethal BAR in his hands, listening to the insane scream of the bird, listening to the rising voice of the officer, the smiling officer who calmly stood waiting

way, but Larry couldn't understand why she felt the need for a heavy coat on a day like this. She was beaming from ear to ear, apparently concerned only with her mother-turtle accomplishment of having parked the car some four feet from the curb. It had not yet occurred to her that the woman with Larry Cole was not his wife, or that the man with Margaret Gault was not her husband.

Anticipating the coming of the dawn, his heart pounding, Larry said, "This is like old home week, isn't it? First I run into Mrs. Gault in the diner, and now we run into you. Would you like a cup of coffee, Mary?"

"No, thank you. How are you, Margaret?"

"Fine," Maggie said. "Isn't this the funniest thing, though? You can walk all over the development without meeting a soul you know, and here the three of us meet miles away from the place." She grinned feebly, wondering if she were driving the point home too hard. She had almost, despite her fear, burst out laughing when Larry called her Mrs. Gault. She was concerned now only with the task of impressing upon Mary that this was purely a chance meeting. Mary, however, seemed to have more important things than infidelity on her mind.

"Did you see me park?" she asked excitedly.

"You did very well," Larry said, trying to be nonchalant but thinking, This idiot will explode the bubble. This idiot will destroy us! "How long have you been driving?"

"Just two weeks. Listen, this is costing me five dollars an hour. I have to get back. Listen, what are you doing here anyway?"

"I was shopping for a dress," Maggie said. "You know the little shop, don't you?" She knew full well that Mary Garandi did not know the little shop; she herself did not know whether there was a little shop or a big shop or *any* kind of a shop anywhere near by.

"Sure," Mary said. She was still smiling, but she looked at Larry inquisitively and he felt the first seed of suspicion as it took root in her mind and then spread slowly onto her face.

"I was in the city all day," he said. "Stopped off for a cup of coffee, and who do I meet? Mrs. Gault." He smiled. He was trying to make this thing a nice neighborhood type outing full of good spirit and brimming with the curiosities of fate and chance. "Do you have your car with you, Mrs. Gault?" he asked.

"No, I took a cab," Maggie said.

"Well, can I drop you off?" he asked. "I'm going home, anyway."

"That's awfully nice of you," Maggie said.

For some reason, the stiff formality of Larry's offer and the polite acceptance of it by Maggie seemed to dispel whatever suspicions Mary Garandi had. "I've got to get back," she said. "Give my regards, will you?" She gave the pea jacket a slap and

215

walked back to the dual-control car. Larry and Maggie watched, speechless. She backed out of her space, waved to them, executed a wild turn, and then cut into the street without signaling and without looking to see if there was any oncoming traffic.

When the car was out of sight, Larry said, "Whew."

"What do you think?"

"I don't know."

"She seemed suspicious."

"Yes."

"What shall we do?"

"Let's get in the car first."

They walked to the car. When they were seated, Larry said, "We can't talk this over too long. She may be home before us, Maggie. She lives right across the street from me!"

"I know."

"Do you think she—"

"I don't know," Maggie said. "I thought so for a while, but then she seemed all right." She paused. "Shall we tell them?"

"I think so. I'll drop you off right at your door. We'll make it a friendly kind of thing. I'll tell Eve I ran into you at the diner. It's the only thing we can do. Mary *may* open her mouth."

"All right, I'll tell Don, too. This was stupid, Larry."

"Yes, but it's done."

"Are you frightened?"

"A little."

"I am, too."

"All right, let's get it over with."

"Call me as soon as you can," Maggie said. "I'll be dying."

"I'll call you."

"All right. Let's go, Larry. Please. I'm very nervous about this. Let me know. Please call me tonight."

He dropped her off in front of her house. They hid nothing. When he stopped the car, he got out, went around to her side, and opened the door for her. Don was not yet home, and he was grateful for that. Some of Maggie's neighbors watched her as she got out of the car, but none of them seemed particularly interested or excited by what was happening. He said goodbye in a friendly way and, in perhaps a louder voice than was necessary, she said, "Thank you so much. Give my regards to Eve, won't you?" and then she went into the house.

When he got home, he told Eve about his supposed day in the city and then said, "Oh, a funny thing happened."

"What was that?" Eve asked.

"I stopped for a cup of coffee on the way home. The diner up on the turnpike. I ran into both Margaret Gault and Mary Garandi. It's a small world, all right."

"What happened?"

"Oh, the usual," Larry said. "We talked for a few minutes, and then I asked them if I could drive them home. I dropped Margaret off."

"What'd you talk about?" Eve asked.

"With whom?"

"Margaret."

"Who remembers? I don't think she's very bright, do you?"

"What makes you say that?"

"Just the impression I got," he said. "What's for dinner, hon?"

The episode, in his home at least, was over.

It remained for him to find out how things had gone in Maggie's house. He planned to go up to the center to call her immediately after dinner. But the Porters dropped in just as he and Eve were finishing the dishes. Trapped in the house, he fidgeted nervously all night long, hoping Phyllis and Murray would leave early so that he could get out on the pretext of needing some air. They did not leave until two in the morning. He could not risk awakening Don at that hour.

He went to sleep, tossing fitfully all night.

The telephone is our burglar's tool, he thought.

Sitting in the phone booth the next morning, he found it impossible to conceive of anyone ever having had an affair before the telephone was invented. This was the assurance and the re-assurance which kept them together during the week-long separa-tion. This was the advance scout which checked and double-checked on possible danger, warned of it, prepared for it. This was the single grappling hook which connected two separately revolving worlds from which two people had somehow been stolen and thrown together. The telephone was an absolute necessity.

And so was the loose change, he thought, reaching into his pocket. Hastily, he deposited his dime and dialed.

Because the phone calls were stolen, they had to be speedily inserted into the normal routine of two separate lives. There was no time to cash a dollar bill or a fifty-cent piece, no time to linger at the cash register where a curious neighbor might engage you in conversation and then surmise you cashed your bill to make a phone call. He could think of only two conceivable reasons for using a local public phone booth if you had a phone at home. Either you were calling your wife to decipher an item on the shopping list or you were calling another woman. He could understand a curious neighbor buying the undecipherable item the first time around. He could not picture that neighbor buying the same story twice. So it was essential that he have ready change in his pockets, change that would take him quickly into a store or a filling station or a restaurant and then quickly to the phone booth. Once inside the booth, he could turn his back to the glass doors and make his call anonymously.

Now, as the phone rang on the other end, as he wondered why Maggie did not answer it, he realized he had learned to hoard small change like a miser.

Nickels and dimes, quarters, he collected faithfully, cached them in his jewelry box with his cuff links. He never left the house without an assortment of change in his pockets. He assumed it was the same for any man involved with another woman, and he wondered what would happen on that fictitious day in the future of America when suspicious housewives across the face of the nation decided to hold an unannounced inspection of their husbands' pockets.

"Hello?" the voice said.

"Hi," he answered. The voice sounded almost like Maggie's, but the shading was slightly off. He almost said "Maggie?" and then something stopped him, something warned him of danger, and he said instead, "Who's this?"

"Who's *this*?" the voice asked.

He was sure now that the woman was not Maggie. He said, "This is Fred Purley of Purley Real Estate. May I speak to Mrs. Gallanzi, please?"

"I think you have the wrong number," the voice said.

"Isn't Isabel Gallanzi there?"

"No," she said, "you have the wrong number."

"Oh, excuse me. I'm sorry," he said, and he hung up.

He called back later that day.

"Hello?" the same voice said.

He recognized the voice at once this time. Abruptly, bringing his voice down an octave, he said, "Lemmee talk to Joe."

"Who?"

"Joe. Joey. Lemmee talk to him."

"There's no Joey here," the woman said. "You have the wrong number."

"Argh, goddamnit," Larry said, and he hung up.

He was unable to reach her for three days, and now when that same infuriating voice came onto the line, the voice that was so close to Maggie's without being hers, he was ready to scream at it.

"Hello?" the voice said.

"Honey, this is Sam," he answered instantly. "You said you wanted ice cream, but you didn't—"

"You must have the wrong number," the woman said.

"Alice?"

"No. You have the wrong number."

"I'm sorry," he said, and he hung up.

He called four more times that day, and each time he got the same woman who was not Maggie. The last time, he had run out of voice variations. When she said "Hello?" he simply hung up.

He did not want to go to Felix, but he could see no other choice open to him. He stopped off at the Anders' house on the way home from the bakery. Felix was outside with June, his youngest child. At the Gault Cape Cod across the street, Larry could see no sign of life.

"Can you talk?" he asked Felix.

"What's the matter? You look in a bad way."

"We were spotted Tuesday," Larry said, "and now I can't get her on the phone. I'm going out of my mind."

"Relax," Felix said masterfully. To his daughter, he said, "Junie, don't pull out the grass." His daughter nodded, yanked up a clump of grass and stuck it into her mouth, clinging earth and all. Felix pulled it away from her and slapped her hand. "Damn kid sticks everything in her mouth," he said to Larry. "She swallowed a whole package of phonograph needles last week. Would you believe it?"

"Felix, could you ask around? Ask Betty? Find out what's happening?"

"Who saw you?"

"Mary Garandi."

"She's harmless. A dope."

"Then why hasn't Maggie answered the phone?"

"Maybe she's in the shower."

"Since Tuesday?"

"Maybe she went away for a while."

"She didn't say anything about it."

"Women are funny. Maybe she went away to think. They like to think a lot. Or at least they like to think they're thinking. Women don't really know how to think. Most of their thought emanates from their—"

"Felix, would you find out, please?"

"I'll try. I can't ask too many questions or Betty'll tip. You don't want Betty to tip, do you?"

"No. But I want to know." Again he looked across at the Gault house. It seemed empty and silent.

"I'll try. Can I do more than that?" He smiled. "How's Eve?"

"Fine."

"Pretty woman," Felix said pleasantly.

"Felix, will you find out?"

"Sure," Felix said. "I'll try."

On Monday morning Felix went to work as usual in the Lexington Avenue butcher shop. He changed his clothes in the back room, and then went out to cut meat. At ten o'clock he was slicing cutlets. With his left hand pressed against the meat, he skillfully worked the sharp blade of the knife through the cutlet, stopping just before it was completely severed, and then flipped it open to form a thinner, larger cutlet. He swept some scraps of meat from the chopping block into the bloody bucket behind it, lifted the waxed paper with its meat, and put it onto the scale.

"A pound of veal cutlets, Italian style," he said. "Anything else, dear?"

The young matron standing before the counter pointed into the glass display case. "How are the sweetbreads?"

"Sweeter than you, dear," Felix answered, smiling.

"Stop it, Felix," the woman said, returning the smile. "If they're fresh, I'll take half a pound."

"Fresh and sweet," he said, and he opened the case. At the back of the shop, the telephone rang. His partner lifted it from the hook and then yelled, "Felix! It's for you!"

"Excuse me, dear," Felix said to the woman. Wiping his hands on his blood-stained apron, he went to the phone. "Hello?" he said.

"Felix, this is Larry Cole."

"Who?" He paused. "Oh, Larry, yes. How's it going, Larry?"

"Did you find out?"

"Find out?" Felix frowned. "Oh! Oh, yeah, yeah, that's right. I was supposed to call you, wasn't I?"

"Well, what is it?"

"She's sick."

There was a silence on the line.

"What do you mean sick?" Larry asked. "Is it anything serious?"

"Just a virus. But she had a fever, and they won't let her out of bed. The phone's downstairs. That's why she hasn't been answering it."

"Who's the woman there?"

"Her mother."

"Oh."

There was another long pause.

"Why don't you go see her?" Felix asked, grinning.

"Maybe I will," Larry said.

"Don't be stu—" Felix started, but Larry had already hung up.

The woman who answered the door could have been no one but Maggie's mother. The same hair and eyes, the same figure, older, not as sharply defined, but the same figure.

"Yes?" she asked. Her voice, too, was very like Maggie's. It held the slight tremolo of advanced years, but as a girl her voice must have been Maggie's exactly.

"Hello," Larry said pleasantly. "I'm one of the Gaults' neighbors. We heard Margaret was ill. I thought I'd stop by."

Mrs. Wagner appriased him silently. "How nice," she said. "Come in."

Larry stepped into the hall. It was the first time he'd been inside the Cape Cod, and he felt rather strange, more like the intruder than he'd ever felt.

"She's uptairs," Mrs. Wagner said. "I'll see if she's decent."

"Mother?" Maggie called. "Who is it?"

"It's just Larry Cole," Larry answered. "Heard you were sick." His heart was pounding. He was sure her mother could hear the pounding.

"Oh, come up, Larry," she said, and there was so much warmth and longing in her voice that he almost ran for the steps. He restrained himself and allowed Mrs. Wagner to precede him. Over her shoulder, she said, "I'm Margaret's mother, Elizabeth Wagner."

"How do you do?" Larry said.

"You live right in the development, do you?"

"Yes."

"How nice," Mrs. Wagner said. "No work today?"

"Hmh?"

"It's Monday. Are you—"

"Oh, I work at home mostly."

"That's very convenient," Mrs. Wagner said. "What do you do?"

"I'm an architect."

"That's a nice profession."

"Yes."

They walked into the bedroom.

She sat in the center of a large canopied bed. She was wearing a sheer bedjacket under which was a nylon gown, and he was ashamed of himself for the first thought which entered his mind. But he could not keep his eyes away from the sharp impact of her nipples against the sheer fabrics. She wore no lipstick, no make-up. For the first time since he'd known her, the tiny scar was distinct and clear, a miniature white cross on her cheek. Her hair was pulled back into a pony tail. She looked very pale and very tired, and she smiled weakly when he came into the room with her mother.

"Hello, Larry," she said.

"Hello, Margaret," he answered. He smiled. He wanted to rush to the bed and take her into his arms. "How are you?"

"She's feeling much better," Mrs. Wagner said, standing at the foot of the bed, looking first at Margaret and then at Larry.

"Are you?" he asked her.

"Yes."

"What've you got?"

"A virus."

"They're murder."

"Yes."

"Did you have any fever?"

"Yes. But I'm all right now. How's Eve?"

221

"Fine."

"And the children?"

"Fine."

"I got sick last week. Don called my mother. He has to work, you know. He couldn't stay home to take care of an invalid."

"I see," Larry said. His eyes locked with hers. Her face looked pure and young and untouched and magnificently beautiful.

"How'd you know I was sick?"

"One of the neighbors mentioned it. Eve would have come by, too," he said, glancing at Mrs. Wagner, "but she had shopping to do."

"Would you like some coffee, Mr. Cole?" Margaret's mother asked.

"If it's not any trouble."

"None at all. I have some on the stove." She smiled briefly and left the room. The moment she was gone, Maggie held out her arms and he rushed to her.

"Darling, darling," he said. "I was frantic. I called and called . . ."

"I know. All those wrong numbers. I died each time. They wouldn't let me out of bed. Larry, Larry, how I've missed you." He reached for her mouth, and she turned her head away. "Don't kiss me. You'll catch it."

"I don't care."

He kissed her, and she clung to him and said, "Did it go all right? That day with Mary?"

"Yes. You?"

"Yes. Oh, Larry, I didn't know how much your voice meant to me. I didn't realize how much I needed it every day. Let me look at you." She studied him and said, smiling, "You look handsome."

"I need a shave."

"I don't care. Your face is so rough, so strong. Put your face against mine."

He held her close and asked, "When can you get up?"

"I have to stay in bed at least another two days."

"Can I see you Thursday night?"

"Yes. Larry, how will I live until then?"

"I know, I know," he said, and his hands dug into her shoulders.

"Will you come to see me again?"

"I don't think so."

"Of course not. This was a silly chance you took. But I'm so glad you came. When I heard your voice—"

"Shhh," he said.

"She's coming. Tell me. Quick."

"I love you." He kissed her unpainted mouth briefly and then

222

moved away from the bed. Mrs. Wagner came into the room with a tray.

"I didn't know what you took," she said, "so I brought all the fixings." Casually, she said to Maggie, "What does he take, Margaret?"

"He . . . I don't know," Maggie said.

They chatted leisurely while they had their coffee. Larry stayed for a half hour and then left. They looked at each other constantly during that half hour. After Mrs. Wagner showed him to the door, she came upstairs and went to the bed.

"So that's him," she said to Margaret.

Margaret said nothing. She lay with her head turned into the pillow, looking out the window.

"And it's happened to you," Mrs. Wagner said.

And with perhaps the first honest words she'd spoken to her mother since the day her grandfather died, she said, "Yes, it's happened to me."

It had, apparently, also happened to Linda and Hank.

It had happened with all the ferocity and all the painfully terrible sweetness of youth. Conditioned beforehand by the overt propaganda of the communications industry, they knew what to expect of love; but its unexpectedness startled them nonetheless.

The street on which they parked that night was completely unsuitable for necking during the winter months. During those months the trees were bare and the street lamps illuminated the entire block with scrutinizing intensity. Now, in April, the trees were filling out, and they cloaked the parked car in dappled denseness.

Hank McLean was not a coward, but he'd had an automobile experience which had caused him to become somewhat cautious. He and his friends had discovered a dark houseless street at the top of a hill, a dead-end street which dropped away to give a remarkable view of the sprawling lighted foothills below. It was a good spot for necking. You were safe from the police there, and the spot was certainly romantic as hell and worked particularly well with girls who needed that extra bit of encouragement before getting in the mood. He had gone there regularly with different girls. Sometimes he'd spotted his friends' cars on the hill, and this had lent a fraternal feeling to the ritual of necking.

One night, long before he'd met Linda, he'd gone there with a girl named Suzie. None of his friends were there that night. Alone, he and Suzie parked at the top of the hill some three feet from the edge of the drop. Suzie was a girl who didn't need encouragement. Suzie was a girl who, legend had it, had almost been kicked out of college because of a rather spirited session in the storage room behind the little theater's stage while a play was in rehearsal. Not that Suzie was a pig. She wasn't. She was a damn pretty girl, and Hank enjoyed her company. She just didn't need encouragement, that was all. She was rather spirited, that was all.

They had begun necking almost instantly. They'd been exchanging kisses for perhaps fifteen minutes when the headlights appeared behind them. Curiously, Hank never once thought it might be the police. This hilltop spot, he was certain, had not yet been discovered by the fastidious minions of the law. He thought for a moment that it might be one of his friends. So he stepped on his brake pedal in three rapid dashes, which, had the car behind him belonged to a friend, would have been answered by a rapid flick of the headlights.

The car's headlights did not flick.

Instead, the car pulled up directly behind Hank's car, almost bumper to bumper. The doors of the car opened and four boys stepped out. It was then that Hank felt his first twinge of fear.

Luckily, it was December, and the windows of his car were rolled up. Just as luckily, and totally by chance, both his door and the door on Suzie's side of the car were locked. The boys surrounded the car. "Open up!" they shouted, and Hank started the engine. One boy began pounding at the window on his side of the car. Hank looked behind him. He could not back away for a turn because the other car was too close. Nor could he move forward because the drop was too near to permit a turn. He had the sudden vision of himself getting beat up and Suzie getting raped. He knew this would represent no particular loss on Suzie's part, but the entire idea revolted him. Suzie was with him. He had, in effect, made a bargain with her when he'd asked her out. He was her escort. And escorts didn't go around letting girls get raped, no matter what the state of their virtue.

He noticed then that there was no one behind the wheel of the other car. He noticed at the same time that the boy on his side was searching the ground for a rock or a stick or anything with which he could shatter the window. "Open up, you bastard!" one of the boys shouted, and Hank realized he had to act now or take what was certainly coming within the next few minutes. He sucked in a deep breath, pushed the gearshift lever into reverse, and then rammed his foot onto the accelerator.

He hit the car behind him with considerable force. He did not take his foot from the accelerator. He felt a surge of delighted relief when the car behind him began to move. He threw his own car into low, moved forward some six feet, almost running over one of the shouting boys, and then went into reverse again, picking up speed as he headed for the other car. He hit it with a solid smash this time, the speed of an extended run behind him. The other car began rolling backward.

A boy leaped onto the running board, shouting and cursing, pounding at the window. Hank's car was an old one, but it withstood the boy's fist nonetheless. With elbow room now, he swung around in an arc, backed off, and then faced his car down the hill. He stepped on the gas pedal suddenly so that the car lurched forward, knocking the boy from the running board. The other car had stopped rolling, captured by the bank at the side of the road; but it was out of his way now, and he gunned his old car forward and raced down the hill.

Suzie was petrified beside him. She sat crouched on the seat, looking through the rear window, trembling. He came very close to loving her while she was trembling. She seemed more like a woman in her fear than she did while exchanging passionate kisses. The attacking boys did not give chase. He took Suzie directly home. At the front door, she kissed him with grateful tenderness. He stopped thinking he might love her as soon as she went into the apartment. But the experience that night had taught Hank a lesson. He discussed it with his friends, and they reached the conclusion that they would thereafter search out streets which were dark but lined with houses.

The street on which he parked with Linda Harder that April night was one which had been uncovered in the corporate search.

He wanted to kiss Linda, but she was in an extremely talkative mood that night. She had been rattling on for the past five minutes about a boy who'd given her a Stevenson button, and Hank was beginning to dislike Intellectuals and Democrats everywhere.

"He was just a fat little boy," Linda said, "but he had these wonderful dimples in his cheeks, and this big toothy smile. I was terribly in love with him, and he never paid me the slightest bit of attention."

"Until the Democrats nominated Stevenson," Hank said.

"Yes. And then he just came up to me one day and said, 'Here, vote for Stevenson.' And he handed me the campaign button. I've still got it. It was the first time he'd singled me out for anything, the first time he showed he knew I was alive. I can't tell you how important it made me feel."

"I'll have to buy you a trunkful of campaign buttons. Willkie, Landon, Roose—"

"I don't need that with you, Hank," Linda said. "I feel important *all* the time with you."

"Do you love me, Linda?" he asked.

"Yes."

"I wonder why people don't think we know how to love?"

"What do you mean?"

"I mean . . . when we're young. Why do they always think it's puppy love or something? Do you know what I believe? I believe we're the only ones who *do* know how to love. I mean it. When you get older, you forget. I see it all the time. My parents and their friends. I think they've all forgotten what love is. I'm glad I'm young. You know? I'm glad I can love you."

"I'm glad, too," Linda said.

"Are you finished with your fat boy?"

"Yes."

"Can I kiss you now?"

"Anytime you want to kiss me, even if I'm talking, you just shut me—"

He kissed her.

It was a curious thing to be kissing Linda. Hank was twenty-one years old, but he'd never been in love before. Moreover, he had always considered necking the prelude to whatever fortune might allow to follow. Linda's lips were very nice lips. She was only seventeen, but she kissed well, and she knew how to use the soft inner cushion of her mouth expertly. Kissing her, even though Hank was a man of the world who knew what this sex bit was all about, he felt sort of dizzy, actually dizzy, just kissing her. He listened to her harsh breathing, and he could feel her face feverishly hot against his and he knew without doubt that this was the girl for him, this wonderfully sweet, gentle girl who kissed like this, this marvelously intelligent, remarkably gorgeous girl who kissed like this, this tender, sensitive, amazingly exotic girl who kissed like this was for him, who kissed like this and made him dizzy.

In ten minutes' time, they both agreed they had better go for an ice-cream soda or something.

Linda buttoned her blouse and put on fresh lipstick.

24

ON THURSDAY night Felix Anders saw Larry's car leave the development and then, not five minutes later, Margaret came down the front steps and drove away in her car.

He was amazed that they could run their affair in such a slip-shod manner and still escape detection. It was a wonder everyone in the world, no less the development, did not know exactly what was going on between them. But even while considering them the most careless sort of fools, he managed to find a tender spot in his heart for them. They were, after all, in love. This spoke in their favor. Like a father picking lice from the hair of two idiot children, Felix Anders felt great paternal compassion for these two tormented fools.

At the same time there was something immensely satisfying about their tortured writhings, something quite pleasurable about watching their silly gyrations and knowing they were rank amateurs playing a game invented for experts. Amateurs amused him. This entire Cole-Gault affair was an entertainment being performed solely for Felix Anders.

And then there was Eve.

Eve was something else again.

Felix walked into the kitchen where Betty was washing the dishes. "Leave them," he said. "Let's go to bed."

"Oh, stop it," Betty said, pleased.

"Come on, come on," he said impatiently.

"I don't like to leave dirty dishes," Betty said.

He put his hands on her buttocks. "Come on."

"No. Later."

"Okay," he said, shrugging, having made his stud-bull impression, having left Betty with the idea that all he desired in this budding world of beautiful women was her enticing little form alone. "I'm going for a walk. I'll be back in a little while."

"Where are you going?" she asked, having become partially interested by his damned wandering hands and toying with the idea of leaving the dirty dishes in the sink.

"Over to say hello to Larry."

"I'll be finished soon" she said.

"Okay," he answered. He kissed her, and he let his hand drift caressingly over her buttocks again. He enjoyed arousing her. He enjoyed being in complete control of the castle which was his home. "I'll be back."

Outside, the stars pecked fiercely at the deep blue-black sky. Felix walked the streets of Pinecrest Manor knowing full well that Betty would be waiting at home in her nightgown whenever he decided to return. He would let her wait a while. A long while. He would let her wait until he was ready. It was better for her that way. It was the only way to treat her.

He had long ago stopped believing it was the male of the species who possessed the deep yearning, the insatiable sex drive. He had come to the conclusion that the reverse was true. There was an empty chasm in a woman, and only a man could fill that chasm. And until the chasm was filled, a woman was essentially incomplete. Women had invented marriage only to insure repeated completion, and then had destroyed their own invention when they'd discovered insurance was not necessary. The chasm could be filled, the completion accomplished, by anyone at all.

Felix smiled and ambled up the walk to the Cole house. He rang the bell once, a short, sharp ring. He waited.

Eve answered the door. She was wearing black Bermuda shorts and a black sweater. Her long black hair hung to her shoulders. Her eyes were intensely blue against the overwhelming mass of unrelieved black.

"Oh, hello, Felix," she said.

Felix stepped into the house quickly. He did not want to ask for Larry while standing on the doorstep. He did not want to be told that Larry was not home and then have no further excuse for entering. Once inside the house, he walked casually into the living room.

"Out for a walk," he said nonchalantly. "Thought I'd stop by and say hello to Larry." Quickly, he sat on the couch.

"Larry's not home," Eve said.

"Oh, that's too bad," Felix answered. He made no motion to rise.

"He went to a lecture at Pratt. He goes every other week or so."

"Well, too bad he's not home," Felix said. "I felt like going for a beer."

"I have beer, if you want some," Eve said politely.

"No, no," Felix said, standing. "You've got work to do, kids to get to bed."

"Well . . ." Eve hesitated. She had already done the dishes and put the children to bed, and so her evening was free. But she'd planned on reading a book she'd taken from the library. She was, in fact, in a particularly uncommunicative mood and was almost glad Larry had gone to his lecture. She did not, however, wish to be rude to Felix. "The children are in bed already," she said, "and I've done the dishes. *Would* you like a glass of beer?"

She hoped he would say no, but instead he said, "If it's no trouble, Eve."

"No trouble at all," she lied, and she went into the kitchen and opened the refrigerator. "How's Betty?" she called.

"Fine," Felix said. "When I get home, I'll tell her you're alone. She may want to drop in."

"Oh, no need to do that," Eve said hastily. She had visions of this becoming one of those development drop-in evenings. That was exactly what she needed tonight. Carrying the bottle of beer, a bottle opener and a glass, she went back into the living room. Felix was thumbing through a magazine, which he put down the moment she entered. He uncapped the beer, poured, and then said, "Aren't you having any?"

Eve shook her head. She smiled to let him know it was perfectly all right to drink without her, and then sat opposite him.

"I always wonder," Felix said, sipping at the beer, "how a woman feels when she's alone in the house and a man comes calling."

Eve shrugged. "The same way she feels when a woman comes calling."

"Well, not really," Felix said. He smiled indulgently.

"Mmm," Eve said, nodding. "Really."

"Do you mean to tell me that an attractive woman doesn't feel any difference when her visitor is a man?"

Eve frowned momentarily. Felix had not sounded at all like himself just then. He had called her an attractive woman, and her frown was partially provoked by surprise—she had not thought

Felix capable of a subtle pass—and partially by the uncomfortable knowledge of which Felix had suddenly made her aware. She *was* alone with a man. And whereas she normally might have considered this an unexceptionable situation, Felix had managed to give it a different slant. Still, she didn't want to seem silly or overly reserved. The frown vanished.

"I guess it depends on the frame of mind of the man or woman involved," she said.

"Well," Felix said easily, "what's your frame of mind, Eve?"

"If a man drops in," Eve said, "he drops in. I'm not looking for anything, and I assume he isn't either."

"What do you mean by 'anything'?" Felix asked.

"Well . . ." Again she frowned. Instead of helping the situation, she seemed to have aggravated it. She was becoming slightly annoyed. She'd never really discussed sex with anyone but Larry, and she didn't feel like discussing it with Felix, who was an absolute stranger and, after all, a man. "Well, *any*thing," she said, hoping she had stressed the word strongly enough to cut the conversation dead instantly.

"Yes, but what do you mean by *anything*?" Felix persisted.

She became suddenly flustered by his perseverance. "Oh, anything," she said, and then she laughed a forced laugh and tried to make her voice light. "I'm just a faithful, one-hunnerd-per-cent American housewife. Very dull. Very boring."

"Very interesting," Felix corrected. "The American housewife is the most fascinating person you can find."

"Well, I'm glad you think so," Eve said, hoping the conversation was moving onto fresher ground.

"Otherwise I wouldn't be married to one," Felix said, laughing.

"Well, Betty must certainly make married life inter—"

"Of course," Felix said, "some situations develop whether the man and woman are looking for them or not."

"Perhaps," Eve said. She felt very uncomfortable now. She did not believe that anyone could dwell so long on a subject unless he had a point to make. She was beginning to receive Felix's message and was convinced he'd come here to deliver it. She wondered for an instant if he'd known Larry wasn't home, and then suddenly wished she were wearing slacks instead of shorts.

"Sure," Felix said, sipping at his beer as if he intended it to last all night. "Sometimes a man and a woman are thrown together and things happen. They just happen. Take a man and a woman on a desert island. How long can they remain platonic friends?"

"That's a slightly different situation," Eve said.

"Different from *what*?" Felix asked, suddenly leaning forward.

"From . . . from the situation you were describing."

"*Which* situation?"

"Where a man and a woman . . . just are . . . where . . ."

229

"Where they become a male and a female?" Felix supplied.

"This is a pretty stupid conversation, isn't it, Felix?" Eve asked. She smiled because he was a guest in her home, but the smile was nervous and unsure.

"Well, I like to speculate," Felix said.

"So do I, but not on situations in which I'll never be involved."

"You never know, Eve."

Eve laughed, but it sounded hollow even to her own ears. "There isn't the slightest possibility that I'll ever be stranded on a desert island with any man but Larry."

"Many women have discovered that there are desert islands on every street corner, Eve." He was staring at her now. Unconsciously, her hand came up to tuck a stray wisp of hair behind her ear.

"That's a . . . a very romantic notion, Felix," she said.

"I'm a very romantic person," he said. "Aren't you?"

"Yes," she admitted, smiling.

"And a woman never knows when romance is going to pounce on her, does she?"

"There's . . . there's . . ." She felt very warm all at once. She rose and went to the television set. "There's not much reason for a . . . a . . . housewife to . . . to . . . to be worrying about romance," she said, surprised to hear herself stammering, thinking, The last time I stammered was in grammar school! She snapped on the set and then bent to select a channel. She felt Felix's eyes on her back and instantly rose to turn the dial from a standing position. "I hope you don't mind," she said, hoping her voice sounded calm and assured. "There's a show I want to see."

"Certainly not," Felix answered. "Time and a place for everything. Right?" He paused. "Right?"

She had not thought he'd expected an answer. "Yes," she said.

"Sure. Good night, Eve," he said warmly. "I enjoyed the beer, and I enjoyed our little talk. Tell Larry I stopped by, won't you?"

Eve moved quickly to the door. "I will," she said, and she smiled graciously. Felix stepped out of the house and onto the front stoop. He waved and then went down the walk. Behind him, Eve closed the door.

Felix looked up at the sky and smiled.

She's smart, he thought. She's a smart girl, and she's playing it exceedingly cool. Good! Smart girls are safe girls.

Smiling, he ambled home to his wife.

25

THERE was, of course, a girl with Altar.

Larry was somewhat disappointed. He liked talking to the writer, and he'd discovered that Altar assumed a different personality whenever he was with a woman. Besides, this girl wasn't even pretty. There was a peasant simplicity to her face which was entirely too honest.

They met at the Howard Johnson's across the bridge. Larry parked and locked his car and then walked over to the convertible. Leaning over the girl, Altar said, "This is Joan. Do you want to lay her?" The girl smiled somewhat guardedly. She took Larry's hand when he introduced himself and then moved over on the seat to make room for him. Sitting beside her, Larry thought back to a ride not so long before with Altar and . . . Agnes? Had that been her name? Rhinelander 4 . . . He could no longer remember. But the girl had truly flustered him that day, and now, knowing Maggie, he wasn't the slightest bit interested in Altar's newest acquisition. In fact, he actively resented her presence.

"The house is coming along nicely," he said. "I think you'll be surprised by the progress."

"You sound antagonistic," Altar said.

"No."

"Accusatory then. I'd have gone up to the site, but I've been busy with other things."

Larry glanced at the girl, smiled, and said, "Yes, I see."

"Not Joan," Altar replied. "Important things. I think we've got a movie sale for *Stone*. A big fat percentage deal."

"I'm glad to hear it," Larry said.

"You sound positively overjoyed."

"Success always pleases me. Do you know any men who've bitten dogs lately?"

Altar chuckled. "You expected a movie sale?"

"Didn't *you*?"

"I suppose so. In a way, I was hoping we wouldn't make one. It scares the hell out of me. All we need now is a book club, and the pattern is complete. I can almost see those bad reviews before they're printed."

"It's heartbreaking," Larry said. "Your life is so dull and meaningless."

"Larry's life is very exciting," Altar said to Joan. "He's been commissioned to straighten out the Tower of Pisa."

"That sounds very interesting," Joan said, as if she thought it were possibly the dullest project in the history of architecture.

231

"Joan is a very enthusiastic girl," Altar explained. "Her enthusiasm, however, is limited to several clearly defined areas. Don't judge her by her silence. She is what is commonly referred to as still water."

"I'm a very exuberant girl," Joan said blankly.

"She works for a movie company," Altar said. "She sorts the mail. She also makes all the decisions which are later attributed to courageous Hollywood producers." He paused. "Actually, she comes from a very creative family. Her mother is in your profession, Larry."

"Oh? Is she an architect?" Larry asked, interested.

"No," the girl said. "She designs sets for the Howdy Doody show," and Altar burst out laughing.

The land was swarming with workmen when they reached it. They drove down the rutted, mud-soaked road to the construction site and then stepped from the car. Joan chose to stay out of the mud. She opened a magazine and began reading while Altar and Larry headed for the house. It was beginning to take real form. Like a giant bird poised for flight, the structure clung delicately to the slope of the land, waiting to spread the wings of its roof. Even in skeleton there was a soaring sweep to the house, the majestic surge of rising wall against angled roof.

"Jesus, it's going to be beautiful," Altar said.

Larry nodded absently. "Do you see Di Labbia around anywhere?"

They searched the grounds for him and then went into the house. Carpenters were busily sawing and hammering. Electricians were paying out lengths of wire. Plumbers were carrying flexible copper tubing which would be twisted into radiant heating loops beneath the floors. There was the smell of sawdust on the air, the reverberating solid bang of metal hitting metal. Trying to keep out of the workmen's way, they climbed a makeshift ladder to the upper level of the house and found Di Labbia in the uncompleted room which was to be Altar's study, a room facing north, with floor to ceiling windows stretching its entire thirty-foot length. The windows were not in yet, but the effect of the window wall was obvious even at this stage of construction. The room seemed to extend itself into the woods, enveloping the outdoors, giving Altar a workspace commanding a wide vista of tree and rock and sloping land and sky. Assuming that Altar wanted to feel like a god while he wrote, Larry had spread the world out at his feet.

Di Labbia was squatting on the rough wood floor with his foreman, looking over one of the printed drawings. He looked up when the two men entered. He was wearing skintight dungarees and a filthy white tee shirt. A hammer hung in a loop on his trousers. He rose instantly, his face splitting in childlike pleasure.

"Larry!" he said. "Hey!" and he extended his hand. He shook

232

Larry's hand vigorously, apparently really pleased to see him. Then he said, "Hello, Mr. Altar. I haven't seen you in a long time. It's really beginning to look like something, isn't it?"

"It certainly is," Altar agreed.

There was pride in Di Labbia's eyes. He clapped Larry on the shoulder and said, "I'm really enjoying this house, do you know that? Come on, let me show you what we've done. I think you're gonna—"

"Frank?" the foreman said.

Di Labbia turned. "Yeah, Joe?"

"Do you want to ask him about this door?"

"Oh, yeah, yeah. Ordinarily, I'd have changed it myself, but I know how you are, Larry." He grinned. "It's this door from the master bedroom to the bathroom. The way you've got it hung, it swings open into the closet. Can we hang it from the right instead?"

"Let me see the drawing," Larry said.

They talked over the door for several moments. Larry agreed the swing was awkward and okayed the change. Di Labbia seemed pleased that he'd pointed out this small error and had it corrected in construction. Watching them, Altar had the feeling that Di Labbia, no matter what he'd said earlier, needed Larry's guidance and supervision—in fact, admired and respected it. They began discussing the reinforcement necessary in the basement to support the flagstone entrance hallway, and again there seemed to be complete understanding and rapport between the two men. Then Di Labbia, like a kid anxious to show off his latest toy, said, "Come on, I want you to see what we've done!" and he led the men downstairs again.

In planning the living space on the lower level, Larry had utilized two separate areas as expressions of opposing experiences. One was a cool formal living room to be enclosed almost completely by glass, with the sliding doors from Slipwell to provide access to the outdoor terraces. The second area was a smaller living room at the opposite end of the house. Conceived in terms of wood and stone, the room was intended to convey a sense of intimately warm enclosure as contrasted to the open, airy feeling of the larger space. An interior stone wall was to separate the room from the adjoining efficiency kitchen. A mason was working on that wall when the men entered the room.

Larry came in behind Altar and Di Labbia, saw the mason, and stopped. He faced the wall, hands on his hips, and said, "What's that supposed to be?"

Di Labbia turned, the proud smile still on his face, the eagerness to exhibit his work still shining in his eyes. "What's what, Larry?" he asked, still caught in the intoxicating grip of what had seemed to be ideal builder-architect rapport.

"That wall," Larry said.

"It's gonna make the room," Di Labbia said enthusiastically. "When you step into this room—"

"You'll be smacked in the face with a wall that looks like the local bank!" Larry snapped.

Di Labbia blinked, puzzled. "What?" he said.

"The drawings call for a random rubble pattern," Larry said, his voice rising. "Your mason's doing ashlar. There's supposed to be a natural feel to this room, and you've got him laying the stone up in neat courses. Look at it! He's got half the wall done already—and all wrong!"

"Gee, that's funny," Di Labbia said. "The elevation—"

"The elevation indicated the pattern clearly!" Larry shouted. "Get the plans! Where are they?"

Di Labbia turned to his foreman. Anxiously, he began leafing through the drawings. When they came to the detail for the wall, Di Labbia bit his lip and frowned. "I can see how he made the mistake," he said. "You only indicated a portion of the wall, and he—"

"That's usually enough for a competent mason," Larry snapped. "Or did you suddenly decide to design my house?"

"Now, don't get excited, Larry. It was a natural mistake. The mason probably figured you wanted things—" He sought a word with his hands—"neat and even in such an expensive house. He probably figured—"

"It's my job to do the figuring!" Larry said. "Why wasn't the drawing followed?"

"It was a mistake," Di Labbia said apologetically, obviously embarrassed. He looked at Altar, his face trying to indicate how natural the error had been, and then he turned to Larry again, eager to reconstruct the earlier, friendlier feeling. But Larry would not let it go.

"Doesn't anybody here know how to read a simple elevation?" he asked. "What kind of a builder are you, Di Labbia? Is everybody asleep around here?"

"The elevation showed only—"

"The elevation showed a rough, round, informal pattern! Your man took it into his head to change the design. And your foreman didn't stop him, and you didn't stop him, and if I hadn't come up today, you'd have built that damn wall to China without being stopped!"

"Larry, it was a mis—"

"Rip it out!"

"All right, I'll rip it out. Don't get so excited. It's only a wall. So we'll—"

"Don't tell me what to get excited about. I don't like workmen meddling with my design."

"But nobody meddled . . ."

234

"What else is wrong around here? What else are you trying to hide?"

He went storming away from Di Labbia and Altar. Like a patient father watching a spoiled son in a tantrum, Di Labbia stood with his grimy hands hanging at his sides, chewing nervously at his mustache. Altar didn't know quite what to say. By association, he felt somewhat like Larry's accomplice. He could hear Larry shouting at the workmen as he moved angrily through the house. When he returned, his full fury had still not been vented.

"Why hasn't he started taking it down?" he shouted. "Must I watch you every minute, Di Labbia? I thought you were an honest builder."

"Now listen—" Di Labbia started.

"What the hell are you? A crook? A cheat?"

"Now just a minute!" Di Labbia said, his voice rising.

"I don't like crooks or cheats! You said you were a builder. All right, *builder*, why don't you—"

"I'm a builder!" Di Labbia shouted, as if his manhood had been questioned. "I'm a damn good builder!" His voice was shrill in indignation now. "Everybody makes mistakes. You designed a door that swung open against a closet, didn't you?" He paused, and then lowered his voice in an attempt once more to recapture the friendship he'd felt earlier. "Didn't I point that out to you?"

"Thanks for nothing," Larry said. "I'd have discovered it myself anyway."

Di Labbia was trembling now with the effort to make things right again. The house had been going along beautifully, so beautifully, and it seemed incredible to him that a mason's stupid mistake could cause so wide a breach. He sought the right words, but they would not come. Instead, in childish retaliation, he said, "When am I getting my Thermopane? How can I finish inside if I can't enclose?"

"Use tar paper," Larry said.

"What about the glass?"

"It's on order. You'll get it, don't worry. You've got plenty to do outside."

"My exterior work'll be finished by the end of next week. I want to get started on—"

"Then use tar paper! Don't create problems. Your big problem now is ripping out that wall."

Di Labbia nodded. With great dignity, he said, "The wall will be ripped out and rebuilt according to your drawing," and then he turned from Larry and walked away.

"Come on, Altar," Larry said, and he strode out of the house. Altar went to Di Labbia to shake hands with him and then ran to catch up with Larry. When he fell into step beside him, Larry muttered, "The crook! I can't stand a goddamn cheat!"

And Altar very softly said, "Transference is a marvelous phenomenon, isn't it?"

When he got out of the car after the long drive to Howard Johnson's, Larry apologized to Altar. The writer gently suggested that perhaps the apology was being misdirected, and Larry promised to call Di Labbia as soon as he got home. He said goodbye to Joan, walked to his own car, unlocked it, and climbed behind the wheel. He sat behind the wheel for a long time without starting the car. The afternoon sun slanted against the windshield, throwing a faint reflection of his face into the car. He looked at the face, a face he once had known. The reflection was transparent, not a true mirror image. Beyond it, through it, he could see people walking in and out of the restaurant. He had the sudden feeling that the person he'd known to be himself, like the face he'd known, was becoming transparent and thin, was fading, and would someday vanish completely.

Today, he thought, I turned on a nice guy doing a job. What do I do tomorrow? Kick a blind man? How many other people will I attack in an attempt to justify something in myself which I know to be wrong? How long can I maintain two separate warring identities within the same body shell? How long can I be two people without being either, borrowing the worst from each to create a monster unlike either? I can't, I can't. I can't go on this way without destroying myself.

I guess I'll have to leave Eve, he thought calmly. The thought did not frighten him or startle him. It came quite easily and reasonably, as if it were the result of irrefutably logical thinking.

If I were a different person, he thought, I wouldn't have to leave my wife. I could allow things to go along just the way they're going now. According to Felix Anders, everyone in the world is cheating anyway, and perhaps Felix is right. Perhaps, after all, there's nothing new under the sun, nothing startling about two basically decent people who have somehow become so involved with each other that all values are now meaningless. If I were capable of adjusting more easily, he thought, I could doubtless adjust to this too and leave things just the way they are. I could allow my marriage to move along steadily on a rising graph line recording a bank of memories—the birthdays, the sick children, the parties, the traffic snarls, the outings, the anniversaries, the Christmases, the jokes shared, the movies shared, the songs shared—and at the same time there would be another graph for Maggie and me, a similar graph with its own memory bank, separate and apart. I could maintain a split identity which overlapped at some points, do just what Felix says everyone else is doing anyhow.

Except that I am not everyone else.

I am me.

And I suppose I'm basically a monogamist, which, according

236

to Felix, is an incredibly naïve thing to be in this supersonic day and age. According to Felix, cheating is the safety valve, the one emotional release which prevents the water boiler of marriage from exploding. According to Felix, marriage is a practical joke perpetrated on young lovers. And if Felix is right, and marriage is a joke, what do I do when and if I leave my wife? I marry Maggie, do I not? I become the butt of the same tired gag again. And why?

Because I was raised as a monogamist. Because I have had love and marriage drummed into my mind, etched on my brain as inseparable units in the scheme of human relations. And being a monogamist, I want only one woman, and I suppose that woman is Maggie.

Well, maybe basically decent monogamists shouldn't go around looking for trouble because there sure as hell is a lot of trouble to find if one decides to look for it. I didn't decide to look for it, but I found it in carloads. Or maybe I did decide to look for it. And maybe I'm not even a basically decent monogamist or a basically decent anything. Maybe I'm just plain rotten.

In which case everyone in the world is just plain rotten and we might as well throw down the barricades and let the Mongol ponies ride through the streets. Because, discounting any ego-tistical notions I may have about myself, I imagine I'm more or less the same as any other male walking the streets. I work hard for a living, and I've got a wife and a family and a mortgage. I come home nights, usually, and I've got my private dreams and disappointments, my illusions, my hopes, my fears. I tell dirty jokes, and I smoke, and I drink, and I react to Marilyn Monroe. I'm an average American male.

I'm Felix Anders, so to speak.

But I'm not Felix Anders, he thought. Felix is playing a game, and I'm not playing. I'm serious, I'm dead serious. I'm drowning in an ocean of morality and all the while I thought I knew how to swim. All the while I thought I was a sensitive, sensible man who could reconcile action with ethics, frivolous speculation with responsible behavior. Perhaps I am not sensible or sensitive, but I am a monogamist and I want only one woman. And at the same time I don't want to hurt Eve. But what makes me believe a clean break would hurt her more than falsely living a failure? Oh, yes, yes, face it, it's a failure, the marriage is a failure. Somewhere long before Maggie there was no more fun and no more surprise. There was only failure. And that's where Felix comes in again because Felix says all marriage is an ugly disappointment, all marriage is the burial ground of identity. And if Felix is right, what makes me think it'll be any different with Maggie?

If Felix is right, won't I start another alliance with another woman five years, ten years, fifteen years after marrying Maggie? Does marriage automatically become a quagmire of boredom

237

and disillusionment from which escape is an absolute necessity? Escape or die? Escape or be buried alive?

But how can I hurt Eve? How can I willfully hurt someone I've loved, lived with, shared with, dreamed with, grown with? How can I hurt someone who is an essential part of me? And how can I consider her an essential part of me and still think of leaving her? And what about the kids? What do Chris and David mean to me? What's my role as father? What's my true relationship to them? Hello, Chris, hello, David, pat on the head, don't wet the bed, don't do this, don't do that, here now give me a kiss before you go to sleep, an accidental relationship. What do they mean to me, and what do I mean to them?

What does *my* father mean to me?

He's a crashing bore who puts me to sleep every time he opens his mouth. Will Chris and David think I'm a bore when they grow up? Will I be able to sit across a restaurant table from a grown-up son and have an intelligent, interesting conversation with him? Or do all parents turn into crashing bores? What's a parent but a judge and a jury and a pain in the ass? What real affection does Chris feel for me? Or David?

Questions, questions, questions.

Where are all the answers? Who's giving out the answers today? Isn't there a man who stands on street corners with answers? A man like Roger Altar who has all the pat endings in a big bag of tricks? But try to apply those endings to reality, just try. In real life, you pick a happy ending, and there are fourteen other people involved who've decided on fourteen different endings. And all the endings are in conflict, and either you stick to your own ending and make a lot of people unhappy, or you take one of their endings and make yourself unhappy.

I don't want to hurt people, he thought.

I really don't want to hurt anyone. Do I have to kill Eve to prove something to myself? And what am I proving after I've killed her? I'm simply proving that I'm willing to indulge my own selfish whims to their most ridiculous extreme. I am destroying her in order to build a new image of myself, which image may or may not be valid.

But it is valid.

It is the only valid image of me.

I want the job in Puerto Rico, and I want Maggie. I do not want one or either; I want both.

I, I, I, the enormous ego of me, the enormous self-centred universe of me! But what else is life about? Isn't it all about me? The happiness of me, and the sadness of me, and the hopes of me, and the shattered or realized dreams of me? Isn't ME the most important concept and hasn't it always been? Why did I marry Eve if not to please ME? Was I thinking of her, was I thinking of how magnanimous I was being in showering upon

238

her the rains of this magnificent being who is me? Wasn't I
thinking of myself alone and of how much Eve pleased ME? Am
I not the sum total of the universe? Doesn't the universe have its
nucleus in each and every solitary individual who shouts "I, I,
I!" against the total oblivion of anonymity?

I, I, I!

I want the job in Puerto Rico, and I want Maggie.

He reached for the ignition key.

And in the second it took him to twist the key and start the
engine, he decided to accept the Baxter proposal, divorce Eve,
and take Maggie with him to Puerto Rico.

26

THE MEN met in a midtown bar on a Monday afternoon two
weeks later.

By that time Larry had formulated a tentative plan of action.
And the one certainty in that plan, it seemed to him, was the
Baxter proposal. He had realized early, and with some loss of
assurance, that he could not definitely count upon Maggie's
affirmative reaction to his scheme. He would, after all, be asking
her to make a decision which he himself had reached only after
grave consideration. He could not expect her to leap into a new
experience blindly, without first giving it serious thought. He did,
in truth, feel she would readily agree to anything he suggested.
But he was certain that the presentation of the Puerto Rican job
as a *fait accompli*, the concept of the island as a sanctuary, would
help her in deciding to sever whatever ties still bound her to Don.
And so he did not discuss his decision or his scheme with her. He
would do that after he spoke to Baxter. The acceptance of the
Baxter proposal was his foundation; upon that he would build.

The bar at five o'clock was full of editors and publishers discussing their fall lists. As Larry waited for Baxter, he found himself inadvertently eavesdropping, hoping to hear some discussion
of Altar's name or the new book. The hot topic of discussion,
though, seemed to be a new novel by a fifteen-year-old Indian
girl who—judging from the wild enthusiasm—had very important
things to say about sex and saris. Larry couldn't imagine what
important things a fifteen-year-old girl had to say about sex. He
mused that he was surely approaching middle age when he began
considering adolescence unimportant, and then in self-defense
tried to learn the title of the book so that he could buy it and read
it with appreciative tolerance for the very young. Apparently
none of the editors or publishers were interested in the title. They

were solely concerned with discovering how a fifteen-year-old Indian girl had come to know so much about sex. They were climactically discussing a particularly inflammable chapter of the book when Baxter walked into the bar.

Larry rose and signaled to him, and he came to the table immediately, his hand extended.

"Good to see you, Larry," he said. "I need a drink. Where's the waiter?"

They shook hands, and then ordered. Baxter made himself comfortable and said, "I was hoping Eve would be with you."

"No, not today," Larry said.

"I like that girl," Baxter said. "How is she?"

"Fine."

"I like her a great deal," Baxter said, and Larry felt a first indefinite twinge of warning. "Ah," Baxter said, "here're the drinks." He waited while the drinks were put down, and then he picked up his glass. "Something wrong with the times," he said. "Do you know that? I really look forward to this drink at the end of the day. Look forward to it? By God, I *need* it! I'm a mild alcoholic, I'm sure. But all I know is that after a day of pounding and pounding and pounding, I *need* this drink. Cheers." He drank. "How's Eve?" he asked.

"Fine," Larry repeated, the warning twinge stronger now. Baxter nodded. "How does she feel about Puerto Rico?"

"Well . . ."

"Or haven't you discussed it with her?"

"Certainly I have."

"Does she seem favorably inclined?"

"Well . . ."

"Or do I seem to be putting undue stress upon Eve's reaction?" Baxter smiled pleasantly and sipped at his drink. "Eloise and I will be going to Puerto Rico to live, you see. This isn't Scarsdale, Larry, and you simply don't commute. We'll be making our home there for at least five years, perhaps longer." He smiled again. "If you accept the job, we'll be working together most of the time. And we'll probably be together a lot socially, too."

The warning twinge was no longer that. It had grown into full-fledged recognition. Larry felt the blood draining from his face. He sat quite still, holding his glass to the table with both hands.

"That's why I'm so delighted Eve is the kind of person she is," Baxter said.

"What do you mean?" Larry asked, knowing his meaning already, knowing it now before amplification. His hands were beginning to tremble. Hastily, he gulped at his drink.

"Don't misunderstand me. Your wife could be the queen of England, and I still wouldn't have offered you the job if you weren't a good architect." He paused. "By the way, how's the Altar house going?"

"Fine, fine," Larry said. There was a tight knot inside him now. He kept staring across the table at Baxter, knowing what was coming, and yet silently, desperately hoping he was wrong.

"Good," Baxter said. "But Eve is important. She's the wife you should have, and the wife I'm glad you have. She'll help you a great deal on the island. And, of course, I'm being selfish. I like her company, and so does Eloise. We want her with us. She's one of the reasons I asked you." His smile widened. "Besides, I was hoping she'd sway you in favor of accepting. Has she?"

"I . . . I don't know. You mean," Larry said, "Eve is . . . is part of this?"

"Well, isn't she?" Baxter asked, his eyebrows raising in surprise.

"Of course," Larry said quickly. "I meant . . ."

"Do you mean if Eve were against it, would I allow you to take the job anyway?"

"Well, yes. Something like that."

"Definitely not!" Baxter said. "I believe in marriage strongly, Larry. And I don't think I've seen two people more perfectly suited to each other than you and Eve. If Eve doesn't want to go, I wouldn't dream of separating you. Maintaining a marriage is the most important thing I can think of. More important than Puerto Rico. Even more important than *architecture*. That's the way I feel about it."

"I see," Larry said dully.

"Why? Doesn't Eve want to go?"

"It's not that."

"What is it then?"

"Nothing. We . . . we just haven't decided yet."

"Oh?" Baxter seemed surprised. "I was hoping that was why you wanted to see me today."

"No, no. I just felt like socializing, I guess."

"Well, I'm glad you came in. I'm always happy to see you. But bring Eve next time, why don't you?"

"I will," Larry promised.

"I like that girl," Baxter said. "She's pretty, and intelligent, and a woman. And she has dignity. I can't abide women who are too blatant about their femaleness. Eve is a quiet woman, the kind I'd like for a daughter." Baxter grinned. "Perhaps I shouldn't be telling you all this. But I'm trying to make our relationship something more than a cut-and-dried business deal. I want to work with you, Larry, but I want us to be friends, too."

"I understand," Larry said, thinking how quickly everything seemed to drop to the common denominator of free choice. There were always simple choices to be made, except the simple choices were always so goddamn difficult. And now it was no longer a question of Puerto Rico *and* Maggie. The choice was between them—one or the other. A very simple choice, he thought, for a man who wants and needs both. Take Puerto Rico, and be unhappy without Maggie. Take Maggie and be unhappy without work. The choice is really very clear and simple: You can either be unhappy or—you can be unhappy.

Choose!

"I hope you'll be letting me know your decision soon, Larry," Baxter said. "If Eve has any doubts, let me know and I'll talk to her."

"No," Larry said hastily. "It isn't that. We're just considering every possibility."

"I see. Well, of course it's up to you. But Eve's a sensible girl, and I doubt very much that she'll let you pass up an opportunity like this one. Not unless I've greatly underestimated her."

Larry tried to grin. "I'm getting an inferiority complex," he said.

"No need to. Whatever we feel for Eve reflects upon you. She's your wife, Larry, and that's what marriage is. A complete sharing. It has to be if it's going to work."

"Yes," Larry said.

Baxter looked at his watch. "Can I inveigle you into dinner with Eloise and me?"

"Thanks, not tonight," Larry said. "I've got to get back."

"Well, then, I've got to rush. Larry, think this thing over seriously, won't you? Time's running short, and I want you and Eve with me. Sincerely, I do. Think it over." Baxter smiled. "When you get right down to it, I'm sure you'll find it's not such a hard decision to make at all."

BOOK THREE

27

THE ONE thing Eve Cole would not admit to herself was that Larry was having an affair.

All summer long the idea spread like a plaster crack in the ceiling of her mind. With each new marital door slam, the crack widened, sending out tendrils which threatened the walls themselves. She kept her eyes away from the ceiling, unwilling to believe that so small a fissure had become so wide a chasm.

At the same time she kept waiting for the ceiling to crash down around her in a sudden implosion of plaster dust and lath. As frequently as the idea of infidelity entered her mind, it was rejected. Skirting the thought, rushing blindly around its boundaries, refusing to accept it, she found confusion rising unchallenged in her mind. Something had come into her life and her marriage, wedged itself between her and her husband with granite immobility. For perhaps the first time in her life, she felt uncertainty that summer, a terrifying, unsolvable doubt which began to upset the everyday machinery of her home.

"Can I go over to Bobby's, Ma?" Chris would ask.

"May I," she would correct automatically.

"Well, *may* I?" and Eve would think for a moment, trying to remember who Bobby was, where he lived, whether there were dangerous streets to cross.

"I don't know," she would say hesitantly.

Chris would look at her in puzzlement and ask, "Well, yes or no?"

"Yes," she would answer. "No. All right. But be careful."

By June the planning of meals became something she detested. Coping with her private problem, struggling with what she was sure was the dissolution of her marriage, she found food and eating insignificant. The last time she'd abhorred food was while she was carrying David, but she was then in the overshadowing midst of steady, slow creation. Her resentment now was a different reaction. The dinner table, which had always been a meaningful part of the family experience, became shallow and empty when the family experience itself was threatened with destruction. More and more, the planning of meals became a tasteless, unappreciated chore.

One night, as she placed a platter of lamb chops in the center of the table, David wailed, "Oh, no, not again!"

"What?"

"We had those *last* night," Chris informed her complainingly.

She stared at the meat for a moment, and then snapped, "Your father likes lamb chops. Now start eating or you'll both go to your room."

At the market she found herself taking the same shopping list item from the shelves twice and then discovering the duplicate at the checkout counter. While driving, she failed to notice lights when they changed to green, was constantly being snapped out of her thoughts of Larry by the sharp honk of horns behind her. At the bank she failed to make a covering deposit in the checking account, with the result that two checks came back marked INSUFFICENT FUNDS.

In July she bought herself a pair of knee-length hose because they were on sale and because she liked the color. When she got home, she realized she hadn't even looked at the size before snatching them from the counter. The socks were three sizes too small for her. She found herself forgetting to leave notes for the milkman, forgetting social appointments, forgetting to return overdue books to the library. And all the while, the one thing she wanted to forget remained immovable in a dark corner of her mind.

When her mother asked her to come out to the beach at East-hampton for a few days in the beginning of August, she leaped at the opportunity. As was usually the case, Mrs. Harder's invitation had certain limitations and conditions. The beach house was thronged with her own friends on weekends, so any weekend was out of the question. The twins had invited some girl friends for Wednesday and Thursday on condition that they'd leave early Friday morning. In any case, *those* two days were struck off the calendar.

"So when *would* you like to come, darling?" Mrs. Harder asked.

"Friday," Eve said.

"Eve, I just told you I'll be having other guests. It'll have to be next week sometime, I guess. Perhaps Monday or . . ."

"Do you have a single bed somewhere?"

"What do you mean?"

"A bed I can sleep in."

"Well, of course, I have a bed you can sleep in. But you're four people counting Larry and the children. I can't put you all in one—"

"I want to come out alone, Mama," Eve said.

"Alone?"

There was a long silence on the line.

Then Mrs. Harder said, "Is anything wrong?"

"No. I just feel like getting away by myself for a few days."

There was another silence.

Mrs. Harder said, "Darling, if something's wrong . . ."

"No, Mama. Do you have a bed for me?"

244

"Come whenever you like, Eve," Mrs. Harder said. "Come today if you like."

"I'll be there Friday afternoon."

"All right." Mrs. Harder paused. "Eve . . ." she said.

"Yes?"

"You're not pregnant again, are you?"

"No, Mama."

"All right, then, I'll see you Friday. Bring some heavy sweaters. It gets cool at night."

When she presented the idea to Larry, he accepted it readily, agreeing a few days' rest was just what she needed. Perhaps she was hoping for an objection from him—but none came.

On Thursday night he helped her pack. And at eight o'clock on a Friday morning in the first week of August, Eve drove away from the house in Pinecrest Manor. It was the first time she'd been separated from her husband in the eight years of their marriage.

There was, not far from the development, a children's amusement area called Joyland.

Joylessly built on two acres of back-topped ground, Joyland boasted its own parking lot and restaurant, and rides ranging from the carousel to a miniature roller coaster. On Saturday, her housework finished, Don busy in the back yard planting shrubs around the new patio, Maggie drove her son to the small-scale amusement park. Patrick had been to Joyland perhaps fifty times since they'd moved into the development, but he never tired of the place. Vicariously, she shared in his childish joy, grinning at him as the carousel whirled by, putting her hand to her mouth when he shrieked on the Whip.

She persuaded him to take a breather by buying him an ice-cream cone in the Joyland restaurant. They were walking outdoors again when she spotted Larry. At first she couldn't believe her eyes. Her mouth opened in a small surprised "Oh." She smiled, her cheek dimpling, took Patrick's free hand and fairly dragged him to where Larry was standing with his sons.

He turned to her in astonishment. "Maggie! What—"

"Hi," she said. "Oh, hi, hi!"

"What are you doing here?"

"Hello, Chris," Patrick said.

"Hello, Patrick."

"What are *you* doing here?" Maggie asked.

"I just thought I'd take the kids—" He shrugged, grinning happily.

"This's my little brother," Chris said. "His name's David."

"Hi," David said. He looked at Patrick cautiously.

"Hi," Patrick answered.

"He's three," Chris said.

245

"Yeah?"

"Yeah, I'm three," David said.

"So I'm five."

"So I'm three," David said, "*Chris* is five."

"I don't have any brothers," Patrick said.

"Well, I got a brother," David said, "and anyway, I'm almost four."

"So what?" Patrick said. "Do you go to school?"

"He's too small for school," Chris said.

"I'm gonna go to nursery school maybe," David said, frowning.

"That ain't real school," Patrick said. "I went on the Whip and everything," he added, dismissing David and turning to Chris.

"Hey, Dad, can we go on the rides?" Chris asked excitedly.

"Sure, sure," Larry said.

He bought tickets, and they put all three children on a ride with miniature tanks and noisy machine guns.

"You look beautiful, Mag," he said. "If I'd known you could get away . . ."

"Don was busy out back. I didn't even tell him I was leaving." She paused. "Have you been managing all right?"

"Yes, fine."

"When's she coming back?"

"Monday night."

They were leaning on the grilled railing which fenced in the tank ride. He covered her hand with his, and she glanced hastily over her shoulder and then turned back to him.

"Did you put up a struggle when she asked to go?"

"No."

"Do you think she might return the courtesy?"

"What do you mean?"

"Do you think *you* might be able to get away for a few days?"

He was silent for a moment. "Maybe."

"I might be able to."

"When?"

She shrugged. "You name it."

"Would he let you go?"

"You let Eve go, didn't you?"

"Yes."

"He'll let me go."

"It'll have to be after the Altar house is finished."

"Whenever you say," she said.

"The ride's over. Here they come."

The children emerged from their tanks like troops come to liberate France. David, in the presence of the older boys, walked with a particularly cocky swagger. In an aside to Chris, he whispered, "Don't tell him I wet the bed." They swarmed about Larry and Maggie, and then ran off in three separate directions, heading for the rides of their choice. Larry and Maggie rounded them up and deposited them together on a ride which featured motorboats in water. David complained because he got the back seat of a boat Patrick was steering.

"Where would we go?" she asked.

"I don't know. Upstate someplace?"

"Let's go somewhere new," she said. "Where neither of us has ever been."

"All right."

"We can pretend we're married for a few days," she said lightly.

And very seriously he answered. "Yes, we can pretend we're married."

They watched the children in silence. David sat morosely at the back of the boat, his arms folded stoically across his chest. Patrick handled the wheel with a yachtsman's elegance, little realizing the boat would move in its prescribed circle no matter what steering feats he performed. Monotonously, the boats moved around and around. The children tugged at the wheels, wrenched at them, yanked at them, spun them, twisted them, but the metal bars connecting the boats to the center hub kept them moving in a regular, unbending circle, around and around.

He felt rather sad all at once. There was an artificiality to the revolving boats, a directed falseness which mocked reality. Watching the children and the boats, he felt a part of the fake, felt the sham spreading until it included him and Maggie. Wasn't the course of their affair as predetermined as the course of the boats? What promise was there for them but a narrow orbit around a hub of deceit? Their universe was restricted by the four walls of a motel and now, expanding—this giant, expanding universe!—it would include a secret weekend perhaps, and then back again to the exile of the motel sign blinking vacancy, emptiness.

The boats moved around and around monotonously.

He had to believe there was more for them, but he could not build such faith on the meanderings of his own mind. There were things he had to know which only she could tell him. Was this all there would ever be for them, the world of the neon motels beckoning vacancy, VACANCY, vacancy, the quick, pretended weekends—was this to be the sum total of all they'd ever known together, would they remember this only as the spaced regularity of vacancy, VACANCY, vacancy?

He had to know where they were going.

"Let's get out of here," he said sharply. "Do you have the car with you?"

"Yes," she said, surprised by the harshness in his voice.

"All right, let's give them a few more rides and then clear out. What time do you have to be back?"

"I have to prepare dinner. Four-thirty? Five?"

"Good."

The children protested but were led off to the car anyway, and Maggie drove out on the parkway to one of the county picnic areas. He watched her while she drove. Occasionally, she took one hand from the wheel to touch his hand where it rested on the seat. The three boys sat in the back. David wanted to sit by the window, but Patrick said it was his car and wouldn't let him.

"Do you feel suburban?" she asked him. "With your wife driving and your three children on the back seat?"

"Yes," he said, "I feel suburban as hell."

"What's wrong, Larry?"

"Nothing."

The picnic grounds were swarming with city dwellers. He took one look at the crowd and said, "Maybe this isn't so wise."

"Mary Garandi again?" she asked. "It doesn't matter. We've got three wonderful alibis with us."

They allowed the children to run free. Idly, they walked side by side behind them.

"I met Don on a picnic, you know."

"I didn't know," he said absently. He was thinking there were only two types of memories they shared: those concerned with the lying necessary to protect their meetings; and those concerned with the passion they knew when they were together. Passion and Deceit, he thought. I'll give it to Roger Altar. It'll make a good title for a collection of short stories about jungle animals. That's funny, all right. That's hilarious. When did mankind stop crying and begin joking about the things that really mattered most?

"I was only sixteen," Maggie said. "Eleven years ago—what a long time to know a person. I wish I'd met you instead, Larry. I wish you'd come eleven years ago."

"Sure," he said, "but I didn't," and there was the same curious harshness in his voice.

She turned to him. "Don't you want to hold my hand?" she asked. He glanced at the crowd. "Oh, who gives a damn about *them*?" she said, tossing her pony tail in a defiant gesture which included the entire world.

He took her hand.

"Are you frightened?" she asked.

"Not of people."

"They're the only things to fear," Maggie said. She paused. "Don took my hand on that picnic. He was very shy, but he took my hand. We were at Pelham Bay Park, and they were ready to start a three-legged race and I needed a partner. So I asked Don. He'd already graduated, you know. In fact, he'd just got out of the Army. He'd been a big wheel at the school, one of the girls said. Captain of the swimming team. We were city champs the year he was captain."

"Is that why you asked him to be your partner?"

"Oh, no, don't be silly."

"Then why?" he said.

"He simply seemed nice. So I went over and said, 'Will you race with me?' And he looked at me for a few minutes without saying anything, and then he got up from where he was lying and just said, 'Sure.' I held out my hand, and he took it. We lost the race. But when it was over, he said, 'My name's Don Gault. What's yours?' I said, 'Margaret Wagner,' and he said, 'Why don't we take a walk? So we did. And that was the start of it. It's funny the way people start, isn't it?"

"Oh, yes, it's sidesplitting," he said.

"Larry, what's the matter with you? Is something wrong?"

"Was he your first boy friend?"

"Yes."

"Did you go to bed with him?"

"No, oh no. He always treated me like a . . . a saint." She looked puzzled for a moment. "Sometimes I think he's afraid of me, afraid of my being a woman." She shook her head. "This is silly. Let's talk about something else."

"Why'd you marry him, Maggie?"

"I don't know. He was pleasant and good looking and . . . and considerate, I guess."

"Did you love him?"

"Who knows what love is at that age? I was only eighteen when we got married."

"But you married him. You must have had a reason."

"I felt safe with him. I guess I needed someone to make me feel that way again."

"Do you feel safe with me?"

"No."

"No?" he said, surprised.

"Because I don't really have you, Larry. I only borrow you."

"And only when you need me."

"I need you *all* the time. You know that."

"Maybe you need us both," he said slowly. "Maybe I'm no good without him there, too," and there he was face to face with the unasked question. The conversation, it seemed, had followed the course of every talk they'd ever had since the very beginning. Without conscious will or direction from either of them, it had moved the issue to the point where the asking of the ultimate question was inescapable. And now, poised for interrogation, he wondered if the question *should* be voiced, and knew that he would voice it no matter what reasonable arguments his mind presented against it. And he felt, too, that nothing would be changed by her answer. Whatever she answered, the unretreating boundaries of their isolated universe would remain ever and always the same. There really was no sense in asking at all. And yet, he put the question.

"Suppose I wanted you to leave him, Maggie?"

"Don't," she said flatly.

"Why not?"

She hesitated a long time, and then she said, "I want it to stay the way it is."

And that was her answer. Not the desired answer, perhaps not really an answer at all. Perhaps just another pretense, another mockery, another shallow attempt to preserve the walls which hemmed them in. And faced with it, he thought, That isn't all, that can't be all!

"Nothing stays the way it is!" he said fiercely. "Everything changes."

"We'll never change," she said.

"That's romantic as hell, but it isn't true. You change or you die, Maggie! Haven't *you* changed since this started? Jesus Christ, *I* can't even *recognize* myself any more!"

She laughed lightly and said, "How'd this get so serious all of a sudden?"

"I want it to get serious, Maggie! For once, just for once, let's take a good look at ourselves. All right? Where the hell are we going, Maggie? What the hell is there for us? Where's our place in this world? Am I supposed to be a perennial lover? I'm a man, Maggie. Goddamnit, there's more to life than just . . . just . . ."

"Just love?" she said quietly.

"No, but there's more than just love-making! Otherwise we're only animals. We're substituting . . ."

"Don't you like to make love to me?"

"Maggie, for Christ's sake, don't be dense," he said fiercely. "I'm trying to tell you it's no good this way."

"Do you want to end it?" she asked calmly.

"No!"

"Then what do you want?" she asked.

"I want to *begin* it. I have to know where you stand and what you expect. I have to be able to pick up the pieces of my life and put them together into a reasonable—"

"I told you what I want," she said calmly.

"What do you want?"

"I want it to stay the way it is," she said calmly.

"It can't stay the way it is!"

"But it has to," she said calmly. "That's the only way I can have you, Larry, and I do want you."

"All of me? Or just the happy swordsman? Do you want the guy who's frustrated and frightened and confused? Do you want the guy who cries alone at night sometimes? Do you want all of me, Maggie, or just the goddamn stranger who makes love to you once a week?"

"That isn't kind, Larry," she said calmly.

"Neither is survival! It's cruel and realistic, and I'm trying to survive! I have to know where I'm going," he said. "I have to know, or I'll love my—"

"I don't want to know," she said calmly. "Let it happen. Let whatever's going to happen happen." She squeezed his hand. "Isn't it enough that we'll be going away together for a few days?"

"No," he said. "It isn't enough."

"It's enough for me," she said. "When will the Altar house be finished?"

"The end of the month."

"This month? August?"

"Yes."

"Could we go away the last week in August? That would be a nice time, Larry."

"If the house is finished," he said. "Look, Maggie, can we just get back to this for a minute? I don't think you realize how important it is to me, or you wouldn't brush it off like . . . like . . . Do you know Baxter and Baxter? The firm that sent me to Puerto Rico? Well, they've asked—"

"I don't care!" Patrick suddenly roared. "I don't like you, either."

"Oh-oh," Maggie said, and she broke into a run. Emptily, Larry watched her, the blue skirt flapping about the firm calves, the ankles strong and slender, the skirt flattening against rounded thighs. He sighed and slowly walked to where she stood with the children in a bristling knot.

"He's smaller than you!" Chris yelled.

"So what? He started it!" Patrick said.

"I did not!" David bellowed.

"You did so!"

"Boys," Maggie said.

"I did not!"

"You did so!"

"Boys, boys," Maggie said more firmly.

"Now let's just calm down," Larry said.

"He hit David," Chris said, "so I slugged him."

"Why'd you do that?" Larry asked.

"I just told you. He hit David."

"Why'd you hit David?" Maggie asked her son.

"He started it."

"I did not!" David shouted. "You're a bully."

"Now stop that, David," Larry said.

"Well, he is. I'm only three, and he picked on me."

"You're almost four," Patrick said.

"You want me to slug you again?" Chris asked.

"I don't like that word, Chris," Larry said.

"Is it a dirty word?" Chris asked.

"No, but I don't like it."

251

Patrick suddenly began crying. Maggie took him into her arms. "They ganged up on me," he sobbed. "Both of them."

"Well, they're brothers, sweetheart," Maggie said. "That's what brothers are for."

"Why don't you get *me* a brother?" Patrick sobbed.

"Now stop crying. Come on."

"They ganged up on me. They surrounded me."

"Tell Patrick you're sorry, Chris," Larry said.

"What for? He hit David."

"I know, but tell him you're sorry."

"But I'm *not* sorry. You told me if anybody hurt David, I should slug him. So why should I be—?"

"Chris, I said I don't like that word."

"Which word?"

"Slug."

"Okay, but didn't you say I should protect David? He's my brother, and Patrick's a stranger, and you said family is family and strangers . . ."

"It's all right, Larry," Maggie said. "You know how children are."

Patrick had stopped crying. He looked at Chris surlily now, embarrassed by his earlier tears.

"You want to be friends?" Chris asked, holding out his hand.

"No."

"Okay, so don't."

"He hit me," David said, seemingly proud that he'd caused the altercation.

"Come on," Larry said, "shake hands and make up."

"He don't want to," Chris said. He stuck out his hand again. "You want to or not, Patrick?"

Reluctantly, Patrick took the offered hand and gave it a jerky shake. The boys began walking back to the car, vaguely communicative, friendly in a hostile way. Larry and Maggie walked behind them silently.

At last she said, "Family is family, and strangers are strangers."

"He meant . . ."

"Yes," she said, as if finally presenting him with the irrefutable answer to his question.

Mr. Harder was very proud of his grown-up married daughter.

"This is the girl who made me a grandfather," he told his friends at the cottage, and his eyes glowed with parental pleasure. Mrs. Harder told him to stop fussing over the poor girl, and then took Eve aside.

"You don't have to be nice or even polite, Eve," she said. "You came for a rest, and you'll get one."

"Thank you, Mama," Eve said.

Mrs. Harder took her daughter into her arms and said, "If there's anything you want to tell me . . ."

"No, Mama."

"All right. Then change and go down to the beach. Get some sun. There isn't a woman in the world who doesn't feel better with an attractive suntan."

On the beach, her problems seemed to vanish.

Swimming in the surf, lying on the sand afterward in her brief wet swim suit, she shut out the world and indulged in an orgy of the senses. The sun baked her, and the mild ocean wind cooled her naked limbs. There was the smell of salt in the air, the lulling whisper of the ocean in her ears. Occasionally a boat would appear on the far horizon, and she would sit up to look at it, feeling detached and irresponsible, suspended in a timeless coma. She took long walks along the lonely shore, searching the trackless dunes for seashells, stopping in complete freedom to study a sudden cloud formation. Pinecrest Manor seemed a million miles away. Here, on the edge of eternity, she felt at peace with nature and herself. As evening pressed on, as the sun vanished and purple dusk stained the sky, she would pick up her canvas bag, the wind whipping her hair over her shoulders, and alone she would walk back to the cottage feeling as wistfully fulfilled as a sixteen-year-old girl.

Her parents' friends contributed to this feeling of youthfulness she experienced. Sitting on the screened porch of the cottage, listening to the drone of their voices, sipping cocktails with them as stars invaded the sky, their advanced years contrasted sharply with the youth she felt surging through her body.

And late at night, lying alone in her narrow bed, looking through the screened window at the gleaming wheel of night, she felt a deep contentment she had not known since the summer began. She felt again like a young and desirable woman.

28

ON THE Monday after Eve returned from Easthampton, Felix Anders committed a series of blunders which might have been forgivable in a lesser man.

But Felix was not a lesser man. In his own estimation, he was possessed of keen observational powers, an excellent sense of timing, and a shrewd ability to judge character. He had learned through the development grapevine that Eve had gone out to the beach alone the week before. Silently, he wondered why Eve had felt the need to get away for a few days and, triumphantly, he concluded that a woman who left home was a restless woman. This was not too difficult to understand. With young Lawrence playing the field, was it not entirely plausible that Eve was being neglected? Felix did not like the idea of someone as attractive as Eve being shunted aside. This was extreme wastefulness which he could never condone.

Besides, he was firmly convinced that she was ripe.

He had seen her on the day after her return from Easthampton. She had acquired a beautiful tan, and her eyes were a shocking blue against her oval face. There was something patrician about this girl's features, Felix thought, something untouchable, something almost rarefied. He would like to hold her face in his hands and watch those cool blue eyes explode in ecstasy. He would like that. She had been wearing a halter and shorts that Wednesday. The halter was very brief, and her breasts crowded it, and he could see the milk-white inch of flesh above the slender halter where the skin had been protected by her bathing suit, where the sun had not touched her. She worked barefooted in the back yard, her legs long and clean, stemming in firm three dimensionality from the turned-up cuffs of her shorts. He had walked past the house and nodded to her briefly. She had smiled back at him, her teeth dazzling white against the tanned skin.

Cool, Felix thought.

And, patiently, he waited.

His calculations on the following Monday seemed true and sharp, but of course he did not have the benefit of either Larry's or Maggie's counsel. He judged the events as they happened and formed what seemed to him logical conclusions. He was relaxing on the front steps of his house at eight o'clock that night, reading the *Daily News*. Dick Tracy was bound to a cake of ice, floating down a river. It looked like the end for Dick Tracy. Felix sighed, and then glanced up when he saw the front door of the Gault house opening.

Margaret Gault came out of the Cape Cod, hesitated a moment, and then rushed down the steps. Felix watched her. There was a smell on this one and Felix reluctantly admired Larry for having recognized it. There was, too, a sure femaleness to her walk, the tread of a jungle cat padding familiar paths. She turned left on the slate which ran past the big maple on the front lawn, and then walked to the garage at the back of her house. Felix watched her. She was wearing a green silk dress and high-heeled pumps. All decked out, he thought, and instantly assumed she was going to meet Larry. He watched the dress move up over her knees as she slid onto the seat of the Chevy. He waited while she started the car, and then watched as she backed it into the street. She seemed in a terrible rush. She didn't even wave to him as she drove away.

Felix busied himself with his newspaper, and waited.

No matter how he read it, it still looked like the end for Dick Tracy.

In ten minutes Larry Cole drove past his house. He honked the horn at Felix and waved. Felix waved back. Hurry up, lover, he thought. She's got a ten-minute start on you.

He folded his newspaper and walked into the house.

"Betty," he said, "I'm going over to Larry's. See if he wants a glass of beer."

"Do you ever think of helping around here?" Betty asked.

"Do you ever think of going into the city every day to cut meat?" he asked. "I may be late. I've got a big thirst."

"You're getting to be a drunkard," Betty said, and she plunked another dish into the soapy water.

Felix went to the bathroom, combed his hair, and left the house. He assumed his calculations so far had been correct. The lovers had left to meet each other. It was close to eight-thirty, which meant that Eve would be through with the after-dinner mess, the children in bed. And even the weather seemed to be with him. Black clouds were piling up in the sky. That meant rain, and rain would drive everyone indoors. Not that it really mattered. There was certainly nothing suspicious about a visit from a friend and neighbor. Still, the rain wouldn't hurt. He glanced skyward, and even as he did, the first drops started to fall in a slow, steady drizzle. He grinned and began walking faster, convinced that all of his observations were as true as the forecast of rain.

He didn't know this was the only safe conclusion he'd drawn, or that he was yet to commit his biggest blunder.

To begin with, the haste with which Margaret Gault had left her house was occasioned by a dental appointment for eight o'clock in Dr. Bennuti's office, an appointment for which she was already late. She was not hurrying to meet Larry. Her rendezvous was with a drill.

Nor had Larry driven past on his way to meet her. Larry was simply driving into town to pick up some art supplies, and he would not be gone all night as Felix had surmised. He was, in fact, not more than two miles away buying pencils and erasers when Felix knocked on his front door.

Nor had Eve, ripe or not, completely finished with the after-dinner duties. True, the children were in bed and the dishes done, but a shower was still on her schedule. She had gone to the bathroom, undressed, tied her hair back with a ribbon, and was adjusting the water preparatory to stepping into the tub when she heard the knocking at the door.

"Who is it?" she called.

The bathroom door was closed, so she could not be certain, but it sounded to her as if someone had entered the house without waiting for the customary "Come in." Even in gregarious Pinecrest Manor, this was a little odd. She put on her robe, opened the bathroom door, and peeked out.

"Who is it?" she asked again.

"Me. Felix."

"Oh," she said. "Larry isn't home, Felix."

"I know."

"I'm about to take a shower. Is it anything important?"

"It'll just take a minute, Eve."

"Well, all right," she said. "Sit down."

"I'm sitting already," he answered.

She closed the bathroom door and debated getting fully dressed again. She decided against it. He'd said he'd only take a minute, and she meant to keep him to that promise. She belted the robe tightly around her waist, turned up the collar to her throat, and then inspected herself in the mirror. The robe was a bulky terry cloth, unrevealing, thick, impenetrable. Satisfied, she put on her mules and went into the living room. Felix stood up when she came in.

"I hope I'm not bothering you," he said.

"Not at all," she answered, smiling politely. "What is it?" He seemed embarrassed to find her in a robe. The thought amused her slightly. She was completely and formidably covered, but nonetheless he avoided looking at her.

"I wanted to find out what you did with those azaleas," he said.

"Azaleas?" She went to the coffee table, took a cigarette from the box there, and lighted it.

"Yes. Out front."

"I don't understand. I didn't do anything with them."

"You handle the gardening around here, don't you?"

"Yes," Eve said. She sat in one of the easy chairs, tucking the robe around her. Outside, the falling drizzle washed the development streets.

"Well, they're coming along beautifully. Betty and I want to buy some, but we want to know first . . ." He paused. "You've got your hair back, haven't you?"

"What?" Eve said.

"Your hair."

Her hand went to the back of her neck. "Oh, yes."

"It looks prettier loose."

"Well, I don't like shower caps," she said. "It gets wet this way, but at least it's manageable."

"Why don't you loosen it, Eve?"

"What do you mean?"

"Why don't you take off the ribbon?"

"Because I'm going into the shower as soon as you leave."

"But it looks prettier loose."

"Well, I'll wear it loose later."

"Let it fall free, Eve," he said. "Let it fall around your face."

256

Eve did not answer him. She looked at him, puzzled.

"You have a very pretty face, Eve."

"Thank you," she said quickly. "About the azaleas, all I did was dig a hole and spread peat moss into the bottom of it. And I kept them watered. That's all I did." She rose. Felix kept sitting.

"When did you plant them?" he asked.

"In the spring."

"Do you think I ought to wait for the spring?"

"I don't know." She shrugged.

"Yes, but what do you think? Should I wait until the spring, or should I plant now?"

"I really don't know, Felix. I don't think August is very good for putting plants in, but it's up to you. The nursery might not guaran—"

"Take off the ribbon, Eve," Felix said.

"Felix, let's not be foolish," she said. "I have to take a shower."

Felix stood up. She watched him as he walked toward her. For the first time since he had entered the house, she felt somewhat frightened. She did not move when he reached out to loosen the ribbon, and yet she felt she was succumbing, powerless to his will. She felt that if she allowed him to take off that silly piece of cloth, it would be the same as if he . . . as if he . . . but she did not move. She felt his fingers plucking at the silk. The ribbon fell. Her hair tumbled about her face. Felix moved back from her, the ribbon in his hands. The room was gray with the drizzle that oozed along the big picture window facing the street.

"There," he said, "that's better." He grinned. "You've got a very pretty face, and very lovely eyes."

Eve smiled nervously. "Well, I'm not going to argue with you about a ribbon," she said, the words spilling from her mouth. "I doubt that the nursery will guarantee anything you plant in . . ."

"Eve . . ."

". . . in August. You should consider that if . . ."

They saw the lightning streak simultaneously. It flashed across the sky with sudden, startling brilliance, a jagged, luminescent yellow-white. And then, after the space of a heart beat, the thunder followed, and the heavier rain was unleashed all at once, lashing across the development streets in unchallenged fury.

"It's really beginning to come down," Felix said.

"I'd better turn on the lights."

"What for?"

"It's . . . it's getting dark in here."

"Don't you like to watch a storm?"

"Yes," she said quietly.

"Then leave the lights out."

Across the street she saw Arthur Garandi run toward his car with a newspaper over his head. He rolled up the windows and then ran back to the house.

"I like storms," Felix said.

Eve said nothing. Their eyes met and held.

"Was it very painful?" Felix asked. "Taking off the ribbon."

In a whisper, she said, "No."

"Was it?" he demanded.

She raised her eyes to meet his. "No," she said, slightly louder.

"Now take off the robe," Felix said.

Lightning flashed into the sky, illuminating the room with its sudden electric glow. Thunder bellowed on the horizon.

"Take it off, Eve," Felix said gently.

She did not answer. She kept staring at him. She could feel her loosened hair against her cheeks.

"Take it off, Eve," Felix said. "You want to, and I know it."

He took a slow step forward. She saw his hands reaching out, but she could not move to stop him. He grasped the lapels of her robe and with a swift motion pulled it open down the front. She felt cold air attack her nipples as her breasts spilled free. Felix backed away from her and studied her appraisingly. She made no motion to close the robe. She stood facing him, staring at him.

"Beautiful," he said, and then he moved toward her again.

She brought her arm back and released it in a roundhouse swing, her open palm colliding with Felix's cheek. The slap resounded in the dim silence of the room. Felix blinked.

"Get out," she whispered.

Rubbing his face, Felix grinned and said, "Let's not kid each other, Eve. I know what you want."

"Get out," she repeated, her voice a deadly whisper.

Felix kept grinning. "Sure, sure. But what we both know is that in about two minutes we'll be in that other room."

"Take your filthy eyes off me," she said, and she pulled the robe shut. She belted the terry cloth and stood facing him, her eyes slitted, her voice going on in its controlled, furious whisper. "Get out of here before I call the police."

"Now look, Eve," Felix said, still grinning.

"Get out!"

"Come on, come on," he said, stepping toward her.

"Oh, you filthy rotten bastard," she said, and tears welled into her eyes, and in a moment of sudden recognition, Felix realized he'd miscalculated. He realized he'd committed a serious blunder. "*Get out! Get out!*" she said, and this time she hurled the words, and he could see she was beginning to tremble, and he was afraid she would scream in the next minute. He turned and went to the door. He did not say goodbye. Silently, he walked out into the rain.

Eve stood in the center of the room trembling. She did not want to cry, but she could not stop the tears. She cried into her open hand, and she said to no one, "Oh, the rotten filthy bas-

added tolerantly, the man had apologized profusely, when the incident was over, and had offered to take Felix to a doctor, which medical aid Felix had heroically refused.

Betty was properly sympathetic and properly indignant. She could not understand why a man drank in a bar—wasn't his home a good enough place for drinking? But if he had to go to a bar, why did he choose a place where drunks threw around beer bottles? Fussily maternal, she had made him a purifying ice-cream soda with vanilla ice cream and Coca-Cola, and then they'd gone to bed. Felix lay awake half the night, thinking. By morning he had formulated an attitude and a course of action.

He admitted reluctantly that he had been wrong about Eve. It wasn't that she couldn't be had; there wasn't a woman alive who couldn't be had. It was simply that she couldn't be had right now. His timing had been off, that was all. Nonetheless, he put Eve Cole out of his mind as a possible acquisition. He had violated one of his own tenets—"Never spit where you eat!"—when he'd approached her. The experience had been unsatisfactory and served to strengthen his own sound judgment regarding neighborhood philandering. Eve Cole, as far as Felix was concerned, was finished business.

On the other hand, Larry Cole stuck in his craw.

Felix had taken the beating, but even while the fists were pummeling him into the booth he'd been thinking, You won't get away with this! He had lain awake the night before plotting his revenge. By morning, he realized that revenge, for the time being anyway, was impossible. Not only impossible but unthinkable. It annoyed him that instant reprisal was to be denied him. Larry Cole had behaved like an absolute ass. A man who was playing around had no right to get offended when a pass was made at his wife. Didn't Larry know the elementary rules of the game? Immediate revenge against this rebel would have been delightful—but for now revenge was impossible.

For if Felix went to Don Gault, as was his first impulse, Larry would instantly know who had betrayed him. He might then divulge the story of the beating to Betty. Was a petty revenge worth the sacrifice of a way of life? Certainly not. Felix enjoyed his extramarital excursions. Should Betty learn about the Eve Cole incident, she might divorce him. Or, worse thought, he might become a prisoner in his own home. It simply wasn't worth it, especially for something which had not paid off.

He wondered if Larry knew what powerful cards he was holding. And then a new, rather painfully amusing thought came to him. It occurred to him that should Don Gault, in any way whatever, tip to the affair, Larry would automatically assume Felix had been the informer. And believing that, there was again the danger that he would go to Betty in retaliation. The situation was a precarious one. Not only was Felix being forced to forego what would have been a delicious revenge, he was also being forced into the role of protector. Don Gault could not be allowed to find out about his wife and Larry. If he did, the repercussions would shake the very foundations of Felix's home.

Felix Anders surveyed his new role sourly and reached the conclusion that it stank.

Someday, perhaps, he could strike back at Larry with impunity. But for now he could only hope that his blunders—like Banquo's ghost—would not come back to haunt him.

It seemed coincidental but significant to Larry that the only two fist fights he'd had since he was twelve years old had both taken place in or around a phone booth and had both been in defense of a woman's honor. When he was a boy, his mother had drummed her own peculiar brand of chivalry into him with the oft-repeated advice: "Never get into a fight over a girl."

He had, in the past several months, got into two fights over two separate girls. One of those girls had been his wife. The concept was somehow amusing. Trudging back through the rain on the night of the beating, he had wanted to laugh aloud with the thought. He'd felt primitively, fiercely, instinctively protective of Eve when he'd left the house twenty minutes earlier. Now with his knuckles aching, with his clothes soaked, with the rain beating on his head in cold frenzy, he wanted to laugh to the skies. What the hell was so strange about defending your own wife? Wasn't that what husbands were for? And yet it was strange and puzzling and amusing. Wanting to laugh, he walked through the rain feeling very heroic and very content and very baffled.

When he got back to the house, Eve was waiting for him. He was going to spare her the details of the fight, but she saw his swollen hands and torn knuckles, and she began to cry instantly. She went to the bathroom for boric acid and hot water and then, gently bathing his hands, she listened to the story. When he was finished, she took his hands from the water and kissed them. Her eyes were glowing. They made love that night the way they had not made love in a very long while.

It was not until the next day that he began to think of the possible repercussions. Would Felix attempt reprisal? He considered the problem for a long time, and then decided he was safe. Felix would never reveal anything to Don because his own position was too vulnerable. Nonetheless, Maggie had to know of the incident if only to put her on guard should Felix behave unexpectedly. He called her that afternoon, and she became the fifth person to know about the beating.

As she put the phone back onto its cradle, she thought, He loves his wife.

The thought was not new to her, and so she could not under-

262

stand why it was causing so much pain. Surely she should have been used to it by this time. Certainly she had gone to bed with the thought often enough, awakened with it just as often.

He loves his wife.

It was a very simple thought, a very simple concept. And yet it hurt, it ached, it hurt like hell. Wearily, she sat at the pine-topped kitchen table, looking out at the bright August sunshine.

Well, Margaret, where do we go from here?

That was the same question Larry had asked, and now she was asking it too, and her answer was still the same: I want it to stay the way it is. Even though he loves his wife. That's all right. You knew he loved her all along. Maybe *he* didn't know it, but you certainly did, so let's not pretend this is a new thought. He beat up Felix, and Felix deserved it. He should have killed him. So be proud of him instead of getting foolish and jealous and depressed. You knew he loved his wife all along, so you've no reason to let it affect you this way.

Yes, he loves his wife.

Yes, well he does. Yes, but it hurts. I don't want him to love anyone but me; it hurts like hell that he should rush out to defend her pure white virgin clean pure damn honor. I wish Felix had got her. I wish to hell he had.

STOP IT!

She sat with her hands clasped tightly on the kitchen table.

Stop it.

Please.

Stop it.

Yes.

Nothing has changed. Everything is still the way it was, the way it will always be. Just this way, just the way I want it, and I don't care if he loves his wife. Let him love her, but let him belong to me without belonging. I will never never never again be left alone! And you will never leave me, Larry, because I'll give you what you want, not all, never that, never that again as long as I live, but enough, enough and you'll never leave me no matter how much you love her, you'll be mine always, I'll never lose again, it will stay the way it is, it will stay the way it is, I don't want it to be over!

She put her head on the table and began to weep.

Her grandfather had owned a shock of brilliant white hair. He was sixty-three years old, but he walked with his shoulders back and his head erect, and she always felt as if he were a very tall tall gentleman when she walked with him, even though he was only five-eight. Her grandfather had a mild German accent, and sometimes he used German words with her, words like "*Lieb-chen*" and "*Maggie-lein*."

He told her the most marvelous stories about Germany and Austria and skiing in the Alps. Sometimes he yodeled for her, just to prove he'd been to Switzerland. He had brown hands. His hands were always brown, with big veins that puffed out. She would sometimes push at the soft cushion of his veins and he would say, "*Gott*, Maggie, you will cut off der blood!"

She had loved her grandfather very much. She would always tell him so. "Papa," she would say, "I love you." He was really the warmest man in the entire world. She loved to walk with him, or talk to him, or just sit on his lap and say nothing or maybe push at his fat hand veins. He was retired, and so he was always there when she needed him. Sometimes he read to her. There were a lot of words he pronounced wrong, and when she laughed at him he would become furious, but she loved him even when his face was all red with anger.

They played a lot of games together, and whenever they played he would laugh with this very loud, ringing laugh. Whenever he laughed she would remember the stories he told her about sitting in a *brauhaus* and drinking good black beer, and she could see him sitting with the big stein in his hands, laughing and laughing. She loved his laugh, and she loved her grandfather with a special unreserved love she gave to no one else in the world.

She called him "Papa" because that was what her mother called him. She supposed in a way, with her father being a salesman and on the road so much, that Papa was almost like another father to her. And, of course, she loved her father too but not the way she loved Papa, not in that special way. He was always there with his gentle brown hands and his booming laugh and his warm voice and eyes. He was always there when she wanted him.

And then, right after Papa gave her the topaz earrings, everything changed.

In the apartment where they lived in the city, her bedroom was right next door to her parents', and she always slept with the door open because she was afraid of a completely dark room. She awoke in the middle of a weekend night, when her father was home. She heard loud voices, and she sleepily realized the voices were her mother's and father's, and she lay saucer-eyed in bed with the blankets pulled to her throat, a little frightened, not yet quite awake, listening to them.

"You don't know what you're talking about," her father said. "This is the stupidest thing I ever heard."

"It's not stupid at all," her mother answered. "*You're* stupid! For the first time in two years I'm telling you the truth, and you're too stupid to understand it."

"What truth? Do you call this truth? Is this what I come home to hear?"

"I'm in love with another man!" her mother shouted. "Learn it! Understand it!"

"I'll understand nothing of the sort."

"I love him, and he loves me. I've been going to bed with him for two years. Does that penetrate? To bed! For two years! I love him, and I want to go away with him."

"Stop it, Elizabeth. You'll wake the child."

"I don't care about the child. I want to settle this with you."

"You don't care about Margaret?"

"I don't care about anything but being with him."

"You're crazy, Elizabeth. Go to sleep. We'll talk about this in the morning."

"I want to settle it now."

"Settle what? What do you want? A divorce?"

"Yes."

"Have you told your father about this?"

"No."

"It would kill him."

"No."

"It would kill the old man, and you know it. You can't do this, Elizabeth. Don't you care about him at all? Or about your own daughter? Have you nothing left? Are you all filth?"

"I love him," she said flatly.

"Love is for the movies! What are you, a high-school girl? Don't talk foolishly, Elizabeth!"

"Won't you understand? My God, *won't* you understand?"

"I understand only that there's more involved here than your stupid little selfish affair! There's your daughter . . . and your father . . ."

"I'm going to tell him tomorrow."

"And you'll kill him."

"I won't kill him, don't worry. My father is a man. I wish I could say the same for you."

"I'm a man, Elizabeth," he said softly.

Margaret heard her mother laugh.

"I'm a man," he repeated.

"You're nothing," her mother said. "Not a man, not anything. You don't know what a man is!"

Margaret lay in the dark with the blankets pulled to her throat. She was very frightened. She had not understood all of what she'd heard, but she felt suddenly as if her parents were strangers, just a strange man and a strange woman who happened to be in the bedroom next to hers. And, trembling, lying with the darkness around her, she thought, I have Papa. Papa loves me. Papa will take care of me.

Her grandfather died the next week.

He died in his sleep, and everyone said it was a natural death for an old man. But Margaret knew what had really happened. Margaret knew that her mother had told him all those things. Margaret knew that her mother had killed Papa.

Her mother did not get the divorce she'd wanted; perhaps the death of the old man really affected her. In any case, she did not

265

go away. She continued to stay in a household that was suddenly filled with strangers. And once, months after the old man had been buried, Margaret walked into the kitchen to find her mother weeping. Her mother turned to her and said, "I've lost him, I've lost him," but Margaret knew she was not talking about Papa. She was talking about this other man someplace. And so she turned her back and left the room. After that there were new men. Margaret learned to sense when her mother was leaving the house to meet another man, but she didn't care by that time.

Her mother had killed the one person Margaret really loved, and now there was no one left to kill, and so she didn't care any more.

At ten years of age she had learned that you could never love anyone too deeply because you were always left alone.

Alone and afraid.

When Don came home from work that night, she told him about the beating even though she knew this presented a possible danger. The Coles were not truly friends of theirs, and he might wonder how she'd got access to the story. But she felt compelled to tell him, and he listened to the story gravely, and never once asked how she'd learned of the attack.

When it was over, he said, "I don't believe it."

"What don't you believe?"

"That Felix would be stupid enough to do a thing like that."

"Do you think Eve made up the story?"

"I don't know."

"Why should she make up a story like that?"

"I don't know." Don was pensive for a moment. Then he asked, "She's got two kids, hasn't she?"

"Yes."

"So how could Felix do anything like that? I don't believe it. Besides, she doesn't seem like the kind of girl who'd get into such trouble."

"But it happened."

"If it happened, it was Felix's fault. He must have a dirty mind."

"Maybe she asked for it," Maggie said.

"I'm sure she didn't. She's a married woman, the mother of two kids!"

Maggie looked at him unflinchingly. "Married women," she said slowly, "have been known to go to bed with other men on occasion. The idea may come as a shock to you . . ."

"It doesn't come as a shock to me, Margaret, but I'm glad I don't know any women like that. And Eve Cole certainly isn't that kind of a woman."

"How do you know?"

"I just know, that's all. You can tell by looking at her. She's

266

the mother of two kids, for God's sake, and I can't see her getting into a cheap stupid situation—"

"All right."

". . . where a fellow like Felix—"

"All right, Don."

". . . would take advantage of—"

"All right!" Maggie snapped. "You've successfully defended her honor!"

"Well, that's the way I feel."

"You missed your calling."

"What do you mean?"

"You should have been a press agent for Mother's Day."

"I don't think that's funny."

"I thought it was pretty funny," Maggie said. She left him and went into the kitchen to do the dishes, wondering what he would do if he ever found out his own wife, a *mother*, for God's sake, was one of those women he was glad he didn't know.

Don sat in his easy chair, picked up the newspaper, and began reading it. After a while, he called, "Do you really think Felix got funny with her?"

"Yes," she said.

"Poor kid," Don answered. "I wonder how she feels."

At first Eve felt nothing but pride.

Responding in a time-worn, timeless, female way, she knew only that her man had gone to her defense. The storm had intensified the protected feeling she'd known. Not only had Larry gone out to defy another man, but he'd casually defied the raging elements as well. The entire concept, she supposed, was completely medieval—the insult, the defense, the victorious return, the comforting, and then the reward. She had made love to him passionately that night. Her own ardor surprised her. Reaching for him, rediscovering him, she wanted to possess and be possessed. She knew pride and passion and ownership that night. That night he was her man.

In the morning everything seemed to have been forgotten.

The bedroom was still cool from the gratifying night breezes. Later in the day the August sun would attack the small ranch and render it insufferably hot. But now it was cool, and she opened her eyes and then sat up and stretched and ran her hands upward on the back of her neck, the long black hair tumbling through her fingers. She smiled contentedly, remembering.

Larry was already out of bed. She got up, went to the closet, and put on a blue peignoir. She hoped the children were already dressed and out of the house. Feeling quite saucy and daring, she went into the kitchen. Larry was standing at the counter spooning instant coffee into their cups. She went to him and stood behind him, her arms around his waist, her cheeks against his back. Then, without warning, she began caressing him.

"Hey!"

"Making coffee?" she cooed innocently.

"Come on, come on," he said. He caught her hands gently and turned to face her.

"Where are the kids?" she asked.

"Outside already."

"Did you give them breakfast?"

"Yes. David wouldn't eat his egg."

"Come into the bedroom with me," she said. "I want to show you something."

"What do you want to show me?"

"Me," she said.

"Come on, sexy. Get dressed."

"I'd rather get undressed."

"I guess I ought to beat people up more often."

"I guess you ought to."

"I guess so."

"I guess so." They stood looking at each other. Eve winked. "Well?"

"The kids'll be popping in and out."

"We'll lock the doors."

"Later," Larry said.

"Why not now?"

"I've got some work to do. A letter to Altar about a legitimate extra, and some other things."

"Oh." Eve shrugged. "Okay." She turned away from him. "Do you want toast?" she asked, and she hoped her disappointment did not show.

Several times that day she went into the small office and hovered about his board, but he did not give her much attention. And several times that day she found a persistent thought nagging her mind. Now that the episode with Felix was over, she began to wonder just what had provoked it. Unable to find within herself any reasons for Felix's bald assumption, honestly believing she had never given him the slightest indication of unrest or dissatisfaction or willingness to submit to his advances, she began to wonder just *what* had given him the idea.

And it was then that she once again thought of infidelity.

And immediately put it out of her mind.

To find it returning again immediately.

She had thought the weekend at Easthampton had banished the idea completely, but here it was back again, seemingly stronger after its short exile. She tried to ignore it, tried to pretend it was not there, but Larry's indifference strengthened the vague idea until it began taking firmer shape.

Was Larry being unfaithful to her? And had he confided this to Felix? And was this why Felix had assumed he could safely approach her?

The idea was fantastic, of course.

But possible.

Preposterous.

But plausible.

She allowed it to gnaw steadily at her mind.

Perhaps, if Larry had made love to her that day—or even that night—she'd have put the idea aside temporarily. But Larry did not make love to her.

Perhaps, too, if Harry Baxter had not called the next day, she'd have put the idea out of her mind permanently.

But Harry Baxter *did* call the next day.

30

WEDNESDAY morning.

The television forecasters the night before had promised temperatures in the high nineties. By eight in the morning the house was already suffocatingly hot. There was a muggy oppressiveness on the air, a clinging, crawling, penetrating, sticky heat that invaded clothing and furniture and flesh. There was a stillness to Pinecrest Manor. The lawns and the sidewalks and the roof tops baked. In the stillness, you could hear telephones ringing halfway up the block. You could hear a dog barking occasionally. The smothering blanket of August hung in the sky, bright, yellow, glaring.

She awoke to the heat.

The first thing she did was take a cold shower. She sent the kids out in shorts, with no shirts. She hoped the heat would not reach her. She wore her briefest halter, her shortest shorts, but still the heat penetrated. And as the morning doggedly wore on, it became more and more evident that the forecasters had been right. She sought the shade outdoors, but even in the shade it was difficult to breathe.

"Larry," she said, "please! Let's pack up and go to the beach."

He agreed instantly. She went into the house to make some sandwiches and then discovered they were out of cold cuts. She made out a list, sent Larry to the market with it, and then went outside to the shade again. Larry had put out the children's plastic pool and they romped and splashed in the water noisily. She watched them with adult envy and then finally went over to sit on the pool's rim with her feet in the water. Across the street, the Signora was sitting on her shaded front stoop fanning herself.

The front screen door opened and clattered shut again. Mary Garandi came out of the house.

"Hot enough for you, Eve?" she called.

Eve nodded but made no comment.

"Why don't you get in there with the kids?" Mary called.

"I wish I could."

"Go ahead."

Eve smiled weakly. She heard a telephone ringing. At first, because of the stillness of the street, because sound seemed to be magnified by the heat that day, she wasn't sure it was her phone. She listened. Persistently, the phone rang. She swung her feet over the pool's edge and walked across the grass to the front door. Standing there, she knew the ringing was unmistakably hers. She opened the screen door and ran through the house to the bedroom. The minor exertion exhausted her. When she lifted the receiver, she was wringing wet.

"Hello?" she said.

"Mr. Cole, please. Harry Baxter is calling."

"He just stepped out for a few minutes," Eve said. "This is Mrs. Cole. May I take a message?"

"Just a moment, please," the girl said. Eve waited. The girl came back onto the line. "Mr. Baxter will speak with you," she said. "One moment." Again Eve waited.

"Hello, Eve?" Baxter said, his voice booming cheerily onto the line.

"Hello, Mr. Baxter," Eve said warmly. "How are you?"

"Fine, thank you."

"And Mrs. Baxter?"

"In the pink. It's good to talk to you, Eve. Where have you been keeping yourself?"

Eve laughed, not knowing whether or not an answer was expected of her.

"Why don't you come in with that man of yours sometime, and we'll have dinner together, the four of us?"

"I'd love to," Eve said.

"How about today?"

"We're going to the beach. It's insufferable here. How is it in the city?"

"Worse," Baxter said, "but I'm sitting here with air conditioning all around me."

"Oh, lucky lucky man."

"Why not come in after the beach? We'll have a late dinner."

"That's awfully nice," Eve said, "but we'll probably be exhausted. Couldn't we make it some other night?"

"Certainly," Baxter said. "I suppose I'm being a little overanxious."

Eve smiled and said nothing, not knowing what he meant.

"But," Baxter went on, "time's getting a little short, you know."

"Yes," Eve said, and then wondered why she had agreed with him. Time was getting a little short for *what*?

"So forgive my impatience, will you?"

"All right," she said, puzzled.

"How do *you* feel about it, Eve?"

"We're happy to come in anytime," she said. "Just give us a little notice so we can get a sitter."

"What?" Baxter said.

"Didn't you mean . . . ?"

Baxter chuckled. "No, no, I was talking about Puerto Rico." He paused. "Or are you just being a shrewd business-woman?"

"Oh, Puerto Rico," Eve said laughing.

"Yes. How do you feel about it?"

"Well, I think it's wonderful you liked Larry's ideas. Has construction started yet?"

There was a long pause.

Baxter chuckled and then said, "Oh, Eve, Eve, I'm too old to play this sort of game."

"What?"

"Can I count on Larry, or can't I?"

"What?" she said again.

"The offer I made him," Baxter said.

"The . . ." She stopped. Despite the heat, she felt suddenly cold. With terrifying intuition, she realized that Baxter knew something she did not know. The instant question that leaped into her mind was "*What* offer?" With remarkable restraint, she kept it off her tongue. Instead, she said, "Oh, yes, the offer."

"What did you think of it?"

"Well, I . . . uh . . . I . . . I'd rather not say. Larry might . . . uh . . . want to tell you himself."

"Uh-oh," Baxter said. "That sounds bad."

"No, no," she said hastily. "It's just I . . . I don't like to meddle in business."

"But doesn't the idea of island planning excite you?"

"Island . . ." She felt weak all at once. She hoped she would not faint. She clung to the receiver as if it alone held her erect. "Yes, it . . . it excites me."

"This is a wonderful opportunity for Larry, Eve. I wouldn't try to fool you. There are a hundred architects in the country who'd cut off their arms to be my assistant on this project."

"The . . . the island planning for . . . for Puerto Rico, you mean?"

"Yes, of course."

"Your assistant," she said blankly.

"Yes. Or didn't you like Puerto Rico?"

"No, I liked it."

271

"What is it then? It can't be taking the kids out of school that's bothering you. Your eldest is just going into the first grade, isn't he?"

"Yes, he . . . he . . ."

"Wouldn't you want to go down there with the family?"

"I . . . I don't know. It isn't that," she said, the size of the offer finally overwhelming her, the importance of it, the *enormity* of it, and the fact that Larry had not even mentioned it to her. Why, why, why? "You'd better . . . you'd better talk to Larry. Shall I ask him to call you back?"

"Eve, convince him for me, will you?"

"Yes, yes, I . . ."

"If you haven't already."

"No. I'll ask him to call you. He'll call you, Mr. Baxter. I hear one of the children. I have to hang up."

"Don't let him miss out on this, Eve. He deserves the opportunity to show what he can really do."

"Yes. Goodbye, Mr. Baxter. He'll call you."

She hung up abruptly, and then collapsed in the chair alongside the phone, feeling certain she would faint. She knew there would be an argument when Larry returned to the house. She did not want an argument, and she told herself, He must have a very good reason, he must, he must, he would not withhold something as important as this from me unless he has a terribly good and valid reason, but she knew there would be an argument. She knew because while she told herself there was a good reason behind Larry's strange behavior, she simultaneously thought, He has another woman.

She wanted to blot out the thought, crush it, squash it, but, elusive as quicksilver, it raced through her mind over and over and over again. She sat sweating, feeling the oppressive heat inside the small house, hearing the sounds of the children splashing outside, feeling a black despair starting within her, combining with the heat to leave her limp. He has a reason, she thought. He *must* have a reason. And then the reason leaped into her mind again, the only reason, the only possible reason and she told herself, Don't cry, goddamnit, don't cry! Breathing heavily, sucking in great gulps of air from the still, hot moistness, she sat and waited.

She heard the screen door clatter shut when he returned to the house.

"Hon?" he called. "Where are you?"

"In the bedroom," she said, and she thought it fitting that they should have this out in the bedroom, that this important thing in their life should be thrashed out in the only room in the house which was truly and privately theirs alone, the way this monstrous thing was theirs alone.

She could hear his footsteps coming through the house. He paused just outside the bedroom door.

"Hi," he said. "I got the stuff."

"Hi," she answered.

"What are you doing in here? Cooler in here?"

"No."

He looked at her, puzzled. "You left the kids outside all alone?"

"Yes."

"In the pool? Honey, they can drown in an inch of—"

"Harry Baxter just phoned," Eve said.

"Oh?"

"Yes."

"What did he want?"

"What did he want, Larry?"

She wondered whether he would try to bluff his way out of this. She hoped he would not. Looking at him, holding his face in sharp, clear focus, she hoped he would not lie.

"Puerto Rico?" he said, and his shoulders slumped.

"Yes."

"He told you?"

"I'm listening, Larry."

"I didn't expect . . ."

"I'm listening, Larry. Goddamnit, I'm listening!"

"What are you getting sore about?"

"Why didn't you mention this to me?"

"I wanted to think about it."

"Alone? I thought we were married? I thought we shared things? Since when did you—"

"Eve, for God's sake, every window in the house is open."

"I don't care! Why didn't you tell me about this? What right did you have to keep it from me?"

"I wasn't going to keep it from you. I wanted to think about it for a while."

"For how long?"

"Eve, please stop shouting."

"I'll do whatever I damn please! If you can keep something as important as this—"

"All right, it's important! I wanted my own ideas to be clear before I broke it to you."

"When did you start doing that?"

"I've always done that."

"It was my impression we—"

"Well, your impression is wrong."

". . . we talked things over—"

"Well, you're wrong!"

". . . together! Stop telling me I'm wrong. *You're* wrong this time! I had every right to know about this offer. Am I your wife, or what am I?"

"You're my wife."

"Then why? Goddamnit, *why*?"

"I told you. I'm not even going to talk to you if—"

"Don't leave this room, Larry. If you leave, you don't have to come back!"

"Then lower your voice."

"When did he make the offer?"

"I don't remember."

"When?"

"Sometime in—"

"When, when?"

"It . . . it must have been February."

"*February!* And this is August! You've had this inside you all this time? Larry, what's the matter with you? What the hell is the matter with you?" and she began crying.

"Oh, here we go," he said.

"Yes, here we go, here we go. I've done nothing but cry about you since . . . since . . . I don't know how long. You rotten . . . thing! What's the matter with you?"

"Nothing's the matter with me. I was simply thinking over the possibilities, that's all."

"Stop it. You're lying. Don't lie to me, Larry!"

"I'm not lying!"

"Aren't you?" She sat in the chair and looked across the room at him. The room was suffocatingly hot—their bedroom—and they faced each other streaked with sweat. Their clothes hung limply to their bodies, as if the clothing too were exhausted after the bitterest argument they'd ever had. Up the street a telephone rang. Outside, Chris and David splashed in the pool. They could hear the drone of an airplane somewhere high above.

"Are you in love with another woman?" Eve asked.

He did not flinch, he did not move. His eyes held hers in what seemed to be utter honesty.

"No," he answered. "And that's the truth."

31

TRUTH or not, they did not speak to each other for more than a week. He was, in a sense, glad for the respite. He knew that once they began talking again, the Puerto Rican offer would be the first topic of conversation. He did not know what Eve was thinking, and he began to wonder if he'd ever known what she thought. He'd suspected that one day the Puerto Rican offer would inadvertently come to light and that he would have to face the fact that he'd withheld it from her. But he had not expected her to forge any link between his concealment and the possibility of another woman's existing. He had been totally unprepared for her baldly presented question and rather impressed by what he thought was his unblinking lie in answer to it.

He knew that once the silence broke, Baxter's offer would again be dragged into the living room. And this time it would not be allowed to bleed unnoticed on the rug. This time it would be rolled over and scrutinized. Answers would be demanded, decisions would be expected. He did not want to decide. He did not want to lose Maggie, nor—he realized with some surprise—did he want to lose Eve. What the hell *do* you want? he asked himself. A harem?

He dreaded the lifting of the silence because he had the uncertain sneaking dread that Eve would accomplish it by announcing she was leaving him. He did not want Eve to leave him. But he recognized the irrevocable error of having concealed Baxter's proposal. What possible excuse could he find to justify such behavior?

And exactly how much had Baxter told her? Did she realize the full scope of the opportunity he'd presented? Was she aware that this could be a turning point in their lives, the possible answer to his professional dreams? And if she knew that, how could he excuse the fact that he had not discussed it with her? A sudden shocking thought came to him. Had she spoken to anyone else? Had Altar ever called on the nights he'd used him for an alibi?

Hastily, he went to the phone and dialed Altar's home.

"Hello?"

"Altar?"

"Yes, who's this?"

"Larry."

"Oh, hello, Larry. What's up?"

"Nothing much. I was planning on going up to the house this week. I thought you might like to come with me."

"Oh, good. I was up last Saturday. Di Labbia's really clipping along. All the outside painting is done, and they'd already started to paint inside. When do you think he'll be finished?"

"The end of the month easily," Larry said.

"I wanted to discuss colors with you," Altar said. "I don't know what color to paint the study."

"Well, that's up to you. I can make suggestions, but the final choice—"

"Maybe black would be appropriate," Altar said.

"Black?"

"Well, *Stone*'ll be published soon. The reviews may be bad."

"I doubt it," Larry said.

"I'm on pins and needles. I'm stupid, I know. I shouldn't feel this way. But I can't help it."

"Just relax," Larry said. "They'll probably be raves."

"God, I hope so. It's only seventeen days, you know."

"What is?"

"To publication date. August thirtieth."

"You mean you're counting them?"

"I'm crossing them off on the calendar. August thirtieth. I get nervous even mentioning the date."

"Take a Miltown."

"I do. Regularly. They don't help. I think I'll get a woman tonight."

"Good idea."

"Aw, that won't help either. I'm worthless until that damn book is published and I see the reviews."

"Don't curse it."

"No, I shouldn't curse it. It's not a damn book, it's a beautiful book, a lovely book. But I can't wait for the damn thing to be published.

Larry laughed.

"Don't laugh! Suppose I didn't like the house you designed after it was all built?"

"It wouldn't matter to me."

"Sure, you'd get your damn ten per cent anyway. I'm surrounded by ten-per-centers. My agent, you . . ."

"The book'll be all right. Don't worry about it."

"Don't worry about it. That's like telling a man with cancer not to have cancer. The Book-of-the-Month Club News arrived yesterday. They gave it a rousing shove."

"What do you mean?"

"*Stone*. Didn't I tell you it was Book-of-the-Month for September?"

"No."

"Well, it is. They send out this thing announcing their selections. Marquand or one of the other people up there usually writes a sort of review on the selection. They sound as if they really like this one."

"Well, that's good."

"Well, it's not so good. They always like their selections. They're certainly not going to give a bad review to their own selection."

"Oh, I see."

"But it's pretty good because it sounds honestly enthusiastic. That's one of the most difficult things to do nowadays. Sound honestly enthusiastic, I mean. Do you think people like to buy books in September?"

"Sure."

"Well, I hope so."

They were silent for a moment.

Then Larry said, "You haven't called here recently, have you?"

"No. Why?"

"I thought you might have spoken to Eve."

"I only talk to wives when I have plans for them."

"All right."

"So, now that I know why you really called, you can hang up."

"Go to hell," Larry said.

"Are you really going up to the house tomorrow or the next day?"

"Did I say tomorrow?"

"You said this week. You can't go on Sunday. Not if you expect to see Di Labbia."

"Is tomorrow Friday already?"

"All day," Altar said, and then he chuckled. "My mother always says that. Ask her, 'Is today Wednesday?' and she'll answer, 'All day.' She's a character in *Stone*. Did I tell you?"

"No."

"I'm worried about that damn book," Altar said.

In his best family-relations-counselor voice, Larry said, "Mr. Altar, go, go to these people, beg their forgiveness, tell them your heart . . ."

"Aw, no sympathy in the world," Altar said. "That's the trouble. No sympathy."

"I'll leave you to your miseries," Larry said.

"Everyone always does. Are we going up to the house or not?"

"Let it wait until next week."

"I figured. Thanks for the call. If I turn on the gas or jump out the window, you'll be sorry."

"I will."

"It's too late to make amends," Altar said, and he hung up.

Larry grinned. Perhaps, he thought solemnly, it *is* too late to make amends. He hung up, and then steeled himself for the eventual shattering of the silence.

The communication for the next week was handled in the classically comic tradition of transmission through the children.

"Ask your father to pass me the butter please, Chris."

"Whyn't you ask him yourself, Ma? He's sitting right there."

"Ask him, please."

"Daddy, will you please pass Mommy the butter?"

"Here, Chris."

"Thank you."

"Thank your father, Chris."

"I did."

"For me."

"Mommy says thanks, Dad."

The silence persisted.

Maggie, unaware of the explosion in Larry's home, busily

277

made plans for the weekend they would share at the end of the month. She had already approached Don and he'd agreed to let her go provided his mother would come to stay with Patrick while she was away. He had not seemed at all surprised by her request, had asked relatively few questions about where she planned to go or what she planned to do. Breathlessly, on the telephone, she told Larry she could leave on Thursday night, August twenty-ninth. Would the house be finished by then? Could he get away by then? He could not tell her of the argument which had been caused by the Puerto Rican offer without revealing the offer to her. And so he said he would ask Eve as soon as the opportunity presented itself.

The opportunity came on Friday, August twenty-third, the night the silence shattered.

He had gone to bed at about twelve o'clock, leaving Eve in the living room watching television. When she came into the bedroom at one, he was still not asleep. She turned on the small lamp, went to the bed, and sat on the edge of it.

"Can we discuss this sensibly now?" she asked.

"Well, well, it speaks," Larry said lightly.

"If you want to continue this, that's up to you," Eve said coolly. "I don't want another argument."

"Neither do I."

"Then let's not be flippant, either of us."

"I'm sorry."

"All right."

There was a long silence.

Eve sucked in a deep breath. "I don't want to discuss why you kept this thing a secret," she said in what sounded like the beginning of a rehearsed speech. "I'm sure you have your own reasons, and apparently your reasons are privately and exclusively your own."

"I thought we weren't going to be flippant."

"I'm sorry," Eve said instantly. "I'd like you to tell me about the offer now. I'd like you to tell me as if it were just presented to you yesterday and not in February. I'd like you to tell me all of it, and then I'd like to make a decision. I'd like us to make a decision."

"I don't know if a decision is possible right now."

"Tell me anyway."

He told her of the proposal. He left nothing out. She sat silently on the edge of the bed, listening. There was no emotion on her face, and he realized, while he was talking, that he had robbed her of what could have been a truly joyous experience by not telling her of the offer when it was first made. It was too late now. The thing had somehow become a cold business proposition about which a high-level decision had to be made. Like the President of the Board, Eve sat listening intelligently, but there was no spark of emotion in her eyes or on her face. If she felt anything, she did not reveal it. If she felt anything, it was contained within her rigid body, bottled there secretly.

When he'd finished, she said only, "It sounds good."

"Yes."

They were silent for a long time.

Then she said, "I think we should take it. I think we should get out of Pinecrest Manor."

"I don't know," Larry said cautiously. "It's a big move."

"Or do you have personal reasons for not wanting to leave the States?"

"Eve . . ."

"I'm sorry. I shouldn't have said that. This is too important. I feel we should take it. I think this is the biggest thing that's ever happened to you. I can't understand your hesitation."

"Well, I've always liked to work on my own. You know that."

"This would be almost the same thing."

"I suppose so. It needs thought."

"It was my understanding you'd been thinking about it since February."

"Yes."

"But you haven't reached a conclusion?"

"No. It's not an easy decision to make."

"It seems very simple to me. Baxter's right. A hundred architects would cut off their arms for this job."

"Well, it's not that simple."

"Apparently not." Eve rose and went to the dresser for her nightgown. She came back to the bed and said, "I think we should take it, Larry."

"I'll think about it."

"When will you know? If we're going to Puerto Rico for five years, there's a lot of planning to be done."

"That's true."

"Well, when will you know?"

"Baxter's not leaving until September sometime."

"Will you know by then?"

"I thought . . ."

"Yes?"

"I thought I might go away by myself for a few days. To . . . to really think it over."

"Will that help?"

"Yes, I think so."

"When?"

"The end of next week, I thought. I thought I'd leave on Thursday night. The twenty-ninth. For the weekend."

"And on this weekend . . . will you make up your mind?"

"Yes."

"Fully?"

"Yes."

"I hope you make the right decision," she said, and he had the feeling she was not talking about anything as simple as Baxter's offer.

The telephone rang.

It shrilled into the silence of the sleeping house, and they both turned to look at it in surprise. The clock read 1:30 A.M. The phone kept ringing.

For a moment it seemed to Larry an evil instrument of torture. He made no move to answer it. Despair had come over Eve's face. She put her gown down on the edge of the bed and then walked to the telephone. She lifted the receiver.

"Hello?"

"Eve?" The voice was cracklingly brisk.

"Yes?"

"This is Mama. Can you and Larry get over here first thing in the morning?"

"What's wrong?" Eve asked quickly.

"Your darling sister has eloped, that's all," Mrs. Harder said.

32

THE MEETING on that Saturday morning, August twenty-fourth, was a grim and purposeful one. It would have seemed frivolous to have held it at the Easthampton cottage. Sensing this with the instinct of a natural actress, Mrs. Harder gathered the clan in the New York apartment.

When Larry and Eve arrived with the children, the Harders had already finished breakfast and were sitting in the living room overlooking Fifth Avenue and the park. The drapes were drawn back, and the hot, flat glare of the sun filled the room. Lois sat demurely on the piano bench. She was wearing a black sweater which somehow seemed to match the solemnity of the occasion and which, for a welcome change, was neither form-fitting nor too snug. The piano, together with the other furniture in the room, was covered for the summer. The Harders had not expected to be in the city again until after Labor Day and would not have been in the apartment had something dire not drawn them there.

One look at Mrs. Harder's face would have informed the most casual observer that something dire indeed had happened. Her face and her body had been browned by the Easthampton sun. Her arms where the short-sleeved cotton dress ended were muscularly lithe from ocean swimming. She looked oddly out of place in the living room where the furniture was covered, ghostly white against her tan. Her face, though, in contrast to her holiday coloration, was grim and set unyielding.

The first thing she said to Eve was "You didn't have to bring the children."

"There was no place to leave them, Mama," Eve said, and then instantly asked, "Is Linda all right?"

"How do I know?" Mrs. Harder said. "I don't even know where she is. A telegram! A girl gets married, and she sends her mother a telegram!"

"I'm sure she's all right," Mr. Harder said. "Hank is an intelligent, capable boy."

Sitting on the window seat overlooking the park, Mr. Harder did not seem terribly disturbed. He seemed concerned, but not disturbed.

"That's just my point!" Mrs. Harder said, whirling on her husband. "He's a boy, just a *boy*."

"We were all boys once," Mr. Harder said.

"Alex, you were twenty-three years old when we got married, and I do not consider that a boy. But Hank MacLean happens to be twenty-one, and that is a boy. A *boy*!" she repeated in emphasis.

"I don't see what difference two years makes," Mr. Harder said.

"There's a lot of difference!" Mrs. Harder snapped.

"Chris, don't go near the windows!" Eve shouted. Mrs. Harder turned sharply. Apologetically, Eve said, "I'm always scared to death they'll fall out."

"They won't fall out the windows," Mrs. Harder said. "This isn't the first time they've been here, and they haven't fallen out yet. I raised three children in this apartment and none of them ever fell out the window."

"I know, but . . ."

"You shouldn't have brought them anyway. This is no place for children. Not when we're discussing—"

"Mama, there was nowhere I could—"

"May we see the telegram?" Larry interrupted.

"Where's the telegram, Alex?" Mrs. Harder said.

"On the table, I think."

"Lois, get the telegram."

Lois rose from the piano bench and walked silently into the hall. It was difficult to tell from her face exactly how she felt about her twin sister's rather impulsive action. Instinctively, she knew that a double wedding would have been more acceptable to the family, and she somehow wished Linda had taken her into her confidence. But at the same time, she realized this would not be treated as another cute twinnish prank, and so, cautiously, she

281

watched and waited. Picking up the telegram, she brought it back into the living room and offered it to her mother.

"Give it to Larry," Mrs. Harder said, waving the telegram aside impatiently, as if it were crawling with vermin.

Larry took the telegram and read it:

DEAR MAMA AND DADDY. MARRIED THIS AFTER-NOON. DELIRIOUSLY HAPPY. SEE YOU ALL SOON. LOVE. LINDA AND HANK.

Larry handed the wire to Eve.

"Deliriously happy," Mrs. Harder said, as if that sentence of all the others had particularly annoyed her.

"The telegram was sent from New York," Larry said.

"Yes. That doesn't mean a thing. It was sent at nine P.M. They could have been married anyplace."

Eve looked up, puzzled. "What difference does it make where they were married?"

"Linda's only seventeen," Mrs. Harder said. "In New York State, you've got to be eighteen. That's the law. *That* much I know. I don't know what it is in other states. But if she got married in New York, we can have it—"

"Why don't we talk to the girl first, for Pete's sake!" Mr. Harder said. "You're already getting the thing annulled, and we haven't even—"

"She's only seventeen!" Mrs. Harder said, and she began to weep.

"She's almost eighteen, Patricia," Mr. Harder said.

Mrs. Harder did not answer. She sat in her chair weeping into a small lace handkerchief.

"Do Hank's parents know about this?" Larry asked.

"They received an identical telegram," Mr. Harder said. "I spoke to Mr. MacLean last night. He seemed like a sensible man."

"What does he care?" Mrs. Harder said. "Is it his daughter? His son hasn't even been in the Army yet. Suppose he gets drafted? What does Linda do then? Become a camp follower? She's just a baby." She turned to Eve suddenly. "Eve, she's just your baby sister."

Eve nodded. Watching her mother, looking beyond her mother to Lois, she felt like weeping herself. Everything suddenly seemed so confused and puzzling, and she did not want to be a part of it. And yet Linda was her sister and had always been her favorite. But sitting opposite Mrs. Harder, Eve told herself, I don't want to get involved. I mustn't. And she felt like weeping.

"Did you call Sam?" Mrs. Harder asked.

"I called Sam," Mr. Harder said.

"Well, where is he?"

"This is Saturday. Even lawyers take a day off every now and then."

"Is he coming?"

"He said he would."

"When?"

"As soon as possible."

"Will he know the state laws?"

"He's a lawyer. I imagine he will know the law."

"How could she do this to me?" Mrs. Harder asked. "How could she do a thing like this?"

The way Linda Harder could do a thing like this was relatively simple.

In a sense, though Mrs. Harder was the staunchest objector to the marriage, she had been in no small part responsible for it. She had raised Eve to believe that a girl should enter her nuptial bed a virgin. Eve had chosen to ignore her mother's advice, but Mrs. Harder remained blithely ignorant of this fact. In her eyes, she had done an excellent job with Eve and so she turned to the twins with the same vigor and the same admonitions never to sit on a boy's lap. If the warnings were wasted on Lois, they were not wasted on Linda. Mrs. Harder had successfully drummed into her the concept that a good girl waits until she is married. And so, watching her rising passion with Hank, Linda was faced with the dilemma of either becoming a bad girl or becoming married.

Her dilemma was enforced by Hank MacLean's attitudes on the subject. He was in many respects much like Mrs. Harder—a comparison he would not have particularly relished. In his mind there were good girls and bad girls and you didn't marry the bad girls. He had no desire to transform Linda Harder, the girl he loved, into a bad girl. Cautiously, both he and Linda had sounded out their parents on the topic of marriage. In both families, the response had been identical.

"Wait. You're still kids. Linda isn't even out of high school yet. Hank may be drafted. Wait."

Well, they couldn't wait. It was as simple as that.

On Wednesday morning, August twenty-first, Linda Harder left the cottage at Easthampton. She had told her mother she would be spending the next few days with a high-school chum named Sissie Carlisle in the city. Mrs. Harder had not objected. Girls visiting girls was a commonplace she had come to accept as the mother of two teenagers. She knew that Linda was a good girl who could be counted on to keep out of trouble. She kissed her daughter warmly, and, suitcase in hand, Linda left. Mrs. Harder didn't know it but the next time she saw her daughter it would be on almost equal terms of womanhood. Indeed, even when she left the cottage that day, Linda looked more womanly than she ever had. Full-breasted, ample-hipped, wearing a tailored suit, with brown calf pumps, her hair back off her face, she seemed far older than seventeen.

She met Hank in New York and together they started the trip to Elkton, Maryland.

Hank had wondered whether a loose interpretation of the Mann Act could make it seem he'd transported her over a state line for immoral purposes. They seriously decided between them that marriage could never be considered an immoral purpose, and then the conversation swung around to the bottleneck again —and the bottleneck was Linda's age. Marriage in New York had been out of the question. The state was a stickler for observing the letter of the law, and they were certain Linda would be asked for a birth certificate. As the train sped southward, they weren't even sure that Linda wouldn't be questioned in Elkton.

"How old do I look?" she asked him seriously.

"Eighteen, at least."

"Nineteen?"

"Maybe."

"Twenty?"

"I guess."

"If I say I'm eighteen, they're sure to ask me for proof. But if I say I'm twenty, maybe they won't think I'm lying. Who would lie by three years?"

"I guess you're right," Hank said.

"Well, it's really only two years and two months." She paused. "We could wait the two months, if you like. Then there wouldn't be any trouble. I'd really be eighteen. Do you want to wait?"

"No. Do you?"

"No. I want to marry you."

They discussed the Maryland state law as it had been transmitted to them piecemeal by people they knew who'd eloped and been married there. As they understood it, they had to be twenty-one and the girl eighteen. If they were not they needed written and notarized permission from their parents before a marriage license would be issued. The state required no blood test but would not perform a ceremony before a forty-eight hour period of residence had been established. The ceremony, by state law, had to be a religious one. Sitting side by side on the train, their suitcases on the rack overhead, they talked in whispers, plotting the perjury Linda would commit.

Elkton was not a big town, and it did not boast of a large railroad station. When they arrived, they discovered that only one car serviced the station, and they had to walk the length of the train to disembark. As they moved up the aisle with their battered suitcases, they were aware of heads turning, of the whispered words, "They're eloping."

When they got off the train, Hank took her hand and squeezed it. "You all right?" he said.

"I'm fine." She grinned. "There's nothing wrong with getting married, is there?"

"There certainly isn't," Hank said. "Let's get the license."

In the taxi, they rehearsed.

"How old are you?"

"Twenty."

"When were you born?"

Over and over again, they repeated the data in whispers, lest the cabbie should overhear them and spoil the plot by informing to an official. In truth, the cabbie didn't seem very much like an informer. He was a round little man who said as they got out of the cab. "Look me up when you're ready. Joe that's my name. I'll take you where you can get a nice ceremony."

In the clerk's office, Hank whispered, "Think you ought to light a cigarette?"

"No," Linda whispered back.

They filled out the license application and handed it to the clerk.

"You're twenty-one?" he asked Hank.

"Yes, sir," Hank said.

"Any proof of age? Birth certificate? Baptism papers?"

"Yes, I have it in my bag," Hank said. He stooped and began unfastening his suitcase.

"Never mind," the clerk said. He looked at Linda. "You're twenty, little lady?"

"Yes," she said. She smiled easily.

"Mmmm," the clerk said, still studying her. It seemed ridiculous to Linda in that moment that this hawk-eyed clerk could, by completely arbitrary will, either ask or not ask her for proof of age, in which case she would either be or not be married.

The clerk was reaching for stamp and stamp pad, still studying Linda.

His face slightly bored, he stamped the application.

"Forty-eight-hour wait before you can get married," he said. "No civil ceremonies allowed. Would you see the cashier, please, young man?"

As they left the office, Linda became aware of the other people in the room for the first time. All of the girls, it seemed to her, looked much younger than she. In the corridor, she looped her arm through Hank's.

"What time is it?" she whispered.

He looked at his watch. "Two-twenty," he said.

"By this time Friday we'll be married." She paused. "Do you really have a birth certificate with you?"

"Sure. I *am* twenty-one, you know."

Linda giggled and pressed herself to his arm.

285

They spent two nights in adjoining rooms at a motel on the outskirts of town. On the first night Hank leaped out of bed when he thought he heard Linda calling him. He stood by the door between their rooms for a long time, listening. Then he opened the door and looked into the room. Linda was sleeping peacefully. He closed the door and went back to bed.

On Friday, August twenty-third, at 2:30 P.M., they were married by a Protestant minister in the back of an antique shop. They thought they might spend the night in Baltimore but decided instead to come back to New York. They had dinner in the city and then sent off wires to their parents. When they checked into the Waldorf-Astoria, they were surprised no one asked them for a marriage certificate. At 9:30 P.M., in their room on the sixth floor, they consummated their marriage. They were very happy.

It looked as if the siege in the New York apartment was going to be a long one, and so the covers were taken off the furniture.

Larry was not looking forward to a long siege. The weekend had somehow come and gone, and it was Monday already and the honey-mooners had still not been located. On Thursday night he and Maggie were supposed to leave for their trip. Nervously, he watched time rushing by as Sam Gottleib, the Harder's attorney, tried to find Linda and Hank.

Working on the assumption that the honeymooners were in hiding, Gottleib avoided calling the better hotels. He checked the motels in New Jersey and on Long Island, the second-rate hotels nestled in New York's West Forties, and then the hotels in the out-lying suburbs of Westchester. It was not until Tuesday morning that he reluctantly began calling the first-class New York hotels. By this time Larry's impatience had reached the breaking point. Trapped in the Harder apartment, he had not been able to reach a telephone. Maggie still did not know that his own plans for the weekend had materialized. She didn't even know they were meeting, no less where or when.

The first hotel Gottleib called on Tuesday morning was the Waldorf.

In two minutes, after three days of fruitless search, he was connected with Hank MacLean. As calmly as he could over the screeches of Mrs. Harder in the background, he demanded that the couple return at once to the arms of their parents. Mrs. Harder insisted on speaking to Linda, but Gottleib wisely restrained her. He did not want her to frighten the girl into real hiding.

By twelve noon on Tuesday, both families were gathered to greet the fugitives. The gathering had all the outward appearances of a wedding party, with none of the inner warmth or happiness. Mrs. Harder served sandwiches. Her brother Fred, who had been divorced twice and knew about such things as these, opened a bottle of bourbon without being invited to do so and poured himself a before-lunch drink. Not wishing to seem rude, Mrs. Harder asked the rest of those present if they would care for a drink. Sam Gottlieb and Joshua MacLean, Hank's older brother who was a med student at Cornell, accepted. The other men declined. David kept asking Eve if someone had died.

At twelve-thirty the front doorbell sounded. Mrs. Harder began weeping. Mr. MacLean, Hank's father said, "There, there." Mr. Harder went to open the door. Linda, wearing an orchid pinned to her suit, smiled and went into her father's arms. Mr. Harder took Hank's hand and whispered, "Congratulations. Take care of her, do you hear?" and then they went into the living room.

The sight of her despoiled daughter sent Mrs. Harder into a fresh wave of hysteria. Mr. MacLean, a thin man of sixty, with white hair and pale blue eyes, kept saying over and over again, "There, there. There, there." His wife Martha, was a red faced woman who seemed rather annoyed by all the fuss. She could see nothing whatever wrong with her son. Any girl's mother, it seemed to her, should have been delighted to have him as a son-in-law.

Linda went directly to Eve.

Eve rose, and the sisters embraced, and Eve was surprised to find herself holding Linda so tightly. Again she warned herself not to become too involved, but still she held her sister close and wished her happiness and silently wished, too, that the marriage were not starting on the bitter note Mrs. Harder had introduced. There was so much yet that Linda had to learn, to experience, and it should have started happily, the way her own marriage to Larry had started. And thinking back to the start and the joy she had known, she felt a new rush of sadness, and over Linda's shoulder she saw Larry and wondered again if she could have been so wrong about the man she loved.

"Where were you married?" Gottlieb asked suddenly.

Linda turned. The lawyer was a heavy-set man in his middle fifties. A Phi Beta Kappa key hung on a gold chain across his vest. He wore a brown pin-stripe suit and a silk rep tie. He wore spectacles which had slipped halfway down his nose. He carried his head cocked to one side in a perpetual expression of mild skepticism.

"We were married in Maryland," Hank said.

"Then you were married illegally," Gottlieb said triumphantly. "The Maryland state law requires that the girl—"

"We know the state law," Hank said firmly.

"Then you must know that your wife committed perjury when she falsely represented—"

"We're married now," Hank said.

"I want it annulled," Mrs. Harder said quietly.

Linda turned to her mother. "Why?" she asked.

"Because you're both children. We'll have no trouble annulling the marriage. You're underage. Once we point this out to—"

"I'm not a child, Mama," Linda said with calm dignity.

"Just because you spent a few nights in a hotel room—" Mrs. Harder started, and Mr. Harder sharply said, "Patricia! Stop it!"

"I want it annulled," Mrs. Harder repeated.

"And we don't," Linda said.

"It doesn't matter very much what you want, young lady," Gottleib pointed out.

"Now, now," Henry MacLean said, "I think the kids should decide for—"

"Mr. MacLean," Mrs. Harder said, "Let's not complicate the issue. My daughter is underage. That's quite enough for me, and quite enough for Mr. Gottleib, and quite enough for the state of Maryland. There's no reason to—"

"Patricia, you are talking like a fool," Mr. Harder said.

"Alex—"

"Now just keep quiet for a minute, can't you?" He frowned at his wife, and she looked up at him with her own frown. "The kids got married. All right, let's not jump off the deep end screaming annulment, annulment." He turned to Hank. "How do you expect to support her, Hank?"

"I've already got a part-time job, Mr. Harder," Hank said. "And I'll be graduating next semester."

"I'll work too," Linda said. "Until Hank graduates."

"For that matter," Mr. MacLean said, "I'll help Hank until he gets on his feet. I think Linda's a fine girl, and I wouldn't want—"

"She's not even out of high school," Mrs. Harder said. "Suppose she has a baby?"

"So she'll have a baby," Mr. Harder said. "Is there anything wrong with married people having babies?"

"I'll be a grandmother who never even attended her own daughter's wedding. How could you do this to me, Linda? Am I a bad mother? Have I ever—"

"Mama, Mama."

"*Eve* didn't do this. Why did you have to do this?"

"Mama, I *love* him," Linda said.

"Oh, don't talk to me about love," Mrs. Harder said.

"What's wrong with their being in love?" Mrs. MacLean wanted to know.

"They're children! What do they know about—"

"But they're old enough to have babies, huh?" Mrs. MacLean asked, raising her eyebrows, her face getting redder.

"This isn't getting us anywhere," Mr. Harder said. "I refuse to treat my own daughter like a criminal."

"I want it annulled," Mrs. Harder said.

"Even if we can decide among us," Gottleib said, "that the marriage might work?"

"There are only two people who should decide that," Mrs. MacLean said.

Mr. Harder smiled at her. "Right! My daughter and your son. The rest of us are just excess baggage. I suggest we break out the whisky and drink to the bride and groom."

"Alex!" Mrs. Harder said sharply. "This thing is not settled!"

"What do you want to do? Call in the district attorney? Send Linda to jail? For God's sake, look at her, Patricia. She's a woman, your married daughter. Kiss her, hold her, Patricia. *Love* her."

"I want it annulled," Mrs. Harder said firmly.

"Could I . . . could I talk to Eve, please?" Linda asked.

Eve looked up. She was beginning to shake her head, but Linda took her hand and led her from the room. They went directly to the bedroom that had been Eve's when she lived with the family. The room was now a second television room, but some of Eve's old decorations were still on the wall—a pennant Larry had bought her at a Randall's Island football game, a Lexington Avenue Express sign which she and Larry had stolen on a scavenger hunt, a framed photograph of her and Larry taken at Palisades Amusement Park, a program from the Junior prom Larry had escorted her to at the Astor. Linda closed the door.

There was something of the past attached to the room, something of the innocent teen-ager lingering about the transformed room, something of the memory of Linda coming in to talk to her when she'd been a little girl, to talk to Eve before a date or sometimes when she returned home late at night. And suddenly, in the room that used to be hers, she could remember a Saturday in spring, the window open and the curtains rustling in a mild breeze. She could remember French notes spread open on her desk by the window, could remember the sound of Beethoven in the living room. And she thought . . .

> *You are truly Eve.*
> *I mean . . .*
> *Had you never been,*

Linda came to her.
"Eve?" she said.

> *Had I never seen*
> *Your face or known*
> *Your grace, there would*
> *For me*
> *Be no eve.*

She embraced her sister with sudden ferocity. "Oh, my baby," she said. "Are you happy, Linda? Are you happy darling?"

"Yes, Eve. Eve, I love him so much. What's wrong with Mama? Doesn't she know we're in love? Can't you talk to her, Eve? Can't you make her see?"

"Darling, darling . . ." Linda sat on the floor at her feet now, and Eve stroked the long black hair and then lifted Linda's chin and looked into her eyes. "Does he love you very much, Linda?" she asked.

"Yes, Eve."

"Are you sure, Linda? Be sure. I feel so old. I feel so goddamn old."

Linda looked at her, puzzled. She took Eve's hand and said, "Is something wrong?"

"No. I'm very glad you're married. It'll be nice having a married sister. It'll be nice being an aunt someday."

"Do you like him, Eve?"

"Do *you* like him, baby? That's what counts."

"Yes, yes. Oh, yes."

"And you love him? You're sure? You're absolutely certain?"

"Yes."

"Linda . . ."

She wanted to tell her sister about marriage. There were so many things Linda should know about marriage, the wonderful things and the horrible things, the security and the uncertainty, the tenderness and the cruelty, the excitement and the boredom, the ease and the difficulty. She wanted to tell her sister whom she loved very much in that instant, who seemed to her clean and untouched, young and innocent, about this wonderful and terrible thing called marriage. And when she tried to tell her, there was nothing she could say.

She could remember events in her own marriage, remember them as if they were happening right then, but they didn't seem important enough to transmit; they seemed only highly personal incidents which were a part of her and Larry but which could not possibly apply to anyone else's life. And again she was confused because an impersonal note had been introduced into the life she shared with Larry, a secretive note which intruded upon the highly personal and private thing which was marriage. She felt almost complete soaring joy for her sister, and only despondent sadness for herself and her own baffling marriage. She wanted to laugh and she wanted to cry, and she did neither. She sat in undecided stunned silence, not knowing what to say or what to do. Her sister was starting upon a cycle the very cycle she herself had entered eight years before. What could she tell her? How could she prepare her?

Could she say, "Baby, baby, life isn't just a bowl of cherries?"

290

Could she say, "There'll be ups and downs, Linda. Ride with them."

Could she call upon all the old clichés, all the banalities, all the tommyrot that was passed from generation to generation, from mother to daughter, from elder sister to younger sister? How could she tell anyone else the proper way to enter the most private and personal arrangement ever devised by human beings for human beings?

Wanting to laugh, wanting to cry, Eve said only, "We'll talk to Mama. You'll be happy, darling."

And she hoped Linda would.

33

HE CALLED MAGGIE as soon as he got out of the Harder apartment on Wednesday morning.

"My God, Larry, where have you been?" she asked.

He told her about Linda's elopement, and she told him how frantic she'd been, waiting for him to call. She'd walked past his house yesterday only to find it locked tighter than a vault. She couldn't imagine what had happened.

"Are we going tomorrow?" she asked. "I haven't known what to say to Don."

"Yes, we're going," he said.

"But how will you get away?"

"I'll just leave. Settled or not. They don't need me here to settle it."

"What about this thing from Puerto Rico?" she asked.

For a stunned moment he was completely speechless. Then all he could say was "What?"

"Felicia."

"Who? What are you talking about, Maggie?"

"The hurricane. Felicia. Haven't you been listening to the radio?"

"No."

"It's supposed to be headed this way," she said. "It passed a hundred miles north of Puerto Rico, and they think it's coming toward the coast. The radio said it might hit us tomorrow."

"What's that got to do with us?"

"I thought you might not like to drive in—"

"I've driven in bad weather before. Where are we going to meet, Maggie? What time?"

"The post office?"

"No, not for this. It's too risky." He thought for a moment. "There's a luncheonette on the edge of town. It's called the

291

Paradise or something. Right next to the bowling alley. Do you know it?"

"I'll find it. What time?"

"Eight o'clock?"

"No," she said, "it'll have to be much later than that. Don's mother isn't coming out until ten. She's having dinner with some friends and then they're driving her here."

"What time then?"

"Eleven?"

"Fine. Maggie, I've got to make this short. I'm on my way up to the Altar house."

"Is it finished?"

"I hope so. This is a final inspection."

"I wish I could go with you."

"We'll be together all weekend," he said. "I'll see you tomorrow night. Eleven at the luncheonette, right?"

"I'll be there. Be careful, Larry."

"I will. So long, Maggie."

He hung up, and then remembered he hadn't told her he loved her.

Summer was dying.

It was the end of August, and the leaves were beginning to turn already on some of the giant trees surrounding the house he had designed. There was a silence to the land. Regally, the house sat atop the slope, commanding the land and the sky. He inspected the exterior and then found six identical keys hanging on a nail in the garage. He took one from the bunch and opened the front door. The smell of fresh paint was still in the house, and another exciting familiar smell, the smell of newness. He closed the door behind him and stood silently in the entrance hall.

He was glad he was alone.

Here, surrounded by something he had created, something which had been born in his mind, something which had come from his hands to take visible form, like static electricity bursting in yellow spurts from the fingertips, here he was glad he was alone.

He walked through the house, into the enormous glass-enclosed living room, into the small, intimate room of stone and wood, upstairs to the study with the world at its feet, and then downstairs again to the kitchen and the dining room and back into the magnificent living room of glass where the wilderness stretched beyond to the edge of the sky.

And then he walked through the house again, a small black note-book in his hands this time, jotting down small corrections to be made. When he finished his formal inspection tour, he sat in the stone-and-wood room on the first floor, sat with his back to the stone wall, and there was a smile on his face and a peculiarly tender wistfulness in his eyes.

He sat alone for a long time.

Then he went out of the house and walked back to the car, and hesitated with his hand on the door handle, looking down the road to where the house reached for the sky, seemed ready to soar upward into the clouds if only it could break free of the foundation. He started the car and drove back to the city. He called Altar from a phone booth and told him he'd just inspected the house. It was a good house and a beautiful one, even though there were some minor changes and corrections Di Labbia would have to make. But as soon as the certificate of occupancy was issued, Altar could move in. He suggested that three hundred dollars be withheld from the final payment until Di Labbia had made the changes. He wasn't at all sure that Altar heard a word he said.

This was August twenty-eighth and *The Fall of a Stone* would be published on the thirtieth.

When he returned to the apartment that afternoon, Mr. Harder opened the door for him.

"Welcome back," he said. "We've landed!"

In the living room, Mrs. Harder was crying and hugging Linda close to her breast. "But why didn't you tell me, darling?" she said. "A mother should know. Her own daughter's wedding, her baby daughter."

Larry took Eve aside and whispered, "What happened?"

"Daddy kept giving it to her," Eve said. "She finally gave in."

"What are you drinking, Larry?" Mr. Harder said, beaming. "I've got another son in the fold and that's an occasion for real celebration. I'm a man who's been surrounded by jabbering females all his life!"

They drank together, the three men. As Larry tilted his glass, he heard Lois whisper, "How was it, Lindy? Did he make you take off all your clothes?" and he almost choked on his whisky.

The family had a late dinner together. In the television room, where Chris and David sat watching the screen after their earlier meal, the forecasters said that the hurricane Felicia had hit the North Carolina coast, passing inland near Morehead City and Beaufort, leaving floods and great destruction everywhere behind her. Felicia was moving northward. If she kept on course, she would pass through Chesapeake Bay and then strike the New York area sometime the next day, Thursday.

David said to Chris, "Ain't Disneyland on yet?"

Thursday came.

In the afternoon they left the children with Mrs. Harder and went out for a walk. The city was gray and silent. The people in the streets felt the coming storm. Unconsciously, they all looked skyward.

For Eve, the city had always been a magic place. The moment she arrived in New York, her step quickened, and her shoulders pulled back, and she held her head more erect. It was a city full of busy people rushing to get someplace. You could feel the quickened tempo the moment you stepped off the train. You could feel it surging along the pavements, echoing raucously in the beep of the taxicab horns, singing in the neon, rushing skyward with the buildings. The city was a treasure box of energy, and you wanted to laugh over your wealth, pick up the jewels of the city and let them trickle through your fingers while your laugh bellowed to the concrete and steel pulsing with life.

The city was there on that Thursday too, but it seemed dull and lifeless and sad to Eve. Walking along Fifth Avenue with Larry, she thought, This is the most beautiful street in the world, but the thought was shallow because she could muster no real enthusiasm for it.

"Mama wants to give the kids a reception on Saturday," she said. "At the apartment. Can we stay until then?"

"You can stay," Larry said.

"What about you?"

"I'm leaving tonight," he told her.

"Leav—? Oh, yes. I'd forgotten."

They walked silently. A wind was rising. It seemed as if it would begin raining any moment.

"Where will you go, Larry?" she asked.

"I'm not sure yet."

"What time are you leaving tonight?"

"About nine."

"So late?"

"I like to drive at night."

"There's a hurricane coming," Eve said. "Couldn't you wait until—"

"It may by-pass us completely."

"And it may not. Doesn't Linda's wedding mean anything to you?"

"Of course it does."

"Then you can stay for the reception? It'll only be family and some friends. It'll seem very strange if you're not there."

"You can tell them I had some important business to attend to. Upstate." He shrugged. "I've been called away before."

"Yes," she said. "But Larry, there *is* a storm coming. Is it so important that you leave tonight?"

"I want to get away," he said.

"I'm not trying to stop you, but you can leave Sunday or Monday, can't you? Why tonight?"

"I'm leaving tonight," he said.

"It doesn't matter what I say any more, does it?" she said, and he didn't answer.

294

They sat at the fountain outside the Plaza. Eve clenched her hands in her lap, and she stared straight ahead of her into the grayness of a city waiting for a storm. She sat with a growing sadness inside her. She sat feeling empty and drained and dead.

She had tried on Tuesday to explain things to Linda, and she could not. Now sitting at the fountain, she tried to explain things to herself and she was faced with the same impenetrable haze, the same inability to reason or think clearly. If only she could think. If only she could lay things out simply—this and this are so, that and that are not—if only she could think.

But the only sure thought she had was that uncertainty was certain. She had put complete trust in a man she thought existed, and the trust had been broken. For some reason this man had chosen to walk alone, ignoring her by his side. Alone. And you could not talk to someone who was alone, you could not reach that person, you could not touch him. He could not hold you close and comfort you, he could not say the things you longed to hear, he could not say, "It's all right, I'm here with you. I'll always be with you." Speechless, faceless, mindless, the man who sat beside her was a stranger.

Facing his aloneness, her own solitude seemed overwhelming. She was suddenly frightened. The world seemed like a gigantic place to her all at once, a strange and forbidding place where she wandered alone and unwanted. There was danger in this place, hidden behind every tortured outcropping of rock, every twisted tree. In the wilderness, she wandered alone, her eyes wide with terror in a world alive with menace. In all this lonely wilderness, there was no one to whom she could turn—no firm hand or smiling face—only a forest of clutching trees and tearing brambles.

Whom can I trust? she thought. To whom can I go? Who wants me? Who loves me? What shall I do! How will I live, how will I survive, what can I do, where shall I turn, whom shall I love, what does one do alone, why am I alone, why am I afraid, I don't want to be alone, I need someone, I'm scared, I can't, alone, I'm scared, I can't, I don't know, I want, alone, no, I can't, yes trust please, love please, me please, take, take, please, I can't, I'm afraid, I'm afraid, please, I'm afraid, please, please, please, PLEASE.

And the tears burst from her eyes like explosions of her soul.

She had cried before. She had certainly cried before. But this time the tears were tears of utter bewilderment, of sorrow wrenched from the depths of her being, sorrow that rose in her throat and burned there, scaldingly hot, to erupt in great wracking sobs, claiming her completely because she did not know why she was crying and so the crying became a final act in itself, with no reason for being and no reason for ceasing.

Larry turned to her, alarmed. "Eve, what is it?" he asked. His eyes darted from her face to the passers-by, and then back to her face again.

"I don't know," she said. She moaned the words. The words were the tortured cry of a wounded animal hiding in the darkness. "I DON'T KNOW!"

He seized her shoulders and shook her, and she stopped for a moment, gasping for breath. And then the crying came again in a series of short machine-gun bursts, her breath *uh-uh-uhing* as she tried to hold back the giant sobs. Her entire body trembled with the effort to hold back the sobs. The tears ran, but her sorrow did not need tears, needed only the twisted, tortured face, the wildly moving fingers in her lap, the gasps for breath as if she were suffocating, desperately trying to suck air into her lungs.

He shook her violently. "Stop it!" he said. "Eve, *stop it!*"

She nodded, but she could not stop crying. Foolishly, all she could say was "The people, the people . . ."

"The hell with the people!" He put his arm around her and tried to pull her to him, but she would not move. Her chest and shoulders heaving she sat like a stone and would not respond to his touch. "What is it?" he asked desperately.

"Are you happy?" she asked. Her voice was very small. It barely escaped her lips, thinly wedged itself between the sobs.

"No," he said.

She nodded her head, and then she shook her head. The crying was beginning to taper off. Nodding, she said, "I want you to be happy."

"All right, but stop crying, Eve. Please . . ."

"Can't you be happy?"

"Yes. Yes, I can. It's . . ."

"Is it me?"

"Eve, please, try to stop crying. Please don't cry like this."

"I can't help it. Is it me?"

"No."

"Is it? Am I making you unhappy?"

"No."

"Because if it's me . . ." A new wave of anguish tore through her. She turned her head from him, sobbing, gasping for breath.

"Eve, Eve . . ."

"If it's me, say so. Tell me, Larry, and I'll let you go."

"Eve, this isn't the time to . . ."

"When? When you come back? Will *you* come back, Larry? Will *Larry* come back, the person I used to know? Where are we, Larry? Who are we? Larry, don't you know how much I need you?" she said, hurling the words on a sob, and then turning on the seat to fling herself into his arms. "Please don't cut me off, please don't kill me. I have to know I'm yours. Please, Larry, please!"

He held her close, and he comforted her and soothed her. The

296

passers-by looked at them strangely, and then glanced skyward again, anticipating the arrival of Felicia.

In a little while it began raining.

He hailed a cab and took her back to the apartment.

34

MAGGIE did not begin dressing until nine o'clock that night.

The rain that had swept the development that afternoon seemed to have abated suddenly, leaving an anticlimactic stillness. The forecasters warned that this was the eye of the storm, the lull preceding the real onslaught of Felicia, but it seemed to Maggie the storm was over, it seemed to her it had passed. Larry had called again that afternoon to say he'd be leaving the city at nine that night, giving himself plenty of time in case the traveling was bad. She was grateful for the lull. He would be starting just about now, and she did not want him to be driving in the rain.

She was in her slip when Don came into the bedroom

"Where's Patrick?" she asked.

"Downstairs. Watching television." Don sat on the edge of the canopied bed, his hands behind him. "You really going, Margaret?" he asked.

"Yes, Don."

"In spite of the storm?"

"The storm is over."

"That's not what they said on television."

"Well, I'm going anyway."

He watched her silently for a while. Then he said, "You've got wide hips, you know?"

"Mmm."

"Real childbirth hips."

"Thank you."

"I wasn't trying to be nasty," he said apologetically. "I meant it as a . . ." He stopped and shrugged, and then fell silent again. At last he said, "You're really looking forward to this trip, aren't you?"

"I'm anxious to get away," she said. "The house can get a person down."

"Oh, sure, I know. Don't misunderstand me, Margaret. I don't mind."

She felt a spark of anger in his words. She rose suddenly as if to hurl a retort, walked swiftly to the closet instead, and took a dress from one of the hangers. She pulled it over her head and smoothed it over her hips and all the while her hands worked she

297

thought angrily, Why *doesn't* he mind? She went to him and said, "Would you zip me up please?"

Don pulled up the zipper at the back of her dress, and then put his hands behind him on the bed again.

"You don't seem very concerned about my going," she said, a sharp edge to her voice.

"I just wish you'd wait for the storm to be over, that's all."

"I didn't mean that."

"What *did* you mean?"

"My going. Not the storm. Just my going." With each word he spoke, she was becoming increasingly more angry. She could not understand the anger, but she knew it was spreading through her unchecked. As she walked to the dressing table, she could feel a frown claiming her face.

"Why should I be worried?" Don shrugged. "Everybody deserves a rest every now and then."

"Not many men let their wives go alone," she said. She sat and picked up her lipstick tube. In tense short movements, she jabbed at it with her brush.

Don shrugged again. "Who cares what other men do? You're *my* wife, not theirs."

"A *lot* of men would feel—"

"I can't see anything wrong with your going away for a little rest."

"*Most* men," she said, "wouldn't trust their wives that far."

"Well, I trust you, Margaret."

"Well, maybe you shouldn't," she said, amazed when the words sprang from her mouth.

"What do you mean?"

"Just that!" she said, and she begged herself to stop, knowing the conversation had come too far already, and yet perversely and doggedly continuing as her anger mounted. "I might be running off to meet another man, for all you know."

"Oh, sure," Don said.

"Why not? Is it so damn impossible?"

"Well, I just don't think . . ."

"Suppose I *was* meeting another man, Don?"

"I don't like this kind of talk, Margaret."

"Would you be jealous, Don?"

"Well, I . . ."

"Would you be infuriated, Don? Could you picture him kissing me, Don, and touching me and—"

"Now stop it. You know I don't—"

"How would you like that, Don? Another man making love to me?"

"I wouldn't like it at all. Now stop that kind of talk. The way you talk, sometimes I think—"

"What?" she said, whirling from the mirror to face him.

"Nothing. But it's not becoming, Margaret. I mean it. You talk like a . . . a . . ."

"A *what*, Don?" she said, her eyes flashing.

"I don't know what, but it's not right for a woman to talk that way. Suppose Patrick heard you? His mother. Talking like that."

"I think I'll pick up a man tonight," she said brazenly, angrily.

"Now come on, stop it."

"I'll find one in the storm and—"

"You won't find *anything*. Now cut it out. You'll go away just the way you're supposed to, and you'll come back to me just the way you're supposed to."

"Suppose I don't come back?"

"You will."

"You're pretty damn sure, aren't you?" she said, and there was so much vehemence in her voice that he opened his eyes wide and stared at her for several moments before speaking again.

Then he said, "Yes. I'm sure."

"Well, don't count on it!" she snapped.

"Margaret, what—"

"Stop taking me for granted! I'm a woman! And one of these days I'm liable to walk out of here and *never* come back!

Don gently said, "Now Margaret, you know that isn't true. You'll always come back to me."

She turned away from him and viciously picked up the lipstick brush again, her fingers trembling. In the mirror, she could see her eyes flashing with rage. Damn stupid fool, she thought. *I'll always come back to him.* Damn smug satisfied stupid fool!

But he's right, she thought. You always come back to him. He's right about that. Didn't you know that?

No, I didn't know that. I damn well . . .

Didn't you know you'd never leave him? she thought.

No! I can leave him any time I want to. I can . . .

Oh, Margaret, don't. Please. Look at the truth, Margaret. You can have Larry and a hundred men after him if you like, but you'll always go back to Don. Don't you know why, Margaret? It's because you were made for each other.

Made for . . .!

Yes, yes, oh surely you know that. You couldn't leave him if you wanted to. And you don't want to. Didn't you say you liked things the way they are? You want everything to stay the way it is, don't you? Don't you?

I won't listen! she thought.

You'll listen, she thought, because you know it's true. You know you're caught in a personal Hell. You're stuck with Don until the day you die, and then maybe you'll really go to Hell, but . . .

I'm not listening! I don't have to . . .

. . . in the meantime, this is fine, this is Hell enough. No matter how much you want to break away from him, no matter who's waiting out in that storm now or forever, you'll never do it.

Stop it, she thought. Stop it. I'm not listening!

You'll never do it because Don is safe! He's the safest goddamn man you could find, and that's why you married him.

No!

Admit it, admit it! Look into your own eyes and admit it. Larry may fill you for a while but you'll always go back to Don because he doesn't want as much. He doesn't want your heart.

No, she thought. *Stop it. Please.*

Yes, yes, she thought, get used to Hell. Get used to staying here and to coming back here and to living with a man who'll never know and never care. But things will stay the way they are. Always. Forever. You'll have company, but you'll be alone for the rest of your goddamn life!

No! She shook her head. No, that isn't true. No, it—

The front doorbell chimed. The sound startled her. She dropped the lipstick brush and then looked up into the mirror at a pale white face she had never seen before.

From the bed, Don said, "Is that my mother? So early?"

She did not answer him. She kept staring into the mirror at the terrified white face, shaking her head over and over again. Don left the room. The doorbell chimed again. She could hear him as he rushed downstairs to open the door.

"Mom!" he said happily. "Mom!"

When Larry left the Harder apartment at nine o'clock that night, the city was as silent as a tomb. The rain had stopped, and there was a strange glow in the sky, a sense of foreboding in the streets. He started for the garage where his car was parked, and then stopped at a newsstand on the way to pick up the early edition of the morning paper. Hastily, he thumbed through it to the book page. The slug at the top of the review read:

Fall of a Stone:
Rise of an Author!

He felt intense sudden pride. He folded back the page and, standing under a street lamp, began reading the column:

> When any reviewer's fortune includes one major novel in any given month, he has reason for rejoicing. When, in the month of August, the traditional doldrum month, he receives two such novels, he has surely heard the heavenly choir. If Roger Altar's new book, *The Fall of a Stone*, is not a masterpiece, it comes very close to being one. It is certainly a mature work of art, and one of the finest books published this year, if not this decade. *Stone*, unlike the earlier August entry which . . .

Larry could not finish the review. He had not been so excited or honestly happy for another person in as long as he could remember. He was shaking with vicarious joy. He had to see Altar at once. He had to share the writer's triumph with him, if only for a few minutes. Quickly, he got his car from the garage and drove downtown. He made it to Altar's apartment in ten minutes. He raced up the steps with the newspaper in his hand, wondering if Altar had seen it yet, hoping he would be the one to bring the good news. He rang the doorbell impatiently, and then knocked on the door. It opened wide. Altar stood there with a drunken grin on his face. He had already seen the review.

"Hot damn!" he shouted ecstatically.

Larry grabbed his hand and slapped him on the back with the newspaper. "Congratulations, you bastard!" he said, and Altar pulled him into the apartment, apparently not at all surprised to see him in New York.

"Hot damn!" he roared ecstatically. "Hot *damn*! You want a drink?"

"A short one."

"Did you see it?"

"*Did* I see it!"

"*Hot* day-am!" Altar shouted. He reeled to the liquor cabinet and feverishly poured a drink, the whisky sloshing over the brim of the glass. He staggered back to Larry hurriedly, thrusting the drink into his hand. "Drink up!" he said. "Did you read it? A work of art! Crisp sharp dialogue and true characterization! Penetrating! That's what the man said! A work of art!" he shouted joyously, tensely ecstatic.

Larry grinned at him stupidly.

"This is it, Larry," Altar said excitedly. "This is it, man! What's left after this? Man, this is the peak, the top, the gateway to heaven!" He poured whisky down his throat ferociously. "I did it, Larry!"

"Yes!"

"I really did it this time!"

"Yes!"

"I knocked them on their asses," he said, his eyes bright and glowing hotly, his head nodding nervously. "I did it, I wrote a work of art, I got a . . ." and suddenly his voice trailed off and the room went silent.

Altar shook his head.

"Who the hell am I kidding?" he asked the wall.

"What?"

"I've been sitting up here ever since I read that review and drinking myself silly and trying to get a boot out of it! I've been trying to make believe that damn review is the be-all and the end-all, and the plain damn honest truth is that it doesn't matter at all, it doesn't matter one goddamn little bit!" He turned to Larry despairingly. "It isn't enough, Larry!"

"But the review said—"

"Yes, and it isn't enough! What's wrong with me? What the hell do I want? Why shouldn't I be deliriously happy right now? What do I do if I win the Nobel Prize someday? Put a bullet in my head? What's *enough* for me? Larry, Larry, I don't know what I want any more!"

"Hey!" Larry said. "Hey, don't be—"

"Oh, what a crock!" Altar said. "Oh, what an empty crock success is! Oh, what a phony, what a two-bit phony. Drink. Drink, y' bastard." He refilled his own glass. "The two American carrots," he said. "The man-carrot is Success, and the woman-carrot is beauty. Those are the carrots they dangle. You wanna know something? Carrots are for rabbits, and they stink! We're *people*. Don't you know that?"

"Yes, I know it," Larry said. "But a man has to strive for success. You can't—"

"You know what a man has to strive for?" Altar asked. "A man has to strive to *be* a *man*, that's all. What the hell does success mean? I got success and what good is it? I'm riding on top of the world! A work of art, the man said! So where am I? I wish I was a guy who cleaned gook out of the sewers. I wish I could go home to a dumpy wife and eat scrambled eggs and tell her what a goddamn hard day I had down in the sewer. That's for me! The sewer and the gook!"

"You don't mean that, Altar."

"I mean every word I say. Success? Bunk. *Bunk!* A canard! Tell them! Tell all the white-collar workers and the junior executives in the Brooks Brothers suits. Tell them success is a farce! Tell them you're never a success until you're a *man*—" Altar burst out laughing—"and the stupid bastards'll answer, 'You're never a man until you're a success!' "

Larry sipped at his drink quietly.

"Here's to the big successful bachelor house in the exurbs," Altar toasted. "Long may it serve as a monument to the blood we spilled and the tears we shed and the prizes we brought home from the sewer. You know something?"

"What?"

"I never won a prize."

"I did."

"How does it feel?"

"It's not so hot."

"Why not?"

"Well, once you've got the prize, what're you going to do with it?"

"Pickle it," Altar said. "Exactly my point. There are no real prizes left in this goddamn world of ours. If there were real prizes, who'd care what some reviewer thinks about what you do?"

Larry looked at his watch. "I have to leave soon," he said.

"What time?"

"Before ten."

"Relax, there's time." He paused. "Or is there? Time's running out, isn't it, Larry?"

"Time's running out," Larry repeated.

"We're getting old, Larry. We better grab a big handful of life before there's nothing left to grab. Listen, don't go."

"I have to," Larry said.

"What's the matter? Don't you like me?"

"I like you."

"I like you too, Larry."

"Good."

"It's very good. I like you. I love you, y' bastard. You're a good guy. And that's the whole secret, Larry. Love. Not success and not beauty and not the gook in the sewer. Love. You know something?"

"What?"

"I'm gonna get married someday. I'm gonna kick all the tarts out of my apartment, and I'm gonna get a wife. A sweet little wife who doesn't give a damn what the reviewers say, and who'll cook me scrambled eggs."

"You like scrambled eggs?"

"I *hate* scrambled eggs," Altar said. "Let's go down the Village and find some girls."

"I've got to go," Larry said.

"Sure, excuse me. Forgive me. Home to your wife. I know. You worked it out, didn't you?"

"Altar . . ."

"Sure, I can see you worked it out. I told you, didn't I? Don't lose your head, just don't lose it. Love, that's the secret. Home to the wife, home to the woman. That's what I'm gonna do. I'm gonna take a woman to bed tonight."

"That's not love, Altar," Larry said.

"I know, I know, that's only the success carrot of love. You got love. What you got with your wife is love. I told you it'd work out, didn't I? Sure. Jesus, I wish I could love some girl. Listen, I love your wife. What's her name? Eve? I love her. I love Eve. The mother of all men, Eve, I love her. Listen, you go home to her, hear me?"

"I . . ."

"Hurry up, 'cause this bitchin' storm's gonna catch her all alone with the hurricane lamps. Hurry up, Larry. Go to her and love her, love that wonderful goddamn Eve! And keep designing those magnificent houses, man, let them pour out of you. And love your wife and bring forth men children only and love your wife! Fill the earth, Larry! Fill it with your houses and your kids and you're on the road to eternity! Go home to Eve, man, and thank God your life doesn't rise and fall on what a review says about a goddamn cloth binding stuffed with paper!"

Larry looked at his watch. "I've really . . ."

"Sure, sure. Wait for me. I'll get my coat and then I'll come down with you. I'm gonna get my coat and drive with the top down and let the damn storm crash all around me! And I'm gonna get me a woman and come back here and let the storm call the music!"

He got his coat and they walked downstairs and they stood together on the sidewalk. The storm was ready to break. The wind furiously hurled newspapers across the sidewalk. There was a sullen roar in the streets. The skies were swollen and ready to burst in fury.

"So the house is finished," Altar said.

"Yes."

"And now what?"

"I don't know."

"The age of uncertainty," Altar said. He nodded bleakly, the wind whipping at his hair. "Only one thing's sure, Larry."

"What's that?"

"People come and go. You meet as strangers . . . and most of the time you part as strangers. And if you ever really get to know another human being, it's a miracle." He took Larry's hand in a firm grip. "I get the feeling I won't be seeing much of you now that the house is finished. I get that feeling. Take care of yourself, y' bastard."

"I will. You too."

Altar dropped his hand. Larry felt there was no more he should say, and he sought words, and then the moment was gone. Altar turned abruptly and started down the street toward his convertible, walking quickly for a big man, his broad shoulders pushing against the wind which swept sullenly through the narrow concrete canyon. Larry watched him as he climbed into the car. He heard the engine start, and then the top of the car came down slowly, slowly.

Larry went back to his own car and began driving toward the bridge.

35

He FELT rather good when the storm broke around him.

It broke suddenly. There was a stillness one moment and then instant and absolute raging fury which shook the car. He was still miles from the bridge when the rain burst from the sky. He could feel the sudden lurch of the automobile as a stronger wind captured it. He clung tightly to the wheel, picking up the challenge of the storm like a dropped gauntlet, grinning into the suddenly flooded windshield. Rain swept across the glass in successive sheets, impervious to the sniping of the windshield wipers. The glass became a blurred dissolving pane of pinpoint lights through which he squinted to see the road. He did not slow the car. With the wind shrieking around him, shrilling at the windows, screaming over the roof, combining with the incessant rain which smeared red, green and white lights across the windshield, he felt he was locked in a safe metal chamber which hurtled straight and true into an indistinct tunnel of howling furies.

The night did not frighten him at all. As he drove into the rain, smiling and squinting through the blurred windshield, he felt in complete control of the vehicle. He felt as if he were starting a great adventure, a lively and interesting journey, at the end of which he would be rewarded for his courage and tenacity. Courageously, tenaciously, he tried to see the road, his foot on the accelerator, pushing the Dodge through the storm. He thought of how childishly naïve Altar's concept of marriage was, wondered how fast the winds outside were, wondered if Maggie had left the house yet. And beneath all his idle thoughts, like a tingling undercurrent of anticipation, he had a sense of something about to happen. The windshield was dissolving before his eyes and he could barely see the road. He could feel the buffeting wind and water wrenching at each straining joint of the automobile, but he felt safely encased in a strong metal cocoon.

He supposed it was only the storm and the egotistical idea of puny man pitting himself against mighty nature; just that coupled with the feeling of aloneness as he pushed through the night, and yet he couldn't shake the persistent feeling that he was on the verge of a magnificent realization. He drove hunched over the wheel, fully expecting a sudden illuminating light to burst into the automobile, exploding in incandescent brilliance around him, a roman candle of truth and revelation. He wondered about sudden truth, rejecting it as a stylized concept for the practitioners of Altar's art. There was no such thing as sudden truth. Verity simply piled upon verity to form one day a shining edifice which only seemed to have materialized suddenly out of thin air. And yet, even rejecting it, he felt as if he were about to touch sudden truth, felt as if he would soon be able to see clearly through the raging storm, see through it into the core of life, and beyond that to death, and into eternity, and into the very soul itself.

He felt the way he'd felt in Puerto Rico, watching the funeral procession.

And suddenly he began to tremble.

His mind seemed crystal clear, brimming with thoughts, flooding with solutions. His mind grabbed for the scattered glittering pieces, clicking them into place until he thought he would burst with the sheer thrill of near-revelation. With luminous clarity, he could remember the first time he saw Maggie and everything that had followed afterward, the meeting of two strangers, the clasping of alien hands. With persistent logic, he wondered why they had reached for each other? What in him had not been satisfied? What in him and the thousands of others who broke the marriage contract caused the unrest? Was it the struggle for Altar's prize, for success, for beauty in a world grown suddenly too complex for a simple animal?

Hadn't his yielding to desire been a simple rebellion, a basic retrogression to something clearly understood in a world of incomprehensible things and ideas? Hadn't the sex been a sure thing in a world of uncertainties? An accomplishment in a world of unrealized dreams and frustrated goals? Wasn't that why he'd sought Maggie and found her?

He laughed aloud at the storm, feeling free all at once, hurtling free and unfettered into the raging teeth of the shrieking monster outside, routing the beast, pointing the nose of the car into the blackness and the rain and the howling winds as the windshield melted in pinpoint oozing blobs of red and green and yellow and white.

Then was there no such thing as love? Was love just another label? Was the whole world and everything in it a giant fabrication, a push-button front, a fakery for fakes? His mind veered from the thought because he was seeing now with penetrating logic, and he would not accept the pessimistic glibness of the idea, would not allow himself to fall into the facile trap of false acceptance, not when truth was piled in glittering heaps of golden coins at his feet. Not when he could pick up truth and let it spill through his fingers in cascades of dazzling revealed splendor. Of course there was love! Maybe romance was a fake, but love was as real as breathing, and what he knew with Maggie was love.

Again his mind backed away, refusing to accept any pat statement in the shining revelation of truth, asking the question: Or is it romance? and then rushing headlong with the question, allowing it to produce the next inescapable query: Isn't this the same romance I knew with Eve? Hadn't it been this way for us when we were still kids discovering each other? Yes! Yes! But I *do* love Maggie, I *know* I love Maggie; still the admission had to be made, and it followed unchecked: his love for Maggie was a thing sheltered and protected by the adolescent concept of romance. He had turned back to a juvenile belief, clutching for the glamour and the excitement—and he knew why. As the car hurtled through the night, he knew why. He'd grabbed for the glitter and the tinsel because the reality was too damned painful and too damned complex. But what had he found, and why was he still looking?

In the tunnel of wind and rain he wondered if you ever stopped looking, if you ever really discovered yourself in all the noise and all the confusion and all the speed, or did you keep looking for the rest of your life? And another truth rolled down upon him in overwhelming certainty, and he knew you didn't find yourself by going back to seventeen. Maybe you looked until you were dead and buried, but there was no going back.

He realized now the fallacy of his reaction to the funeral procession in Vega Alta. He had been watching the drama of life and death that day. He had placed himself in the supported coffin and watched it going down the street, knowing it would be out of sight soon, knowing that his own life was moving forward unrealized, unfound, and that someday he would be buried. Soon, soon! And facing the utter finality of death, he had wanted to reach out for life, to hold it close in an embrace, stop the steady advance of life which was rushing him unfulfilled to the grave. He had wanted to turn back time, stop the insidious clocks, find himself before it was too late.

He had found Maggie Gault instead.

And the Signora had said it at a party in February, when he'd been too drunk to understand her. The Signora had said, "Margaret Gault isn't the pot of gold."

Now, as the lights of the bridge appeared blurringly in the distance, as the hurricane Felicia grasped at the car with undiminished fury, he thought, No, Maggie isn't the pot of gold. I love her but she isn't the pot of gold and maybe there isn't any pot of gold at all. Maybe you never find it, or maybe you always keep looking for it, but one thing's certain. You'll never find it if you go back over ground you've already searched. I know for sure I'll never find it this way. I love you, Maggie, he thought, but I know for sure.

That was the sparkling, shimmering moment of golden truth, and he nodded his head and thought, I'm going home to Eve.

The approach to the bridge was ahead. Through the blurred windshield, he could see the approach on his left and the curving ramp ascending in a high sweep above the storm. And straight ahead was the road which led back to Eve, the road to Manhattan's cross streets. The white sign appeared suddenly in the storm, its black lettering swept relentlessly by the wind and rain: LAST EXIT BEFORE BRIDGE.

I'm going home to Eve, he thought.

And he pressed his foot to the accelerator with new determination, and he nodded again because truth had come to him at last.

"I'm going home to Eve!" he said aloud in the stillness of the car.

Last exit, the sign read. Pained, he saw the sign fall away on his right. Powerless to stop himself, he swung the car to the left, onto the ramp leading to the bridge and Maggie. The decision

307

arrived at in pain, discarded now with pain, he drove onto the ramp decisionless, unable to stop, captured in the car as it mounted the wide, ascending curve of concrete. *Last exit*, the sign had read, but seeing the exit he had ignored it, had instead succumbed, powerless to something within him which was incapable of committing the final act of severance. He could not cut Maggie out of his life, could not leave a part of him bleeding and raw on the pavement. He knew then that truth could descend in lightning bolts, shower purging sparks upon him, and he would still be helpless to break whatever held him to her.

And, realizing this, he began crying.

The windshield, dissolved already in the incessant wash of the rain, became a muddy, shifting, protoplasmic mass as he blinked to keep back the blinding tears. He wept from the very roots of his being, the tears welling into his eyes and streaming down his face as he sped into the storm and onto the high span of the bridge. He could no longer see ahead of him. The road seemed to be one he'd traveled before and often, the repetitious, monotonous, ungratifying landscape of an alien land in which he was a familiar stranger. Decided but decisionless, committed but lacking real commitment, he wept bitterly. The rain cascaded against the roof; wind tore at the windows. Helplessly, he clung to the wheel, weeping. Blindly, he followed whatever crude instinct propelled him through the night, rushing to reach her side, rushing to Maggie, Maggie, Maggie, Maggie.

Perhaps the car went into its skid only because it was suddenly sideswiped by a fresh fierce gust which blew in over the open water to the span of the bridge, causing the tires to relinquish for an instant their tenuous grip on the slick pavement. Perhaps he remembered for a split second his earlier decision and impulsively pushed his foot onto the brake pedal in an attempt to follow the demands of reason by executing a now-unreasonable, all-impossible turn. Or perhaps—perhaps the familiar road was suddenly recognized as a road without an end; perhaps, confronted with a bewildering despair he had never known before, he turned the car deliberately toward the edge of the bridge.

The car turned sharply and then entered a sideswinging skid, its speed undiminished. He remembered something about always turning into a skid, but if he knew how to correct the sudden slipping motion, he made no attempt to do so. And then the moment for action was gone, and he recognized with a small shock that he had lost all control of the automobile. The shock passed almost at once. He sat in nearly expectant resignation as the car swung sideward in what seemed to be an endlessly long arc, swinging, swinging, swinging, and then striking.

He felt the impact as the car hit the guard railing, heard the splintering sound of glass and the crunching tear of metal above the noise of the wind. Held low by the weight of the engine, the

308

nose of the car clung to the dark pocket where concrete met steel. The rear end buckled and leaped into the air of its own momentum and then was captured by the wild rush of the wind at hurricane force, lifting, lifting the back wheels and then flipping the car over like a toy. His chest rammed hard against the steering wheel, and he felt sharp, unbearable pain as the car completed a somersault which sent it spinning over the steel railing. He clutched for the roof of the car, and then the seat, felt the automobile lurch clear of the steel rail, upright again for just an instant, and then hurtling free, unhampered, loose on the wild night air, dropping for the river below.

Pinned behind the wheel, he thought. This is it.

Helpless in the spinning automobile, he thought, I'm going to die, for God's sake, I'm going to die.

The thought surprised him and amused him. It was such a damn funny, shocking thought, he was going to die like this, what a goddamn corny, ridiculous, stupid way to die! He was amazed by it, and yet he felt somehow that his reaction was rather thin, the false shock at the entrance door to a suspected surprise party. He sat with pain knifing his chest as the world revolved around him and the wind screamed in his ears, and he thought, This is the way it happens, you sweat and you worry and you work and you wonder and then you die for nothing, no cause, where are all the prizes, if you never really lived, how can you learn to die so soon?

I wonder if Chris will go to college, he thought.

Eve, he thought. Eve.

I must call Baxter. We'll do Puerto Rico. We'll make it, don't worry, we'll make it.

With the unbearable pain in his chest, and the car spinning forever to the swirling black waters below, falling like a stone, he thought, Poor David still wets the bed. Oh, Jesus, my poor

36

The music for Pinecrest Manor's Third Annual Beer Party was live.

The leader of the band was a man who sold insurance in the development. He played trumpet rather forlornly and was followed sadly by four musicians who had come all the way from Queens and who looked upon these suburban shenanigans somewhat dimly. In Queens, people knew how to live.

The musicians read their sheets but they didn't play with any particular gumption because October was a sad month and besides this wasn't even a union-scale job. Not that there was any danger of a union representative asking them for their cards at this obscure American Legion hall. But scale should have been $22.00 per man, with double for leader, and the band was getting only $20.00 per man, with the leader—because of his civic attachments—forsaking the double salary. And so, though the music was alive, it wasn't very lively.

The musicians had arrived at 8:00 P.M. and were set up and tuned by eight-fifteen even though the party wasn't scheduled to start until eight-thirty. A few early birds arrived on the dot. There were always, the musicians mused, a few early birds who arrived everywhere on the dot, as if unwilling to miss even a moment of the forthcoming festivities. The real exodus from Pinecrest Manor to the American Legion hall, however, did not begin until nine. By that time, all the baby sitters and mothers-in-law had received their detailed instructions.

There were, to be sure, some last-minute hassles with children in some of the development homes. But the children were being raised to understand that the night was a mysterious time of adult pleasures. Hadn't Mummy and Daddy spent the whole day trying to make the kids happy, hadn't they gone on all the rides at Joyland and eaten hot dogs and popcorn and had heaps of fun? So go to sleep, you little bastards. We don't come to *your* parties, do we?

At nine o'clock, as if by prearranged signal, the front aluminum storm doors of the development ranches, Cape Cods, and split-levels opened. The women emerged smiling in their finery, and the men followed them even to the cars. The sprinklers were going on the front lawns even though it was October already. The right to sprinkle was a God-given one which only reluctantly retreated before the approach of winter.

The sedans and the station wagons—of which many were in evidence—and the convertibles backed out on the concrete driveway strips and headed for town. There was a deep peace in the air over the development, an almost tangible feeling of heavy contentment. The street lights glowed warmly in the orderly streets. The lawns which had received their addict's fix of 10-6-4 sparkled greenly under the glistening saturation of the sprinklers. There were warmth and beauty and bliss in Pinecrest Manor. On the front seats of the automobiles, the bottles of booze were wrapped in brown paper bags, the couples' surnames inked onto the labels. There would be setups available at the American Legion hall. This was going to be a damn fine affair!

There was a lot of milling around in the entrance hallway, the couples who'd arrived alone trying to decide where they would sit and with whom. There was, too, the usual cloakroom bottleneck, but this was straightened out in time and it didn't take long for friends to find friends. Chairs were pulled up to the long

310

wooden tables, and everyone sat down in the cheerless wooden box which was the American Legion hall, and each neighbor looked at his neighbor with a patient, bored, anticipative expression which seemed to say, "Well, I'm here. Entertain me." The men went for setups and then opened the whisky bottles. The band began playing. Drinks were poured. Chairs were shifted. Laughter resounded throughout the hall.

"Looks like a nice crowd," Betty Anders said. The trumpet wailed into the room mournfully.

"It's awfully hot in here, isn't it?" Doris Ramsey asked.

A man rushing back to his table dropped a bottle of ginger ale. It hit the floor and shattered. Wild applause and cheering congratulated his clumsiness.

Fran Levy said, "I think they ought to have these things more often."

"That's a good idea," Betty said. "We ought to suggest it to the Civic Association."

"We need more ice," Felix said, and he rose and left the table.

"I think this is going to be a big bore," Doris said suddenly. She smiled. "Present company excluded, of course."

"What the hell," Max Levy said. "We'll make our own fun."

"We'll *have* to," Doris said.

"Everything is what you make it" Max said judiciously.

"We passed by a new development yesterday," Arthur Garandi said. "Oakdale Acres. Mostly split-levels. They've got it laid out nice. Winding roads. Nice."

"How much is the house?" Paul Ramsey asked.

"I think it's sixteen nine-nine," Arthur said. "I'm not sure. We didn't stop."

"That's a lot of money," Doris said.

"It always kills me when they say nine-nine," Ramsey said. "What they really mean is seventeen thousand. Why don't they say so?"

"It sounds cheaper the other way," Mary Garandi said.

Felix came back to the table with a bucket of ice.

"Do you know what a lot of people are doing?" Max said. "They're buying those big estates on the shore. Getting them for a song."

"What's a song?" Betty asked.

"Forty thousand. Something like that."

"That's a song, huh? Sing to me a little."

"Those are white elephants," Mary said. "Cost a fortune to heat."

"Yes," Felix said, entering the conversation, "but you get an awful lot of land and a really big house. Nineteen, twenty rooms."

"Who needs so many rooms?" Mary asked. "Besides, why is everybody talking about other houses? Is anybody moving?"

311

"I guess it's on everybody's mind," Felix said. "Now that Eve's put up the house for sale."

"That's different," Mary said. "What do you expect her to do? Stay here with the two kids? Without a man?"

"Let's not talk about it," Betty said. "It gives me the shivers."

"Do you think she'll be able to sell the house?" Max asked.

"No question," Felix said. "These houses have a very good resale value. She'll probably make a little money on the deal."

"It's a shame," Mary said. "That poor woman. You never know when something like that is going to happen, do you? That poor woman."

"Let's not talk about it," Betty said.

Ramsey cleared his throat. "I've heard a little talk about Larry," he said. "Not that I want to spread any rumors."

"What kind of talk?" Max asked.

"Oh, just about what he was doing out in that storm," Ramsey said.

"What do you mean?" Fran asked.

"Well, just talk," Ramsey said, "and I don't want to spread any rumors. But there was some mention of another woman."

"You're crazy," Felix said immediately.

"I'm only saying what I heard."

"Well, what you heard is wrong. I think I knew Larry better than any of you. Isn't that right, Betty?"

"They spent a lot of time together," Betty confirmed.

"And a straighter guy never existed," Felix said. "I'd like to know who told you a thing like that, Paul."

"What difference does it make? I just heard it around."

"If I knew who told you that, I'd go over and tell that guy a thing or two, you can bet on that."

"Forget it," Ramsey said. "I just heard it around."

"This was a real sweet man," Felix said, "I'm not kidding you. I've met a lot of people in my life, but Larry Cole was one of the genuine real sweet men. I'd have done anything for that guy. All he had to do was ask. I'm not kidding. I mean it."

"I didn't know you were such close friends." Max said.

"Well, who talks about friendship? It's either there or it isn't. But it burns me up how people can change a legitimate business trip—he was out in that damn storm on his way to see a client—into something with . . . with . . . hints of another woman! It just burns me up! Boy, sometimes I wonder where everybody's mind is!"

"Well, forget it," Ramsey said. "It was only something I heard."

"You know how hard that guy worked? Do you think it's easy to sit there on your own, without that steady salary coming in every week? He had to hustle for every cent he ever made. That's what he was doing in that damn hurricane! Lining up another client so he could feed his family. You should have heard him

312

when he talked about Eve and the kids. You should have seen his face! This guy was devoted! One of the real sweet people, believe me."

"I always liked him," Max said.

"It's a shame," Mary said. "A thing like that. Such a young man."

"Listen, it makes no difference to me one way or the other," Ramsey said. "I mean whether he was fooling around or not. Everybody else is doing it, anyway."

"Oh, shut up, Paul," Doris said.

"Well, he's not exactly wrong, Doris," Max said.

"Sex is here to stay," Ramsey said, shrugging. "Let's admit it."

"That's the right idea," Max agreed, trying to raise the party out of the mud of morbidity.

"The right idea," Fran scoffed. "My husband. The sex machine."

"Who?" Max said, pretending to be offended.

"The sex machine with the missing part."

"*Who's* got a missing part?"

"Well, maybe not missing. But hard to find."

Everyone laughed, and the laughter seemed to dispel any remaining remnants of the previous talk.

"Those people in Massachusetts who had those key parties knew what they were doing," Ramsey said.

"How about it, Felix?" Doris said, winking. "You want my key?"

"Sure, sure," Felix said.

"Take her up on it, Felix," Betty said, grinning.

"Sure, sure."

"Listen, I'm available," Max said.

"Ask him, Doris," Fran said. "He'll run a mile."

"Go ahead try me," Max said.

"Nope. Either Felix or nobody," Doris said, winking at Betty this time.

"Look out there on the floor," Ramsey said. "Everybody dancing with everybody else's wife. That's the only reason they come to these affairs."

"Speak for yourself, John," Felix said.

"I'm only making an observation," Ramsey said. "Look at them. Cheek to cheek. Who's more honest? Those sneak thieves on the dance floor out there or the ones in Massachusetts who swapped keys?"

"The ones in good old Mass," Max agreed instantly.

"Certainly."

"I don't think so," Felix said.

"Felix is very moral," Betty said solemnly. "Really. He is."

"It's not that I'm a prude, but I've got old-fashioned ideas about marriage. Adultery is dishonest. *And* immoral. *And* illegal."

313

"I'll bet you," Ramsey said slowly, "that half those guys out there who are dancing with another man's wife would like to take her to bed."

"Now watch it, Paul," Felix said seriously. "That's no kind of talk to—"

"I'm only trying to make a point."

"Then make it, and let's talk about something else."

"All I want to know is this. What's more honest? A flirtation? Or an affair?"

"He's got a good point," Max said.

"I fail to see it," Felix answered bluntly.

"Look out there on the dance floor," Ramsey said. "You see that tall guy with the glasses? That girl he's dancing with isn't his wife. Look at where his hand is."

Everyone looked.

"All right, all right," Felix said.

"Who's more honest?" Ramsey asked. "Them or the ones who go to bed? Who's crazy?"

"Is that your point?" Felix asked.

"That's my point."

"Okay, you made it. Now let's talk about the weather or something."

Ramsey chuckled. "I always distrust the ones who don't want to discuss it," he said.

"Sure," Felix answered, smiling.

"Doesn't anybody want to dance?" Arthur asked.

"Come on, honey," Felix said and lovingly he took Betty into his arms.

The Picasso print of the boy leading the horse had been his favorite and now the moving man lifted it gingerly from the wall and carried it past Eve to the front door. She could remember when they'd bought the print. It had been a bitter cold day in January and they'd stopped at the museum only to escape the frigid streets. She watched as the man put the framed print into the truck, and then another man carried out the Saarinen chair which had cost them something like three hundred dollars, their one extravagance when they were first married and furnishing the three-room apartment they had in the Bronx.

She watched the chair move out of the house, and she marveled at how quickly the place she had called her home could become nothing but a bare shell stripped of whatever personality its owners had given it. Standing in the living room as the moving men rushed past her like a silent demolition crew, she felt lonelier than she had at any time since the accident. She tried to put the horror of that night out of her mind now, the phone call from the harbor police, and then the wild rush to the hospital in the hope they'd been wrong, please, please let them have been wrong,

314

and the terrible pallid stillness of the mortuary, the somber, embarrassed attendant and the swift, clean pain of looking into the dead face of what had been her husband and knowing it was over.

I must not think about it now, she thought. Life goes on. I must not think about it.

Alone, she stood in the living room as the furniture which had surrounded her life was moved into a truck backed to the curb. How easily they take apart a home, she thought. How easily they pack a life into the back of a truck. This afternoon she would move into the apartment on Fifth Avenue with her parents. Her furniture would go into storage, and she would become a guest in the apartment which had once been her home. If she ever thought back to Pinecrest Manor again, it would only be with pain. Her loneliness was a completely engulfing thing. She did not know what was ahead for her. A job, she supposed. She could not, after all, ask her father to assume the responsibility of her and her two children, nor did she want to. A job then, and perhaps her own apartment eventually and a nursery-school arrangement for David, and a woman to help with the house. A new life alone. She had always believed her life was set, its course charted. And now . . .

The living room was empty.

Leadenly, Eve looked at the blank walls.

She wondered again about that night in August, and again she told herself that he really truly was going on a trip alone, and that he was coming back to her at the end of that trip. And this she believed, and this she would always believe until the day she died.

One of the moving men came to her. He wiped his forehead and said, "That looks like it, lady. Is there anything else?"

Eve shook her head and said, "No, there's nothing else."

And then she walked out of the house and did not even try to look back at it.

The girl with Roger Altar was a honey blonde with bright blue eyes. She unbuttoned her blouse and said, "This is a great house. I've never been in a pad like this one. I really dig it."

"Good," Altar said. "I had it built just so you could dig it."

Outside the bedroom windows, the woods were a riot of fall color. The girl threw her blouse over a chair and walked to the windows. "It's the end," she said. "Who ever thought nature was so crazy? Did you design this house?"

"No," Altar said.

"Who designed it?"

"A man named Larry Cole," Altar said.

"A friend of yours?"

Altar hesitated. "Yes," he said at last. "A friend."

315

"We can really have a ball in this house," the girl said. "This is the absolute most. Crazy!"

"Yeah," Altar said.

For a moment his mind had gone back to the night of the hurricane and the last time he'd seen Larry. And for a moment he was possessed of an impulse he'd had ever since that night, a desire to rush to the telephone and call the widow of his architect and say, "Eve, I want you to know how sorry I am. Eve, I want you to know how much I thought of your husband. I just want you to know."

He had never made the call. And once, sitting down to write a letter to Eve Cole, he had discovered that he—a professional writer—could not put what he felt into words.

The girl went to the big bed and rolled on it luxuriantly.

"Sunlight and love," she said. "What a wild mixture!"

"Would you like a drink?" Altar asked. "I can use one."

"Sure," she said. "I'm game for anything. I dig this pad."

Altar mixed the drinks silently. The girl stretched her arms to the ceiling, ecstatically digging the pad all over again. He handed her one of the drinks.

"Where do you get ideas for books?" she asked him.

"Oh, you just get them," he said.

Someday he would make that call. Someday, he promised himself, I will call Eve Cole and pay my respects. Someday before it's all forgotten.

"Let's ball," the girl said.

The pavement was covered with fallen leaves of red and yellow and orange and russet and gold. She walked with her head bent, and the wind grasped at the leaves and sent them rasping along the pavement, parting in whispers before her high-heeled stride. Her blonde hair blew free in the wind. With one hand, she held her collar pressed to her cheek, covering the small scar. High in the naked treetops, the wind sang a wild, keening song.

There was a wind on the night he died.

She could remember it rattling the front door of the small luncheonette. She could remember the young boy who sat at the end of the counter with a cup of coffee. She could remember the storm flailing the streets, and she could remember clenching and unclenching her hands in her lap as the clock steadily advanced past eleven. At twelve o'clock, the proprietor told her he was closing and asked her if she wanted a lift home. She had refused with an ever-mounting sense of dread, and then had stood in the doorway of the closed luncheonette and watched the storm gradually subsiding. By one o'clock she knew that he was not coming to her, and she went home. She learned of the accident from Betty Anders the next day. She almost screamed aloud, and then with carefully disguised anguish, she listened to the details.

316

The news was all over Pinecrest Manor. She heard the story a hundred times that day, and that night she wept in the darkness of the bedroom and Don made no move to console her. When she awoke the next day, the Cape Cod seemed empty. She kept waiting for the telephone to ring, but it did not. She kept waiting for his voice and his expected "Hi," but it never came. She cried again. She could not seem to stop drying. In the middle of a simple household chore, the tears would suddenly spring to her eyes. She cried for a week, and then there were no tears left to shed. Then she felt only the terrible emptiness of being alone again.

Now, walking with her head bent, with the leaves scattering before her on the pavement, she wondered if things did really end after all, if everything always came to a suddenly terrifying halt. She wondered about her own life, about the long empty years ahead, alone. And she shuddered, hunching her shoulders against the wind.

A car pulled up alongside the curb. She did not turn to look at it. Slowly, the car cruised next to the sidewalk, rolling slowly with her pace. The horn honked. She did not look up. The horn honked again. She paused and then turned to look at the car and the driver, squinting into the afternoon sun.

"Hello, Margaret," the driver said.

She recognized him and smiled nervously. "Hello," she said, her voice very low.

"Want a lift?"

She hesitated. In the sun-washed interior of the Oldsmobile, Felix Anders was smiling, his eyes very green, his teeth very white.

"Come on," he said.

She hesitated another moment. Her lashes began to flutter. She pressed her coat collar into her cheek with her right hand. Then she moved swiftly to the car door and opened it. She leaned over stiffly. In a very cold voice, she said, "I'm only going as far as the center."

Felix Anders smiled.

"Sure," he said. "Get in, stranger."

317

A SELECTION OF FINE READING
AVAILABLE IN CORGI BOOKS

☐ 552 07965 0	SOHO NIGHT AND DAY (illustrated)	*Norman and Bernard*	30p
☐ 552 08611 8	FEEDING THE FLAME	*T. Lobsang Rampa*	30p
☐ 552 08228 7	WOMAN: a Biological Study	*Philip Rhodes*	25p
☐ 552 98178 8	THE YELLOW STAR (illustrated)	*Gerhard Schoenberner*	105p
☐ 552 08456 5	COMPLETE BOOK OF JUKADO SELF DEFENCE		
	(illustrated)	*Bruce Tegner*	30p
☐ 552 98479 5	MADEMOISELLE 1+1 (illustrated)		
		Marcel Veronese and Jean-Claude Peretz	105p

Western

☐ 552 08532 4	BLOOD BROTHER	*Elliott Arnold*	40p
☐ 552 08567 7	SUDDEN—DEAD OR ALIVE	*Frederick H. Christian*	20p
☐ 552 08589 8	UNDER THE STARS AND BARS No. 63	*J. T. Edson*	20p
☐ 552 08065 9	GUN WIZARD No. 32	*J. T. Edson*	20p
☐ 552 08132 9	THE SMALL TEXAN No. 36	*J. T. Edson*	20p
☐ 552 08193 0	CUCHILO No. 43	*J. T. Edson*	20p
☐ 552 08475 1	NO SURVIVORS	*Will Henry*	25p
☐ 552 07561 2	KILRONE	*Louis L'Amour*	20p
☐ 552 08007 1	CHANCY	*Louis L'Amour*	20p
☐ 552 08158 2	THE BROKEN GUN	*Louis L'Amour*	20p
☐ 552 08568 5	MAVERICKS	*Jack Schaefer*	20p

Crime

☐ 552 08605 3	BELOW SUSPICION	*Jack Dickson Carr*	25p
☐ 552 08554 5	FIND THE BODY	*John Creasey*	25p
☐ 552 08606 1	VERSUS THE BARON	*John Creasey*	20p
☐ 552 08588 X	A COMPLETE STATE OF DEATH	*John Gardner*	25p
☐ 552 08472 7	THE INNOCENT BYSTANDERS	*James Munro*	25p
☐ 552 08520 0	KISS ME, DEADLY	*Mickey Spillane*	20p
☐ 552 08425 5	THE SHADOW GAME	*Michael Underwood*	20p

*All these books are available at your book shop or newsagent; or can be ordered direct
rom the publisher. Just tick the titles you want and fill in the form below.*

— —

CORGI BOOKS, Cash Sales Department, P.O. Box 11, Falmouth, Cornwall.
Please send cheque or postal order. No currency, and allow 4p per book to cover the
cost of postage and packing in U.K. 5p per copy overseas.

NAME ....

ADDRESS ....

(JAN. '71) ....